Mystery in the Title

THE MIRANDA ABBOTT MYSTERY SERIES

I Only Read Murder

Mystery in the Title

A MIRANDA ABBOTT MYSTERY

Ian Ferguson
& Will Ferguson

HarperCollins*PublishersLtd*

Published by HarperCollins Publishers Ltd

First Canadian edition

HarperCollins books may be purchased for educational, business or sales promotional use through our Special Markets Department.

HarperCollins Publishers Ltd
Bay Adelaide Centre, East Tower
22 Adelaide Street West, 41st Floor
Toronto, Ontario, Canada
M5H 4E3

www.harpercollins.ca

Library and Archives Canada Cataloguing in Publication
Title: Mystery in the title / Ian Ferguson & Will Ferguson. Names: Ferguson, Ian (Author of How to be a Canadian), author. | Ferguson, Will, author.
Description: Series statement: A Miranda Abbott mystery
Identifiers: Canadiana (print) 2024030215X | Canadiana (ebook) 20240302176 | ISBN 9781443470803   (softcover) | ISBN 9781443470810 (ebook)
Subjects: LCGFT: Cozy mysteries. | LCGFT: Novels.
Classification: LCC PS8561.E7545 M97 2024 | DDC C813/.6—dc23

Printed and bound in the United States of America
24 25 26 27 28 LBC 5 4 3 2 1

Mystery in the Title

CHAPTER ONE

A Fateful Thump

Miranda Abbott confronted the killer.

"I thought I knew you," she said. Every word, every syllable, was wrung from the tortured depths of her soul. "I thought I might even love you . . ."

She was looking directly into a soft, diffused light that picked up several conflicting emotions shining in those eyes. Those green eyes. That auburn hair, those celebrated cheekbones.

"You're a smart man," she said, her voice betraying the faintest touch of trepidation overcome by a quiet resolve. "A clever man. But maybe a bit too clever, a bit too smart. Killing Pascal de Montaigne with an icicle bayonet was brilliant; you removed any possibility of fingerprints and then disposed of the murder weapon by turning up the heat in the vault after you left. Faking a suicide note? That was too clever by half. First, I asked myself, why would a career criminal like Pascal, a fence for high-end objets d'art, known for his joie de vivre, kill himself? And why would he do it using a weapon that vanished? And why would he stab himself in his *right* ear? He wasn't called 'Sinister Pascal' because he was evil. *Sinister*, you see, also means left-handed! That was the clue that unraveled your malevolent plans. Mon amour, I've already contacted les gendarmes. It's all over for you ... But before they get here, you have one last chance to tell me where you stashed the missing money."

She pursed her lips as her expression shifted from one of pensive courage to mild irritation.

"Line!" she shouted.

"That's a cut," sighed Andrew.

Bea couldn't help herself; she sprang to her feet and burst into applause. "I think that was your best one yet!" she said.

Andrew Nguyen, Miranda's long-suffering assistant, lowered his smartphone with a world-weariness that belied his youth. He switched off the ring light, a Westcott 18" LED with adjustable stand—and how much had that cost her? better not to ask—as Bea scampered across to pull back the curtains, flooding the sitting room once again with sunlight.

They were ensconced in a cozy nook in Bea's B&B amid the mist-festooned Pacific Northwest, far from the catacombs of Paris or the dastardly machinations of Pascal de Montaigne. Potted begonias and tea sets, mainly, with nary an icicle bayonet in sight.

"It's Monet," said Andrew, "not 'money.' They're searching for a 'missing Monet,' not missing money."

"That's the part that keeps tripping me up."

Miranda Abbott was auditioning for the lead in a *major* motion picture, *From Paris with Pathos*, a love story art-heist action drama that would see her hopping from Monaco to Barcelona and then to France (or Montreal, if the tax credits were better there) as soon as she landed the role. *When*, not if. This was a role designed for an actress—a star!—of Miranda's caliber and experience. Her agent back in LA had tipped her off about it, pretending to have slipped it into an otherwise pointless conversation over the phone—"*I see Clooney's shooting in Monaco next fall. Go figure.*"—which Miranda had immediately leapt upon. She was good at picking up on clues. She had played a sleuth on network TV for six years, as well as in that strange realm known as "real life."

Indeed, framed in a place of honor in Bea's kitchen was the front page from *Variety* magazine, HOLLYWOOD HAS-BEEN SOLVES MURDER, which Miranda passed with a tingle of pride every day. *Hollywood!* she noted. *Solves!* she thrilled. Front page, no less!

Unfortunately, "unpaid amateur sleuth" did not cover the rent on her room, or the sort of wardrobe someone of her stature required. And, despite a brief flurry of interest in her as an accidental detective, neither did the offers, or lack thereof, that followed.

Andrew deleted the last take, cued up the video app on his smartphone again.

"Should I throw in a karate kick as well?" Miranda asked. "At the end, for a bit of pizzazz?"

"Um, maybe not," said Andrew, as tactfully as possible. "But only because it's not, you know, in the script."

"Andrew, darling, I've never been *shy* about sharing my ideas with the producers of *any* project I've worked on, suggesting ways to improve the screenplay, or how to best light me, or which angles to shoot me from."

Shy? No. Miranda was many things—she contained multitudes—but shy wasn't one of them.

"I think you want to focus on the quality of the performance rather than the physicality of the role," Andrew said. It had been some time since the curvaceous Miranda Abbott had been able to execute such a move and he didn't want to see her try now.

Trim and impeccably dressed, Andrew was a wizened veteran of such moments.

"From the top?" he asked.

"From the top!" Miranda cried.

Bea went to close the curtains and Miranda said, sotto voce, "Bea, perhaps we could keep the applause to a minimum this time? As used to adulation as I am, it does throw me off my timing, which is so, so crucial for an actress."

"I'm sorry," said Bea. "I just get caught up in the moment."

Gray hair, neatly bobbed, with smile-creased eyes, Bea Maracle was Miranda Abbott's biggest fan—or, more accurately, Pastor Fran's biggest fan, Miranda's alter ego from that classic TV show *Pastor Fran Investigates*, off the air for more than a decade and a half yet still fondly remembered and regularly viewed here at Bea's B&B.

If anyone could karate-kick an icicle-wielding bad guy, it was Pastor Fran.

"So," said Miranda. "No karate kick?"

Andrew sighed. He did that a lot lately. "No karate kick."

She shook the tension out of her shoulders. Took a deep, calming breath.

"This could mean a lot for us," she reminded him. "Cannes, the red carpet, a comeback worthy of my fans. Remember, I don't make fans, fans make me!"

A Miranda Abbott aphorism. Andrew had started jotting them down in a small notebook he carried.

"If I land this role, I shall be Number Two on the call sheet at the very least." During the glory days of *Pastor Fran Investigates*, Miranda had been Number One on the call sheet for six years running. She had since dropped off it entirely, and was determined to claw her way up that sheet again. No sane person would care about their number on a sheet of paper, but no one could ever accuse actors of being sane. Never mind that the role she was auditioning for was described as "a lithe twenty-something ballerina." Miranda hadn't been twenty-something in, oh, twenty-something years, or more. But was she unduly worried by this? She was not. "It's all in the lighting," she'd told Andrew. Hence the newly purchased ring light that Andrew had procured for her.

Andrew's parents had fled Vietnam in a leaky boat. For this? he thought. They escaped persecution and braved shark-infested waters so their oldest son could become a glorified babysitter to a *former*–heavy emphasis on *former*–TV star?

His parents had learned their English from *Pastor Fran Investigates*, and he and his overachieving younger brother had been forced to sit through the weekly mystery every Friday, the biggest mystery being, why did a wandering pastor always turn up in a small town at *exactly* the moment someone was murdered? Suspicious, no? "Better not to think about it," his brother had grinned. "Y'know, Mom and Pops learning American culture from someone who is probably a secret transient murderess. Between her and Jessica Fletcher, you have half the murders in small towns accounted for."

Andrew lived in the pantry at Bea's B&B. He'd relocated from LA for *this*? he often thought. A temporary arrangement, he had been assured, just until Miranda could afford a proper suite at the Duchess Hotel, the town's fine establishment on Tillamook Bay. (Miranda, like every actor, was forever one role away from extravagant affluence.) "Don't think of it as a pantry with a cot in it," she'd said. "Think of it as a boutique office-slash-living-quarters. Do you have any idea how much that would run back in LA?"

"But we're not in LA," he'd protested, in vain–and his protests were mostly in vain when it came to the mercurial Miranda Abbott.

Miranda, meanwhile, had commandeered the "upstairs suite" of the B&B, what Bea strangely referred to as "my bedroom." (Bea had since moved to one of the smaller guest rooms, one that did NOT have an ensuite or a full dresser or a closet full of Bea's clothes.) Today, Miranda had commandeered the sitting room as well, transforming it into a film studio.

"Paris, here we come!" said Miranda. "Or Montreal, depending on the tax credits available! From the top!"

The movie she was preparing her audition tape for was a co-production of some sort, hence all the French terms and French names that littered the script, none of which she'd had any difficulty pronouncing. Les gendarmes? No problem. Objets d'art? Easy-peasy. Pascal de Montaigne? A piece of proverbial cake. Monet? Yikes. Kept coming out *money*.

"Monet, Monet, Monet," she said, warming up for another round—and even then, it became *money, money, money*. "I'm ready to go again."

Bea made sure the curtains were fully drawn, and Andrew turned the ring light on again, making sure to adjust diffusion to the most flattering setting.

"Take 27," he said (with a sigh).

Miranda held up a small white board. Written in erasable ink was the name of the project ("From Paris with Pathos"), the role that Miranda was auditioning for ("Yvette-Eloise Toussaint"), and, in large block letters, TAKE ONE.

This was Miranda's idea. However many tries it took before she was satisfied, the slate would always read TAKE ONE, as if she'd simply read the script, memorized her lines, and delivered on her first attempt.

How had she gotten the script in the first place? Not through her agent, of course. Marty hadn't been able to turn her sudden notoriety as a crime solver into the sort of A-list offers she deserved, but through her assistant Andrew's cunning connections. "Someone leaked it online," he had said with a shrug. "I downloaded it." False modesty, she was sure. Andrew was a very astute player in the biz.

It was sometime between Take 32 and Take 47 that a thump sounded in the front of the B&B.

"Oh, that'll be the mail," said Bea, scurrying off to get it, while Miranda and Andrew took five.

It would prove to be a very fateful thump.

Miranda had flopped down in one of Bea's elegant but faded Queen Anne chairs. "Why am I doing this?" she asked Andrew.

"The role?" he said. "You're asking me why you're auditioning for this role?"

"I know *why*," she said. "I don't know *why* why." She had a habit of speaking in riddles that almost made sense. "It should be offers only. I shouldn't have to go out hat in hand like some B-list celebrity."

B-list? thought Andrew. We should be so lucky.

Still, his affection for her, in spite of everything, perhaps *because* of everything, wouldn't allow him to be cruel. Or honest. And in the case of Miranda's post-fame career, the two were closely aligned.

"You're absolutely right," he said. "Hollywood should be calling *you*. And they will, I'm sure. They just need a little . . . nudge. That's all."

She smiled sadly. "Thank you, Andrew. I do appreciate that you care enough to lie. That's very kind. When Bea comes back, we'll do the final take. I promise."

Speaking of which . . .

In a burst of breathless energy, Bea came rushing in waving the latest copy of *Variety*. "Your movie!" she said. "It's on the front cover!"

"What do you mean?" said Andrew, who knew exactly what it meant.

Sure enough, the cover did indeed feature *From Paris with Pathos* with George Clooney and Meryl Streep splashed across it, airbrushed to a Platonic Ideal under the heading BOFFO B.O. PREDICTED AS WHAMMO CLOONEY-STREEP ROM-COM-HEIST-MYSTERY-ACTION-THRILLER WRAPS!

"Good thing you're auditioning!" said Bea. "You better get that in soon!"

Andrew looked to Miranda, but Miranda said nothing. Instead, she stood, head high, and straightened her shoulders in a simulacrum of courage. An actress preparing to exit Stage Left. She was wearing her favorite satin blouse, deep green to set off her red hair, with a shoulder scarf perfectly designed for flinging . . . but none came. No dramatic moves, no defiant retorts.

"I think I'm done," she said. Only that. *I think I'm done.* "Thank you, Andrew. Thank you, Bea."

"But don't you want to do one more of the takes?" said Bea. "We're all set up and ready. Right, Andrew?"

Bea didn't care how many times Miranda did the same scene over and over again, she was thrilled to watch every single time. And every single time she would chime, "I think that was your best try yet!" She'd been picking up a bit of show business argot of late, and was trying to remember to call them "the takes."

Miranda was in no mood for more takes. "Please inform the staff that I shall be dining alfresco, on the veranda." She gathered her clutch purse, pulled her scarf to where it belonged, and left.

Bea and Andrew exchanged looks. Staff?

"Are you the staff or am I the staff?" Bea asked.

"I think we're both staff."

"And the veranda . . . ?"

"Front porch," he explained. Andrew spoke Miranda.

He turned off the ring light as Bea opened the curtains. The morning light once again flooded the sitting room, now steeped more in sadness than sun, it seemed.

"I thought she'd be happy," said Bea, referring to the magazine. "I hurried in with the news."

"If they've 'wrapped,' it means it's a little too late to audition."

Did he really have to explain this to her?

"Oh. I see."

"Don't feel bad. It's not you, Bea."

It's the universe. It was arrayed against Miranda, it seemed. Memories of Andrew's parents, elated when he was first hired as a personal assistant to the former Pastor Fran. "What is she like?" they would ask. Pastor Fran? She was strong, decisive, invulnerable. Miranda Abbott? Not so much.

"I'll put on a pot of oatmeal," said Bea. "An' crack open some SunnyD." Breakfast was overdue.

Miranda, meanwhile, feeling forlorn and vaguely betrayed, had retired to the veranda (aka Bea's front porch) with its overhanging baskets of asters and fall pansies, and was looking out at the waters of Tillamook Bay. Amid the reel and cry of seagulls, sailboats moved across the silvery surface, gliding in on westward winds, the air crisp and clean. The town of Happy Rock lay snug in the curve of the bay, nestled between the lighthouse at one end and Bea's B&B at the other.

There would be no Monaco, no Lisbon, no Paris—no Montreal, even. Miranda Abbott, star of stage and screen, was marooned in Happy Rock.

Above the harbor, ivy-clad and regal, stood the grand Duchess Hotel, haunted it was said—as most buildings were out here. (A building that hadn't managed to pick up a ghost or two along the way was considered unworthy of the area. It was almost listed as a real estate feature: *3 bedrooms, cedar shake roof, plenty of parking, resident ghost.*) Next to the hotel, equally haunted, was the alabaster elegance of the Opera House, home to the local Little Theater Society. But these grand architectural gestures aside, the town was as drowsy as a waking dream. It was always three in the afternoon in Happy Rock. It was a town of modest Victorian storefronts and latticework trellises, with mossy cabins half-hidden in the back lanes.

Fishermen cast their lines from the barnacled pier, reeling them in, casting them out, reeling them in, the motion almost hypnotic–not unlike the town itself. Happy Rock had a way of lulling one into a state of sleepy surrender. A sign above the pier read CATCH & RELEASE ONLY, and Miranda often wondered, having been caught, would she ever be released? Did she want to be released?

Damn that Meryl Streep! She's always stealing roles from me.

Miranda took out a small bell from her clutch purse, the type receptionists use, and placed it firmly on the wide arm of the chair. With a single decisive tap, she rang it. This wasn't over! Not by a long shot!

Bea appeared, confused.

"You bought a bell?"

"I had Andrew order it for me from The Cloud. Same place he found the lighting kit." Miranda assumed The Cloud was some sort of specialty shop back in Beverly Hills, and she lowered her voice, lest she give away any of Andrew's secrets. "He has an app, you see." She wasn't exactly clear on what an app was, but she knew Andrew had one, and that it allowed him to perform any number of feats.

"And, ah, what did you want?" Bea asked with a nod to the bell. The porridge was on low boil, the SunnyD had been decanted. Breakfast was almost ready.

"The telephone!" cried Miranda in the manner of a Shakespearean king calling for a horse.

Oh no, thought Bea. Here we go.

CHAPTER TWO

Rendezvous at the Murder Store

"**I** will call that disreputable agent of mine and set things straight once and for all!" Miranda vowed. "Don't worry!"

"I wasn't," said Bea. "It's just... I'm not sure the phone will reach out here. Are you sure you don't want to use Andrew's cell phone instead? He doesn't have to pay long-distance fees and..." Miranda hadn't been paying any of her room charges during The Lull, as she called it.

"One cannot slam down a cell phone in anger," Miranda explained. "I will be calling that simpering invertebrate of an agent. And when I do, I shall hang up on him!"

True. It was much more satisfying to slam down a handset than end a call by angrily swiping at a screen. But would the landline reach the veranda?

"It must! It shall!" Miranda cried.

And so it did. Bea managed to stretch the cord all the way from the sitting room, taut as a lute string, to where Miranda was sitting, regal on her Adirondack throne. The telephone was an old-fashioned black rotary unit. Bea had added a ridiculously lengthy cord because of Miranda's habit of taking calls wherever she happened to be, upstairs or down.

Andrew appeared, and she had him dial—and dial and dial. It was a very lengthy number. "LA!" she said.

"Long-distance," Bea replied.

The pas de deux began as soon as Marty's alleged receptionist answered the phone. (It was quite obviously just Marty speaking in a high-pitched voice.) "Marty Sharpe Talent Agency, Home of Tomorrow's Stars Today. Please hold—"

Thirty seconds of Muzak (the *Pastor Fran* theme song, ironically enough; Andrew remembered it well).

"Hello. This is Marty Sharpe's office, how may I direct your call?"

It was Marty. There was no one other than him to "direct" the call to. Andrew knew that, Miranda knew that, Marty knew that Andrew and Miranda knew that, but this was LA; perception was everything, reality just an annoying detail to get past.

As soon as Marty came on, Andrew said, "Hold for Miranda Abbott, please." "Hold for Miranda Abbott, please."

The rule was, whoever waited last was of lower status. Andrew could actually hear Marty Sharpe's eyes rolling on the other end.

"That you, Andy?"

Miranda snatched the receiver from Andrew and commenced yelling.

When she paused to draw breath, Marty said, in awe really, "You honestly thought you were going to audition for the Clooney pic? Even by your standards, Miranda, that is really some pie-in-the-sky fantasizing. Bravo. Quite remarkable. Truly. Whenever I think you can't get any more delusionary, you prove me wrong."

"Marty, I swear, I will come down to LA and personally kick your tiny little balls into orbit."

"Okay, okay. Listen. I may have something for you. The Kalama-zoo Redd-E-Alert. It's only one line, but it's a beaut! *I have fallen… but I CAN get up, thanks to the Kalamazoo Redd-E-Alert 2000.* Of course, you'd have to fly out to Kalamazoo for the audition."

"Offers only, Marty!"

"You have to audition, like regular folk."

"I am NOT regular folk. I am a star."

"*Were* a star."

When Andrew overheard that, he began his countdown to deto-nation. *3… 2… 1*

"How dare you! I played Pastor Fran on *Pastor Fran Investigates*! I had a number one show on network TV. You can't talk to me like that. You're fired, Marty! I'm firing you. Do you understand? You have been thoroughly and utterly fired!"

"Yup. Got that."

BAM! She slammed down the receiver. Those old phones. Sturdy.

Miranda's face was flush with ire. Andrew's less so. He'd seen this play before.

"Oh, dear," said Bea, always worried that Miranda would some-day fire Marty and he'd stay fired. Then where would Bea's secret dream of a *Pastor Fran* reboot be? Time for some oatmeal, she reck-oned. "Now, Fran—er, Miranda—maybe we should just . . ." But her voice trailed off, as it always did whenever she saw the police chief's patrol car pull up.

The law had come calling, the vehicle rolling to a slow stop in front of Bea's veranda. Officer Ned Buckley got out carrying a newspaper-wrapped package.

"Halloo!" he said, coming to the porch rather than through the back door, holding the package up. "Chinook salmon, fresh from the fall run on Nestucca Bay."

Some people bring flowers, some bring wine. Officer Ned

Buckley, Chief of Police, HRPD, brought a great big dead fish.

Ned was a soft fellow, in every sense. Soft-spoken and soft of eyes, soft of girth and soft of chin. But Miranda had learned not to underestimate him, even if the uniform was a little snug around the waist and the belly a little round.

With Bea being a widow and Ned single and clearly smitten, Miranda never could tell what was holding them back—except for the fact that Ned had known Bea's husband. They'd been friends, had grown up together. "Bob was a good man," Ned always said. It was the highest compliment he could give.

Bob's presence—or rather, his absence—hung over Bea's life like a winding sheet, like a scent of aftershave that never quite faded. When Bea had converted her cottage-like home into a bed-and-breakfast after Bob's passing, as much for the company as the income, she had considered naming it after both her and her late husband—B&B's B&B—but decided against it. "It might prove confusing," she'd said.

So Bea's B&B it was.

Ned handed the fish across the veranda. "For tonight," he said. "Pastor Fran Friday!"

It was Wednesday, not Friday, but no one minded. The day of the week for a Pastor Fran Friday was flexible. Bea and her late husband Bob had purchased the entire *Pastor Fran* Collection on VHS—including both Christmas specials and the hard-to-find compilation tape *A Pastor Fran Potpourri*—and with the star of the show in residence, Bea would regularly select a blast from the past to watch over TV trays of baked salmon and caramel popcorn. (Bea baked the salmon; Ned brought the popcorn. Not the most nuanced of gastronomical couplings.)

As long as she stayed at Bea's, Miranda was resigned to such rituals, sitting snug with Ned and Bea in the dark, watching her younger self defuse bombs and karate-kick villains with a vigor she could hardly recall. It was like watching someone else entirely. An alternate version of herself.

For Miranda Abbott, Pastor Fran Fridays would always be more poignant than nostalgic.

Miranda's hopelessly urban—and urbane—assistant Andrew Nguyen found Ned Buckley endlessly fascinating, like a rare bit of fauna long thought to be extinct: the friendly small-town cop, imbued in the local vernacular, who said things like "Gol'darnit" and "Well, ain't that a to-do?," who called lunch "dinner" and soft drinks "soda pop."

"Workin' on a case?" Andrew asked, dropping his g's, just like a local.

"Power went out in the Duchess. If you can call that a case."

The hotel's entire east wing had lost electricity briefly during the night.

"Wouldn't that be more of a utilities issue," asked Andrew, "rather than police?"

"Well, you know how it is, anything goes wrong up there and right away they're on the blower askin' for me."

Blower, thought Andrew. He also calls a telephone "the blower." Soda pop, dinner, and the ol' blower.

"I'll run the salmon in," Andrew offered, taking the drooping package from Ned as he handed it across the porch railing. Ned was clearly there on other business.

"Come around," Bea said to the police chief. "Tea? I have chamomile."

"Can't stay, I'm afraid. Was at the Murder Store," he said, with a nod to Miranda, before turning his attention back to Bea. "And I found something you might like."

It was a paperback, well-thumbed, with a lurid orange cover, cheesy 3D font—and a painting of Miranda on the front, leaning into a darkened room, leaning into danger. A *Pastor Fran* TV novelization, as written by the indomitable and completely fictitious Stone Rockwell.

"Oh my!" said Bea, taking the book from Ned and turning it over in her hands. "*The Case of the Cold-Hearted Casanova*. I don't have this one!"

"Signed by the author," Ned noted proudly. What he didn't mention was "begrudgingly." Signed very begrudgingly by the author.

"I didn't think he carried those," Miranda said dryly. "I thought they were beneath him."

The Murder Store, as Ned and most of the town referred to it, was Happy Rock's preeminent bookstore, one that specialized in mysteries and thrillers. Enclosed in an old house on Beacon Hill, with creaky floors and narrow corridors, the bookstore—named I Only Read Murder—seemed very much like it was drawn straight from the pages of one of the mysteries it sold.

It was manned by a cranky owner, unforgivably handsome, who lived above the store like a literary hermit, pecking away on an electric typewriter that should have been in a museum. His name was Edgar, aka Stone Rockwell, aka Doug Dirks (when he was writing plays), aka the head writer on *Pastor Fran Investigates* all those years ago, aka Miranda Abbott's husband.

Or, one should say, her soon-to-be ex-husband.

"Edgar was askin' after you," Ned said.

"Oh. Was he now?" This threw Miranda a bit. So, HE was asking after ME? Interesting...

"Yup, wanted to know where the heck you were. Though of course, it being Edgar, he didn't say 'heck.' He has a more saltier vocabulary than that."

Andrew returned, having stowed the salmon in Bea's fridge, only to have Miranda say to him, "Darling, as my personal assistant, are you aware of any appointments I might have today? Do check your day-timer."

He pulled out the notebook he kept in his pocket, blank except for the occasional scribbled Miranda Abbott aphorism, and pretended to flip through her non-existent schedule. "Let me see, other than filming the audition tape for a movie that's already wrapped … Nothing. You have a free day." She had a lot of those lately.

She turned back to Ned, who was standing on the steps to the veranda. "Ha!" she said. "See? Edgar is woefully mistaken! I have no arrangement to meet with him, least of all today!"

"Be that as it may," said Ned. "He is waitin' on you at the Murder Store. He's there with Atticus, waitin', the both of them."

"Atticus Lawson? The lawyer who has a paralyzing fear of public speaking? The worst lawyer in Happy Rock? That Atticus Lawson?"

The *only* lawyer in Happy Rock, thought Andrew. Pretty much.

"Do you know any other Atticus Lawsons?" Ned asked, genuinely puzzled. "Seems like an unusual name."

"Leave me!" Miranda cried, finally able to pivot with a proper fling of her scarf. "Leave me now, Ned. I have nothing further to say to my husband or his mercenary cabal of legal hyenas."

She had a sense of what it might be about. They all did. Dimly, at the back of her mind, Miranda recalled a terse phone call from Edgar a few days earlier, reminding her that the two of them still needed to …

"Fine!" she said. "I shall meet with Edgar and Atticus, if only to explain how utterly mistaken they are in terms of any prearranged meetings on our part. Ned! To the bookstore!" She rose dramatically.

Ned sighed. "Now, Miranda, what have I said about using my patrol car to run errands? I'm not a taxi. I'm a police officer. I'm the chief of police officers."

"Of course you are, that's why I asked you. I wouldn't ask you if you weren't, but you are, so I did." Riddles that almost made sense. "We must make haste, Ned. We are already late."

"How can you be late for an appointment you didn't make?" he asked.

"I don't make appointments," she said.

"I know, I know," said Ned. He was getting a Miranda-induced headache. "Appointments make you. Right?"

"That's the first thing you've said that's made any sense," she said. "Well done, Ned. Now Andrew, darling, you can wait here till I return." She lowered her voice. "Perhaps check your app while I'm out, see if there are any further Clooney-related auditions coming up. Oh, and remind me to fire Marty later."

"But... you already did."

"Yes, yes, yes," she said, getting impatient. "That's why I asked you to remind me."

Andrew was now getting a Miranda-induced migraine of his own.

"What about the oatmeal?" Bea fretted.

"I shall have it on my return. This shan't take long."

And she was right... It didn't take long. It took ages.

THE TROUBLE BEGAN almost immediately, when Miranda entered the bookstore on the trill of a bell. Edgar had cleared one of the discount tables—remaindered hardcovers and discontinued series—and was waiting with Atticus at his side.

Edgar's eyes were blazing with annoyance. She knew that look well. Edgar was an easily annoyed man, one of his many flaws. Lean, with a strong jawline, which, if not chiseled, was at the very least well-filed. Hair, short and graying at the temples. Jeans and a plaid shirt—had he ever worn anything else, other than the occasional corduroy jacket?—and eyes impossibly blue. Her husband still, even if he didn't want to admit it.

Atticus Lawson, with his turkey neck and polyester jacket, was not nearly as impressive. "Hiya!" he said, a sheaf of documents on the table in front of him.

Ned Buckley, having driven her up, followed Miranda into the bookstore with a friendly, "I'll be in the next room if you need me, poking about in True Crime."

The bookstore sprawled between rooms, took up the entire first floor. The hallways and corridors were lined with shelves stacked floor-to-ceiling with books, both new and used. It was expansive— and crowded. Much like her marriage, she thought.

Miranda had returned to Edgar after fifteen years in Hollywood, thinking they could pick up where they'd left off, but no, he spoke instead about "water" under some "bridge," about "ships" that had somehow "sailed." He was utterly unreasonable.

Edgar gestured to a chair, but she remained standing. "I accept your apology," she said. Only then did she sit down, and regally so.

"Apology? For what! We've been waiting an hour."

"An hour and a half, actually," said Atticus, who charged by the half hour.

Edgar slid a pen across to Miranda. "Just sign the damned divorce papers."

"I want custody. Joint custody."

Edgar, tense. "We've already talked about this. You have visitation rights. That's all. It would be upsetting for her, going back and forth."

"Last time I walked by, Emmy was rooting around in the garbage like a dog!"

"She *is* a dog. That's what dogs do!"

Emmy being Edgar's golden Lab.

"Fine," said Miranda. "I'll sign…"

"Good!"

"If you apologize."

"You're hopeless!" Edgar roared. "Apologize? For what?"

"You cheated on me."

"We've been separated for more than fifteen years!"

"Exactly. I turn my back for one moment…"

"It wasn't some sleazy fling," said Edgar. "Cindy and I were together for three and a half of those years. We *almost* got married, but–" Edgar seemed to catch himself.

Miranda flipped through the documents. "A no-contest divorce? Ha. I should get half of everything."

"Half of my debts too? Be my guest. The bookstore has been mortgaged. Twice. It's a labor of love at this point."

"Well then…" She thought for a moment. "I should get half your books, then."

"Half?"

"Every second book should be mine, hardcover or paperback, new or used." She turned around in her chair to the wall of books next to the table. "So, if there's a mystery series, like this one, for example–Mrs. Petunia's Perfect Capers–I would get books 1, 3, 5, 7, 9, 11, 13, and so on."

"There are 178 of them!"

"Exactly. I could sell them."

Edgar was working up another head of steam. "Sell them? How? *To who?!*"

"Whom, darling. Sell them to *whom*. Well, I suppose I could sell them to… you, I guess."

"You want all the odd-numbered books in a series? Do you hear yourself? Do you hear what you're saying? That's idiotic! Even by your standards!"

In truth, she didn't want anything from him. Not books, not money. Just regret, that's all. Just the smallest sign that he was sad about it, that she had meant something to him once upon a time. Miranda didn't realize that she hadn't meant *something* to Edgar. She'd meant everything.

CHAPTER THREE

Carpe Diem, Baby!

The bookstore was on Beacon Hill. It had a perfect view of the harbor, like peering down on a postcard, thought Miranda. A haunted postcard, much like the hotel, like the town. Even Edgar's bookstore was haunted—though not only with the ghosts of those who had faced an untimely demise inside, but with the ghost of their marriage as well.

She had stormed out of her meeting with Edgar and Atticus—Miranda Abbott never "left" a room, she either stormed out or floated away like silk unfurling on a breeze. Everyone talked about making an entrance. For Miranda, it was equally important to make an exit.

"It will snow in Happy Rock before I sign those papers!" she'd declared.

"It does snow in Happy Rock," Atticus had said, clearly confused. "Every winter. Quite pretty, actually."

But by that point, Miranda Abbott had already flung her scarf over her shoulder and herself from the bookstore.

"Ned! We are leaving!" she said, but Ned was two rooms away in True Crime.

"In a sec," he called out.

For Ned, True Crime was like homework. He preferred romances, truth be told, but Edgar didn't stock those.

Miranda waited outside, next to Ned's patrol car. From the harbor below, a seaplane lifted off against a thick backdrop of Douglas fir, evergreen and forever dark, even in sunlight. In the town itself, the first tinge of autumn color had arrived, highlights of orange among the larch and ash. It was beautiful. A beautiful prison. Whenever she caught herself falling for it, Miranda reminded herself that she was only here temporarily. Her heart still belonged to Hollywood. (And Hollywood belonged to her!)

And yet...

Ned came down the steps, holster flopping, his latest stash of books tucked under one arm, car keys in hand, police cap pushed back.

"He got a new batch in this morning," Ned explained. "Said I might like 'em. Tricky true-life mysteries, the sort I enjoy, is what he said." ("He" meaning her husband—or ex-husband, or whatever it was Edgar was.)

"I have to get out of Happy Rock," she said.

"Portland? Bus left already. Next one's not till dinner." And in case she thought he was going to drive her all the way to Portland, he quickly added, "And I got a lot of police work to catch up on, what with the power outage at the hotel and some rosebushes that were trampled."

Ah, yes. Trampled bushes and faulty hotel breakers. The excitement never stopped here in Happy Rock.

"Not Portland, Ned. LA. Where I belong."

Ned's expression softened as he unlocked the back of the patrol car (Miranda preferred to sit in the rear, as one might with a chauffeur). "But you do belong here," he said.

That's what I'm worried about, she thought.

She didn't speak on the drive back, down the winding, leafy lane from Beacon Hill, around behind the Duchess Hotel and then along the harbor road toward Bea's.

The oatmeal had gone cold.

Andrew was rinsing out his bowl and Bea was fretting, as she always did—fretting was her default, Ned had noted, especially since Bob died. "Shall I cook a fresh batch?" she asked.

Miranda smiled. Bea is so kind. I scarcely deserve it, she thought.

"I'll have it later," Miranda said. "It is not a problem. I once ate cold oatmeal for a month when I was preparing to play Oliver in an all-female stage production of *Oliver Twist*." (She hadn't landed the role because she was not "believable" as a ten-year old "orphan.") "I may even make some of my famous lemonade," she threatened.

Ned shuddered. He looked around the kitchen, desperate for a way out. Miranda's lemonade was not so much famous as infamous. A slurry of processed sugar mixed with a gallon of lemon juice, a handful of salt (inexplicably), and sometimes a dollop of cream, which instantly curdled.

"Please god no," said Bea. "I mean, *Gosh, please don't*. I've got plenty of SunnyD. No reason for you to be put out."

"Nonsense! It's the least I could do."

"But—well, it turns out I've developed an allergy to lemons. Drat it, anyway."

"Yes!" Andrew chimed in. "Myself as well. I saw Doc Meadows. He said, 'Son, you best avoid lemons.' You know how he talks, all folksy and whatnot."

"He said that? Ancient sacred knowledge?" Miranda asked, voice in a hush. Doc Meadows was Salish.

"Yes!" Andrew said. "Very ancient, very sacred. No lemons. That's what he said."

"A Salish aversion to lemons? I'd never heard of that before. How utterly odd." She turned to Happy Rock's finest. "Ned?"

"Can't. Canker sores."

"For the last four months? You should really see Doc Meadows as well, get that checked."

"Will do," he said. "Gotta get back to the station. Salmon tonight?" he asked Bea.

"You bet!" said Bea. She would bake it, and together they would watch Pastor Fran crack another case.

With that, Ned slipped away before Miranda could book any more rides with him.

She turned to Andrew. "To the sitting room!" she cried.

"Landline?" he asked, resigned.

"Exactly!"

They went down the hall and Bea fretted some more and Andrew dialed that same number, which seemed to grow longer every time.

"Long-distance again, I see," said Bea with a pained smile.

"Please hold for Miranda Abbott." Andrew handed the receiver over to her.

"It is I!" she said. "We have much to discuss."

"I'm not your agent anymore," said Marty. "You fired me, remember? Again."

"Oh. Well then, I am *un*-firing you."

"You're un-firing me? Again?"

"Yes."

Andrew was sitting next to her. He leaned in, whispered to Miranda, "You 'un-fired' him? I think that's called re-hiring."

She replied with a perfect Miranda Abbott aphorism. "Firing and hiring are the same sides of a different coin!"

Riddles that almost made sense...

Andrew flipped open his notebook, wrote that bon mot down too.

A rustle of paper from Marty on the other end. "Okay, seeing as how I have been *un*-re-fired, I may have something for you."

"It had better be good," she warned.

"Commensurate with your stature as an actor."

"That's much better," she replied, placated for the time being and missing the hidden ambiguity of that statement. "Continue."

"A detective show..."

"Go on. I'm listening."

"Filmed in Burbank."

"Series?"

"A one-off, but it could become a backdoor pilot."

"And whom will I be playing?"

"Not *playing*," he said. "Auditioning for."

She let that go with a grit of her teeth. "The role, Marty. What is the *role*?"

"A wry, gum-snapping waitress at the local diner. Would be a recurring character if it goes to series. No lines, but she's in almost every scene that involves the diner."

"No lines?!"

"Think of her as Our Goddess of the Coffee Pot. A potentially iconic role. Some of the greatest roles in cinematic history had no lines, I remind you."

"Name one!" And before he could cite Chaplin or Mary Pickford, "*After* the silent era."

"Well, if you're gonna put it like that," he griped. "Words or no words, it's a terrific part. The character is very reactive. Very wry, as I said."

"The name," said Miranda, voice flat.

"The name?"

"Of the character." She already knew what he was going to say.

"She doesn't have a name right now, not exactly, not *per se*." When in doubt, use Latin. "It's more of an *acta non verba* situation. For now, she's listed as Waitress #1. Think about that! *Number one*, Miranda. No second fiddle for you at the diner. Carpe diem, kiddo!"

"Et tu, Marty? She has no lines!"

"But think what you can bring to the role, Miranda. Think of how you can use your eyebrows to convey the subtleties of what she is feeling."

"I don't care if it is a backdoor pilot, Marty. I'm not auditioning with my eyebrows!"

Bea Maracle wasn't sure what a backdoor pilot was, but it sounded a bit risqué. She hoped not. Though she did love a man in uniform. Pilots, firemen. Police.

"I shouldn't have to audition at all!" Miranda shouted. Bea could feel the slam-down coming. "It should be offers only at this point. Offers only! You're fired, Marty."

"Oh, dear," said Bea, worried as always that this time it would be permanent.

"Don't you worry," Miranda said after she hung up. "They'll come crawling back. They always do."

The landline rang. Miranda and Andrew were so startled, they jumped.

"That was fast." Andrew was concerned. Marty never made callbacks, said they were for suckers.

Again the phone rang, and again Andrew flinched.

"How very strange," said Miranda. "He never calls this number." Never calls at all, in fact. She wasn't concerned so much as confused.

Bea Maracle, however, was neither concerned nor confused. She answered for them.

"Hello? . . . Yes, that's right. Bea's B&B . . . No, just the three Bs . . . Oh, I see . . . She's here now. Just a sec and I'll fetch her." Bea held the handset to Miranda.

Miranda reached for the phone, but before she could take it, Bea remembered her show business etiquette.

"Hold for Miranda Abbott, please," she said primly, and then passed the phone to Miranda. "Something about a movie," Bea whispered.

Ha!

"I knew you'd come crawling back!" Miranda yelled, triumphant. "You had better have something good for me or so help me, I will tear you a new one!"

"Um, yeah," said an unfamiliar voice. "I may have something. Is this Ms. Abbott?"

An awkward pause. "It is I."

"I just talked to your agent, one Martin J. Sharpe, but he said he's been un-fired and then re-unhired, or something, and he wasn't sure if he still worked for you."

"My relationship with Martin is . . . complicated."

A warm chuckle. "I understand completely. Agents, right?" The voice on the other end of the line was friendly—not Hollywood friendly, not air-kiss-you-on-the-cheek-while-I-trash-you-behind-your-back friendly, but *actual* friendly, like in the real world. "It's a pleasure to speak with you, Ms. Abbott. And an honor. I've been a fan of yours for many years. My name is Alan Zabic. I'm with A to Z Film Services. I work with Pindaric, and I've been brought on as Unit Production Manager to oversee one of their upcoming projects. Pindaric Productions? You've heard of them?"

"I'm familiar with Pindaric." Miranda was not familiar with Pindaric.

"Wonderful. Well, as you know, Pindaric creates made-for-television movies of the week, often based on novels, mid-budget productions, but always of the highest quality. They do Christmas MOWs and Valentine's Day MOWs, any number of holiday-themed shows. I've been involved with several of those, they're always a lot of fun, but this project is part of their mystery series. Cozies, for want of a better word. You know, an amateur sleuth, female, usually plucky, with a small-town murder solved in the penultimate chapter and equilibrium restored. That sort of thing. They're surprisingly popular."

An MOW? Please tell me this isn't the same one Marty was pitching, she thought. "Does the, ah, character have any lines?"

Alan laughed. "You're very funny. I knew you'd be funny. You always brought such humor and humanity to your parts. Of course she has lines!"

"And a name?"

Another laugh. "I would hope so. It's Clover McBride, the lead character. You'd be starring alongside–"

And there it was.

The Name.

Not a person, not an actor, a *name*.

"Harry Tomlin?" Miranda gasped, not sure she'd heard correctly. "Five-time-Oscar-nominated Harry Tomlin, star of *Shipwreck Bugaloo*, *Mermaid 2*, *Normandy Ho!*, and *Tears for the Innocent Prisoner Who Didn't Deserve to Die*? The same Harry Tomlin who's been voted The Nicest Man in America™ by *People* magazine four years running? That Harry Tomlin?"

"Do you know any other Harry Tomlins? You're hilarious, Ms. Abbott! And here I was, nervous to call you."

"Why would you be nervous?" she asked.

"Are you kidding? You're Miranda Abbott. You must have dozens of bigwigs lining up every day, pitching you projects. I'm amazed you even took my call."

Miranda was as susceptible to empty flattery as the next actress, possibly more so, but the strangest thing was, he sounded … almost

... *sincere*. This was such an alien emotion among film people that Miranda had trouble placing it at first. But yes, he was being—of all things!—sincere.

"I see," she said, waving to Andrew for a pen and paper. He quickly handed over his blank notebook. "And when will the auditions be held?" she asked.

She was already thinking wardrobe and stylist and which monologue to recite, and she scribbled a note to Andrew while she was still on the phone, meaning *Book us a flight to Los Angeles right away, okay?* What she actually scribbled was *LAXASAPOK??* To which Andrew could only scribble back: *wtf??*

"Auditions?" said the voice on the line. "Oh, I'm sorry, I didn't make myself clear. This isn't for an audition."

"No?" she said, growing wary.

"This is an offer."

"I see."

"I was happy to get Harry Tomlin, but if I could land you as well, that would be a major, major coup."

"May I confer a moment with my colleagues?" Miranda said, cool as all get-out. She then muffled the phone with one of Bea's throw cushions, the one with HOME IS A HAPPINESS OF THE HEART in needlepoint.

Andrew looked at her. "And?"

"A starring role," she said. "Alongside Harry Tomlin! Not an audition. An offer."

"Harry Tomlin?" Bea exclaimed. "But he has his own line of salad dressings!" This was the highest level of fame one could attain in her eyes.

"Huh," said Andrew, trying to process the information that was coming out of Miranda. His head tilted slightly to one side, like a dog hearing a fire engine siren in the distance. What could these sounds I'm hearing possibly mean? "You sure he said Tomlin? You sure he said co-starring? And are you sure he said 'offer' not 'possibly consider'?"

"Yes, yes, and most assuredly yes," she replied. "Now, contact Marty on your mobile phone and tell him he's un-fired."

Andrew was already on it, thumb-texting in a blur, as Miranda placed the cushion delicately to one side. The back of the cushion read LOVE IS THE LOVELIEST WAY TO LIVE with a cherub and a heart. When Miranda spoke, she tried not to grin or smile too much; you could hear that in a voice, and she didn't want to seem desperate.

"Mr. Zabic, is it?" Miranda wasn't sure she remembered the name on the other end of the line.

"It is, indeed."

"I could look through the script, see if it meets my high standards, and then let you know if it is possibly a project I might perhaps be interested in."

"Wonderful!"

Andrew was making "I'm writing with a quill pen" gestures.

Oh, right.

"I don't care for emails, however. Too impersonal. And the personal is all too often *impersonal* these days, don't you think?"

Bizarrely, he seemed to understand. "Of course. I won't send it as an attachment. I have a freshly printed hardcopy, bound and ready for you to read."

"You may messenger it to me. I'll have my personal assistant give you the address momentarily. Andrew, darling—"

But the voice on the line stopped her.

"Yes, well, here's the thing…"

"Yes?"

"I'm actually parked outside."

CHAPTER FOUR

"Call me Zab"

The door to 313 was unlocked—again.

Chester Cornelius, newly appointed acting general manager of the Duchess Hotel, hesitated. He felt a chill at odds with the stuffy corridors he was walking down. The faded paisley carpets, the wallpaper in an indeterminate shade of puce, the endless hallways, the lace curtains that looked like they might crumble at the slightest touch, the bulbs that flickered overhead and the floorboards that groaned below: the entire east wing, four stories stacked atop each other, stately in their day but now threadbare and frayed, was a diorama of dust.

He swallowed, locked the door to Room 313. Again. It was as though something was trying to get out. A simple turn of a key, and the room was secured. Again. No card swipes here. Not in the east wing, anyway. Actual keys in actual locks.

So why had the film crew booked it? The movie director, the one who'd been scouting locations on the sly—Leni something-or-other—had asked specifically for the *east* wing, "for atmosphere," as she put it. They would be filming and staying in the east wing, having reserved every room, grand or small, on every floor. Even the Suicide Suite, though of course that wasn't its real name. To unwitting guests, it was simply Room 313.

Chester was a gangly man, all knees and elbows and Adam's apple, constrained in a burgundy jacket with sleeves too short and a collar too tight. He heard the rattle of something moving behind a wall. A scraping sound. One of the dumbwaiters, no doubt, rattling upwards, carrying linen most likely.

The hotel staff would be hurrying to get ready for the Hollywood types who were about to descend on Happy Rock. This would be a fortuitous windfall for the Duchess. The film crew was paying top dollar, well above market value, which in turn might finally allow Chester to get approval for the funds needed to renovate the east wing, bring it up to par with the west, casting aside outdated fixtures and lingering ghosts alike.

A movie! Here in Happy Rock! It was all very exciting. There were even rumors of a bona fide movie star. Hence the Roosevelt Suite on the third floor, reserved for tinseled royalty with its Evita-style balcony looking out over the rose garden and glass-encased atrium below. The Roosevelt was also, unfortunately, directly across the hall from Room 313. Better not to mention the gruesome murders that had occurred in the Duchess over the years: the grisly suitcase murder, the ghastly newlyweds' murder-suicide, not to mention the Victorian maid who'd stepped off that very balcony in the Roosevelt Suite or the traveling salesman who'd been found hanging from the rafters in the Suicide Suite. None of that was relevant. They were shooting a movie! Right here in Happy Rock!

He checked the handle to 313 one last time, made sure it was indeed locked, then hurried off, like a man pursued by an undefinable fear.

...

AT THE VERY moment that Chester Cornelius was scurrying away, Miranda Abbott and her stalwart assistant Andrew were peeking through the tiniest of gaps in Bea's drapes.

A sporty baby-blue Aston Martin, the kind James Bond might drive, was parked out front, and leaning against it, in a Tommy Bahama shirt and L.L.Bean chinos, with a grin as wide as the sky, was a tousle-haired man with a California tan—not spray-on, even from here they could see that. He held a smartphone in one hand and a script in the other, and he must have seen the curtains move, because he held the script up in lieu of a wave.

Both Miranda and Andrew had the same thought: *That's an attractive man.* Although Andrew was noticing the smooth cheeks and smile, while Miranda was noticing the smile lines and full head of graying hair.

"Oh, for goodness' sake," said Bea. She yanked the curtains open, and Miranda and Andrew were caught, frozen in place, crouching in front of the window like cartoon spies.

Outside, Alan's smile became warmer, his eyes crinklier, and Bea Maracle took notice.

"That's a good-looking man," she said.

Alan Zabic. A to Z, indeed.

Bea waved for him to come around and, patting her hair into place, went to the back door to let him in. She brought him in, and even in close-up he was handsome. Heck, even his *watch* was handsome, a classic white-gold and mother-of-pearl Rolex Cellini, if Andrew wasn't mistaken.

"So you're the Bea in B&B," said Mr. Zabic. "Or should I say, the Bea's knees."

When you're attractive, every quip is treated like a comment worthy of the Algonquin Round Table, and so it was with Bea, who giggled and sputtered, and—was she blushing? She was!

"I'm Andrew Nguyen." Hand extended. "I'm Miranda's personal assistant. Andrew. That's my name. Andrew. It's Andrew. Andrew Nguyen."

Direct eye contact and a firm handshake from Mr. Zabic—and for a moment Andrew was the most important person in the world. Just for a moment, but it was enough.

Mr. Zabic then turned his attention, all his attention, onto Miranda.

His smile became a grin, and the grin a beam of pure light. "Miranda Abbott," he said, pronouncing her name the way some might say *Santa* or *the Loch Ness Monster* or some other mythical creation they never thought they'd actually meet, weren't even sure existed.

"It is I. It is. I." Miranda realized she was repeating herself as badly as Andrew had.

Alan Zabic smiled. That same unblinking eye contact, that same disarming sincerity. Miranda held out her own hand as though expecting (hoping) he would kiss it, but, misinterpreting the gesture, he said, "Oh. Right. Of course," and he handed her the script instead.

Not just any script, though. It was bound in genuine Corinthian leather and printed on the finest washi parchment paper in matte ivory:

MURDEROUSNESS AND MYSTERIOUSNESS
AT YE OLDE TYME HOTEL!!

screenplay by Lachlan Todd
based on the novel
The Quiet Dignity of the Old Hotel: A Mystery
by P.K. Pennington

The screenwriter. *Lachlan Todd*. Miranda knew that name. Surely it couldn't be Luckless Lachlan, Edgar's old rival? They'd had a feud of some sort years ago, Lachlan and her husband. Surely it couldn't be *that* Lachlan.

But then, how many Lachlan Todds would one person know?

"Please do have a seat," said Bea, hands aflutter. "It is called the *sitting* room, after all." And she giggled. Oh, how she giggled.

Alan sat down the way wine slides into a glass and the three of them crowded in, Andrew and Bea wedging into the settee, as Miranda Abbott poured herself equally elegantly into the high-backed armchair across from him.

"Now, Mr. Zabic—"

"Please. Call me Zab. All my friends do."

"Mr. . . . Zab. As flattered as I am by your offer and your interest, you should be aware that I am currently considering several major projects."

"Really?" chirped Bea. "That's wonderful. Because you told us you had nothing, absolutely nothing on the horizon. You fired Marty, remember, because— *Ow!* Andrew!"

He had kicked her shin. He would do it again if he had to. Sometimes one had to resort to violence.

An icicle of a smile from Miranda was thrown Bea's way. She then turned her lofty gaze back to Alan "Zab" Zabic.

"As I was saying . . ."

But he stopped her with a raised hand. "I understand. It's presumptuous of me to expect an actress of your caliber to readily agree. But Miranda, will you do me one favor?"

"Anything!" said Bea, jumping in, answering for Miranda. "*Ow!*"

There it was again, that deep, compassionate eye contact. Miranda almost melted. What witchcraft is this?! she thought. To think, just that morning she'd had to face her ex-husband's angry glare, so much harsher.

"Will you at least *think* about it, Miranda? That's all I ask."

"I shall."

"Excellent!" said Zab. "This calls for a celebration. Champagne?"

"SunnyD?" said Bea.

Oh no. There would be none of that. Miranda Abbott rose like the royalty she was and said, with the grace that was hers, "I shall make you some lemonade, Mr. Zabic."

"No!" said Bea and Andrew, more or less simultaneously. "I mean, that is..." said Bea.

"That is to say," said Andrew, "I'm sure Mr. Zabic—"

"Please, call me Zab."

"—Zab, I should say, is very busy and, well . . ." Andrew's voice trailed off. Could an actor lose a role over lemonade? Andrew didn't want to find out.

"I don't mind, not at all," said Zab, damn him anyway. "I would *love* a glass."

Miranda beckoned Andrew to assist. "Darling, join me in the kitchen."

"Are you really sure now is the time for lemonade . . . ?" he said, following her down the hall to Bea's kitchen.

"Nonsense. My lemonade was the talk of Beverly Hills in my day."

Talk, yes. But what exactly were they saying about it was anyone's guess.

Miranda flung open Bea's 1970s-era refrigerator in canary yellow ("Harvest Gold" more officially), which Miranda had always assumed was an aesthetic choice—"Wonderfully retro!" It wasn't. Nothing Bea did was ever *intentionally* retro. From this fridge, Miranda extracted the required arsenal and assembled it on the

counter the way a mad scientist might in preparation of a particularly potent potion. Miranda Abbott didn't believe in "recipes" or
the "measuring" of "ingredients," and instead chose a more intu-
itive approach, much like her acting. A single tall glass. A chug-
chug-chug of raw lemon juice, the smallest splash of water, several
heaping tablespoons of sugar, her patented "dash of salt" (dash
meaning "fistful"), and it was ready.

"A tray, darling, silver preferably. Ornate, but not too ornate, and
certainly not ostentatious."

Bea didn't have such a tray, silver or otherwise, ornate or not. She
did have a baking pan and paper towels that Andrew folded into a
sort-of swan.

"Wait," she said, draping a folded tea towel over Andrew's fore-
arm. "Perfect."

"I look like a waiter."

"Exactly!"

When they returned to the sitting room, with Andrew shakily
trying not to spill the baking tray and its single glass of lemonade,
Bea Maracle was all but sitting in Mr. Zabic's lap, having somehow
squirmed her way out of the settee and into the love seat he was in.

"That's a very kind offer," Zab of the tousled hair and sun-creased
eyes was saying as Miranda and Andrew entered. "I would have
loved to stay here while I am in town. I can tell that your B&B is a
lovely, restful place. Unfortunately, they've put me up at the Duchess Hotel and I do need to be there for cast and crew."

"Cast?" said Miranda.

"Crew?" said Andrew.

"The Duchess?" said Bea.

"Did I not tell you? We're shooting our MOW right here in Happy
Rock."

And now Andrew almost did spill the drink. The tray wobbled

and so did the glass. Here, then, was the first inkling, the first sense that something was not quite right. Why would the Great Harry Tomlin—and Andrew was fairly sure *Great* was Tomlin's legally required first name—ever agree to shoot a low-end movie of the week? With a second-tier production company? In Happy Rock? Andrew had a feeling there was more to this than met the eye, even if it was a disconcertingly handsome eye with unblinking contact. And why, underneath Zab's cheerful geniality—his bonhomie, if you will—did Andrew sense a certain desperation, a sadness even?

"Ah, Miranda's famous lemonade!" said Zab, noticing the tray. He plucked the glass, which caused the tray to wobble again in Andrew's grasp. He raised it up with a hearty "Cheers!" and took a long, deep drink.

Andrew and Bea held their breath. For a split second it looked like their guest's expression had gone completely blank. But then the smile returned—and he drained the glass.

"Delicious!" he said.

Andrew's eyebrow went up. And stayed up.

What Andrew didn't realize was that his own dubious reaction was the beginning of a divisive storm, one that would threaten to rend Andrew and Miranda apart.

"Can't wait for you to meet the director," Zab said to Miranda. "Her name's Leni Vedette. Very talented, very passionate. A real visionary. She's the one who sussed out the locations for us. But listen to me! You haven't even agreed to star in our little movie yet." He looked around the mismatched but homey bric-a-brac of Bea's sitting room and smiled—*sadly*, Andrew thought, which seemed oddly suspicious. "But don't worry, if you *do* say yes—fingers crossed!—and you do come on board, I can assure you we wouldn't dream of uprooting you. I would imagine you have a suite worthy of your status, right here at Bea's."

"I do," said Miranda.

"It's called my bedroom," said Bea.

"The suites here all have cozy monikers like that," said Miranda. "'Bea's bedroom,' or 'the attic,' or"—a nod to Andrew—"'the pantry.' It's part of the charm."

"Which is exactly why I didn't book one of the Duchess Hotel's luxury suites for you, Miranda, like the one Harry asked for. I knew you wouldn't be interested."

"Erm—" Miranda would not have been wholly averse to staying in a room resplendent, in a hotel iconic, but—*no*. Miranda saw the hurt look in Bea's eyes that she was even considering it. "Exactly so," said Miranda. "I am wonderfully happy here at Bea's. I wouldn't dream of staying anywhere else."

She saw Bea's relief, and it was almost worth it, giving up a luxury bath and empress-sized bed and a balcony overlooking the bay. Almost.

"Really?" said Zab, genuinely surprised. "Okay. But if you change your mind, let me know."

It was at this point that Ned Buckley popped his head into the sitting room. "Halloo, everyone! I knocked, but no one answered."

Bea waved him in, introduced him to Zab.

"Ned is the chief of police," Bea said proudly, giving Ned's arm a squeeze. She was often finding reasons to squeeze Ned, Miranda noted, the way she did bread dough or throw cushions.

"Well, well, officer!" said Zab. "Guess I better keep my head down while I am in town. Wouldn't want to run afoul of the law."

"Unless you're trampling rosebushes out beside the Duchess, I think you'll be fine," Ned said with a shake of the head. "Damnedest thing—if you'll pardon my language."

Zab's face clouded over. "The rosebushes?"

"Yup, someone must have been wantin' to break in. But the door they were trying to jimmy—if that's what they were doing—only leads to the linen room. Not a lot to steal there. Probably just teenagers," said Ned doubtfully. "Probably just mischief. Either way, gotta stay vigilant. Crime never sleeps here in Happy Rock."

"I suppose not," said Zab, but they could see his thoughts were elsewhere. "Anything else?" he asked. "About the hotel, I mean. I'm always fascinated by police investigations, however minor."

"Just the power outage, if you can call it that. More of a glitch really. A hiccup."

And now Zab was chewing his lip—and Miranda thought his lips looked very chewable indeed.

"Anyhoo. You should stay for dinner," said Ned.

"Yes!" Bea agreed, a little too eagerly.

"Havin' salmon," said Ned. His voice dropped as he confided, "A nice plump chinook, right outta Nestucca Bay, never even been iced, fresh as all get-out. Got connections with the Salish Nation, y'see. I get 'em before they go to market."

Everyone knew that Ned's "inside connections" were just Doc Meadows and his family, who always gave Ned a coho or chinook when they got back from a salmon run, but Miranda hated to puncture Ned's carefully constructed mystique about the source of the salmon, so she said, "Ned is a man of mystery in so many ways."

Ned stammered, "Well, I don't know about that. But, hey! Alan, was it? Stick around for the salmon and you'll get a show too. We're watching *Pastor Fran*. Bea here has every episode of Miranda's old TV show on VHS tape. Isn't that right, Bea?"

"Sure do! Even the Christmas specials."

"And what do you have in store for us tonight, Bea?" Ned asked.

"'The Case of the Trapdoor Toreador,'" she said.

"I know that episode!" said Zab. "Undercover as a bullfighter!"

"We shot it in Puerto Rico," said Miranda. Memories of long ago, of Miranda, younger, spryer, learning to pivot with a scarlet cape...

"Loved it!" said Zab. "Co-starred Lindsay Wagner as Lady Generalissimo, if I'm not mistaken. With a cameo by Robert Goulet. The Season Three finale." Then, slightly embarrassed, "Like I said, I'm a fan."

Robert Goulet, older but still elegant, moving closer at the wrap party, sweet, breathy sentiments in her ear, mustache tickling her neck, Miranda declining, "I'm a married woman," and Robbie, gracious, bowing out...

"Yes. Right. The bullfight one," said Miranda, shaking herself free from the past. "Do stay."

But Zab stood up, thanked them for the hospitality—and the lemonade—adjusted his Rolex and said, "Regretfully, I can't. I'm meeting with the director tonight. She's giving me a walk-through of our locations, along with the hotel manager. Chester, I think his name is. I can't really get out of it, wish though I may."

And then he stopped. Stood there looking through the window to his sporty Aston Martin parked outside. The door to the car was slightly ajar, and his voice went quiet. "Tell me, Chief Buckley. Do you get a lot of crime here in Happy Rock?"

CHAPTER FIVE

Enter the Sheriff

Butter, that was the key, thought Bea. "With enough butter, everything is good!" Julia Child liked to say.

Bea filleted the salmon into four generous slabs, wrapped them in foil with pats of butter, herbs snipped from her own garden, and thin slices of lemon, more for garnish than flavor, and then laid it out on the very baking pan Andrew had used earlier as a serving tray. (Miranda had offered to further douse the portions with lemon juice from her private stash—"I've got lots!"—but Bea had declined.)

Through the window, evening was settling on Tillamook Bay. The lighthouse was turning, turning, and all was good in the world. Miranda Abbott had landed a lead in a movie, and the savory smell of salmon simmered in the kitchen.

And yet...

"What do you think happened?" Miranda asked.

Ned was checking on the salmon for the fourth time in as many minutes. "You mean the car door? No idea."

Ned had gone out with Alan Zabic to check on his Aston Martin, see if anything was missing. Nothing was. Would have been a pretty brazen theft for Happy Rock, midafternoon down by Bea's.

"It's an old car," Zab had said, self-deprecatingly. His vintage Aston Martin probably cost more than most of the homes in Happy Rock. "The door does tend to stick. I must not have closed it all the way."

Ned had noted a stack of papers and legal documents spilling out from a manila folder on the passenger seat.

"To me, it looked like they'd been rifled through," Ned told Miranda as they waited for the salmon to cook. "But Mr. Zab, he quickly shuffled the pages back into the folder, said, 'Nope, nothing missing,' and skedaddled. Thing is, the interior of that car was spotless. No discarded coffee cups, no mis-folded accordion maps. Very tidy, our Mr. Zab. Tidy and organized. Those loosely thrown papers? You have to figure someone else went through those—in a hurry."

"But whatever it was they were looking for, they failed to find," said Miranda.

"At least according to Mr. Zab. He didn't spend much time going through 'em, just shoved them back in, so it's kinda hard to know how he could have been so certain."

"He certainly seemed rattled by it," said Miranda.

"He did," said Ned. "Almost–" He caught himself. He had been about to say "Almost terrified."

Ding!

The timer. Huzzah!

Bea bustled in, oven mittens on. "Salmon's ready!"

As Andrew set the table, he said, as casually as he could, "Did Mr. Zabic strike any of you as being, well, sad?"

"Sad?" said Ned. "How so?" Fearful, maybe.

"Or desperate. He wanted to sign you so quickly, Miranda."

A flash of red-headed temper from his employer. "Just because someone offers me a rush role in a movie alongside a six-time Oscar winner does not make that person desperate!"

"Five," said Andrew. "Harry Tomlin. Five times nominated. Never won. And no, casting you doesn't make Zab desperate, it's just…" He couldn't let it go. "Why Harry Tomlin? Why would a big star like that agree to shoot a measly MOW in Happy Rock?"

And now the flash became a flare. "Are you saying that working with me is somehow *beneath* him? Are you saying, oh, an MOW is great for *you*, Miranda, but not the amazing Mr. Tomlin? Is that what you're saying?!"

That was exactly what he was saying. "That's not at all what I'm saying."

Bea and Ned exchanged glances. Uh-oh.

Andrew laid down the last of the flatware on Bea's vinyl, green-and-yellow-checked place mats. The same pattern as the vinyl tablecloth, but of a different color scheme, which made it dizzying to look at. Sort of like dining atop a test pattern.

"But don't you find it odd?"

"No, Andrew. I do not! You are forgetting that I had a number one show on network TV for six years! Six!"

"Five," said Andrew. That sixth season, the ratings had plummeted due to an unfortunate dustup at the Golden Globes between Miranda and Bea Arthur. Alcohol had been involved. This was long before Andrew's time as her personal assistant, of course, but through the power of YouTube … "I absolutely know you were a star, Miranda. My family watched you every week when I was little. But that's not the point."

"Is it not? Well then, what *is* the 'point' then, Andrew? Enlighten us! We are all waiting with bated breath for you to *get. to. the. point.* Isn't that right?"

She turned to the other two for support, but they quickly averted their gaze.

"I'm just here for the salmon," mumbled Ned.

Bea pretended not to have heard, busying herself with getting the fish out of the oven along with asparagus and potato wedges.

"It's nothing about you, Miranda," said Andrew, still poking that bear. "It's Harry Tomlin I don't get."

There were rumors, of course. Rumors of shady connections with certain "olive oil importers," wink wink. (We all know what *that* means, thought Andrew.) Perhaps The Nicest Man in America™ was not quite so nice as his public persona might suggest.

"Wasn't he recently threatened with a lawsuit?" asked Andrew as they sat down to tuck in.

"I choose not to lower myself to such gossip," said Miranda—but only because she hadn't heard about it, and thus had nothing juicy to share. Miranda had long ascribed to that other Oscar's adage (Wilde): *The only thing worse than being talked about is NOT being talked about.*

"It was something to do with the charitable returns on his salad dressing revenue," said Andrew, spearing a side of asparagus.

Ned interjected with, "Bea, this is delicious! As always."

And with that, the tension eased as rumors of Harry Tomlin's financial woes and Zab's apparent desperation faded, and the four of them agreed instead, both in turn and in unison, on how delicious the salmon was.

"Julia Child," Bea confided. "But when you have a fish that fine, it's hardly an effort. Thank you, Ned. As always."

"Connections," he said with a telling nod. Our man of mystery.

When they were done, they let their plates soak—Miranda assumed that the night staff cleaned up; the dishes were washed by pixies apparently—as they retired to the living room for an episode of *Pastor Fran*.

Ned had poured himself a big glass of SunnyD before heading in and Miranda, puzzled, asked about his cankers.

"Doc said it's really just lemons I have to avoid. Too citrusy."

"Well, do let me know when you're better. When you are, I'll prepare some—"

Ned, too quickly: "It's chronic! Is what he said. So, probably, never."

The four of them settled into Bea's too-soft couch, with a tub of the Candy Shoppe's caramel popcorn between them. Andrew dimmed the side lamp, and Bea went over to push the night's tape into the VCR and then hurried back to nestle in next to Ned before the credits started.

That ol' familiar VHS tracking line wiggled across the screen as the warbling soundtrack came up to speed. With a sudden sting of music, it began. That iconic opening: Miranda Abbott in a soft-focus close-up wearing her trademark priest's collar (her character was technically a "pastor," not a priest, but the predominantly Jewish writing staff never really bothered to distinguish between the two), as she pulled back a confessional-booth curtain on a sudden zoom-in that revealed a swarthy villain with his hand clasped over a mutely screaming girl. Miranda Abbott, peering down a darkened alleyway. Miranda Abbott, leaping from a helicopter. Miranda Abbott, high-kicking the gun out of a villain's meaty fist. Miranda Abbott, defusing a bomb (dynamite sticks tied together with a comically large alarm clock attached). Driving a hot rod across sand dunes. Strutting down a catwalk, undercover at a swimsuit pageant. (She always laughed when they tried to put her on a catwalk. She was too short, too curvy, too robust to ever pass as a malnourished fashion model, but this was TV. Anything was possible.) And here she is, looking over her shoulder as she steers a speedboat (in that red bikini she liked so much), as a second speedboat full of swarthy criminals in suits and thin ties cut across her wake in hot pursuit.

And all the while, during this opening montage, the gravelly voice-over intoned those immortal lines that Bea and Ned (and Andrew) could recite by heart. Indeed, they often chimed along out loud as it played: *"Our Lady, who arts on the mean streets of Crime City! Hallowed be her fists. Our Kingdom come, her Justice will be done, in the alleyways and backrooms as it is in Heaven."*

Splashing out at the camera as if in 3D came her name: *Miranda Abbott as... Pastor Fran!... in... PASTOR FRAN INVESTIGATES!* Tonight's episode: *Case of the Trapdoor Toreador!* Written, not by Edgar, Miranda noted, but by none other than Luckless Lachlan himself. She should have known. If she recalled correctly, this episode involved a trapdoor hidden in the middle of a bullfighting arena (the title sort of gave it away), and Lachlan always went for the big, impossible twist. Edgar wrote to the character, tried to give Pastor Fran more emotional depth and Miranda more to work with. When a Lachlan Todd script landed on the table, however, Miranda knew she'd have fewer lines but more action. The rest of the writers, meanwhile, stuck to the usual car chases and dagger-in-the-back, falling-out-of-a-closet gasp! scenarios. (The wonder would have been if there *wasn't* a corpse in the closet. It happened so often Miranda wondered why her character reacted at all. *Here we go, another closet, another corpse with a dagger in its back. Ho-hum.*) But even Edgar's episodes usually contained at least one karate chop. She enjoyed the physical stuff as much as the emoting. The kicks, the high dives, the ballroom pirouettes. God, those were good times.

It was all so long ago...

I look so young, she thought as the VHS uncurled to its inevitable conclusion. In the world of Pastor Fran, the good were always rewarded and the bad were always punished. It was a comforting world, even if it was a lie, pleasantly told.

The evening ended on a sense of melancholy for Miranda, as Pastor Fran Fridays always did. The only point of excitement—and nostalgia—was when Ned suddenly stabbed a finger at the screen.

"Pause!" he said, even though he was in charge of the remote. "Right there!"

He rewound, played the scene again.

Sure enough, one of the male toreadors, improbably tall and inexplicably fair given his profession and supposed Iberian ethnicity, suited up in a bullfighter's hat and tight silk pants that showed off a fella's calves to best effect, with an embroidered short jacket and requisite cape, pouting sensuously as though he were the star of the scene rather than one of the background players, was...

"Poe Regal!" Ned cried.

He pronounced it the correct way, emphasis on the second syllable of *Regal*, "Ree-GAL," not "gull." The sign of a true fan.

Future action star and, later, scandal-ridden punchline of late night talk show monologues, Poe Regal looked sort of Swedish, sort of Germanic, sort of Norwegian, always moody. Smoldering good looks, as they say, with that savage widow's peak, visible even under his toreador's cap, those piercing eyes like polished blue opal. It was him. Even if he wasn't listed in the credits. (Ned checked.)

"Extras aren't listed," said Miranda. "If they have any lines, even 'Hello' or 'Excuse me,' they become 'actors.' They have to be paid—and credited. He was neither."

Not back then, anyway.

But at one point, Poe Regal would have been on par, if not with Stallone, at least with Van Damme. Ned rewound the tape, watched the scene flit by again.

Miranda, still not convinced, leaned in, but—yes. That was indeed him.

"Huh. I never knew," she said.

"Didn't you two work together later?" Bea asked.

"Yes," Miranda said softly. "Twice. He had a guest spot on *Pastor Fran* in Season Six, and later we did that horrendous film together, *The Shimmer Spy*. We had a love scene that took four days to shoot. Four days. On the first day it had been awkward, on the second silly, on the third almost sensual—and by the fourth we hated each other." But that wasn't true. Not entirely. "Water under the bridge, as they say."

Before the *Shimmer Spy* movie, Poe Regal had been the star of his own TV show, *Kung Fu Sheriff*, for seven years.

"It was suspiciously similar to the role he'd played on *my* show," Miranda noted. "When he was cast as 'Ju-Jitsu Deputy.' So not a spin-off, but certainly a knock-off. Was he grateful? No. Did he ever thank me? He did not."

"Say, Bea," Ned said, all excited. "Don't you have some old *Kung Fu Sheriff*s as well?"

"I do!" she said. (Bea said "I do!" a lot around Ned, Miranda noticed, often with an undue gusto.) "Haven't watched them in years, though." Bob liked them. Bea was more a *Pastor Fran* fan. *Kung Fu Sheriff* had been a little too gritty for her tastes. Still, she went through the cabinet and, sure enough, found an early episode on VHS. Tried not to think of Bob.

"*Kung Fu Sheriff*?" said Andrew. "Hmm. Never heard of it."

"Oh, you're in for a treat!" said Ned.

And Ned was right, though not in quite the way he had imagined. Andrew Nguyen had a deep tolerance for, even a love of, TV kitsch. But *Kung Fu Sheriff*? This was kitsch on an entirely different plane. This was the very ideal of kitsch. This was kitsch in the eye of god.

From the grizzled cop forced to hand in his badge, to the *"Nooooo!"* cradling of a wounded partner in one's arms, to the *"Don't you die on me, man"* (preceding the aforementioned "Nooooo!"), to the kid with leukemia in a wheelchair who says *"You can do it, Mr. Sheriff, I know you* (cough, cough) *can."* On shows like this, no matter what illness you had, you always ended up in a wheelchair. With a cough. It was shorthand for suffering.

SunnyD and caramel popcorn, and herb-infused salmon. They had started the night with Pastor Fran but ended with the Sheriff, as Andrew tried not to snort with laughter every time the Sheriff wristlocked another perp, chewed yet another toothpick, or peered into yet another dusty Texas horizon, as Ned sat, rapt, and Bea quietly frowned her disapproval over the trip to a strip club that seemed to be required in every other episode of *Kung Fu Sheriff*. No nudity, this being network TV. But it was certainly implied. Which made it "edgy" back in the day.

Ned asked Miranda as the show ended, "He ever show you one of his wristlocks?"

"That's all he did. Wristlocks were kind of his thing."

"Studied aikido with an aikido master in Okinawa for twenty years, is what I heard," said Ned.

Despite the title, the "kung fu" practiced on the show was about as accurate as Fran's "pastor" collar. Likewise, as a working sheriff in rural Texas, Poe Regal's character regularly crossed state and country lines to apprehend miscreants, even going as far as Acapulco at one point to nab a gang of Mexican drug smugglers, which suggested that the writers on the show were as poorly informed about what being "sheriff" entailed as Miranda's were on what exactly a pastor did. They'd even referred to her character as a "parson" in one script. ("Parson, pastor, priest, what's the diff?" they'd said, scoffing at her when she'd pointed it out. To which Edgar, in his role as head writer, had threatened to throw these lippy writers out the window one by one and see whose help they called for on the way down.)

As for Poe Regal?

"He did indeed claim to have studied aikido in Okinawa," said Miranda. *Claimed* being the operative word. Twenty years of studying, and he never seemed to have gotten past wristlocks. He claimed a lot of things, thought Miranda. Including my heart . . . briefly.

Love and hate, after all, were only the same sides of a different coin.

CHAPTER SIX

"I Have No Husband!"

Miranda rolled over in the down comforter, woke to find herself hugging–not Poe Regal–but one of Bea's wonderfully fluffy pillows. Miranda had been dreaming about The Kiss again, the most impressive kiss of her career, and not even caught on camera.

Sunlight through cotton curtains. Ceramic tchotchkes along a dresser embellished with embroidered messages: LOVE IS THE HAPPY HAPPINESS OF THE HOME. More cherubs, more valentines.

A warm and pleasing glow–ruined by a dull, persistent thumping. Not of her heart. But by someone up in the attic. She covered her head with a pillow but couldn't escape it. Then the bedside phone rang, shrill and demanding, and Miranda slouched across to answer.

"It is I," she murmured. "Please leave a message after the–"

"Don't beep! It's me, Andrew. In the pantry? We have a problem."

This was followed by a cheerful pounding on the door. And yes, everything Bea did was cheerful, including pounding on the door of the room she still insisted on calling "my bedroom."

Thump, thump, *trill!*, bang.

Miranda sat up, yelled at all three at the same time. "What is it?!"

"Breakfast!" said Bea, far too cheerfully, from the other side of the door.

"Marty called. We have a problem!" Andrew shouted, distraught, over the phone.

The thumping upstairs continued without explanation.

"Fine." Miranda swung her feet out and into her Neiman Marcus bedroom slippers, pulled her silk robe in around her, held the phone out in front of her. "One at a time! Bea, thank you, I shall dine in the sunroom." The sunroom and the sitting room were the same room. "Andrew, I shall be down momentarily. We shall discuss whatever the current crisis is in a civilized manner over croissants and freshly squeezed tangerines."

"Oatmeal and SunnyD," Bea yelled from behind the door. "Same as always."

Sigh.

Miranda descended like Vivien Leigh down the staircase at Tara, stepping around the DustBuster and potted ferns, the stacks of magazines (to go to recycling later), sailing through the Golden Harvest kitchen and down the hall, then sweeping into the sun-and-sit salon, where Bea had laid out her breakfast on a TV dinner tray.

Even down here, the thumping in the attic could be heard.

Andrew was already waiting, knee bouncing, with a concerned look on his face. He was clutching a legal document of some sort. Miranda could see the yellow *Sign Here… And Here…* plastic tabs. She knew a contract when she saw it. So what was the problem?

"Speak, darling!" she said. "What is that toadlike agent of mine up to now?"

"He doesn't believe any of it. Laughed out loud when I called. Said I had fallen into a folie à deux with you. A 'shared delusionary disorder.' Said, 'First Clooney and now Harry Tomlin? What kind of fantasy world do you two inhabit?'"

"I hope you fired him."

"I did."

A personal assistant wouldn't normally have the authority to fire their employer's agent, but then again, most personal assistants didn't live in the pantry. (When his kid brother had asked, over the phone, "So what's it like up there, your living arrangements?" he'd said, "Rustic.") Nothing about Andrew and Miranda's working relationship could be described as "normal." Indeed, Andrew had been slightly unnerved when Marty joked about a possible folie à deux. Andrew worried about much the same thing. Had he been caught up in the Vortex of Miranda as well?

"And what is that?" Miranda asked, patting her mouth with a napkin. She was referring to the contract Andrew was holding. "From A to Z Productions, I presume."

"It is, and that's the thing. I went through it, and, well . . ." He frowned. "It looks—good. I mean, *really* good. I'm not an agent, but I've seen enough of these. And I couldn't spot a single sneaky bit. None."

"Really?"

Miranda was taken aback by this. Even the best of contracts included at least one "sneaky bit," whether it be a slyly worded requirement for reshoots without reimbursement or an open-ended "exclusivity clause" that stopped an actor from doing any other work during the terms of the contract, even commercials or guest spots or celebrity game show appearances, without kicking back part of the fee to the company. Every Hollywood contract was a snake pit. The challenge was to sort the truly venomous vipers from the garden-variety garter snakes.

"Everything in the boilerplate that Marty would have objected to was already crossed out," said Andrew. "There was even"—he leaned in, almost whispering—"a pay-or-play provision." Meaning, even if Miranda got fired—or even if the project was never completed—she would still get paid.

"I see. And the rate? Above Equity, I would hope."

"Yeah. You could say that." Andrew flipped to the relevant page, handed it over to her.

"Oh, my. That's a lot of zeros."

"Yup. The initial signing fee is a healthy six figures. After that . . ." Another zero.

"And Marty knows about this?"

"Are you kidding? He doesn't even think it's real. He never even saw the offer."

"Then we shall sign without him! Andrew, I want you to arrange a consultation with the finest legal mind Happy Rock has to offer!"

"Um, that would be Atticus."

"Done!"

The thumping above had finally stopped, much to Miranda's relief. Not just the thumping but the high-pitched *whirr* of what must have been a power screwdriver. (A sound that would later weigh heavy on Miranda's mind, though she didn't know it at the time.) *Thump, thump, whirrr.* And now, thankfully, silence.

The heavy footfall of boots coming down the stairs brought the familiar figure of Tanvir Singh into the sunroom.

"Is Bea around?"

Tanvir was a tall man and an impressive presence, with a beard streaked in distinguished gray. He was wearing a striking orange turban today—or *dastār*, as he politely pointed out—and around his hips, slung the way a gunfighter might hoist a holster, was Tanvir's tool belt.

Bea appeared. "Oh, hello! How did it go?"

"All done," he said.

Tanvir, head of the local chamber of commerce, was owner and chief proprietor of Tanvir's Hardwares & Bait Shop (if you wanted a power sander *and* a bucket full of worms, Tanvir's was the place for you. That was their motto, in fact: EVERYTHING FROM TOOLS TO WORMS) and Bea had hired him for some renovations, apparently.

He smiled at Miranda. "Want to see your new room?" he asked.

Bea was trying frantically to shoot signals Tanvir's way, to no avail.

Miranda was confused. "My new room?"

"In the attic. I put in a skylight, wood paneling, some high-end frieze carpeting with plushwalk underlay—Bea had suggested shag, but I made an executive decision to go with the frieze. And anyway, not sure if they still make shag. I know we haven't carried any in years. Looks very nice, though. Has a lamp and a small dresser. Come and see."

"But ... I already have a room."

Bea had been watching Miranda's reaction intently. What Bea said now had clearly been rehearsed ahead of time. "Miranda, you know how famous hotels will have a Sarah Bernhardt Suite, in honor of the great actress? Well, I thought it was high time for Bea's B&B to create its very own Miranda Abbott Suite, in your honor, just for you!"

Bea waited anxiously, a strained smile on her face.

A beat.

And then: "Oh, Bea! How thoughtful! My own suite!" Tears in her eyes. "Thank you, Bea. I won't forget this." To Andrew: "Please move my belongings to the Miranda Abbott Suite!" And to Tanvir: "A wonderful surprise. I shall make you some of my patented lemonade to celebrate."

"Can't. Religious reasons."

"Oh. Yes. Of course."

Religious, all right, thought Tanvir. It's god-awful.

Andrew had brightened at the news. "So, Bea, now that Miranda's moving out of her current bedroom, can I have it?"

"No!" Bea said sharply—which was unusual for her. "I will be taking that room back. Effective immediately."

Bea's B&B had four rooms to let, not including the attic, which was now Miranda's Suite. Andrew's unpaid-for pantry was not among them. And so, to the pantry he went. And to the pantry he remained. The only consolation, he mused, was that someday it might well be christened the Andrew Nguyen Suite.

Moving Miranda from Bea's bedroom to the Miranda Abbott Suite (i.e., attic) took less time than might have been expected, and it struck Andrew as ineffably poignant, how little she owned. All her worldly possessions were here at Bea's, and all it took was three trips up and down the stairs. She had once owned a house in the Hollywood Hills, but had ended up here with a few boxes of mementos, some toiletries, and an eclectic wardrobe, largely out of date, which Andrew hefted into the closet upstairs.

But that was about to change with the good news about the MOW. So why did Andrew still feel a certain unease?

The meeting with Atticus didn't take much more time.

In his narrow law office above the flower shoppe, Atticus flipped through the pages of the contract and said, "You do realize that once you've signed a contract, there's not much I can do."

Andrew hissed, "I told you so."

For all her cries of *"arrange a consultation with the finest legal mind Happy Rock has to offer!"* Miranda operated under a "sign now, read later" strategy.

She brushed aside her assistant's concerns. True, she had already affixed her signature and returned Alan Zabic's copy of the contract, but she was now asking Atticus to evaluate the deal. It made perfect sense to her.

"Contracts are made to be broken!" she said.

"Actually, they're not," said Atticus. "It's sort of the exact opposite of that. Contracts are designed *not* to be broken. Kind of the point of having a contract."

Ned Buckley had run Zab's copy of the agreement over to the front desk of the Duchess, grumbling that he was not a courier, before driving Andrew and Miranda over to the law office, grumbling just as equally that he was not a taxi driver either.

And now Miranda and Andrew sat, awaiting a verdict after the fact.

"Looks pretty solid," said Atticus. "Mind you, I normally do real estate and, um, divorce petitions."

That stung.

He stopped at one page, near the end. "What's 'breakage'? It's mentioned in Addendum A, but isn't really defined. 'The producers have agreed to pay breakage.'"

"Oh, that's an industry term," said Miranda, though she herself wasn't clear on what it entailed.

"It means," said Andrew, "that on a modestly budgeted film, like this one started out to be, if the budget increases, if they sign a major star, say, the Bond Completion Company—the guys who take the risk—have agreed to guarantee an increase in coverage to match the increase in budget. It's a way to adjust upward."

"It also says you will be paid a percentage of the final budget," said Atticus. "So that would be *after* any breakage adjustments?"

"That's correct," said Andrew. "There will be a ceiling, though. She will be paid a percent of the total budget *up to* a certain amount."

Atticus flipped back. "Ah yes. Here it is. There *is* a cap. Still a nice chunk of change—potentially. Especially if there is a bona fide star attached. Now, I heard," said Atticus, resting on his elbows, eyes saucer-wide, "that a major movie star *is* coming to Happy Rock. Is that true? I mean, client confidentiality an' all. It's just, we've never had an actual star here, so that would be pretty darned exciting."

Ouch.

Miranda rose, had to restrain herself from jabbing Atticus in the eye with a letter opener, thanked him instead for his time, and then, turning to Andrew, said, "Beckon Chief Buckley! Have him meet us below. We are going to the Murder Store!"

"About my fee—" said Atticus.

She brushed that aside as well. All this talk of money. So crass!

"My 'thank you' is thanks enough and more than enough to be thankful for. Or don't you not agree?"

"Um, I, *yes*? I don't not agree."

"Exactly!"

IF MIRANDA THOUGHT her husband would be thrilled by the news—that she would once again be starring in a *major* film production, that her Hollywood dream was not yet over even if it did require working from a script written by Edgar's nemesis—she was mistaken. First off, Edgar wasn't even in his bookstore when she arrived.

Chief Buckley dropped Miranda and Andrew at I Only Read Murder, insisting that they walk back to town on their own. "It's downhill," he said. "Twenty minutes, tops. And it's a beautiful fall day."

But Miranda was already on her way into the building, calling back, "Just wait there, Ned! This won't take long!"

Just long enough to let Edgar congratulate her. Just long enough for him to tell her he was wrong and should never have asked her to sign those divorce papers. That she was right when she had returned to Hollywood, and that she was even more right when she came back to him, and that she was rightest of all when she referred to their marriage as being "interrupted," not ended. That was how much time she needed.

Miranda entered the bookstore on a jangle of bell, with Andrew following her in a moment later. The store was empty except for Owen McCune in his greasy coveralls and muttonchop sideburns, who was perched in the corner reading a paperback with the cover curled back.

"Oh, hey there," he said, looking up. "Didn't hear you come in. Lost in the story, as it were. Heck of a good read, this one. It's about an auto mechanic who solves crime. Joins forces with a hardboiled detective plumber, against a villainous electrician. Course, the mechanic is the real hero."

"Speaking of which, shouldn't you be at your garage right now?" said Miranda. As far as she knew, McCune's Garage was a one-man show.

"Taking a break," he said. "There was too much work piled up. Cars to the right of me, cars to the left. Phone ringing off the hook. Figured I could use some me time. I'm minding the store for Edgar. He'll be coming down soon. Ah, and here he is."

Edgar entered, a cup of chamomile in hand, a large hardcover tucked under his arm. Saw Miranda and his face went all sour.

"Is this about the MOW?"

"It is!" She was about to tell him, *Don't worry about alimony, I won't be taking every second book in the store, in fact, I shall be able to help you out.*

"Look, I needed the money, okay?" he snarled. "I got mortgages, plural. Inventory. Heat. Plus an ex-wife who is harassing me. That's why I agreed to do it. Happy now? I mean, you came to gloat, right?"

"What on earth are you talking about?"

Andrew had the same question. "Edgar, I'm not sure—"

"The rewrite. They want me to restructure the entire thing. The MOW. It's a P.K. Pennington adaptation. Can't remember which one, but it has *Mystery* in the title."

"They all have *Mystery* in the title," said Miranda.

"Anyway, Luckless Lachlan—remember him? He turned in his usual travesty of an abomination. They're sending the script over today, want me to completely revise the story."

"Ah, yes. Lachlan Todd. I seem to recall you two having a falling-out. Was it"—her voice dropped—"over me?"

Edgar stared at her in annoyed bafflement. It was a look Miranda had been used to seeing in their years of marriage.

"My problem with Lachlan had nothing to do with you, Miranda. He's a horrible writer, and a prima donna. *Oh, don't touch my immaculate prose!* Remember those ridiculous scripts he used to write? I think there was one where the bullfighter used a secret trapdoor in the arena to escape under the cloud of dust the bull kicked up."

"I, ah, seem to recall that episode." Memories of Poe Regal . . .

"Lachlan adapted the P.K. Pennington novel, horribly, of course. And they want me to take over. Lachlan's threatening lawsuits, as usual, but I could care less. I need the money and it's an easy assignment. I just have to alter the story to make it more about Clover McBride."

"She is I!" said Miranda.

"Who is you?" Edgar asked.

"Clover McBride is me. I'm playing her in the movie—"

"MOW."

"It's still a movie, Edgar. Of the week or not."

"Wait. You're playing the lead?"

Miranda beamed. "Number Two on the call sheet."

"Wow." Edgar didn't know how to react. "Marty really came through for you."

"Marty Sharpe had nothing to do with it. It was Alan."

"Alan Zabic?"

"The very same. He offered me the part—"

"He hired me to rewrite—"

"—without auditioning."

"—without a pitch."

"Huh." This was Andrew, who was also thinking: When you put it that way, it sounds unlikely...

"Mr. Alan Zabic contacted you?" Miranda asked.

"None other. He said the script needs an overhaul. Wants to put your character—"

"Clover McBride."

"—front and center."

"Do you realize what this means, Edgar?! We will be working together again, as star and writer. Just like the old days!"

This time, Edgar *did* know how to react. His eyes narrowed, his jaw clenched, and he all but spit out his words.

"You're starring in a movie of the week that I have been hired to rewrite—specifically for you?"

Since this didn't seem like an actual question, rhetorical or not, but rather a pithy recapitulation of the situation, like Jack Reacher, Miranda Abbott said nothing.

"And I thought this gig couldn't get any worse!" he cried.

Grrrr.

Owen McCune carefully folded over the corner of the page he was reading with a greasy thumb and put it back on the shelf for later. "Thanks, Edgar. Gotta run. Good seeing you, Miranda."

After he left, Miranda pointed out that maybe, just maybe, if Edgar actually *sold* his books instead of letting people read them for free, he might not be in such financial straits.

"'Get any worse'! That's rich coming from you."

"Give it a rest, Miranda!"

"Or what? You'll write me out of my part? Throw me to the wolves?"

"Not wolves. Luckless Lachlan. Let him deal with you!"

It was at this unfortunate moment that a pair of pink-faced tourists came into the store, smiling away. "Hiya! Do you have any guidebooks to—"

"No!" Edgar shouted. "I don't sell nature postcards or souvenir guides to Tillamook Bay or books about bird-watching or fishing or sailing or anything else unrelated to murder. All I sell is murder. Did you not see the sign out front? Was that not a clue? Look around you, every book in here has at least one dead body in it."

"But—but we're here in Happy Rock on holiday," the wife squeaked. "We were looking for some light reading, something local."

"Here." Edgar grabbed a book from the nonfiction shelf. "It's about a series of grisly murders that took place in the hotel."

"The Duchess? But that's where we're staying."

"The chapter about the Suitcase Killer is especially entertaining. The blood dripped from one floor to the next. That's how they caught him. Though they never did find the victim's head. Shall I ring it up for you?"

But they were already backing out slowly toward the door.

"So, you're starring in the MOW," said Edgar after the addled tourists had been chased off. "Are you sure? You do tend to jump to conclusions. Did someone say, 'You are hired'? Did they use those exact words?"

"I signed the contract this morning."

"I see. You can sign those papers, but not the ones for our divorce?"

"I thought you of all people would be happy for me!" she said.

"Life is full of disappointments."

She shoved the door open and Andrew scrambled to keep up. Outside the store, Ned was waiting. Leaning against his patrol car, he was admiring the view from Beacon Hill.

"Was your husband in?" he asked.

"I have no husband!"

CHAPTER SEVEN

Chester vs. the Seagull

For Jane Bannister, what would turn out to be the most important day of her career had begun on a less auspicious, more pungent turn. Jane had been sent on assignment, notepad and camera in hand, to the S.J. Fertilizer emporium, downwind from the Duchess Hotel, to report on a fertilizer-related story for *The Weekly Picayune*, newspaper of note in the Greater Tri-Rock area.

Jane had graduated from the Portland School of Journalism and Communications that spring, without losing any of her naïveté or succumbing to cynicism. More's the pity. She could have done with a little cynicism. Jane had sent out dozens of CVs and cover letters—*I believe my exemplary grades and extracurricular activities speak for themselves*—beginning with the *New York Times* and eventually working her way down to the *Ashland Daily Tidings* in Ashland, Oregon (which turned out to be defunct—the newspaper not the town), and eventually here to Happy Rock, where the only newspaper in town had recently lost its only reporter.

"Happy Rock isn't the place for you," her roommate had warned. "We used to go there in the summer when I was a kid. Had every kind of ball available, my dad used to say: oddballs, screwballs, goofballs."

"That's simply not true," Jane had insisted without any corroborating empirical evidence to the contrary. Now that she'd arrived, though, she'd come to suspect that there were indeed more eccentrics per square foot in Happy Rock than in any other town in the Pacific Northwest, and that included Applegate, Home of the World's Only Bigfoot Trap.

Her qualms had started with her boss, who wore an actual fedora with an actual PRESS tag on his actual head whenever he was "out on the beat." (Bake sales and walkathons mainly, though he did break the occasional salmon exposé. SALMON SEASON DELAYED UNTIL TUESDAY DUE TO BUREAUCRATIC INCOMPETENCE, NEPOTISM, AND INCONGRUOUS INEPTITUDE! ran one headline.)

"I don't care whose toes I step on," he'd said, chomping on a cigar. "Town fishing commission be damned."

Okay, so he didn't actually chomp on a cigar, but he should have.

The fact that his ex-wife worked at the fishing commission had nothing to do with it, he assured her.

"Welcome to *The Weekly Picayune*, Scoop." He pumped her hand like he was priming a cistern.

"Jane," she'd said. "My name. It's Jane."

"Plain Jane? Hmm. Don't like it. Doesn't suit you. I'm gonna call you Scoop. You know why? Because that's your beat. You're young, you're hungry, you're youthful, and you have an appetite for it"—he tended to speak in redundancies, she noted —"and I think you're gonna do grand, great, good even. You've got that rough-and-ready journalistic instinct about you, I can tell. Perry Jameson, that's my name, but you can call me Chief, as in 'Editor-in-.' Any questions before I throw you into the pit of fire, the cauldron of flames?"

"Well, I guess, Mr. Jameson—er, *Chief*—my only real question is, and please don't take this the wrong way, do you actually know what the word *picayune* means?"

"Of course. It's a Spanish coin of little value. Hiram Henry arrived in Happy Rock from Louisiana with a single picayune in his pocket. Founded the paper in 1887. Built his fortune as a newsman out of that one coin—and illegal fur trading. Why do you ask?"

"No reason."

"Enough of the chitchat and chin-wag. Manure store has a new fall line out. An exclusive. I want it in the Saturday paper. Your first byline, Scoop."

"My name—it's just Jane. And, this is a *weekly* paper, correct? So isn't every paper the Saturday paper?"

"That article isn't going to write itself, Scoop. Off you go. Y'got the jitters. I can tell. Don't worry. You can do this. I believe in you."

The S.J. Fertilizer Supply Company was located in a historic three-story, red-brick building along the bay, away from the town and enveloped in a funk of its own making. Dim inside, with thick air and a swirl of smells you could taste on your tongue, the shoppe presented its wares the way a spice merchant might. A potpourri of manure, as it were.

Trying not to gag, Jane sought out the proprietor, a skinny kid who couldn't have been much older than high school.

Melvin the manure sommelier. "A family dynasty," he said with undue pride. "I mind the store. But I also develop new products. Consumers demand improvements constantly."

"Do they?" Choke.

"Oh yes, our customers—we prefer *aficionados*—are very discerning. My newest blend, Jacobson's Amatory Admixture—that's copyright by the way, so if you use it in your story, please add one of those little *c*'s—is infused with pheromones."

"Pheromones?"

"We thought, sure it's manure, but why can't it be sexy too?"

Why? Um, because it's manure? she wanted to say.

He wafted his hand across a mound of the stuff, the way one might waft perfume, breathed deeply, and said, "You're of the female persuasion. How does this aroma make you feel?"

"Queasy."

"Queasy with love?" he said hopefully.

Her phone vibrated. It was her boss, telling her to get to the hotel right away.

"Gotta run," she gasped. Saved by the text!

The Duchess? Jane had a good idea what this was about. The circus had come to Happy Rock—in the form of a film crew that had rolled in on a convoy of trailers and equipment supply vehicles. Star spotting had become a sport. Harry Tomlin's old stunt double was seen on the hotel grounds, walking on wonky hips that seemed to move the wrong way, a souvenir of a memorably spectacular crash that had gone bad. (He was famous as much for what he'd survived as for what he'd done.) This was a man who had once spun a speedboat 360 degrees in the air for a Harry Tomlin picture. People did things for Harry Tomlin. He was, after all, The Nicest Man in America™.

As Jane was discovering the joys of manure, Andrew, meanwhile, had spotted the soundman Silas Ivar wandering around town, headphones on, recording the murmur of the street. Silas was notoriously difficult to work with, insisted on both recording and mixing all audio on "his" films, as he put it, had alienated every director in the field, yet was still treated with something akin to awe in the industry. An artist, twice nominated, once winning. An Oscar-winning sound recordist? On an MOW? Someone was banking on this movie making a lot of money.

Andrew had asked Miranda, as casually as he could, "I saw Silas Ivar down by the Cozy Café, recording seagull squawks along the pier. Does that make sense?"

"Seagulls?"

"Silas."

"It's film, darling. Nothing makes sense. We traffic in fantasy, remember. It's our job."

"I saw Jacquelyn de Valeur as well. A regular United Nations of cinematic power, ha ha."

Jacquelyn was a darling of the French postmodern *anarchie* avant-garde movement, an uncompromising cinematographer known for making death look beautiful—and beauty look like a corpse warmed over. She'd been spotted striding about with her interpreter in tow, a mousy young woman who spent as much time apologizing for Jacquelyn as she did translating. *"Cette ville de merde devra faire,"* Jacquelyn would declare. "A very beautiful location," her interpreter would say.

A young ingénue had also been spotted swanning about, though none could remember her name. *"She was in that thing with that guy!"* A lower end in the ranking of celebrity, but still.

And now a press conference had been called.

In the Duchess Atrium, a glass-enclosed sunroom off the east wing, Acting General Manager Chester Cornelius was laying out a floral arrangement, sheaves of autumn roses—gold and red—from the hotel's own hothouse, atop a long linen-clothed table in front of a line of tabletop microphones. Facing the rose-laden table were rows of garden chairs awaiting the paparazzi.

And the paparazzi had come out in full force! For all his financial and legal woes, or perhaps because of them, Harry Tomlin was still a draw. Jane Bannister felt self-conscious, concerned from the way people moved away to make room for her that the odor of *eau de*

Melvin had clung to her. She overheard some of the other reporters—she tried not to think of them as "the real journalists"—talking amongst themselves. The subject discussed seemed to be "Why the hell would a star of Harry Tomlin's magnitude agree to appear in a movie of the week?" and/or "Why the hell would a star of Harry Tomlin's magnitude agree to appear in a movie of the week filmed in this backwater burg?" It made her sad to think this hurtful line of questioning might actually come up during the press conference.

Chester, however, was pleased beyond words. The atrium's original skylight had been faithfully restored mere months before, and would now be a showcase for the media. A crew from LA was outside in the hall, waiting to be let in, and rumors abounded that Harry Tomlin Himself might be dropping by as well. Chester could well imagine himself showing Mr. Tomlin—"Harry" he would insist on being called—around the historic hotel, could image them becoming friends even. Harry was, after all, The Nicest Man in America™. It was a glorious, sun-drenched day. And then Chester made the mistake of looking up.

On the glass above, he saw a single white dab. A recognizable splatter, like a dribble of yogurt. Seagulls, the bane of Happy Rock.

Dammit!

Let it go, Chester, take a breath. Let it go. But he couldn't. That single smear of seagull excrement threatened to undermine the perfection of this moment. And he couldn't very well ask the housekeeping staff to climb a rickety ladder outside to scrape it away. They were mostly locals, working weekends while in high school, and they just snapped their gum and stared at him whenever he asked them to do something. He was afraid of teenaged girls, had been his whole life. The groundskeeper was away. So it was up to Chester.

If he had known what was about to happen, he would have stayed below.

Miranda Abbott, meanwhile, had waltzed into the hotel lobby and the warm embrace of the waiting press. Before she could announce that it was indeed I, a pair of familiar faces greeted her.

"Doc!" she said. "Ned! I didn't know you two were involved."

"Me? I'm just here for the hoopla," said Doc Meadows with a lopsided grin. A lanky man, affable, with a perpetual half smile always in play, he was more than Happy Rock's finest GP. He was the fourteenth generation of healer from the Coastal Salish Nation, north of Tillamook Bay.

"You've put your hair in braids!" said Miranda. "Looks very dapper."

Embarrassed, he said, "The wife. She likes it that way. Says it's more manly."

"Well, Doc," said Miranda. "You're plenty manly however you wear it. And you, Ned? Here for the hoopla as well?"

He was in full police uniform, but he was always in full police uniform. The only way Miranda could tell when Chief Buckley was off duty was when he wasn't sporting his holster. He was wearing it today.

"Not a fan of hoopla, truth be told," he said. "Here as a favor to Alan Zabic. He wanted a police presence for the press conference. He already brought in security guards, a whole whack of 'em, all the way from Stockton. Stationed at every entrance. You would've passed them on the way in."

"Team of paramedics from Portland is standing by as well," Doc noted. "Wonder what Mr. Zabic is so worried about?"

Police and paramedics and paparazzi, oh my! "Standard in the industry," said Miranda. "No need for concern. Oh, there's my cue!"

She was being called into the atrium, and she filed through and onto the raised dais where the table with the microphones and floral arrangements lay, facing the press who were now massing in front of her, waiting for their opportunity to question one of the Last Great Movie Stars™ and The Nicest Man in America™.

Already assembled were Alan Zabic and the director of the film, Leni Vedette, looking like a bad-tempered scarecrow with suitably frayed features and a straw-like bristle-cut hairdo, dressed in mustard. And two of the three stars: Miranda Abbott and the ingénue, the one who was in that thing with that guy. Notably absent was Harry Tomlin. This was to be expected, the biggest star was always the last to arrive. His empty seat was on one side of Miranda, the ingénue on the other.

Standing at the back of the room, behind the cameras and crowded press corps, were Ned and Doc, beaming their approval at her. Doc Meadows gave Miranda a "thumbs-up, you'll do fine" gesture.

Oh, please, she thought. I've done plenty of press conferences over the years, I hardly need reassurance. So why did she feel a butterfly fluttering inside? It had been a long time since this much hoopla—as Doc would put it—had attended anything she'd done. In fact, the last such event to have any real buzz would probably have been her post-Golden Globes apology tour. *"I would like to take this opportunity to apologize to Ms. Arthur and wish her a speedy recovery..."*

They waited. And waited.

The minutes ticked by, until Zab leaned into the mic and said, nervously, "Mr. Tomlin will be here soon. Not to worry. Sorry about the delay," then began frantically typing on his phone. *Where was he?*

Miranda had stopped by Harry Tomlin's suite earlier, ready to charm her (only slightly more famous) co-star, but he hadn't answered the door. As she waited in the hall, she'd thought, They should do something about these ugly carpets. Paisley and roses.

Sheesh. Three raps on the door with no response and she'd left, a strained smile still in place.

At the press conference, the ingénue was also on her phone, though out of boredom more than anxiety.

Miranda and the young actress had gotten off on the wrong foot. The ingénue, on meeting Miranda, had said, "I just want to say how much I admire you!" So far, so good. But then added: "I think it's really brave of you, putting yourself out there like that at your age. To take up acting so late in life, it's wonderful."

Aghast, Miranda had replied, "This isn't my first role."

"It's not? My bad. I should have googled you."

Never a letter opener handy when you need one...

But we have to get along, Miranda told herself. So now she gritted her teeth and said, by way of conversation and with a nod to the young woman's smartphone, "Calling Harry as well?" And, with a knowing smile, "On your app?"

"Who?" the ingénue asked.

"Harry Tomlin. The star—or, rather, co-star—on this film."

"Oh, right. The old dude. Nah. I'm just scrolling through my name. I have an alert set up. A vanity search."

Miranda was intrigued. "Like a clipping service?"

"I guess."

There's an app for everything, thought Miranda.

Finally, the director Leni had had enough.

"We'll start without him," she said tersely, ignoring Zab's plea to wait just another five minutes. He then went back to his phone, more frantic than ever.

"Questions," said Leni Vedette, prickly and to the point. "Go ahead."

But no one wanted to ask her anything, which only made things more awkward, more tense. It was Harry Tomlin they wanted to see, not the director of such socially conscious art house fare as *The Joy of Menstruation* and *The Misery of Marriage*, and the always popular *Men: Threat or Menace?*

Outside, in the sun, looking down from the atrium skylight and unaware of the drama unfolding below, Chester Cornelius had stretched across the glass with a squeegee he'd commandeered from housekeeping. The ladder wobbled and swayed under him as he reached... and reached... barely keeping his balance, until, finally, he managed to swipe the seagull offering away with nary a smear in its wake. Phew!

A still day. Windless and absolutely calm. And he had removed the only mar on the proceedings.

The ladder swayed and then—miraculously—stabilized, as though an unseen hand were holding it. A helpful ghost, perhaps? He didn't look down lest that was indeed the case. (Some things were better not to know.) Instead, he pulled out a terry cloth from his pocket to wipe the smudges he'd left when he was leaning on the glass. Done! One last smudge. But when he rubbed the cloth across it, the smudge didn't go away, grew larger in fact. It was only then Chester realized that it wasn't a smudge; it was a shadow. He looked up just in time to see—

A smashing crash, and Harry Tomlin plunged through the skylight, right past Chester, who was left clinging to his ladder trying not to fall.

In the atrium below—pandemonium. The glass shattered, shards showering down and people screaming as Harry hit the floral arrangement in the middle of the table with a heavy thud, scattering petals and then flopping backwards into the empty chair next to Miranda.

Through the missing pane in the skylight, still clinging to his swaying ladder, Chester Cornelius, acting general manager of the

Duchess Hotel, peered down in dismay. "Not the roses!" he said.

The press had stampeded for the exit as pieces of glass fell, pushing their way out of the room as a mob, and in the vacuum that followed Harry Tomlin's sudden arrival, Jane Bannister quietly took out her phone and called it in. "Chief? It's me. Jane. I may have a scoop for you."

CHAPTER EIGHT

The Fall Guy

Typical! thought Miranda after Harry Tomlin had landed in the chair next to her. Has to upstage the rest of us with a more dramatic entrance.

In fairness, she didn't yet realize he was dead, assumed it was a stunt of some sort.

The realization came a heartbeat later, when Harry's head lolled forward at a *highly* unnatural angle. (Falling three stories backwards through a sheet of glass and then bouncing off a table, even if it is one cushioned with roses, will do that to you.) He then slid off the chair, flopping onto the carpet behind the table.

A stunned silence... and then everything happened at once.

The ingénue screamed. Zab fell backwards in terror. Leni sat frozen, staring at the scene with a director's eye, cold and appraising, before she too realized what had happened and recoiled as well.

Doc Meadows shoved his way through the crowd of panicked paparazzi, who, having gotten over their initial shock, were now surging forward to see if Harry Tomlin was really, truly dead.

Doc came around the table. But there was little he could do. Pulse, none. Respiration, likewise. Body, still warm, but temperature draining quickly. He gently opened one of the eyelids. Pupils fully dilated. Cause of death? Most likely a fatal compound fracture of the cervical vertebrae, what would more normally be called a bad case of snapped neck. But that would be for the Portland medical examiner to decide. Not a lot of blood, which was a nice change. Internal injuries for the most part.

"Doc?" said Ned, coming forward. "Is he…?"

"Yup." Doc checked his watch, turned on the recording app on his phone. "Matthew Meadows, MD, declaring time of death at 10:41 a.m."

The team of paramedics swarmed in, the fleeing crowds having warned them what happened, and they rushed to Doc's side to help stabilize the patient, extended the gurney—but it wasn't a patient. It was a body. Doc presented his medical ID, confirmed that the person was deceased.

Everyone there was looking down at Harry. Ned Buckley was looking up.

Through the missing pane in the skylight, he could see an open window on the third floor with a sheer curtain hanging from it. "Mr. Cornelius!" he said, shouting up at Chester, who was still clinging to the side of the atrium outside. "Which room is that one?" He pointed.

Trembling, Chester managed to open his eyes and peer up over his shoulder. "That's the—the Roosevelt Suite. Third floor. Can I get a little help?"

Ned could see the ladder leaning against the glass. "You'll be fine. Just take it slow, and if you do fall, try to fall outward into a shrub. A shrub will be softer."

Chester swallowed. Began his shaky descent as Ned turned to his friend.

"Doc, you stay here with the body." To the paramedics: "Get the security team in. Have them lock it down."

Ned headed out of the atrium and into the hotel proper on a determined stride as Miranda sought to catch up.

"Wait!" she cried.

For a heavyset man, he moved fast. Down the hall toward the elevator.

"What do you think is it?" Miranda asked, trying to keep up. She had helped Ned solve cases before, even if he was a tad unappreciative.

"Probably nothing," he said, not breaking pace. He reached the elevator, stabbed at the button. "But possibly something. Stay. Here."

The press, having regained their composure, spotted him and charged headlong down the hall. "Chief Buckley!"

He stepped into the elevator, one of those creaky glorified closets you find in older hotels, and Miranda leapt in beside him, the doors closing on the mob before they could reach it.

"Do you suspect foul play?" she asked.

"This isn't an episode of *Pastor Fran*." He pressed third floor, and the elevator lurched. "A man fell."

"Fell . . . or was *pushed*?"

"Again. Not an episode of *Pastor Fran*."

What Ned hadn't factored in was how ungainly slow the elevators were at the Duchess Hotel. The mob had run up each floor, seen the elevator not stopping, and then run up to the next. They were waiting, red-faced, cameras poised, when the elevator doors opened on the third floor.

A stutter attack of camera shutters and shouting greeted them. Miranda couldn't help herself, she flung back her scarf and smiled.

"KGW Portland!" "A comment!" "Chief Buckley!"

Absent from the mob was reporter Jane Bannister, who was even now holding the ladder for Chester as he made his last uncertain steps to the ground—not wholly altruistically on her part. "Do you have a few moments?" she asked. "I'd like to talk to you about what just happened." She was about to get her second scoop of the day. An eyewitness to a falling star.

Back on the third floor, though, Ned was getting annoyed. He marched down the hall, harried by the braying pack, and along the way he passed a few baffled visitors and the soundman Silas, oblivious as always with his headphones on. Silas gave a "What's going on?" look as everyone hurried past.

The door to the Roosevelt Suite was locked. Ned hammered at it with a fist. Nothing. He turned, saw a pair of housekeeping staff with a linen cart parked at the end of the hallway who were craning their necks, curious about the hullabaloo—to say nothing of the hoopla—that was now underway.

"You two!" They pushed their cart over. "How long have you been here?" he asked.

"Hello? We were on our break," one of the teen girls said, snapping her gum defensively. "It's the law, y'know. We get a ten-minute break every two hours. That's the law."

"And how long were the two of you out in the hall during your ten-minute break?"

"About twenty minutes," she said, and the tone was clearly *What's it to you?*

"I need to get into this room," he said. "Now."

Snap snap. "Can't help ya with that." Snap.

"We don't have access to that suite," the other one said with an eye flutter of exasperation, as though talking to Ned were an ordeal.

"Why not?"

"Security or somethin'."

"Then who cleans it?"

"Dunno. His staff, I guess. I mean, he's like famous or something."

Was, thought Miranda. *Was* famous. They had been here the entire time, were untainted witnesses, didn't know what had happened in the atrium three floors down.

"Did you notice anyone go in or out of the suite while you were in the hallway?" Miranda asked.

Ned growled. "Miranda. I am asking the questions, okay? This doesn't involve you. Now then, girls, did you notice anyone go in or out of the suite while you were in the hallway?"

A shrug.

A shrug *no*? Or a shrug *yes*?

"There was just, like, us." Snap. "No one left or went in. Okay?"

Ned had them call down to the front desk on their walkie-talkies to ask for a supervisor to bring up a key, another ordeal they had to get through. They cheered up, though, when Ned told them not to go anywhere. Could hardly change bedding or clean clogged shower drains if one were delayed on official police orders.

The media scrum was pushing in behind Ned and he turned with a snap of anger. "Stand back. All of you."

As they waited for a key to arrive, Miranda looked down at the faded hallway carpet and noticed a new red carpet—well, red rug—that the staff had laid out at Harry Tomlin's door in anticipation of his Grand Emergence for the press conference. Typical! The male star gets all the perks. She would demand one in front of her room as well. Then she remembered that they hadn't put her up in the hotel. Had kept her at Bea's. It hit her: Harry Tomlin would never cross this final red carpet. What had happened here? A mishap? Suicide? Or something more sinister?

Her sleuth sense, finely honed from her years of playing one on TV, was tingling.

The hotel supervisor wended her way through the mob. A frazzled woman in a frazzled blazer, she said, "I'm sorry, Mr. Buckley. I don't know where Chester–I mean Mr. Cornelius–is. He has one of the skeleton keys. They unlock all the rooms in this wing. He keeps his key in his office. But he's not there now. I'm not sure what he's doing."

"Something *lame*, prob'ly," one of the gum-snappers said in that clearly audible whisper every mean teen has mastered.

"But I have this key from reception instead," said the supervisor as she fumbled with the lock.

Ned said, "No pass cards?"

A frazzled smile. "Not in the east wing. Still old-school over here."

"How many skeleton keys are there?" Miranda asked in full Pastor Fran mode.

"Ignore her," said Ned.

"Um, well, like I said, the manager, Mr. Cornelius, he has his own key. And we keep another one at the front desk in case a guest gets locked out. That's the one I brought up. Why?"

Ned gave Miranda a frownful look. "Miranda, what have I said about interfering with police business?"

"That under certain circumstances it was acceptable? I'm paraphrasing, of course. Reading between the lines, as it were."

He peered up and down the hallway ceiling. "Security cameras?" he asked the supervisor, but he had a hunch what she was going to say.

"Not in the east wing, no. When we renovate it, we will, but–" She was struggling with the lock. "There!" The heavy door swung open.

Ned turned around to address the press.

"I expect everyone to stay out here in the hall. No one enters. Understood?"

"That's right!" shouted Miranda. "You shall remain in the hall!"

82

She was standing next to Ned, fists on her hips in an authoritative stance. "People! Settle down. This is a potential crime scene. You need to keep back."

She started into the room with Ned.

"Not you," he said. "Especially not you."

"I'll, uh, wait here, then, in the doorway. Make sure no one gets by."

"You do that," said Ned, entering the suite, treading carefully, hand on holster.

Miranda watched from the threshold as Ned methodically checked every room, from the bedroom to the bath to the walk-in closets—which, from where Miranda was standing, looked bigger than her entire suite at Bea's.

A large oil painting of the lighthouse at Laurel Point sat above the dining area in a heavy rococo frame, looking out of place, Miranda thought. Indeed, much of the decor in the vaunted Roosevelt Suite seemed tatty and in need of an upgrade. The wallpaper, for one, was a vintage damask that had turned a dull, muddy green with time. Miranda could see a brighter segment above the fireplace, a large square where a painting must have been taken down and never replaced. The wallpaper there was still bright, almost metallic, and sheened. It only served to highlight how faded the rest of the walls were.

Faded beauty, thought Miranda. The saddest kind.

Ned, meanwhile, had now stepped out onto the balcony. A wooden balustrade, sturdy and curved with decorative finials, it looked like something Juliet might pine from. The heavy drapes had been pulled aside, but one of the sheer inner curtains was hanging over the edge. This was no doubt what Ned had spotted from the atrium below. He spent a long time out there, leaning over, looking first down and then up, and then at the sheer fabric that had spilled out. And then—incredibly—he licked his finger!

Held it up like some old-timey mariner reading the wind.

Miranda could see empty liquor bottles and pills lined up along the table beside the suite's writing table. The Nicest Man in America™ clearly had his vices, secret or otherwise.

Photographers—from the gutter press clearly!—tried to squeeze past, but Miranda held them in place with a firm, "I think not!" She always could command a room with her voice.

When Ned stepped back out into the hall and closed the door, he refused to take questions, and they lost interest and drifted away, leaving only the frazzled hotel supervisor and the two ennui girls behind. But they had little more they could add, just that the room was indeed locked, and that no one had entered or left the suite before Harry made his swan dive. Ned thanked them, then asked the supervisor to keep the door locked and off-limits to anyone.

The supervisor agreed and then shouted, "Okay, girls. Back to work!" with a chop-chop handclap. They rolled their cart away in a plodding slow-motion facsimile of effort, at about the same pace one chews gum.

"There was no note," said Ned as he and Miranda walked back to the elevator and began their rickety descent. "No wind either."

"Wind?" said Miranda.

"Completely still outside. Flagpoles below had not a flicker in them. I want to know how that curtain got outside the balcony window, why it was hanging over the side. If you were going to throw yourself from a balcony, you would do it. You wouldn't get tangled up and pull the curtain over the edge with you like an untucked shirt."

"You think it was an accident?" said Miranda.

"I suppose," but he didn't sound convincing, least of all to himself.

"He never made a sound," said Miranda. "Not a peep. Did you

notice that? Silent the whole way down. I didn't hear anything before he crashed through. Did you?"

"No. So?"

"He was an actor, Ned. What kind of movie star doesn't milk his final scene? Doesn't *emote*?"

The elevator doors opened like a revelation.

"You're right," said Ned. "That was his big finale. He would've played it to the hilt."

Back at the atrium, Ned showed his badge and security let them in. The scene of the earlier carnage was now eerily calm.

Doc Meadows was standing over the body, head bowed, palms up, chanting a prayer song in the language of the Coastal Salish, *"Tiwi'ulh cun ce… u tu xe'xe' stiwi'ulh… "* And then quietly, *"l'a'ma'thut cun."*

Ned waited for his friend to finish before he approached. The sound of shoes on broken glass gave them away.

"Hey, Ned," said Doc, looking up. "Hey, Miranda."

"That was beautiful," said Miranda.

"My gramma sang it better. I was never much of a singer."

"I liked that last bit," said Ned. "What was that?"

"Oh, *l'a'ma'thut cun*? That's like saying, look after yourself or have a good trip or, when referring to death, a safe journey home." Which brought them back to the body at their feet. "What do you figure, Ned? Slip or suicide?"

"I'm treating this as a crime scene, Doc, even though no crime appears to have been committed. The room was locked, and he was inside, alone. Either flung himself from the balcony, or stumbled and fell."

"I can hear it in your voice, Ned. We've known each other a long time. You think there's more to it. Here. Let me show you something."

Doc rolled Harry's body over onto its side. The actor was dressed in a loose jacket and tightly tailored slacks, bare feet. The fabric of the jacket was shredded in several places.

"Went through the skylight, back first, hit the table, and then somersaulted into the chair. The human body is very bouncy. The broken neck most likely killed him, but if not the neck, the back, and if not the back, internal trauma. You'll need a coroner," said Doc. "And a seamstress."

Ned leaned in, saw what Doc was pointing to.

"I'll give Harpreet a call, see if she's free."

"Sir!" It was one of the security guards yelling to them from across the atrium. "I have an Andrew Nguyen outside. And a woman kinda scary. They say it's urgent."

Ned waved his hand to let them in.

When Harry Tomlin crashed the party at the Duchess, Andrew had been on the phone, pacing back and forth in the hotel lobby, arguing with an irate Marty Sharpe. "Breach of contract? What breach? She fired you, Marty."

"And then she unfired me. You think you're going to cut me out of a Harry Tomlin picture? How much is she paying you?"

"Nothing. She is paying me literally nothing. And anyway, you laughed when I told you about the offer. You laughed and then you hung up."

"Affectionately! I laughed affectionately. And I hung up on you *ironically*."

"She's already signed the contract, Marty."

"And I'm still entitled to my 10 percent–plus reasonable expenses!"

While all this was going on, a sharply drawn woman in a power suit, heels, and a take-no-prisoners stare was watching with an unblinking gaze. Her lipstick was a scarlet slash, her hair was shellacked into place, and she was obviously—and unabashedly—listening in on Andrew's end of the conversation.

"A commission?" Andrew was speaking into the phone. "You want a commission? For what?"

But then, suddenly, and before Andrew could stop her, the woman in the power suit took three strides across and plucked the phone from Andrew's hand.

"This is Gillian Hardner, executive assistant to Mr. Harry Tomlin. To whom am I speaking? Marty Sharpe, is it? Well, Marty, listen carefully, because I am only going to say this once. If you get in the way of this project, if you do anything whatsoever to slow it down or gum up the works, I will personally have your guts removed and made into garters, which I will then wear at your wake. Do you understand? Good."

She hit END CALL and handed the phone back to Andrew.

"And you are?" she said.

"Andrew. Miranda Abbott's personal assistant." He extended his hand and she nutcrackered it.

"So where is Harry? My flight was delayed. High winds. I only now landed."

"Mr. Tomlin? He'll be at the press conference. It's going on right now."

And at exactly that moment, a thunderous crash was heard from the other side of the lobby.

"That was the atrium!" said Andrew, breaking into a run.

Gillian walked. And she still beat him there.

CHAPTER NINE

A Torn Jacket

Tony "The Nose" Olio placed his fisherman's cap carefully on the counter at the Cozy Café and took a deep, satisfying breath. The clean air up here agreed with him. Cleansed the palate, in the olfactory sense of the word. He'd entered this busy little café above the harbor in full Olio mode, with a camel-hair greatcoat draped over his shoulders and a three-piece suit in pinstripe. Normally, he would have sported a homburg as well, with silk hatband and discreet side feather tucked in—it was almost his trademark, that hat—but Tony had left it in the slate-gray Chrysler 300 sedan that was parked outside. The sedan with the leather interior and tinted windows.

He'd worn a newly purchased Greek fisherman's cap instead. The extent of his disguise. (Tony was neither Greek nor a fisherman, but he'd been told this was a nautical town and one did want to blend in.) He'd been getting sidelong looks and whispered asides ever since he arrived anyway, only later realizing—when someone had half-jokingly asked if they should "ask for your autograph, maybe?"—that they'd mistaken him for someone connected with the film shoot.

His eyes had narrowed. "Why would you come to this conclusion? I am a simple fisherman here to fish. Do you not see the cap I am wearing?"

The other fellow had dropped his voice and said, "It's the rings on your fingers. Dead giveaway."

Tony had looked down at his beefy hands, the gold on them.

"I mean, who wears rings on three fingers of each hand?" said the other fellow. "You're one of the stars, right? Hush hush. I get it. No worries. I won't tell a soul. Playing one of the villains, are you? A henchman of some sort? Why else would you be wearing that overcoat as a cape. Classic mobster, am I right?"

So now Tony had had to corkscrew the rings from his fingers as well. The lesson was clear: everyone in town was paying attention to strangers. *What if this person isn't a tourist, but an actual celebrity?* This was both good and bad—mainly good. He was being watched everywhere, true, but he also had a built-in assumed alibi.

On the counter, next to the Greek fisherman's cap, Tony placed a single sheet of paper, face down. And smiled.

Mabel (or maybe it was Myrtle; the two owners of the café were pretty much interchangeable as far as customers were concerned, never mind that Mabel had been in the WACS and had skydived into the World's Greatest Funk Festival in '79, or that Myrtle had never left Happy Rock, to customers they were a single unit, "Mabel & Myrtle," like salt & pepper, blood & bone) came over wielding a greasy, oversized menu.

"What can I do you for?" she asked.

A shark's smile, spreading. Tony Olio had oversized facial features, like an Easter Island profile. "Is that cinnamon nutmeg with a hint of brown sugar caramelized on top that I smell?"

Mabel was impressed. (Or maybe it was Myrtle.) "Indeed it is. Myrtle baked it fresh this morning." (Okay, so it *was* Mabel.)

Most of the items at the Cozy Café came in huge, generically labeled tubs and were prepared mainly with a can opener. The "gals," as they were known, had an inside track with the company that provided food for the school cafeterias in the Greater Tri-Rock area. Their pea soup, notably, came in giant barrels, not unlike crude oil, though with less nutritional value, it was said.

The pies, however? Those were handmade and oven-warmed, with pastry crusts as flaky as a poetry reading and light as a morning breeze, with fillings that oozed flavor.

"You got a good nose," she said.

I do indeed, he thought. A nose for many things. Business, money. Trouble, as well.

She went off to cut him a slice—"I'll put a scoop on it for ya, and you'll be wantin' coffee as well" (it wasn't a question)—and Tony turned the page over to admire his catch. A catch, not of the fishing kind, except perhaps in the broadest sense. Maybe that fisherman's cap had brought him luck?

He had spotted the production manager's blue Aston Martin parked outside a B&B soon after he arrived. Hard to miss in a town stocked mainly with pickup trucks and green-energy hatchbacks. Lumberjack hippies, what a strange alliance, he thought. A vintage Aston Martin V8? Might as well have been a semaphore signaling "Over here!"

From Zabic's sports car, Tony had extricated this single sheet of paper: *A to Z Film Services & Pindaric Productions*.

A call sheet.

At Number Three on the list was a name that seemed mildly familiar—*Maybe she was that girl he saw in that thing that one time?*—and at Number Two was Miranda Abbott, a name that rang a bell—*Wasn't she in a Poe Regal picture once?*—and there, at Number One, in black and white: Harry Tomlin. So the rumors were true. He was in Happy Rock. Even better, the call sheet had listed the cast's complete contact information, including hotel room numbers.

Slowly, methodically, Tony tore the call sheet into confetti-sized pieces. When Myrtle (or Mabel) came over with the coffee pot and a slice of Happy Rock's finest, Tony brushed the paper into his hand, closed it up in his mutton-sized fist.

"Y'want me to take that for you?" she asked, referring to the clutch of torn paper he was now holding.

He shoved it into the pocket of his vest instead, said, with a smile, "I'll take care of it."

Before Tony could cut a wedge of pie and/or ice cream with his fork, before he could bring the coffee cup to his nose—he smelled everything, deeply, before he dined—before any of that, a commotion rippled through the café.

Tony turned and heard, and then saw, an ambulance fly past along the harbor road. It was heading toward the Duchess Hotel, which was perfectly framed in the café window like a watercolor drenched in sunlight.

A man burst in, shouted, "There's a kerfuffle up at the ol' hotel! Maybe even a brouhaha!"

Customers ran out. But not Tony. A kerfuffle? A brouhaha? Anything less than a donnybrook didn't interest him.

The pie smelled better than it tasted. But then, most things usually do.

If not a brouhaha, definitely a ruckus.

As Andrew Nguyen and Gillian Hardner, she of the power suits and scarlet lipstick and unblinking eyes, reached the entrance to the hotel atrium, the doors were flung open and a stampede of competing voices poured out. "Someone's fallen through the sky-light! Get help!"

An unfortunate window washer, Andrew assumed. Hope he's okay. Andrew was going to fight his way into the atrium to check on Miranda, when Gillian grabbed his arm with the same immobi-lizing strength she had shaken his hand with earlier.

She pointed past the mob to the French-door windows that opened onto the rose garden outside.

"Who," she said, "is that?"

Outside, a robust woman, dressed in artfully arranged layers, hair tumbling back in a raven-sheened abundance, was squinting up at the atrium through a camera viewfinder, holding her eye to it like a pirate scanning the high horizon with a telescope. An incon-gruous image outside amid the confusion inside.

"That's the cinematographer," Andrew said.

"No. It isn't."

Gillian strode across the hall, cutting a swath through the crowds and straight-arming the French doors. Andrew scrambled behind.

The hotel atrium was a multi-planed glass enclosure, a sort of Victorian geodesic greenhouse that was attached to the hotel proper, and the woman with the raven hair and the viewfinder had trampled the garden as she tried to line up the best framing. Up above them, clinging to the glass atop a long and dubious ladder, was Chester. He called down to them—"Little help?"—but was duly ignored by Gillian.

"What do you think you're doing?" she demanded of the other woman.

The other woman barely glanced over at her. *"Enlevez le rouge à lèvres, salope,"* she muttered.

"Um, Ms. Hardner, this is—" Andrew was about to launch into a businesslike introduction, but was cut off.

"I know who this is. And I know what *salope* means too. Why are you here, Jackie?"

Jacquelyn de Valeur, still peering through her viewfinder at Chester, said, *"Shh. Cet imbécile va tomber à sa mort à tout moment."*

At which point a mousy woman in muted browns appeared, as though from nowhere, and said, "Ms. de Valeur says she's keeping a careful eye on the gentleman on the ladder, praying that he will return safely."

Chester, realizing that he was being scoped from below, repeated his plea, to little avail. "Little help?"

"Jackie, you know damned well that you have been let go. This isn't your picture. Harry is bringing in his own crew."

The darling of the French postmodern avant-garde movement said, in thickly accented English, "I sink not."

To which the mousy interpreter dutifully repeated, "She thinks not."

"Harry will be speaking to Alan Zabic about this."

Jacquelyn gave Gillian a sly look and, with a mocking twitch of her lips, said, "You sink so?" This was followed by a burst of French that the interpreter balked at translating.

"Oh my. She says . . . She says she just saw Harry."

"Where?"

"Plummeting from that window up there."

Andrew and Gillian stood, stunned. Stared up at the open window, then down to the glass roof of the atrium with its broken pane, and then back to the evil cinematographer. (A redundancy, that.) Was that the crash they'd just heard?

"Is this some sort of sick joke?" said Gillian, voice cold.

At which point the intrepid Jane Bannister appeared, hurrying past them. "Hang on!" she shouted, running over to hold the ladder for Chester, who took his first hesitant step backwards. Jane yelled up to him, "I want to speak with you about the late Mr. Tomlin."

Andrew and Gillian exchanged looks. *Late?* And here they bolted inside, heading for the atrium at a dead run.

Which is how they came to be standing over the body of the *very* late Harry Tomlin, having wormed their way past the security guards stationed outside and having joined Ned, Doc, and Miranda at the scene of the—crime? accident?

"Who did this?" Gillian demanded.

"He fell," said Miranda.

"No. He didn't."

Miranda would remember that. The lack of shock on Gillian Hardner's part. Like she was expecting it.

Ned was looking to the glass walls of the atrium to the same woman outside. "I will have to speak with her." He pointed to the interpreter. "And her." Chester was wobbily back on safe ground. "And him." They saw Jane talking to Chester, notepad in hand. "And her. Plus that fellow with the headphones we saw on the third floor. Andrew, are you free to give me a hand wrangling witnesses?"

"Sure thing, Ned."

Ned said, "Mr. Zabic had asked me to keep an eye out for any 'unsavory characters.' I said, 'Unsavory characters? They're from California. They're *all* unsavory.' I'll be talking to Mr. Zabic as well, to find out what he meant by that. What he was worried about."

"So not an accident?" said Doc.

"We'll see once Harpreet gets here and examines that jacket. And who might this be?" he asked, politely but professionally, of the lady with the red lips.

Remembering his manners, Andrew stammered, "Ned Buckley, this is Gillian, she was Harry's assistant."

"Executive assistant," she corrected.

"Yes, right, *executive*."

"And when did you arrive?" Ned asked.

"Moments ago. From the golf course."

They didn't have a public airport in Happy Rock. One flew to Portland then took a rattle-bang bus in, or hired a driver or rented a mule or stole a hot-air balloon. Flying in directly meant using the small landing strip at the Golf Course Country Club outside town. Flying in meant taking a private plane. Wealthy patrons did sometimes descend from the heavens to play a round or two; the inventor of Soap-on-a-Rope was rumored to have flown in once, though that may have been wishful thinking on the townspeople's part.

"Wow. Mr. Tomlin has his own plane?" Andrew said, then kicked himself immediately. Of course Mr. Tomlin had his own plane.

"Not plane. Jets," said Gillian. Plural. "I came in on his Eclipse 500."

"So where were you when it happened?" Ned asked, gesturing to Harry's body.

"As I said, officer, I had just arrived and Alfred here—"

"Andrew."

"—and I were together in the lobby when we heard the noise. So, no. I wasn't in the room or anywhere nearby when the accident occurred."

"I'll need to speak with you later just the same, to find out if he had any enemies."

She smiled tightly. "Enemies? He was The Nicest Man in America™. Hadn't you heard? I'll be in the hotel bar, officer." She hadn't bothered to remember his name. "If you'd like to arrange a curated discussion later on, I'll have one of my staff set up a meeting."

She has her own *staff*? thought Andrew.

"Not a meeting," said Ned pleasantly—though his eyes suggested otherwise. "Just a chat."

An icy smile in return. "Either way, it will need to be scheduled." And she departed.

Miranda turned to Ned. "Strange. Dapper. Yes?"

"Miranda, you have to finish your sentences," Andrew reminded her. "Remember? We talked about this."

But Miranda refused to let language master her. She mastered language! Nonetheless, she expanded on her question. "Mr. Tomlin. He was a dapper man, yes? Always well-dressed, as I recall."

And as soon as she said this, Andrew saw it: *the jacket didn't match the slacks.* Harry's jacket, an almost luminescent lime green, was large, oversized. Partly shredded from the glass, true, but it was still clearly an ill-fitting match with the trim burgundy slacks he had on. Burgundy and green? Who wears burgundy and green? The colors clashed, and so did the cut of the garb. Harry Tomlin always wore trim suits to show off his older but still fit physique. The body had tight pants, tight shirt—but a baggy jacket. Seemed strange. As for the bare feet, Andrew reckoned there were probably a pair of deck shoes up in Harry's room or somewhere on the grounds, having fallen off during the fall. (Neither, as it turned out.)

"Andrew," said Ned. "Forget the witnesses, go keep an eye on Ms. Gillian Hardner. Buddy up to her, make sure she doesn't go anywhere near Mr. Tomlin's suite. That room needs to stay sealed."

"Got it!" Andrew Nguyen, on assignment!

Andrew headed out on his mission, and the security guard posted at the entrance of the atrium called out to the police chief. "Sir! There's a Mrs. Singh here to see you. Said you asked for her?"

"Send her in."

Harpreet Singh, Tanvir's better half, owned a sewing and fabric shoppe called Singh's Things across from her husband's hardware store on the leafy lane that would be considered "uptown." Downtown was the Shell station and food store. Their daughter had been back for the summer to help out, but was in Portland now that the fall semester had started. (She was studying pharmacy, which her mom automatically upgraded to "doctor.") So Harpreet had been alone in the shoppe when she got the message–but duty calls. She'd flipped the Back in Five Minutes sign over and come right down, five minutes being a flexible concept in Happy Rock, meaning, essentially, "sometime today ... probably."

She was dressed for autumn, with a headscarf draped in golden orange, and a heavier tunic and billowy *shalwar* trousers, cuffed at the bottom. Harpreet was known far and wide for her fashion sense. But in this case, it was something grimmer that she was being asked to consider.

Ned intercepted her before she could get too close. Hand on her shoulders, he looked into her eyes. "You don't have to do this, okay? But I have a question about something Doc noticed. The way the cloth was torn on the jacket. And I thought you might be able to help us."

She could see the bare feet sticking out, and she gasped. "Is that person–dead?"

"I'm afraid so."

"*Ōha nahī* ! Is it someone we know?"

"It's the actor Harry Tomlin."

Her eyes lit up. "The movie star! Here, in Happy Rock? Oh my goodness. So the rumors were true. Do you think I can get a selfie with him? Oh, right"–she noted Ned's reproachful gaze–"maybe not. But I could still tell people I met him. Sort of."

CHAPTER TEN

A Message in Chalk

The late Harry Tomlin was lying on his side, and Doc was pointing to the shredding on the back of the jacket.

"See how the slashes are all in the same direction, at the same angle?" He nodded to the missing pane of glass above them. "He went through that, back first. The sheet of glass shattered."

The atrium ceiling was made entirely of large panes held in place and supported by a gridwork of beams. Very Victorian. Along the metal edge where Harry went through, you could see a ragged line of broken glass.

"That's what would have ripped the jacket as he went through. Then he landed over here, on his back, in the roses, and then, well, bounced up and over and into the chair."

A backwards somersault, into place. He had then slid off the chair onto the floor.

"Like I said," Doc noted. "Human body. Very bouncy."

The slashes across the back of the jacket looked like claw marks, and were indeed lined up in diagonal striations. They were sticky with blood as well, and wadded with rose petals.

"The blood was still running when I turned him over, tried to resuscitate. Not arterial blood. Superficial lacerations. The jacket took most of it. But still, fresh blood. That tells us he was most likely still alive when he fell. It's only now starting to coagulate."

Ned frowned. "So he didn't die and *then* fall. Didn't have a heart attack and then took a tumble. Nor was he killed first and then thrown over. There was no sign of a struggle up in the suite. No furniture knocked over. A lot of liquor bottles and pill containers, but those weren't scattered or anything. So he wasn't flailing about in his last moments. And he wasn't wrestled over the side of the balcony, either. Maybe an overdose? Got tangled in the curtain, flipped himself on the railing by mistake?"

"Portland coroner's toxicology report will let us know about any narcotics or medications present," Doc said. "Was no sign of anyone else up there, Ned?"

"I checked the room and the balcony. Up and down. No other windows nearby, and no other balconies along that entire section of the hotel. He was in the suite, and that's the only part that projects outward. Above it, below it, only windows flush to the wall and too far away for someone to crawl into—or out of. I'll check with the hotel staff on whether those other windows can open wide enough for someone to slip through, but I suspect not."

"Meaning?" asked Miranda.

Ned had almost forgotten she was there. He sighed. "Meaning, it was most likely an accident. Or self-inflicted. A locked room, with no one inside and no ready access to the balcony. There is no mystery here, Miranda. Hate to break it to you."

"Except..." said Doc.

And it would prove to be a most nettlesome *except*.

"Here, on the back of the jacket," he said. "Something odd."

This was where Harpreet came in. Ned turned, saw her looking down at the body with a sickly expression. He said to Doc, "Maybe spare any more talk about lacerations and coagulating blood, okay?"

"Understood," said Doc. "I forget that not everyone finds this stuff as fascinating as I do."

Harpreet edged closer.

"This is what I can't figure," said Doc.

On the back of Harry's lime-green jacket, between the shoulder blades, was a single decisive slit, small, no more than two inches long. Would have been easy to miss among all the other slashes, except that this one ran straight up and down, while the other cuts were at an angle.

"As someone conversant in such things," Doc said, addressing Harpreet, "could an errant shard of glass have caused that?"

Her voice had a quaver in it, but as the topic shifted to her area of expertise, she gained confidence. Leaned in, careful to avoid glass or rose petals or any, um, viscous liquids.

"Hmm," she said, and that too would prove to be a fateful *hmm*. "I know nothing of broken glass and falling bodies, of course. But you see the fabric on the other cuts, how frayed they are compared to this other, single cut? If I had a magnifying glass…"

Ned produced one, handed it over.

"You carry a magnifying glass?" said Doc, not sure if he should be impressed or bemused. He settled on amused. "Regular Sherlock Holmes, aren't you?"

"I keep it next to the handcuffs and flashlight."

Harpreet was peering intently at the cuts in the fabric. The back of the jacket was matted in blood from the scratches and cuts, but she was looking past that to the fabric itself. "A wool-polyester blend, sturdy, padded shoulders, single vent, medium weight but on the heavier side, lower thread count, reinforced stitching. Durable. Not pretty."

"The cuts?" Ned reminded her.

"Oh, yes. The glass didn't really slice the fabric, it ripped it. Quite ragged, when you get up close. But this cut here, right between the back shoulder panels?" She was referring to the small slit Doc had been puzzled by. "That cut was done cleanly. If he was standing, you probably wouldn't have noticed it, would have been hidden by the seam. But because the jacket is twisted around, that small cut in the fabric has sort of gaped open and come into view. That's probably the only reason you saw it, Dr. Meadows."

"So not glass?"

Harpreet rose on a creak of her knees. "Not torn. It was deliberate."

Unstated was the obvious conclusion: a blade.

"Could it have been a knife?"

She tilted her head in apology. "I don't work with blades, I'm afraid. I work with scissors and shears and snips and razors, not knives."

"Razors?" said Doc.

"To separate seams or slice away loose threads or remove buttons. I have nicked myself many times over the years," she said with a laugh. "But a tailor's razor blade couldn't slice through material that thick, that cleanly. Now then"—she flitted her eyes in Ned's direction—"about the selfie?"

Ned said, "Are you sure you want us to roll him over so you can look into his face?"

She blanched. "Maybe not."

Ned thanked her, as did Doc, but before she could leave, Miranda said, "I have a question. What does this mean?"

She was pointing to the sleeve, where Harry's arm lay flopped along his side. Everyone had been so fixated on the cuts to the back of the jacket that they'd missed a faint marking just visible on the lining of the sleeve cuff.

Ned turned the cuff up and there, in chalk, was written *WDPT*.

Those letters, thought Miranda. They seemed familiar. She was sure she'd seen them—or variations thereof—somewhere before. Maybe at her seamstress in Burbank, back when she was getting custom-made dresses? Or at Martinizer, when she no longer was?

"Do you know what that refers to?" she asked Harpreet.

"Hmm. It's definitely tailor's chalk. But as to the meaning? It could be a personal shorthand, a notation of some sort. Every seamstress has their own. Maybe it just means 'wide pant.' This jacket was off the rack. A large jacket. It could be a mark from a dry cleaner's. Maybe a note that this particular jacket went with a wide pant. WD PT."

"Do you think this jacket matches the rest of his outfit? I don't mean in size, but style."

"Well," said Harpreet with a bob of her head. "Not everyone has fashion sense."

But he did, Miranda thought. Harry Tomlin most certainly did.

"There's someone who will know," said Miranda.

She joined Harpreet, and the two of them walked out together into a full scrum of reporters, who were surging forward against an increasingly aggravated security team.

"No one is going in there!" they yelled, stepping aside only to let Miranda and Harpreet push past into the melee.

Microphones and cameras waved in their faces. "Can you confirm that Mr. Tomlin is dead?" "What is happening in there? The people have a right to know!"

People meaning the media, thought Miranda. *Media*, meaning vultures.

"No comment!" Miranda said with a regal flow.

"I have nothing to say either," said Harpreet. "Except that the Fall Sale at Singh's Things is now underway. All fabrics 30 percent off, but only till Tuesday, so act fast!"

The reporters scribbled this down.

One reporter had not followed the pack, though. Miranda spotted the young woman from earlier—Jane, was it?—in the lobby, interviewing Alan Zabic.

Harpreet slipped out, ahead of a mob of bargain seekers, she was sure, to get back to the store and flip the Five Minute sign over.

Miranda, meanwhile, sought out Harry Tomlin's executive assistant and she found her at the hotel's Bengal Lounge, deep in conversation with a clearly enraptured Andrew.

"So, wait a sec, you're saying Harry Tomlin covered your airfare *and* your meals?" Andrew was saying.

The Bengal Lounge was named for the now-tatty tiger skin that was stretched over the fireplace. Featuring threadbare sofas and teak elephants, the Bengal was an ode to another era. The King of Siam had stayed at the hotel with a full coterie of courtiers back when the Duchess had first opened a century before—the teak elephants were a gift from His Most Enlightened Majesty—and in many ways the lounge remained as a time capsule of those days. One could imagine men in pith helmets and handlebar mustaches chopping their way through the potted palms and ferns. Even the cocktails had anachronistic names, with the recipes mostly involving tropical juice and gin. Lots of gin. Andrew was drinking a Bombay Zinger, Gillian Hardner a Gunga Gin.

Miranda joined them unannounced, as was her habit, sweeping into the rattan chair next to Gillian and proffering her hand like a favor bestowed.

"Miranda Abbott. Yes, it is I."

Gillian gave her the same ouch-inducing clench she'd given Andrew, and said, "Harry mentioned he would be working with you."

"Did he now?" *Mentioned, no less!* Thoroughly flattered, Miranda waved to one of the elderly waiters who were shuffling about the potted palms in vests and bow ties, and ordered a We ARE Amused

Margarita, with pickled onion for the garnish rather than the tradi-
tional wedge of lime.

"Yes, ma'am," said the waiter. "Anything further?"

"A question. I was led to believe that they were getting rid of this
lounge entirely," said Miranda. "I understood they were going to
tear it out and update the decor. Something more... this century."

"That's right, ma'am. But the film company asked us to preserve it.
Wants to use it as a location. Paid the hotel *not* to renovate it, in fact."

"That was very kind," said Miranda.

"It was indeed," he replied, and off he shuffled.

Turning back to Gillian, Miranda said, hand across her heart, "I
am so terribly sorry about your loss."

"She was just saying that Harry Tomlin covered her travel *and*
meals."

Miranda ignored Andrew's blatant attempt at renegotiating the
terms of his (non-existent) contract, and asked Gillian instead, "The
jacket he died in. Is that something he would normally wear?"

Gillian replied, rather curtly, "If it isn't Brooks Brothers, no."

"He was wearing someone else's jacket, then. Why?"

"That's the question, isn't it?" Gillian thought a moment and said,
"This is a fairly small town, right? Everybody knows everybody?"

Miranda nodded. "Pretty much."

Andrew, who was slurping the last of his gin-and-papaya through
a curly straw, said, "Not without its charm, though."

"Any strangers been hanging around lately?" Gillian asked.

"Just the crew," said Miranda. What an odd question.

And then, more to herself, Gillian Hardner said, "No, it wouldn't
be the crew or his co-stars. He was beloved by them."

That's right, thought Miranda. The Nicest Man in Whatsit.

"Earlier, Alvin and I—"

"Andrew."

"–had a run-in with the infamous Jackie de Valeur. What is she doing in town? And, if I'm not mistaken, I spotted the equally notorious sound 'artist'–and I say that with quotation marks around the word *artist*–Silas Ivar. Again, why would either of them be here?"

Miranda was as confused as Andrew by the question. "Because they're working on the project. Same as Leni."

The flare of anger in Gillian's eyes was almost incandescent. "Leni *Vedette*? The director? She's here as well?"

They nodded. Miranda's drink arrived and she gulped down half of it in one go. This did not bode well. She had seen films fall apart before. A star, one could replace. But an entire crew?

"Leni Vedette was let go," Gillian insisted.

"But she was at the press conference," said Andrew.

"And I shall be speaking with Mr. Zabic about that. Guts. Garter. Wake."

Andrew whispered to Miranda, "That's the same threat she made to Marty."

Miranda's drink had been generously garnished with a pair of pickled cocktail onions. She swallowed them whole, the way one might an aspirin. This was bad. This was death-by-a-thousand-cuts bad.

"But," she said, "my dear Ms. Hardner, if Mr. Tomlin, for reasons I won't get into as we are all aware of them and they do not bear repeating, is no longer attached to this project…"

"Doesn't matter. Zab made a commitment. A *legally binding* commitment. You know about the Happy Crew?"

They didn't.

"Everyone knows about the Happy Crew."

"Oh, right, of course," said Andrew, bluffing badly.

"*That* Happy Crew," said Miranda. "I thought perhaps you were referring to a different Happy Crew."

Neither one of them had a clue what Gillian was referring to.

"It's why Harry Tomlin pictures always went so smoothly. On budget and in time, with everyone getting along. He worked with the same crew every time. They were a team. A happy team. From cameras down to sound recordist. Even craft services. When Harry agreed to do this film, that was one of his conditions. It always is. Alan Zabic was pleading, 'Oh, but I already put together a brilliant artistic ensemble, true visionaries, think what they could do!' But Harry wouldn't hear of it. Said his crew was his crew, and he would never ditch them. Zab—as he calls himself—signed an agreement. Play or pay, no matter what happens they get paid." A thought struck her. "Was Wayne Grey on the call sheet? The stunt supervisor."

"The cowboy with the wonky hip and the knee that bends backwards when he walks?" said Andrew. "Yes. He's here."

"Good. So Zab didn't screw that one up, at least. Harry and Wayne Grey are old friends. Harry insisted that Wayne be hired on every project—even if there were no stunts involved. Remember that rom-com about the independent bookstore for insomniacs? Wayne Grey was on set the entire time, overseeing the stunt team. Only stunt required was a fat man getting knocked down holding Christmas presents, but Wayne still got hired, still got paid." And for the first time, a certain softness came to her eyes. "Harry was like that. Always thinking about others. You know that Wayne used to be Harry's stunt double, right? I mean, before the incident."

"The incident?"

"On the set of *Parkour Paralegal*. Harry's last big-budget action flick. Wayne fell. Broke seventeen bones, including three of his vertebrae, plus a fractured pelvis and a jaw that had to be wired shut for seven months. It's amazing he survived. But Harry got him through it. He always did." And now her eyes were welling over. "He was a good soul." A sob caught in her throat. She stopped herself, said, "Nothing we can do about it now, except make sure everyone gets paid off before they pull the plug."

"The plug?" said Miranda. "What plug? There is no plug. Why are we talking about plugs? This is just a smallest of bumps on the widest of roads."

"You call the death of the star a bump in the road? The whole reason Pindaric Productions signed off on this silly MOW is because Alan Zabic convinced Harry to do it, as a favor. Do you know the last thing Harry texted me? He'd been drinking, and all it said was: *Oh how the mighty have fallen.*"

"Ouch," said Andrew, the word *fallen* seemingly prescient in retrospect.

"He was—he was slumming?" Miranda felt a stab in the pit of her stomach.

She had been thinking that Harry Tomlin's death had to be either an accident or foul play. She hadn't considered the third possibility. Why would he possibly kill himself? He had just gotten the lead role in a movie. Ah, but not a movie. A movie *of the week*. Straight-to-TV fare by Pindaric Productions. Andrew had looked up the company, these were the same people who brought you *A Kissable Christmas* and *Easter Comes Early*. They'd also done *Valentine's Day-Dream* and *Arbor Day Ardor*, to say nothing of their St. Patrick's Day family fare, *The World's Largest Leprechaun*. So Harry hadn't been as thrilled to be cast as she had? Harry was a five-time Oscar-nominated actor. Of course he hadn't been thrilled. He might even have been despondent. And with this came the terrible realization that a peak for her could be the low point for someone else.

Oh how the mighty have fallen.

CHAPTER ELEVEN

Audio / Visual

"Is it true," asked Ned, waxing philosophical at Bea's kitchen table, "that people can record silence?"

Miranda, sitting across from him over an early evening chamomile and scones, said, "It's called room tone, Ned. And it's very annoying." She had memories of sound recordists holding up an entire scene with a single raised finger. *Hold for room tone.* "It's the background hum and unique sound of a location. No room is ever entirely silent. And they are all unique. Every potential location is recorded and the tone is logged so they can use it later, during the sound mixing. I think they run a reel-to-reel tape of room tone under the scene, though I imagine now it's all digitalized." She was starting to get the hang of the lingo, from *apps* to *digitalized.*

"It seems slightly dreamy, mapping out the silence of a place." He bit thoughtfully into his scone, chewed in a slow, ruminating fashion.

He had spent the better part of the day rounding up and interviewing possible witnesses. The Happy Rock PD was stretched thin. It was really just him and Officer Holly, who was now holding down the fort—or police station, more specifically.

"She has twins," said Miranda. "She didn't mind the longer hours?"

Holly's toddlers, a dual-set of ankle-biters, were the terror of Happy Rock.

"That's *why* she didn't mind," said Ned.

He'd deputized Andrew instead so that Andrew could help line up the interviews, take notes, file the reports.

"Just temporarily," Ned had emphasized.

"Cool! Do I get a badge?" His little brother would be *sooo* jealous.

Ned had sighed. No badge. Just a way to avoid having any testimony ruled invalid later on due to Andrew's presence. It was one of the perks of being chief. He'd sworn Andrew in as deputy, had him sign documents that outlined Andrew's—very limited—range of authority, plus a confidentiality agreement. "Like an NDA!" Andrew had said. It was the first one he'd ever been asked to sign and he was thrilled to do so, with a flourish.

Andrew was even now holed up in his boutique workshop, better known by its quainter name "the pantry," thumb-typing the day's police notes in a flurry on his smartphone, a laborious process.

Ned was reflecting on the crew they had interviewed today. Silas Ivar, the sound "artiste," as he insisted on being referred to, was a gaunt man, thoroughly bald, with suitably oversized ears.

"Looked like every chemistry teacher I ever had," Ned said.

Silas had been one down, on the second floor, when the accident occurred. He'd been recording the buzz of the lights in the hallway.

"Every silence has its own sound," he'd said, which was what had struck Ned as a tad esoteric, to say nothing of contradictory, so Silas had explained, "The sound of the hallways in the Duchess will be markedly different from a hallway in a modern office building. Most commercial fluorescent tubes in the US run at around 60 Hz, but with this older wiring, due to heightened electromagnetic restrictions, it's nearly *twice* that, which creates a distinct buzz, *slightly* higher in pitch than that of standard frequency, but not as..."

At which point Ned had stopped listening.

"Did he rewind his tapes, see if he picked up anything?" Miranda asked.

"No tapes. Like you said, it's all digital. Time stamped and everything. There were no glitches or missing segments. He was recording right through it, and he was happy to help. Scrolled the audio files with us. It was like a visual chart, a sort of contour map of what he'd recorded, showing the volume levels. Very high-tech."

"And?"

"Nothing. No loud bangs or noises, no footsteps, no muffled voices. No evidence of a struggle or of anyone shouting. Just the usual hum and static."

"That's room tone," said Andrew, emerging from his pantry lair. He poured himself a cup of chamomile, joined them at the check-patterned tablecloth. "Mr. Ivar was recording *ambient* sound. He would have avoided busy corridors, would have been annoyed if he had picked up any actual noises. When he scrolled through for us, we could hear—or rather see—a bunch of running footsteps and shouts that suddenly appeared on the recording when the crowd came charging through the third-floor hallway. Mr. Ivar stopped recording after that."

"That was at 10:46 a.m. As far as the sound recordings go, there's no sign whatsoever that Harry Tomlin was anything but alone in that room," Ned observed.

"And visually?" asked Miranda. "Sound is all very well and good, but do we have any visual evidence that Harry was actually in that suite? It's odd, don't you think, that the soundman didn't record anything. Not even Harry's footsteps up above. His mic would have been aimed at the hallway celling. And the ceiling of the second

MYSTERY IN THE TITLE

floor was, of course, the floor of the third. And he heard nothing? The silence may be more revealing than we realize. Perhaps that very silence suggests the room was empty. I went up to his room before the press conference, rapped on the door. No answer—and no sound from within. And the chain wasn't up when we finally got the key and opened the door."

"I noticed that," said Ned. "But I figured it was morning, so no reason to put up the chain. Except..."

Miranda smiled. "Except that Alan Zabic was nervous, skittish even, about Harry Tomlin's safety. If there was a stalker, or worse, wouldn't Harry have locked himself in more securely?"

"Not if he didn't take the threats seriously," said Ned.

Or, thought Miranda, if Zab hadn't told him. Did our Mr. Zabic know more about a possible danger to Harry Tomlin's life than he let on?

"Either way," she said, "we don't know that he fell from *that* room. Might he not have fallen, or leapt, or been flung, from the hotel roof?"

"We have visual confirmation," said Andrew, warming to his role. He scrolled back on his phone, read out: "*Jacquelyn de Valeur, cinematographer, witnessed the victim plunge out of the window at approximately 10:40 a.m.* She had spotted the curtain hanging out of the balcony earlier," Andrew explained. "Had framed it for a moment in her viewfinder—she does that, framing the world, looking for compositions constantly. A moment later, the curtain billowed and Harry Tomlin toppled out over the side."

"*Toppled*?" said Miranda. "Not *fell*? An interesting choice of words."

"Well, that may have been her interpreter's phrasing."

"Interpreter?"

When Miranda was zooming in on something, she tended to

latch on to the most crucial word. It was an actor's trait, where one looks for those words with greatest punch. In this case: *toppled, silence, interpreter.*

"She's French, y'see," Ned said sympathetically, as though it were an unfortunate affliction. "French, through no fault of her own. Speaks through this tiny little woman."

"And she was there when Harry 'toppled' as well? The interpreter?"

"Now that you mention it, no. Jacquelyn said the interpreter came out from behind the roses afterwards. I guess, if you're Jacquelyn and you're outside and away from everybody, there's no need to have your translator at your side."

"Well, technically, Jacquelyn wasn't alone outside," said Andrew. "The hotel manager—Chester, I think his name was—he was clinging to a ladder. Harry smashed through just inches from him. He's lucky."

"Unlucky, I would say," said Miranda. "To have been up there in the first place. And did this Mr. Chester have any insight into what might have happened? It seems he had a bird's-eye view."

Andrew began scrolling back through his notes, but Ned saved him the effort. "He said he saw a blur and a crash. That's it. Not much help."

"It's looking more and more like an accident," said Andrew, tucking his smartphone away. "Case closed, right, Chief?"

"But that doesn't explain the silence," said Miranda. "Or the unfashionable jacket he was wearing."

"What silence? We already went over that." Ned was confused, thought maybe she was circling back to the issue of the room tone, but no. Miranda was nothing if not dogged. She rarely retreated. It was what had made her a star. And it was also what made her such a daunting sleuth. The skill sets complemented each other.

"When he fell," she said, "he was silent all the way down."

"Oh, that," said Ned. "We're waiting on the official report, but Doc ran some tests already. The alcohol level in his bloodstream was off the charts. Our friend Harry was sozzled. Drunk out of his gourd. Scream? Doc said it's a wonder he wasn't singing the whole way down."

"Found it!"

It was Bea, coming into the kitchen, wielding a VHS tape like it was a trophy.

"*Pastor Fran*. Season Five. Episode Nine. 'The Poisoned Lariat'!" Which, again, sort of gave away the ending.

"Ah, yes," said Miranda. "We shot that one at a dude ranch in Tule Springs. The lasso was dipped in poison or something, correct? It was why the villain always wore leather gloves when he handled it."

"That's exactly right!" said Bea. "Doused in arsenic. You looked so cute!"

"The cowgirl outfit. A fringe buckskin vest, a pink hat, pink cowboy boots—and a miniskirt. Not the smartest choice for ranch wear." They were always doing that back then, trying to come up with excuses to squeeze her into a miniskirt or a revealing top. *Pastor Fran! Undercover at the Cheerleader Academy!* or *Pastor Fran: Undercover as a Malibu Lifeguard!*

"Chafed my thighs something awful," she said, referring to her cowgirl getup. "Riding a horse in a miniskirt will do that."

When she'd asked if she could ride sidesaddle, they'd said, "That would be sexist! Times have changed, Miranda."

The Pastor Fran cowgirl action figure had sold well enough, though, even if they hadn't chafed the thighs on it.

This wasn't a Pastor Fran Friday, although Miranda was still happy to switch from chamomile to Chianti. Bea hustled everyone into the TV room, where she fast-forwarded through the show like it was an episode of *Benny Hill*. Miranda bobbling on a horse, bad guy lurking, lariat twirling, Miranda bobbling, bad guy lurking, Miranda bobbling, bad guy lurking from a different angle, and then–

"There! Do you see?"

She was pointing to the cowboy behind the reins of a wagon, looking sullen and dusty.

"Please tell me it's not Poe Regal again," said Miranda–mispronouncing it.

"It's Re-*gal*," Ned whispered, as though the man were in the room with them. "Not Re-gull."

"That's him!" said Bea, delighted. "I knew it! That's Wayne Grey, Mr. Tomlin's stunt double."

"*Former* stunt double," Andrew amended.

"I saw him ambling around town"–*ambling* being a kind way of putting it; he hobbled more than he ambled–"and I just knew he was in one of the *Pastor Fran* episodes. He rides the wagon over the cliff, remember? You leap for safety in the nick of time."

"Never met the man," said Miranda.

"But he grabbed the reins as you jumped clear, remember?"

Miranda took a steadying breath. "Bea, how many times do I have to explain to you. I didn't do any of the stunts. I never rappelled down a canyon or smashed through a plate glass window ahead of a massive fireball. If I rode a horse, it was only up to a canter–after that, someone else took over. I did the karate kicks and the ballroom dancing, and any high-water dive that would get my shirt reasonably wet, but other than that– If I had met Mr. Grey, it would have been only in passing. That was never me on that runaway wagon."

"But–but there was a close-up of you fighting with the reins."

"Shot in a studio, with a pair of stagehands rocking the wagon back and forth."

Bea hit PLAY and, sure enough, Pastor Fran leapt, the cowboy took the reins, and the entire rig went over the edge into the water.

"God, I hope they didn't hurt the horses," said Miranda. Those were callous days. But no, the horse swam to safety, and Wayne Grey the cowhand struggled until–

In plunged Pastor Fran, alas, too late to save him (he went under with a single hand reaching skyward), but not too late to get her outfit nice and clingy when she climbed back out.

"I spent a lot of time surfacing from water in slow motion," she said. One shot of her had become a best-selling poster, adorning college-boy dorm rooms everywhere on account of that day being particularly cold and the fabric particularly thin.

Wayne Grey had once moved with such grace. And now? After an accident that should have left him dead, he could barely swing his legs into his truck. What a cruel, cruel industry it is, she thought, and took another sip of her wine.

Ned rose. The briefing was done, and the fact that Harry Tomlin's stunt double had once worked on *Pastor Fran* didn't seem quite the revelation Bea seemed to think it was. Ned reckoned that pretty much everyone in Hollywood had worked with pretty much every-one else at some point. Just a small town, really, not unlike Happy Rock–without the fame, the private jets, or the million-dollar paydays. But other than that, pretty much.

"Best be going," he said. "Officer Hinton will have closed up the station for the night, but I need to be on call. Thanks again for your help, Andrew."

"*Deputy* Andrew," he said, half joking, half not.

The sadness came later, after the third glass of wine.

So caught up in the details of Harry Tomlin's demise had Miranda become that she'd forgotten the hard truth behind it. With the star dead, it was likely that she was out of a job. Again. So was Edgar.

Not that Edgar was thrilled about adapting a script for Miranda to star in, but it was still a payday, and with the financial straits the bookstore put him in, Harry's death had hit her husband too. It had been a catastrophe all round.

Andrew found Miranda alone in the sunroom looking out to the Duchess Hotel, outlined in lights above the harbor like a diva's dressing room mirror. He took the seat next to her.

"A partial moon," he said. A partial moon and no stars.

"They'll be shutting down production, I imagine," she said. "Now that Harry Tomlin is gone, no point going on. My comeback canceled by a single fall! Why does everything happen to *me*?"

Kalamazoo it is . . .

"Bring me the phone, Andrew dear. I'm calling Marty. He had a commercial for me last time we spoke."

"It's night."

"He'll answer."

"No, he won't."

But, lo and behold, when Andrew stretched the landline out to the sunroom and dialed that long, long number, Marty picked up on the first ring.

"Thought that was you!" he said. "An Oregon area code? Could only be one person."

Marty was "working on Pacino," as he put it. She knew what that meant: not "for a role" but in needlepoint. Marty Sharpe's painfully slow, painfully inept hobby.

"Part of my Hollywood Legends series," he said. Not that it mattered. His needlepoint portraits all ended up looking squashed and vaguely froglike. (When she pointed this out to him once, he didn't speak to her for three months.)

"Wait, am I still your agent? I can't remember." He worked

through the ongoing tennis match . . . *"Fired, un-fired, re-fired, re-unhired."*

"I am un-refiring you. I need a gig. Anything. Pride is a raisin best eaten dry!"

Pride is a raisin best eaten dry? That was one for the archives.

"You need a gig?" said Marty. "You have a gig. Remember? That Harry Tomlin MOW you cut me out of. Never knew you had it in you, kiddo. Never imagined ol' Miranda was a barracuda. Was a time being cut outta that kind of a payday would have surprised and enraged old Marty. Nowadays nothing surprises me, and I don't get that worked up anymore. Don't have the energy. Unless . . . You're not calling to gloat, are you?"

"Gloat? Why? Harry Tomlin is dead! Hadn't you heard?"

Marty, dryly: "Yeah, people may have mentioned it in passing." It had been in all the news non-stop.

"Well, as my newly re-unfired agent, just make sure I get a kill fee of some sort, however small." *Kill fee* being an especially apt expression in this case.

"What kill fee? The show is going forward. The MOW studio is livid, but they have to push it through or face huge financial penalties. Word is, it's all because of you! It's in all the trades. Miranda Abbott will stay in the picture! Looks like someone has taken a shine to you, kiddo."

She felt like Sally Field. *You like me! You really like me!* But who?

Just then, there came what Edgar would have referred to as a chapter-ending knock on the door.

CHAPTER TWELVE

Scouting Locations

But no. Not Edgar.

When Bea answered her back door, it wasn't Miranda's grumpy husband (ex-husband? un-refired-but-then-rehired husband?) who was making an unexpected evening visit to the B&B, but rather that impossibly handsome man, Alan Zabic. He of the tousled hair and sun-creased eyes.

"Oh, Mr. Zab!" Bea said in a sudden exhalation. "How wonderfully wonderful to see you!"

Ned Buckley chose, graciously, to ignore the titter of delight running through her voice. And Miranda's. And Andrew's, for that matter, when they all came stampeding into the kitchen to see who it was.

"Hello, Zab," said Ned, adjusting his cap. "I was just heading out. Thanks again for meeting with me earlier. It was very helpful."

He'd spoken with Zab about Harry Tomlin, and it hadn't been helpful, except in the broadest sense. Zab had given vague and evasive answers when it came to Harry's state of mind prior to his demise, as though avoiding something—which in itself was revealing. Ned had long ago learned that what people don't say is as crucial as what they do say.

"Bea was showing us a familiar face in one of the old *Pastor Fran* episodes," said Andrew, a little too eagerly. "Want to come in? Watch it with us? It's not an official Pastor Fran Friday, but we can always make an exception, ha ha ha." Did he really just say "ha ha ha"? It was those eyes, dammit, those hypnotically deep-green eyes. A fella could fall into those eyes and never come out.

"Not *old*," Miranda insisted with a flutter sent Zab's way. "Not old at all. Those shows were scarcely a day ago, it seems."

"Of course they are," said Ned, cutting in. "Pastor Fran–like Miranda herself–is ageless."

Now it was Bea's turn to be perturbed. Was Ned *flirting* with Miranda? (What she didn't realize was that Ned was thinking, Two can play this game.)

But after the events at the press conference, Zab wasn't his usual beaming, flirt-worthy self tonight. He looked distracted, distressed, discombobulated even, certainly disconcerted. He was holding a file folder, and he said, "Actually, Ned, it's you I've come to see."

Ned was taken aback by this.

"I went by the police station, but it was closed, and I didn't want to use the emergency after-hours number, so I stopped by the café to see if you were there, and everyone seemed to feel that, if you weren't at the station, odds are you were with Bea. They even joked, 'In this town, you're better off calling Bea's place rather than the emergency number if you want a quicker response.'"

Ned blushed in spite of himself. "Well, you tracked me down. What's up?"

"May I?" Zab took a seat at the kitchen table. Laid the folder in front of him, took a deep breath as the others pulled up chairs. "Ned, as a police officer, if you knew something, do you have to include it in your report? Even if it's—ambiguous, let's say."

Ned remained noncommittal. "I would have to know what that something was, Zab."

"It's just—Harry has three previous wives to support. Plus his salad dressing empire. And, well, I don't know what sort of life insurance he had, but I assume there is no payout if, well..."

He opened the folder. Inside it was an envelope with *Zab* written on it.

"This had been slipped under my door at the hotel. It was there when I came back up after the calamity of that press conference."

Inside the envelope was a sheet of paper with the Duchess Hotel letterhead, featuring an etching of the grande dame at the top along with the town motto, *There Are Furs Aplenty Yet to Poach*, written in cursive Latin. The elegance was at odds with the scrawled message below it: *Zab, I'm going to do it! —Harry.*

"But—'it' could mean anything, right?" said Zab, like a man pleading a losing case.

Considering that after Harry Tomlin had slipped this note under the door, he'd gone back to his own suite and then plunged to his death, the 'it' seemed clear.

"I'll take that," said Ned, lifting the letter gingerly by the corner. He slipped it back into the folder. "We'll dust it for prints, compare them to the ones we lifted from Harry after he died."

Zab blanched. "You took Harry's fingerprints? But why?"

"We dusted the room, want to compare any prints we find with his."

"The note," said Miranda. "You were the one who found it?" The nuance clearly being, *So we have to take your word for it?*

"Yes—no. I mean, it was under my door, but I wasn't the one who found it. I walked in, still in a daze after what had happened. I was with Leni Vedette, the director on the project. We were both in shock, went back to my room to figure out what to do next, and when she followed me in, she said, 'Zab, you almost stepped on something.' When I turned, she handed it to me."

"So the letter was still in the envelope when she gave it you?"

Zab nodded.

Miranda exchanged looks with Ned. They both knew what that meant. Leni's prints should only be on the outside of the envelope, not on the actual note. If they were *inside*... Ned would make a call on Ms. Vedette, get an ink impression from her as well. From her prickly nature, the director would not submit gracefully, Miranda assumed.

"I read the note, and Leni said, right away, 'You have to take that to the police.' I mean, it's definitely Harry's handwriting, but still. I told her, 'You don't understand, if his death is ruled a suicide...' 'Doesn't matter,' Leni said. And she's right. I mean, if it is evidence..." He looked heartbroken.

"When you opened the envelope," asked Miranda, "did Leni handle the letter?"

He thought a moment. "Yes, she did. She snatched it out of my hands at one point—you know how she can be—turned it over to see if anything was written on the other side. Gave it back to me with a snort. 'Not much of a farewell,' she said."

Damn, thought Miranda. There goes that possibility. Leni had—inadvertently—ensured that her fingerprints would be all over the letter too. Still, there should be three and only three sets on that page: Harry's, Zab's, and Leni Vedette's.

Zab looked at Ned. "Can I speak to you about Harry, off the record?"

"Sorry. No can do. Anything you say to me about Harry Tomlin or his death is on the record."

"I'll make some tea," said Bea.

"I'll help," said Andrew.

They then hung round the kitchen counter, well within earshot, pretending not to listen.

Zab was on the brink of tears. "Harry was going through a rough patch. He'd started drinking again. Having his old stunt double Wayne Grey on set wasn't helping. I never should have added stunts to the script. We just wanted to jazz things up a bit. But with Harry, if any stunts whatsoever were called for, no matter how minor, Wayne Grey was brought in to oversee them, even though he himself couldn't do any of it anymore. I think it was just a way for Harry to keep Wayne on the payroll."

"A thoughtful man," said Ned.

But Miranda wasn't so sure . . . She knew how Hollywood really worked. And favors were rarely done without something expected in return. Kindness was always transactional in LA.

"How exactly did Wayne Grey get injured?" asked Miranda. "The specific circumstances around it."

"It was on a Harry Tomlin picture. A fall between buildings. Wayne was supposed to leap across an alley, from one rooftop to the next. Fell during a practice run. Which wouldn't be an issue, except that he missed the foam pit below. Landed hard. The cameras hadn't been rolling, so they didn't even catch it on film. 'Fell for nothing,' he joked."

"And now?" asked Ned. "With Harry dead?"

"Won't come out of his room. He's in despair."

"They were friends?" said Ned.

"More than friends."

"How so?"

"They shared the burden of their lives, let's say."

But Ned was not a man patient with ambiguity. *Don't be coy, Mr. Zabic.* "What do you mean? Exactly."

"Well, after Wayne's accident, Harry helped him. Relentlessly. Got him through recovery and rehabilitation. Wayne had to learn to walk again, and what a long ordeal that was. Harry helped all the way. Every step—almost literally. Wayne had Harry by his side non-stop. I think he felt guilty about it."

But just who Zab meant when he said *"he* felt guilty" wasn't entirely clear.

Ned reminded him, "You wanted to talk about Harry. Something to add to your previous statement?"

Sheepishly: "I'm afraid I wasn't entirely forthcoming with you when we spoke earlier, Ned. But you have to understand, I'd just received that note and was worried that what I said might be, well, misinterpreted. But now that it's out in the open, I guess there's no reason to be evasive. Harry was in a dark place. I tried to help." He looked up, worried. "Something's going on."

"With Harry?"

"With the entire production." He looked to Miranda. "You know what it's like when a project just falls apart, right?"

Ouch.

Memories of *The Shimmer Spy*, of Poe Regal teaching her how to kiss properly. The scathing reviews that didn't dampen his career but certainly hurt hers. *"Miranda Abbott should have stayed in the convent where she belongs!"* one reviewer put it. As though the character she had played on *Pastor Fran* had been a nun! She'd written a letter: "I played a pastor for six years on network TV, NOT a nun, flying or otherwise." She'd often been confused with Sally Field early on, even with her red hair and her, shall we say, more bounteous figure. "I demand you retract this preposterous statement!" So they did—while running the same scathing review again with the words *"the convent"* changed to *"whatever hole she crawled out of,"* a Pyrrhic victory to say the least.

"Truth be told, I threw Harry Tomlin a lifeline," said Zab. "It was a dream project for me, working with someone like him. And he was in debt, owed massive alimony, his business ventures were in trouble. I agreed to pay him his full Hollywood rate."

"Why?" It was Andrew. He couldn't help himself. He'd been hovering near the kitchen counter, but now gave up any pretext and joined them. "For an MOW, that alone must have doubled the budget."

"It did," said Zab. "That was the idea." Then, seeing their confusion, he continued: "It transformed the picture, elevating it from a mere movie of the week, turned it into a major event, got us all sorts of buzz and interest. Did you see the paparazzi that were out? They flew in from LA and New York. It was going to be a triumph. But instead . . ." He went quiet. "Sometimes I think this entire production is cursed—by someone."

"Or some*thing*," said Bea, giving up any pretext as well, shuffling herself back into the table. "They say the hotel is cursed, you know. Murders and mayhem and—" She stopped just short of saying "suicides."

"But why shoot there in the first place?" said Andrew. "Don't get me wrong, Happy Rock is very bucolic and photogenic, but as a location? It's sort of out of the way, no?"

"There were"—and here was Evasive Zab again—"a lot of reasons."

Ned, still no fan of ambiguity, clocked that as well. Andrew had a point. Why Happy Rock? And Zab had sidestepped it.

"Harry was rueful, let's say," Zab admitted. "He knew that MOWs are filled with B-list actors and second chances. Once-great stars, clinging to a dwindling fan base. Harry was embarrassed. He said, 'Guess I'm on the way down.' In more ways than one, as it turns out."

Miranda chose to ignore the implications of this, and when Zab realized what he'd just said, he quickly added, "But that's not what this was. This was a way to pull together a masterpiece. To rise above the format. I wanted to create a truly world-class picture. Just once. A picture with the best cast, the finest crew, and a script that would have real grit to it. I wanted to transform a much-maligned form, the MOW, into art. I confess that I used Harry's financial woes to leverage him into a role. But I paid full price. No haggling. As I did with you, Miranda."

All those zeros, lining up. Yes, it had been a heady offer, and one with no audition. Could it be that he had come to Happy Rock because of her? *Looks like someone has taken a shine to you, kiddo.* No. Theirs was a purely professional relationship. *The show must go on!* That was the reason behind Zab's insistence. And anyway, she was a married woman.

Sort of.

Andrew, however, was still dubious. Zab had assembled the best creative team, and yet . . . "Harry's executive assistant Gillian told me that you agreed to fire the original team and replace them with Harry's handpicked Happy Crew." The Happy Crew in Happy Rock. Seemed apt.

"No! That's not true," said Zab, clearly hurt. "I would never do that. I kept the original team and agreed to pay Harry's crew too. I kept Leni as director, Jacquelyn as cinematographer, Silas as sound artist. Sure, I flew in a caterer from LA, but we paid Harry's crafts services team as well. There were no hard feelings. Harry signed off on all of this. That was just Gillian being Gillian."

"And yet she was late for the press conference. Didn't that seem odd for an assistant?" Miranda asked.

Andrew took this one. "Her flight was delayed due to weather."

"I wanted to ask about that," said Ned. "I checked with the golf course. A to Z Film Services booked a charter flight *before* the cast and crew arrived. There were four passengers on the manifest. You on that flight, Zab?"

"No. I drove up. But I can tell you who was. It's not a secret."

"All the way from LA? In that sporty little Aston Martin of yours?"

"Indeed!" He smiled at the memory. "Along the coast. It was good to get out of LA, the smog and congestion. The air is so crisp up here, so clean. You're all very lucky. I hope you know that." And dammit if it didn't look like he was going to burst into tears.

Here is a man on the edge of a breakdown, thought Andrew.

"If I could live up here, I would," he said with a forced smile. "Maybe I'm secretly scouting locations of my own."

"Scouting locations?"

"For a place to live! Maybe I'll move here. I'm joking, of course." But it didn't seem like he was. He cleared his throat. "Leni Vedette and Jacquelyn de Valeur, along with her interpreter. They were on that flight, came in early to scout actual locations."

This would explain the trampled rosebushes, thought Ned. He had noted how oblivious—how uncaring—the French woman was to whatever was underfoot. Always good to close a case. As for The Case of the Jimmied Door? Unrelated perhaps. But two separate cases, back to back like that? Trampled roses *and* a jimmied door? That's considered a crime wave in Happy Rock. Hard to see those as a coincidence.

"She ever try to pry her way into one of the hotel's side doors?" asked Ned.

"Jacquelyn? Why would she?"

"Probably right. No need to. Must have been teenagers all along. You said four. Leni, Jacquelyn, and the interpreter. Who was the fourth?"

"On the flight? Silas Ivar."

CHAPTER THIRTEEN

"I Have No Personal Assistant!"

Why would a sound recordist need to scout a location? This was the first thought that came to Miranda when she woke up the next morning in her eponymously named suite (née "the attic at Bea's B&B").

A cozy enough nook, quite charming with its quilts and vintage dresser and slanted roof with a view of the harbor and the hotel. (All of Happy Rock had a view of the hotel, it seemed.) Tanvir Singh had done a splendid job converting the space into a sort of Pacific Northwest cottage vernacular. She really must compliment him next time she ran into him, Miranda thought. She had always assumed that the world ran primarily on compliments—and she wasn't entirely wrong.

Seagulls reeling outside, sunlight spilling inside. Miranda was up before breakfast—a rarity, where Bea was usually puttering about long before Miranda lounged herself out of bed and down the stairs in one of her trademark satin gowns, secretly hoping for eggs Benedict, settling as always for oatmeal and SunnyD.

Not this morning, though. Miranda had been prodded awake by a nagging doubt and she now sat at her decorative *bureau à gradin*—or "desk" in the local parlance—looking out over the harbor through the small windows of her suite, brushing her Titianesque hair as she considered that intractable question: *Why would a soundman be involved in scouting film locations?*

Typically, these would be chosen by a locations scout in conjunction with any combination of the following: (a) the producers, (b) the director, (c) the cinematographer. Sound wouldn't enter into it. Sound recordists deferred to image; that was the way films generally worked.

"Sound 'sculpting,' he calls it." That was how Zab had explained Silas Ivar's insistence that he join the initial trip to Happy Rock, but it still seemed odd to her.

Something else.

After Zab had left last night, with that same firm handshake and intensely sincere eye contact of his—and hadn't he seemed to hold Miranda's eyes and hand just a heartbeat longer than he had the others'?—Andrew had been clearly concerned. His forehead knitted, he frowned tightly. She knew that look. Something was bothering him.

"Oh, what is it now?" Miranda had sighed. Her personal assistant had been so skeptical about everything lately; it was really quite annoying.

"His watch," said Andrew, and as soon as he pointed it out, Miranda saw it too.

Or, rather, didn't see it. Zab's magnificent wristwatch had been missing. A pale loop on his otherwise tanned wrists had marked its absence.

"Must have left it in his room," she said. "Or sent it off to be polished."

It had seemed plenty polished last time they saw it, though, and Andrew pointed this out.

"Yes, but the moist air and salt water up here would have tarnished the gold."

This was followed by a long, discursive, and surprisingly heated discussion about whether gold did in fact tarnish (it did) at the same rate as silver (it didn't), which had left Miranda flustered and even more annoyed with Andrew.

"Why are you so obsessed with this?" she'd asked. "If it was missing or stolen, he would have mentioned it to Ned, and Ned would have filed a report. If it was left in his room or dropped off at Jewell's Jewellers" (Yes, her name was Jewell, and yes, it had taken her several months to come up with that name) "for a quick buff, it is no concern of ours."

But Andrew suspected there was more to it than that, and he'd sat stubbornly in the corner, thumb-typing like mad–a skill Miranda had always found remarkable–until, "See!"

He showed Miranda an image from eBay. It was Zab's watch, or at least one that looked like it.

"It went up for auction yesterday. *Must sell! Best offer: white-gold and mother-of-pearl Rolex Cellini.*"

Miranda glared at him. "It is none of our concern what someone does with their own belongings."

"But *why* is he selling his watch? Because he's in trouble. Because this entire film shoot is a disaster and he's desperately trying to raise funds to save it, to keep it going."

"And so he should. The show must go on!"

"Why? Why must the show go on? Everyone says that, but no one says why."

"Can you not be happy for me, Andrew? Must you fling your damp blanket on everything good that comes my way?"

And now it was morning, and the phone on the *bureau à gradin* rang suddenly, making Miranda jump. A hard-shell plastic 1970s model in tangerine orange, it had the dial in the handset. It rang again, a loud trill, and Miranda knew who it was before she even picked up. Few people had the extension number to the Miranda Abbott Suite, so it was either Bea, Ned, or—

"It's me, Andrew. In the pantry?"

"Who?"

"Andrew. Your personal assistant."

"I have no personal assistant!" She slammed it down with panache. No one could slam a phone down like Miranda Abbott could.

If he had just left it at the watch, things might have simmered down. But no, he'd had to bring up the red carpet as well—or red rug, rather—after Zab had left. This is what had set off the full fireworks.

"Why did you mention that to him?" Andrew had asked. "The red carpet, I mean. Or lack thereof."

"It was a simple question," she'd said. "I had noticed that Mr. Tomlin had been given a red carpet, whereas I hadn't."

"You're not staying at the Duchess. And anyway, it was a mat, not a full carpet."

Zab had explained how Gillian, Harry Tomlin's ferocious assistant, had demanded over the phone that a red carpet be given for Harry's entrance at the press conference. Scrambling, Zab had asked the hotel staff and all they'd managed to come up with was one of their bright cardinal-red mats. Quite nice, but a far cry from a real red carpet. Nonetheless, Zab had set one up outside Harry's room, assuming that Gillian would see it. She missed the press conference, though, and Harry, of course, had taken a quicker way down and had never even seen it, let alone trod upon it.

When Miranda asked if the other actors had gotten the same

treatment, Zab had stammered that no, he hadn't thought to, and that if anyone was deserving of a red carpet, it was Miranda Abbott, naturally.

Andrew had cringed at the entire exchange, and once Zab had left and the mystery of the missing watch had been sorted out, he'd needled her about this as well.

"It seemed sort of petty," Andrew had said. "I mean, considering what they'll be paying you for an MOW, a red carpet or a rug or a mat hardly seems–"

"Enough!"

Ned had already left for the night, but Bea was still in attendance at the kitchen table, and she had been distraught at the turn the conversation had taken.

"At moments like this, I always ask myself what Pastor Fran would do," she said.

Miranda had been staring icicle daggers at Andrew. "Pastor Fran is more forgiving than I am."

And now, here he was the next morning, calling up from his workspace-slash-office as though nothing had happened.

She placed her Mason Pearson boar bristle hairbrush to one side, leaned her chin on the back of her interlocked fingers, and stared out to the hotel across the harbor.

A long-bore rifle of some sort. That would do it.

A single shot, fired from a distance, it would not be picked up by Silas's microphone inside the hotel. And not a bullet, but a blade, directly into the back, between the shoulder blades. And then? Ned had found no weapon in the locked room of Harry's suite, so the blade would have had to be withdrawn. A retractable wire of some sort, like the fishermen casting their lines along the pier. Pulling the knife out and away. This was the only way she could see Harry being killed. The point of access to the room was the balcony, three floors up. Only problem was, the balcony overlooked an open bay, with no building of comparable height. Where would the killer have found the elevation to fire said knife-rifle? From a seaplane? Absurd. Those planes rose and descended very sharply. It would have taken a master marksman to pull that off, if at all. A hovering helicopter? There had been none outside the hotel that day. The sky had been calm and clear, in fact. More problematic was how the knife could have gone *through* the sheer curtain and into Harry *without* cutting the curtain's fabric, yet still stabbing Harry through his jacket. And, having been stabbed from behind, why would Harry have turned and then fallen? Maybe in the grips of a death spasm? That was possible. But still. It seemed unnecessarily complicated. Perhaps the truth all along was that Harry Tomlin, in an unfashionable oversized jacket, had gotten plastered, misread the room, and tripped. Or worse, had been in such despair that he had thrown himself through the curtain, onto the atrium below.

Another jarring ring and Miranda jumped again. *Damn, these phones.*

"Hi. It's me, Andrew. In the pantry? Wait, wait! Don't hang up. I'm calling to remind you that you have an appointment today."

Media? Makeup? A photo op? A table read?

"It's with your—" He couldn't remember what descriptor to use. "Edgar."

"My husband?"

"Yes. Your husband."

"I don't have a husband."

"Ex-husband, I meant to say."

"I don't have an ex-husband either."

Andrew, head spinning, said, "Whatever he is, he'll be here in five. Texted to say he's leaving the bookstore right now."

But by that point, Miranda was already sailing toward her boutique washroom in her boutique suite. Five minutes? Time enough to prepare! One needed to look one's best for one's ex, even if one's ex wasn't an ex, to show him what he's missing!

Forty minutes later, Miranda came down the stairs and into the kitchen, where Edgar was waiting, drumming his fingers and smoldering, not in passion, but in irritation.

She sat across from him, draping herself into a chair and saying, simply, curtly, "Edgar." Still handsome, she thought. But so are most villains.

"Miranda. You're looking well." Still beautiful. But so are tiger sharks.

"Thank you, Edgar. And how is Emmy?"

"Good, good. She's learning to sit."

Miranda, wistfully. "They grow up so fast."

"They do," he said.

Even though Emmy was "technically" Edgar's dog, Miranda had asked for joint custody. Edgar had offered her visitation rights only. "It wouldn't have been fair to Bea," he said. "Asking her to put up with Emmy, as she already has to put up with you."

A sliver of a smile. "Always the gentleman."

"I was kidding." He didn't sound like he was kidding. "You know that sense of humor of mine."

"Ah, yes. Much like a UFO, darling. I hear an awful lot about it, but I've never seen it firsthand."

"That," he said with an accusatory finger, "is my line! I wrote that."

"Pastor Fran said it," she countered.

"You're not Pastor Fran!"

"Exactly!"

Off kilter, he threw his hands up. "What does that even mean?"

"It means what it means, and that"–she smiled–"is what it means."

Outside, she heard a friendly woof.

"I have to go into Portland for the day," said Edgar, fighting to regain his composure. "Won't be back till early evening. If you can watch Emmy, that would be much appreciated. Take her for a walk, give her the right mix of Alpo and dry. Her toys and bed are back at the bookstore." He slid the key to the store across to her.

"And what is waiting for you in Portland?" she asked. "What could be so important that you would take an entire day away from rewriting my movie? Another sordid dalliance with one of your many trollops, I presume?"

"Trollops? Dalliances? What are you on about? It's the annual Pacific Northwest Mystery Ink Convention. A trade show for proprietors of bookstores that specialize in crime fiction—a dying breed, both literally and figuratively. Otto is giving the keynote, and I'm not going to miss that."

Otto being Otto Penzler, the owner of Mysterious Press, who had recently been reissuing classic mysteries of the '70s, '80s, and '90s. Notably absent from the titles were the *Pastor Fran* novelizations.

"Are you going to speak to Otto about adding your books to his—"

"No!" said Edgar sharply. "I'm going there to hear him give a talk. That's it."

Miranda didn't realize that Otto had indeed pitched Edgar—several times—on the idea of resurrecting the pocketbooks Edgar had written a lifetime ago under the name Stone Rockwell. Edgar had said no. The mistake had been in Otto adding, "We can tour you with the star of the show as well. I'm sure she'll be up for it."

"And Lachlan Todd?" she asked now, turning the blade. "Will *he* be there?"

A snarl. "Why would he?"

"Well, if it is *successful* writers they are featuring..." She let the sentence finish itself, then called out in the general direction of the pantry, "Andrew!"

Her former assistant appeared. "Yes?"

"Can you bring Emmy inside, please? Someone seems to have tied her up outside as though she were a common criminal. I'm surprised the SPCA hasn't been called."

"Um…"

"Oh, right." Andrew had issues with canines. Or rather, one specific canine.

Emmy was a sociable animal who made friends with anybody and everybody she met, but she'd never taken to Andrew. The first time she met him, she'd reacted not with her usual wag of the tail and slobber of tongue but with raised hackles and a series of increasingly louder barks. Ned had chuckled and said, "That dog's a good judge of human nature," which had been intended as a joke, but Miranda could see how much Andrew's feelings had been hurt, both by the comment and by Emmy's response to him. Andrew had tried his best to win the dog over, even going so far as to switch out his cologne, just in case it was the smell of him the dog was responding to, rather than his personality, but to no avail.

Miranda was about to say something soothing to Andrew, then remembered that (a) they were fighting and (b) he was no longer her personal assistant but was, merely, a fellow lodger at Bea's.

"Never mind," she said, rising with a suitably regal disdain. "I will rescue the poor creature from neglect myself."

Outside, Emmy, with leash lightly tied to one of Bea's backyard Adirondack chairs, gamboled with delight on seeing Miranda, who addressed her primarily in rhetorical questions, as was the societal convention in such situations.

"Who's a good girl? Who is? You are! Yes, you are."

Miranda gave Emmy a few vigorous scritches behind the ears, which, next to a good tummy rub, was Emmy's favorite thing.

Edgar had followed Miranda out, was standing in Bea's pleasantly disheveled back garden when he spotted a sedan crawling past, slate-gray with tinted windows.

"I know that car."

"Mm?" said Miranda, who was now play-wrassling Emmy by her ears.

"That gray sedan. It was loitering outside the bookstore earlier."

"Cars don't *loiter*," she said, not bothering to look. "They prowl."

If there was anything she'd learned from Pastor Fran, it was that.

CHAPTER FOURTEEN

Zab's Secret . . . Revealed

At the very moment that Edgar Abbott was handing over temporary custody of Emmy, with a flurry of instructions and directives—*Don't let her play too long, she gets tuckered out, and avoid the lane behind Bea's, there's a cocker spaniel there she doesn't like, gets her wound up, and don't forget it's two-thirds dry to one-third wet at 2:00 p.m. sharp, and she can have a doggy treat but only if she...*, none of which Miranda retained—at that very same moment, strange happenings were occurring at the Duchess Hotel.

Chester Cornelius, already spooked by the incident involving Harry Tomlin, was walking the hallways of the third floor, keenly aware that the Duchess was haunted. Had another ghost been added to its menagerie? The international press had swarmed into Happy Rock, determined to portray the town as a cauldron of violence—and Harry Tomlin's apparent accident as a suicide. It was not the type of coverage Cornelius was looking for in a hotel.

As he approached the Suicide Suite and, across the faded carpet from it, the sealed door to the Roosevelt, he slowed down.

He was on his rounds, had come to check and make sure the ill-fated entrance to Harry's Death Suite (as the staff were already calling it) had remained sealed and that the wide gum-tape Ned had run along the edges was intact. The tape was still up, certainly—large strips, all the way around—with a notice posted informing any would-be lookie-lous that this room was off-limits for "the duration of the ongoing police investigation." No sense of when that might be.

Flowers had been laid in front of the door to the Roosevelt, carnations and daisies in plastic-wrapped bouquets from the grocery store—Chester recognized several of the arrangements, had often thought forlornly about all those people who had someone to buy flowers for, while he had no one—but what made his heart skip and his spine shiver was not the floral offerings or the taped door, but the message someone had scrawled across said door from one edge right to the other, in thick black letters: EXTRA HARD.

He stopped. Swallowed. Did they mean the death of a beloved movie star was "extra hard" on people? Or was there a sinister intent behind those words? Or, and he blushed just thinking about it, was there a more provocative meaning? A reference to—and now he *was* blushing—bodybuilders of some sort?

He called the police station on his cell phone, had the number on speed dial.

"Chief Buckley? It's me, Chester . . . Yes, Chester *again* . . . No, I didn't hear any more ghosts, not this time . . . It's just—I may have a case of vandalism for you to investigate. Someone wrote a message on one of our doors . . . In marker, I think . . . Oh, I see . . . Yes, I imagine you do have more pressing issues to deal with than . . . It's just that—it's *where* the vandalism occurred that struck me as possibly of interest to your ongoing . . . Hello? Hello?"

Chester put his phone away, was about to hurry onward with those extra-long Ichabod strides he took, when he heard a loud thud at the end of the hall. He turned just in time to see the stairwell door closing.

"Hello? May I help you?" he said, calling out to the empty hallway, unduly polite. Courtesy was called for, even if it was a phantasm.

Chester hurried down the hall, entered the stairwell just in time to hear the door close on the second floor below. So down and around, down and around he ran, coming out onto an empty hallway. More rows of silent rooms. A single potted plant at the other end.

He might have turned back, might well have given up the chase, except that the potted plant at the end of the hallway...sneezed.

WHILE THIS STRANGE occurrence was happening at the Duchess, Andrew Nguyen was tailing a different sort of phantasm.

Shunned by Miranda, who had headed off with Emmy at her side—joyfully leash-less, both the actress and the golden Lab—Andrew had decided to strike out on his own, to get to the truth about Alan Zabic once and for all.

It had been an impromptu decision. Andrew had seen him walking past—walking, not driving his celebrated blue Aston Martin—along the harbor, and had fallen in behind him. Andrew wasn't sure exactly what he was looking for, but he knew that a big-budget MOW shot in Happy Rock, Oregon, featuring Miranda Abbott at full pay, made no sense. There was something he wasn't seeing, some key he wasn't aware of—and Zab might well lead him there.

A fairly mundane stroll, as it turned out. Zab stopped for ice cream at I Scream, sat on the boardwalk admiring the sailboats, fed the last crumbs of his waffle cone to the seagulls, wandered past the shops and shoppes behind the hotel: the chocolatier and the hardwares, it all seemed to catch his fancy. He looked . . . and Andrew was taken aback by this . . . happy. His gait was less choppy, more relaxed. At one point he spent a lot of time studying the property listings posted in the local realtor's window. Took a few steps, then came back. Wrote down some information and, soon after, popped into Atticus Lawson's.

Andrew loitered inconspicuously in front of Singh's Things, watching the entrance to the law office in the reflection, and soon enough Zab was back out again with a spring in his step.

Not only was Atticus Lawson afraid of public speaking, he hated confrontation—common knowledge in Happy Rock—which did hamper him in a courtroom setting. So when Andrew slipped in, took the stairs two at a time to Atticus's crowded second-floor office, he knew what to do.

"What did he want?" Andrew demanded.

"Um, er, can't say. Attorney–client privilege."

"He hired you?"

"Not in so many words, er, no."

"So there is no attorney–client privilege." Andrew stared at him until he cracked. Atticus was noxiously bad at keeping secrets. Another character flaw in a field that prized discretion.

"He's thinking about buying a place!"

"Here in Happy Rock?"

Atticus nodded. "A cottage or a home. Said he's tired of LA, and I said, 'But you could go anywhere you like. Why here, of all places?'"

"Way to solicit business, Atticus. The local tourism office should hire you. *You could go anywhere you like. Why not here?* And what was his reply?"

"Just that there was something about Happy Rock that drew him in. Even asked about LOJIC."

Andrew, mishearing him, said, "Logic?"

"Not logic, LOJIC." They sounded exactly the same. "Loyal Order of Joyous Igneous & Cretaceous Bricklayers. He asked how he would go about joining our lodge. I said, 'Well, it's an elite organization, Mr. Zabic. Not sure anyone can just sign up. You'd have to ask Owen, he's the Grand Bricklayer.'"

"Owen McCune? The mechanic? He's the Grand *Bricklayer*?"

"That's right."

Nothing in this town made sense. "He say anything else?"

Atticus stared at his desktop, avoiding eye contact. Another unfortunate habit for a lawyer. "Not in the field of legalities, not so much, no."

Andrew waited him out.

He looked up. "He was asking about Edgar."

"About the bookstore?"

"No, about Edgar—and Miranda. Real casual-like, as though he were just shooting the breeze, but you could tell that he kind of, sort of, well, wanted to know."

"Know what?"

"Whether the two of them were, y'know, still a couple. Whether he had a chance, I guess."

"And what did you tell him?"

"I said it's complicated. He looked a bit crestfallen, but perked up when I added that Edgar had been in to see me about divorce papers recently." So much for attorney-client privilege. "Cheered him right up, and he left with—"

"I know," said Andrew. "With a spring in his step."

If Happy Rock were a musical, the standing cast had just expanded by one, Andrew realized. Alan Zabic was about to become a regular. The question was, what would this do to the Miranda-Edgar dynamic? If nothing else, Edgar's bluff would finally be called.

Andrew was sure, in his heart of hearts, that Edgar didn't want to sign the divorce papers any more than Miranda did. Nothing focuses a mind more than knowing someone else is waiting in the wings, ready to step in, take over your role as love interest.

Andrew himself had come to Happy Rock with a broken heart. Maybe that was why he desperately wanted Miranda to be happy. That way, at least one of them would be. The answer had been in front of Andrew all along, as clear as it was undeniable. Why had Zab cast Miranda without so much as an audition? Why had he moved the entire film production to Happy Rock? To be near her. To see her as she really was, in her natural surroundings, so to speak. Zab had fallen in love with Happy Rock. But he'd fallen in love with Miranda first. Of course he did, thought Andrew, eyes wet, how could you not? She was Miranda Abbott. She was one of a kind.

Nor was Zab the first person to flee heartbreak to Happy Rock. Andrew had done the same thing. It still stung, like a toothache that flares up then goes away, only to return when you least expect it. Andrew had been engaged once. A home in West Hollywood had beckoned. But Andrew's future husband had pulled the rug out from under him, leaving him not on the altar, but pretty damn close. He'd moved on. Andrew never had.

And in that moment, Andrew's affinity with Alan Zabic solidified. Edgar might not appreciate Miranda. But Zab clearly did. A reckoning was on its way.

Andrew had been wrong all along. Zab wasn't sad. He was lonely. Not a conniver, certainly not a killer. He was just a man, adrift. We are all of us broken, thought Andrew. All of us wounded, in our way.

"Ahem." Atticus cleared his throat. "Anything else?"

"No," said Andrew, smiling through the pain. "That was plenty."

...

IF ONLY LIFE were that simple!

If only true love conquered all. But Zab had ghosts of his own to contend with, and solving the mystery of Harry Tomlin's fall from grace and through a glass atrium was about to take on a greater urgency. Because, as Andrew walked back down the stairs and onto the sun-warmed streets of an autumn day, a car rolled past. Slate-gray with tinted windows, it was almost prowling the sleepy streets of Happy Rock. Looking for what?

"*Gotcha!*" said Tony Olio, who, having abandoned his earlier disguise, was once again sporting his proud homburg as he drove.

He passed Andrew and the chocolate shoppe, had passed Singh's Things and Jewell's Jewellers, was planning to turn around at the next street, where the greasy Quonset hut of Owen McCune's Garage sat squatting on the corner, when he spotted it. Inside the garage: a baby-blue Aston Martin.

Gotcha, indeed.

Tony pulled over and parked—watched. And waited.

And what of our intrepid newshound Jane Bannister? What was she doing during this skulduggery? She was about to break a major story in the way that only small-town press can.

"Good work, Scoop," said her boss back at The Weekly Picayune News Office & Printing Company (they also did flyers, business cards, and party invitations), he of the redundant exhortations. "Well done! Good job! You were dogged, you were tireless, you were..." He searched the air for the proper word to best capture her dogged spirit. "... *dogged* in your pursuit of this story. I knew you had it in you. Furthermore, I knew you were capable of it. Congratulations and—"

She waited for it.

"–felicitations!"

Jane had managed to maneuver every major person involved with the film shoot into giving her an exclusive interview, from the cinematographer to the ingénue to the director to the production team. She even managed to corner the morose stunt coordinator Wayne Grey, who was still grieving the loss of his body-doubled friend. Jane Bannister had been unflinching, unwavering, had asked each one of them directly what they thought. Of Happy Rock.

"Gonna run it on the front page of the Saturday paper!" he said.

"But, sir," she said. "The bake sale?"

"This is bigger than the bake sale! This is grander! Larger, even!"

Bumping a bake sale from the front page? That *was* big.

He would keep his word, as well. Scoop Bannister, only a few days on the beat, had landed a primo feature heralded in D-Day-sized font: VISITORS HAVE FAVORABLE IMPRESSION OF HAPPY ROCK. Whether it was "nice weather" or the "cute little shoppes" or the "lack of any real traffic, which is kind of nice" or "the fish at the hotel was tasty, salmon was it? or trout? Either way, it was very nice," there was nothing that moved small-town papers better than outsiders saying nice things about the town in question. That, and fishing commission scandals. But her boss had been banned from future committee meetings, so Hollywood hotshots having good impressions of Happy Rock it was!

And what of that strange fern? The one that had sneezed earlier?

Chester had approached it cautiously–if it was a ghost, it was a fairly benign one; potted plants don't really make for terrifying ghouls. He was wary, but still cognizant of his role as an unofficial ambassador for the Duchess. One didn't want any guest, even the undead or the horticulturally possessed, leaving one-star reviews.

"Gesundheit?" he hazarded.

Poltergeists can sneeze? Who knew?

The fern didn't answer. But the fronds moved.

Okay, he thought. That's a start. He came closer, and it was only then that he realized it wasn't the fern but someone who was hiding behind it who had sneezed. He knew of only one person small enough to disappear by standing behind a potted plant.

"Paulette? Is that you?"

She stepped out, looking bashful.

"You remembered my name. No one remembers my name. Not even Jacquelyn, and she's my boss." It was the mousy interpreter, in her mousy skirt and mousy haircut, diminutive to the point of non-existent. "Most people just refer to me as 'the interpreter.' I guess that's the point, to be in the background, never to call attention to yourself. But sometimes it feels as though I don't even *have* a name. You remembered, though." She was shyly beaming.

A slight bow of the head from Chester. "It is my pleasure to remember such things. We met the very first day, Paulette, and I haven't forgotten. But why were you watching me, and why did you hurry away when I approached?"

"I didn't want you to think I was following you."

"I see. And what was it you were doing?"

"I was following you."

"Oh. I can see how that might have been misunderstood. But if you wanted to speak with me, you need only to ask." Unless it's about a ghost, he thought. That was a topic he'd rather avoid. "Is there something you need?"

Her face became pink. "It was me," she blurted. "When you were on the atrium, cleaning the glass. It was me, when Mr. Tomlin fell out the window. I was the one."

"I don't follow."

"It was me holding the ladder for you."

His face lit up. "I remember that! I was swaying and then, suddenly, the ladder stabilized. Was that you?"

"It was. Just for a moment, though." She pouted slightly. "Jacquelyn called me back because of some people running out who wanted to know what Jacquelyn saw. Which wasn't much."

"And you?" asked Chester. "Did you see anything?" It had only been a blur and a crash to him, but from her vantage point, looking up from below...?

"Only that you wear nice socks," she said.

And now his face went pink. "Argyles," he explained. "They're argyles. I owe you a belated but heartfelt thank you, Paulette. You may well have saved my neck. I should do something for you to show my appreciation." And, because he had just scooted past Harry Tomlin's door on the floor above, forgetting all about the graffiti but remembering the bundles of bouquets, he hazarded, "Maybe I could give you some flowers?"

"Flowers? Gosh, no. *Ce n'est pas un problème.* You don't need to do that. Honestly, really, you don't have to."

"Oh. I see," he said, taking her word for it. The fool.

CHAPTER FIFTEEN

Stabbing a Dummy

Edgar's Victorian home on the top of Beacon Hill, with its mansard roof and widow's walk, was—suitably enough—filled with dead bodies. Corpses, contained between covers, hard and soft, in pages that dripped with mayhem, both real and imagined, from true crime to cozies.

The "I Only Read Murder" bookstore sprawled through the first floor. Edgar lived on the second. The third floor was more or less storage: four rooms with a pull-chain lavatory at one end that hadn't been upgraded since it was first installed, no doubt, and floorboards that creaked underfoot. At I Only Read Murder, even the carpets creaked. And everywhere, permeating the very wood, it seemed, was that familiar smell of books, both new and used.

Miranda had let herself in, was wandering the third floor, which was still waiting on Edgar's decision as to what these rooms would eventually become. He had considered renting them out as a writers' retreat, had also considered turning them into an Airbnb, but had hesitated out of respect for Bea. She was already struggling against websites and online reservations, and Edgar didn't want to add to her competition. Independent business owners needed to stick together. So the third floor remained a kingdom of dust and possibility. There was no rush. Edgar had—in keeping with the Rule of Three—been ruminating, postponing, and procrastinating about these renovations for over ten years, which would be a bad habit if Edgar were still making a living as a screenwriter, procrastination, delaying, and overthinking having ended more writers than the bottle.

Emmy the golden Lab had accompanied Miranda on her perambulations, happy to be included. But suddenly Emmy's hackles went up, and she started to growl at the top of the stairwell. Miranda heard the tinkle of the bell hanging over the front door, two flights down, and Emmy headed for the stairs leading to the bookstore, barking in her big-girl voice, warning any intruder that she was not to be trifled with!

Miranda hurried down the stairs after Emmy, who had just as suddenly stopped barking. When Miranda reached the main floor, Emmy was sitting pretty, her tail swishing back and forth on the floor. *It's Owen! Owen! Hey, look, it's Owen. Yay!* (Though how much of that was due to Owen's naturally friendly nature, how much to the myriad of interesting odors on his stained mechanic's overalls, and how much to the large, half-eaten burrito he held in one fist was hard to say.)

"Hey, Miranda. Minding the store?"

"Edgar's in Portland. Some sort of conference."

"Huh. That's weird. I thought he was heading to Seattle."

Seattle was where She-who-must-not-be-named now lived.

"Say," said Owen, taking a mouthful of burrito. "Isn't that where Cindy lives? You know, the lady that Edgar was with? Cindy. The one he almost married. Cindy."

Damn you, Owen McCune!

"What are you eating, anyway?" she asked, both repulsed and fascinated by it—much like stumbling across a murder scene.

"This? It's a breakfast burrito. Get 'em from TB Foods, in bulk, frozen."

"Breakfast? So... eggs, ham?"

"Nope. Refried beans, salsa, and seasoned ground beef. At least, I think it's beef. Hard to say."

"And how does that make it a breakfast burrito?"

He thought about this. "Well, it's a *burrito*. And I'm eating it for *breakfast*. I can cut you a slice if you like. There's a kitchenette in the back, all kinds of knives."

And it struck Miranda that neither Ned nor Doc nor herself had ever asked what *type* of knife had been plunged into Harry Tomlin's back. She headed for the small kitchen—past the shelf of POISONS, CONCOCTIONS & OTHER INSIDIOUS METHODS OF MURDER (Edgar had an eccentric approach to organizing books)—where a small Formica table, a sink, some cups, and a kettle lay. Miranda rummaged through the drawers and soon amassed quite the arsenal: a filleting knife, a butcher's knife, several steak knives, a serrated bread knife, a pronged tomato knife, even a paring knife.

She gathered these up in an I Only Read Murder book bag and came back out to where Owen was tossing the last of his burrito to Emmy—who was now very much in love with Owen.

"Can you look after the store for a while?" she asked.

"Sure. It's too busy at work anyway, could use a break. What's up?"

"The game is afoot!"

She dialed from the phone at the desk that served as a cashier's counter.

"Ned! It is I!... Of course it's an emergency! I need a ride to Harpreet's. Oh, and Emmy will be joining us."

She left Owen in charge, sitting in one of the many faded leather chairs that were dispersed throughout the store. Owen had taken down the mystery novel he'd been reading, the one that featured the canny auto mechanic detective and his plumber sidekick, turned to the page he'd folded down earlier, and was settling in for a good long read.

One could rob the store blind while Owen McCune was immersed in a good story, she was sure, but no time for that!

"Miranda, what did I say about treating the Happy Rock PD as your personal driving service?" Ned asked when he pulled up.

But she had already leapt into the back and whistled for Emmy to join her.

"This relates to police work," she said, dragging the clanking cloth bag in next to her.

"What's in the sack, Miranda?"

"Our murder weapons! Gathered from the bookstore kitchen-ette."

"You think Edgar killed Harry?" Ned shook his head. Even for Miranda, this was a flight of fancy.

"Not the actual weapon, but the *type*. Harpreet will tell us!"

But Ned refused to drive until she explained.

"On *Pastor Fran*, we always used collapsible stunt blades," she said. "But remember the Halloween episode Bea showed us a few weeks ago, in the run-up to fall?"

"The Case of the Scarecrow Killer?"

"Exactly. And the twist was that the scarecrow was the killer. Remember the scene where I had to stab the chest of the scarecrow to make sure the killer wasn't still inside?"

"Yeah, that was odd," said Ned. "You would think there would have been easier ways to check."

"Dramatic license, Ned. Now, I had to use an actual knife for that scene. The network was nervous about it, and very concerned."

"For your personal safety?"

"More for the liability. If I got injured, it would have slowed down the shoot and cost them a bunch of money. So I had to stab decisively, two hands on the handle, one thrust, directly into the straw-stuffed shirt. The knife," she said, "got stuck."

"Stabbing straw is a lot different than stabbing a person."

"Of course. But the fabric was pulled in with the blade when I stabbed. It got stuck, and when I yanked the knife back out, the fabric was stretched out around the cut. But the cut on Harry's jacket was clean. Would barely have been visible if he hadn't gotten twisted around when he bounced. What sort of blade would make such a clean slice through that specific fabric? Harpreet will know. She may not know knives and murder, but she certainly knows fabric."

Which is how a very dubious Ned Buckley and a very enthusiastic Miranda Abbott set up a cloth dummy at Singh's Things to practice stabbing on.

"Do not worry," Harpreet had assured Miranda. "This is an old dummy. I use it mainly as a glorified pincushion. Now then, the jacket was definitely a blend."

She went through bolts of fabric till she found one that was the same weave, weight, and feel as Harry Tomlin's. She added the lining as well, something shiny and light.

"We begin!" said Miranda, unrolling her selection of knives.

Turns out, stabbing through fabric with different-sized blades into a cotton-filled dummy is a lot of fun. In each case, though, the fabric did pucker. Harpreet would readjust, find a fresh section, and they would take turns stabbing it again. Then they would ask Ned to, in case his girth added a bit of oomph to it. But the cuts were too wide or too narrow, and the blades were too thick to enter and exit cleanly.

Ned had gone from dubious to skeptical to openly unconvinced.

"Let's wait till we have the forensic report from the Portland office, shall we? They are trained in these things."

"Yes! But you forget that I was involved in hundreds of these cases, over the span of several years," Miranda reminded him.

"On *TV*," he reminded her back.

"*If you know the weapon, you can narrow the suspects,*" she said, repeating a Pastor Fran maxim.

"There was no weapon," Ned said. "Remember? I searched that entire suite. Officer Holly came in, did likewise. Nothing."

"Hmm," said Harpreet.

Hmm, indeed.

"So . . ." Miranda said. "The killer must have taken it with them."

"There was no killer!" Ned was getting exasperated. "He fell."

"While wearing an unusual jacket," said Harpreet. "Seems very unlikely."

"If wearing an unusual jacket is evidence of a crime, half of Happy Rock's LOJIC members would be under lock and key."

The lodge members wore notoriously clashing plaids. Harpreet actually winced at the mention of it.

Fortunately, for Ned anyway, the radio on his police belt squawked. It was Officer Holly, shouting to be heard above her twins—she'd clearly taken them to work today—saying, "Got a call, Ned. Someone's trespassing at Owen's Garage."

"How would we know?" Ned asked. This was a genuine question. Owen never shuttered his place, cars were littered here and there, people came and went. It was a social club as much as it was a place of business.

"'Cause Owen is not there. And whoever it is appears to be trying to break into one of the vehicles."

"Roger that."

"And Ned? Be careful. The caller said it was a big fella."

Ned turned to Harpreet and Miranda, who were examining the results of their latest stabbing. "Gotta run," he said, though with Ned it was more of a chugging walk than a run. They barely noticed him leave.

"Hmm. What if it wasn't a knife at all?" said Harpreet.

"An icicle bayonet?" said Miranda hopefully. "Fired from a helicopter?"

"I was thinking more along the lines of..." She went to her sewing table. "Fabric shears. Or"–she pulled out what looked like a very sharp, very small pizza slicer–"a rotary cutter. The cut on the back of the jacket was only an inch or two long. Here, let me show you." She took the much-stabbed swath of cloth off the dummy, laid it out on a cutting table atop the lining, and, with a single, pressing half turn of the wheel, sliced through the fabric. Cleanly, clearly, and at the right length. She then tried a narrow-bladed fabric shear, jabbing through and then snipping. A similar effect. Very much like what was hidden on the back of that horrible lime-green jacket Harry Tomlin had died in.

Miranda compared these two slits with the ones the knives had punched through. The difference was stark.

"Would be very hard to kill someone with a rotary cutter, no matter how sharp. But fabric shears? That's it! He was stabbed with a sewing implement. *Exactly like the ones you own.*"

"Don't look at me," said Harpreet. "Why are you looking at me? I was nowhere near the place."

Miranda called Doc Meadows instead, caught him between patients.

"Harpreet and I have figured it out! A killer seamstress–who is *not* Harpreet, I hasten to add"–this off her friend's distraught expression–"has been roaming the hotel."

A long pause. "You talkin' about the ghost of the Duchess Hotel?"

"Which one?" Miranda said. There were so many.

"The one that haunts the east wing. Can be heard stitching, stitching, late at night. Hotel was occupied by invading British soldiers during the Fur Wars of the 1820s. She refused to talk, sewing her lips shut instead. Died without a whisper."

"But—wasn't the original hotel built in 1887? And doesn't the current one date from 1901?" Miranda walked by the plaque all the time.

"The ghost probably waited, then moved in once it was finished."

Ghosts, hotels, nefarious redcoats. "I'm talking about the murder of Harry Tomlin," she said. "He was stabbed in the back with a pair of fabric shears."

"Would have to be a pretty amazing set of shears," Doc said. "Magical almost, to go through the jacket but not the shirt underneath."

"What?"

"That cut in the jacket was made *before* he put it on. Was no corresponding cut in the shirt—or the body. Just superficial scratches and minor lacerations. No stab wounds whatsoever. He died from what we in the medical profession call 'falling three stories through a glass surface onto a table.' Portland coroner has ruled it an accidental death. He was drunk. He fell. It happens. But good theory on the crazed seamstress, though." He chuckled. "I always like a good story."

She hung up, feeling winded.

"Who would stab an empty jacket?" she asked Harpreet.

"Someone with a grudge against suits?" was all Harpreet could come up with.

So it wasn't murder, thought Miranda. There was no knife-shooting riddle to be solved, no sewing shears to be plunged into an unsuspecting back. Only a movie star on the way down—in every sense.

...

WHILE HARPREET AND Miranda were reconciling themselves to a simpler version of events, Ned Buckley was facing a less imaginary presence.

He'd pulled up to Owen's Garage and walked in, only to come upon the "big fella" in question. The man was lurking inside, having crab-walked along the culvert-like walls of the Quonset hut, and was peering through the window of a certain vehicle: one vintage baby-blue Aston Martin.

Broad of shoulder and wide of chest, he was wearing a camel-hair coat draped like a cape and a homburg on his head.

"May I help you, friend?"

The man looked up, startled—then opened his mouth in what could easily have been mistaken for a smile. A thick jaw and a beetle brow. "Thank you, officer, but I'm just checking on my vehicle. Thought I left something inside. I see now I didn't."

Ned dropped his hand onto his holster, like a gunslinger who doesn't need to draw his weapon to make his point. "I do believe you are mistaken. I know who that vehicle belongs to, and it isn't you, friend."

Every time Ned referred to the man as "friend," he could see his jaw clench.

"My apologies, officer. I should have said, I was checking on what *I hope* will become my car." The man pointed to the sign in the window of the Aston Martin: For Sale.

Why would Zab be selling his car? And why would this fella be skulking about? Memories came back of that first day at Bea's, when Zab had first arrived, how worried he'd been that someone might have broken into his vehicle.

"This garage is private property," said Ned. "So I'm afraid I'm going to have to ask you to show me some ID, friend."

"Private property, yes. But also a place of business, no? I didn't see the owner around, so I came in, assuming this was acceptable. Surely in the great town of Glad Stone one can enter a place of business during regular store hours without being harassed by the police."

"Happy Rock. You got the name of the town wrong. And am I to understand that you are declining to identify yourself to an officer of the law?"

The feigned smile became a feigned grin. "Not in the least. Here, allow me." He walked over, every step a hulking advance, and presented his driver's license to Ned.

"And what do you do for a living, Mr. Olio?"

"Please, call me Tony. I dabble. A lot of charitable work as well." He held his hands out, palms up in an expansive gesture. "Just trying to do my bit to make the world a better place."

"Well, Mr. Olio, I'm going to ask you to leave this property and return when the owner is in."

"Of course." A shark-toothed smile.

Adjusting his camel-hair coat, the way a matador might his cape, the large man wished Ned a good day and was leaving when Ned stopped him. "Good money?"

He turned like a turret. "I beg your pardon, officer?"

"In charities. Good money in that?"

"Ah, but that is my passion. I wouldn't dream of taking compensation for my charitable work. I'm an importer-exporter."

"And what sort of items would you be importing, Mr. Olio?"

"Oh, all sorts of things. Olive oil, mainly."

CHAPTER SIXTEEN

Love Interests

It was the time of day that cinematographers call the Magic Hour, when the sun had dropped behind the horizon but not yet set. A time without shadows, when the sky seems to glow.

Along the harbor, by the Opera House, a silhouette was walking toward Miranda. She knew that slow but determined gait. Knew it well. So did Emmy, who broke into a full gallop, charging headlong toward the silhouette, bounding up joyously when she got there.

Miranda smiled. He's only been gone for a day and already she misses him.

The golden Lab's tail was flailing as the ear scritches and rhetorical questions came anew. "Who's a good girl? Are you a good girl? Did you behave while I was gone?"

"How was Portland?" Miranda asked, seeing if he would keep the lie going.

"Portland? It was great. Otto sends his best."

"Portland. Not Seattle?"

They walked along the harbor wall, Emmy leaping and bounding and tripping over herself with sheer happiness.

"Seattle? Why would I have gone to Seattle?"

"Oh, I don't know. To see someone, maybe? Like Cindy, who I won't dignify by naming."

"You just did. And anyway, do you really think I could get up to Seattle and back in one day? That's a four-and-a-half-hour drive along the coast."

"Hmmpf. Who knows what you're capable of?"

He laughed. "If I didn't know better, Miranda, I'd say you were jealous. But no, I didn't go to Seattle. I haven't seen Cindy in years."

What he didn't tell her was that he had considered it, had considered calling Cindy's bookstore in Seattle, asking if she wanted to meet him halfway, in Portland, for the trade show, but her store only sold romances—she was never interested much in murder—and Edgar was still, in spite of his best efforts, a married man. *You have to let go.* This is what Cindy had said to him. And she was right.

The Duchess Hotel was lit up in its connect-the-dots array above the harbor, and as Edgar and Miranda approached, they slowed down without realizing. There was always an element of Brigadoon about the place for them. Edgar and Miranda had spent their honeymoon at the Duchess, belatedly. They'd both been so busy in LA that it was only when *Pastor Fran* was canceled that they had been able to arrange their overdue romantic getaway. It was how they'd first discovered the town, the bay, the bookstore on the hill. Edgar had fallen in love with Happy Rock, had taken over the bookstore from its elderly owner. And Miranda had returned to LA to restart her career, to kick it back into gear. But that engine had refused to turn over, and now—well, here she was.

They stood looking at the site of their last true moments as a couple, and a wave of nostalgia—painful and sweet, as nostalgia always is—washed over them.

"Remember the Bengal Lounge?" he said, as though it were gone, as though they were looking, not at a hotel, but at their past.

"Fuzzy Navels," she said, and they chuckled. It was what they'd drunk themselves silly on during their honeymoon, before that final, fateful night.

"Want to stop in?" he asked. "Have a drink for old times' sake?"

"What about Emmy?"

"I'll run her home. You go in, get us a seat. Order a Fuzzy Navel. Or two. Or three."

If only he had stopped there!

Miranda smiled at him, warmly, but Edgar, being Edgar, couldn't help himself. He always did have a tin ear when it came to reading the mood of any moment.

"When I get back to my place, I'll pick up the papers as well," he said, and the warmth drained from Miranda's face. "We can sign them and raise a toast," he said, oblivious to the frosty stare of his wife.

"You want us to sign our divorce papers ... *at the same place we honeymooned?*"

"Um, sure, why not?" The symmetry appealed to the author in him. "Seems apropos, no?"

"Apropos? *Apropos?*" She pivoted, head high, and marched away, leaving him behind.

"Wait—what? Come back," he shouted. "Let's talk!"

"I wouldn't divorce you if you were the last man on earth!" she yelled back.

This was where the night should have ended—with a dramatic exit, stage right. But the night had other things in store for her. Strange things ...

It began with the red carpet outside Bea's back door. Not a carpet. Not exactly. It was one of the Duchess Hotel's rugs.

What the…?

The Mystery of the Red Carpet was solved soon enough, though, when Miranda came into the kitchen. There, at the table, was the radiant Alan Zabic.

Bea was fluttering about him like a flirtatious cockatoo, and he looked up when Miranda came in.

"Why is there a red carpet from the Duchess in front of the door?" she asked.

"Oh, that," he said, blushing. "Just a gesture. I thought you deserved it."

Miranda was flattered, but nonetheless had to ask, "Did the hotel say you could take it?"

He grinned. "They didn't say I couldn't *not* take it."

"Zab stopped by for another impromptu Pastor Fran evening," Bea explained. "He was looking for you."

"I was in the neighborhood anyway," he said, trying to be cool about it.

"But I told him you were doing a favor for *your husband*." Bea let those last two words drop like a bag of wet cement. She then batted her eyes Zab's way.

"Are you okay?" he asked, concerned at Bea's tic. "An eyelash?"

As a widow of many years, Bea was out of practice when it came to flirting. Fortunately, she was saved further embarrassment by Ned's timely arrival.

"Hey there, Zab." Ned placed his cap on the kitchen counter, poured himself a tall glass of SunnyD. "You selling your car?"

"What? Oh. Right. Yes, I am. A sports car like that is not a very good choice up here in the rugged Northwest. So I thought, might as well get something more practical. A Jeep maybe. Like Edgar drives."

Ned frowned. "Right. It's just—why is it parked at Owen's Garage?"

Zab had an answer for that as well. "I told Owen he could keep 10 percent of any sale. I just want to get rid of it."

"Why the rush?"

"No rush. It's just—"

"What's with the interrogation, Ned?" said Bea, scolding him.

"Sorry," said Ned. "Bea's right. A police habit."

"Zab brought sushi!" said Bea, displaying a fancy wrapped tray from the film's high-end catering company. "And popcorn."

"It's from Popcornopolis in Beverly Hills, all-natural flavorings. And the sushi is to die for."

"Oh."

Miranda caught the hurt look on his face. Ned was the salmon guy—he had "inside" connections (i.e., Doc Meadows)—and he was also the popcorn guy. Not "gourmet, naturally flavored, couriered-in-from-La-La-Land" popcorn, but properly sticky confections from the local candy shoppe. Even worse, this was NOT an official Pastor Fran Friday, because Ned had not been consulted. Bea always called him first. Always.

"Zab was asking about one episode in particular," said Bea, "wanted to know if I had it, and I said, well heck, I sure do, 'cause I have every one, even the Christmas special and the hard-to-find compilation tape."

The episode in question was titled "The Scientist Who Had a Secret Twin," about a marijuana gang who infiltrated a medical lab by using a scientist who had a secret twin (the big reveal, as noted in the title) in order to make their illicit drugs. The four of them— Ned, Bea, Miranda, and Zab—retired to the living room to watch it, each with a personalized bag of popcorn.

"I ordered salted caramel for you, Ned, yam-flavored wasabi for Bea. And honeysuckle and lemon-dew for Miranda, and— Where is Andrew? Is he not watching?" asked Zab.

Things were still strained between Andrew and Miranda.

"He may join us later," said Bea, who clearly didn't know. "Let me just find that episode."

Ned struggled with pretending to enjoy the popcorn. Who puts salt on caramel? he thought. Salt, yes. Caramel, sure. But together? Miranda, however, dug in. "You can really taste the lemon!"

"Our Lady, who arts on the mean streets of Crime City! Hallowed be her fists. Our Kingdom come, her Justice will be done..."

It was an episode that featured Pastor Fran's rival, the recurring character "Laurén Morocco, the gumshoe debutante"! Literally.

"I never understood that," said the woman who once played a karate-chopping pastor on TV, "a detective who solves crimes in a clingy evening gown and actual gumshoes. What a ridiculous concept. Why'd you choose this one, Zab?"

He nodded to the cast list for this week's episode, which was now splashing across the screen. Several actresses had played Ms. Morocco over the years. But only one actor had played a jiujitsu deputy.

And guest-starring ... Poe Regal! ... as ... Deputy Marshal Matt Macleod!

It was the guest appearance that would launch Poe into his own TV show. Miranda caught her breath. There it was again, that fleeting memory of lips, a kiss, a sigh ...

"You worked with him. What do you think?" Zab asked.

She measured her words carefully. "I know he's had his troubles of late."

"I'll say!" Zab chimed.

Poe Regal had been fired from the last three movies he'd managed to land, had been arrested on several charges—including aggressive loitering, sea-dooing while under the influence (*plus* indecent exposure when his speedo slipped during the sea-doo incident, thereby mooning a kindergarten group on a nearby banana boat, *plus* reckless endangerment when the waves from his aforementioned sea-doo swamped said banana boat), as well as owning a katana with a blade longer than three feet, driving a stolen handi-bus the wrong way down Mulholland while yodeling, for reasons that weren't clear—and been caught on tape in a low-end Mafia-for-hire movie deal, plus his chain of Tex/Mex/Asian fusion fast-food restaurants, Kung Pow Sherriff, had failed spectacularly, and, worst of all, he'd been stripped of his People's Choice Award.

"But—" said Miranda, and it was an important *but*. "Everyone needs a second chance. Or, in Poe's case, a third, fourth, or even sixteenth chance. He was always a gentleman."

"Didn't you do a movie with him?" Zab asked. "I thought you two had clashed constantly on set."

On set, yes. Off set...

"So you retain a certain... fondness for him. Even now?"

"I suppose." Speaking of the downward trajectory of leading men, "What is happening with the production now that Harry is gone? Everyone is in a holding pattern, not sure what to do. Doc Meadows let slip that the coroner's office has ruled the death accidental."

Relief flooded Zab's face. "So his wives *will* be eligible for the life insurance." He looked to Ned with abject gratitude. "Thank you, Chief Buckley. I was wrought with guilt after I showed you that note."

"It's being ruled death by misadventure," said Ned. "Insurance company could try to fight it, but odds are they'd lose."

It all worked out in the end, thought Miranda. Other than the murder. Regardless of the ruling, she knew there was more to Harry's death, and even with the film now back on track, she was determined to get to the bottom of it.

On Bea's TV, Pastor Fran was resisting a smooch from Poe

Regal. "Whats'uh madder sweetheart?" Poe mumbled. "Married or sum'thin'?"

"Yes," said Pastor Fran—and here Bea mouthed the words with her—"to the Lord."

"Didn't they do their own spin-off?" asked Zab. "Before *Kung Fu Sheriff*? The two of them. The gumshoe debutante and the jiujitsu deputy. *Macleod and Morocco: Private Eyes for Hire*?"

"They did," said Miranda. "Or I should say, they tried. Never got past the pilot. Poe's prima donna tendencies were already beginning to show, sadly." Thank god, I was never like that, thought Miranda (erroneously).

"That's right," said Zab. "Poe Regal threw his co-star under the bus, got himself cast as the lead in *Kung Fu Sheriff* instead. Which did seem a tad derivative of jiujitsu deputy, truth be told. I think there was a lawsuit of some sort over the similarity of the characters. Would that have been one of your husband's creations?"

"No, that would have been Lachlan Todd's. And anyway, the network would have owned the character. Edgar wouldn't have had a say in the matter, either way."

Speaking of the trajectory of former husbands...

There was a sharp rap at the back door. "I'll get it," said Bea, leaping from her seat and upturning her yam and wasabi popcorn (intentionally it seemed). "Oops!"

Bea hit PAUSE and hurried out, came back a moment later with Edgar, who stood glaring at Miranda. "I need the key," he said. "To the store."

"Oh, right. Andrew—" And she caught herself. She was about to ask her personal assistant to rummage through her purse in the kitchen, when she remembered that she had no personal assistant.

"And what did you feed Emmy?" he demanded. "She's been farting all night."

"Just what you said: half dry, half wet. And maybe a little bit of Owen's burrito this morning."

"From TB Foods? He's still eating those?" said Ned. "Those are toxic."

Edgar gave Miranda a look that said, "See? Even Ned here knows that those burritos are unhealthy and shouldn't be given to a dog with a delicate digestive tract." (Edgar could say a lot with a single look.) Only then did Edgar notice Zab sitting on the couch next to Miranda.

"How are the rewrites going?" Zab asked. He sounded genuinely interested, unlike every other executive Edgar had worked with, which should have been reassuring. But pressure was mounting. The meter was running.

The film crew was wandering around town with nothing to do. The cafés were packed, Ned was complaining about the wanton littering—to say nothing of the loitering—and all of it seemed to pivot on Edgar's rewrite. Until the script was done and the lead actor cast, the movie was in an (expensive) idle mode.

"Hard to write when I don't know who I'm writing for," said Edgar. "Any word on who will replace Harry Tomlin? Harry was a beloved character actor, known for his nuance. He could add layers to a line of dialogue that even the writer didn't see. Will be hard to replace. Especially as a love interest for Miranda."

"*Clover,*" said Zab. "A love interest for Clover McBride, the character, not Miranda the actor."

"Yeah, well, Miranda never was one for separating the role she played from who she was." Miranda didn't know if that was a criticism or a compliment, and Edgar didn't give her time to work it out. "So, any word on who the new leading man will be, Zab? It's got to be expensive, keeping the entire crew on the clock. The meter is running. We have to know."

"Heck, maybe *I* should play Miranda's romantic lead," said Zab, a laugh that died in an awkward silence.

Crickets.

Zab cleared his throat and said, "Joking, of course. I'm not an actor. Don't worry, we're talking to several big stars." But his face was red, and Miranda was pretending not to notice, which only made it worse.

And suddenly Edgar noticed how very *close* Zab was sitting to Miranda. And how very handsome Zab was. Why had he not noticed that before?

On Bea's TV screen, a version of Miranda was frozen in place, on pause and looking young. She was wearing a tight, form-fitting lab coat—trust the producers to make even a lab coat sexy—while holding up a test-tube helpfully labeled TOP SECRET ILLEGAL MARIJUANA EXTRACT.

"I remember this one!" said Edgar. "One of Luckless Lachlan's scripts. The one with the two scientists, both of whom were the other one's evil twin. Quite the twist. Do you mind?"

Edgar came over and squeezed himself in between Miranda and Zab. He defiantly took a fistful of Zab's plain buttered popcorn and said, "Roll it, Bea!"

My, my, thought Miranda. Looks like someone is jealous.

It could hardly be considered a love triangle, though, given that Zab and she were colleagues, nothing more, and that Edgar was determined to end things with Miranda anyway.

The episode concluded, as they all did, with redress and justice served, in this case by having Poe Regal and Miranda (aka the jiu-jitsu deputy and the traveling female pastor) team up to bring down a band of nefarious scientists—much to Laurén Morocco's chagrin. (This was shown by having the actress who played Morocco stand, fists on hips, shaking her head angrily. This was how chagrin was shown on network TV back in the day.)

And as the closing credits rolled, Miranda leaned in, whispered to Edgar loud enough for Zab to hear, "Edgar, darling, I shall come by your place tomorrow and sign the papers. The *divorce* papers."

"Fine," said Edgar, though his eyes said otherwise.

CHAPTER SEVENTEEN

A Bouquet of Deadly Roses

It was only after Edgar left and Ned had departed, as Zab dawdled by the door, looking for an excuse to stay—it was only then that Bea made a comment, just in passing, which would have immense repercussions and would lead, eventually, to a killer cornered and a life in peril.

"I enjoyed that episode!" said Bea. (That wasn't the comment.) "You were so full of energy, Miranda!" (That wasn't it either.) "Where did you learn to kick so high?" (Nope.) "In high heels, no less!" (Not that.) "I didn't even know lab coats came in miniskirt length." (There it was!)

"Everything I wore was fitted," Miranda explained. "And hemmed mid-thigh, even the lab coats."

Only later would Miranda catch the significance of this.

"Well, Bea, it's been an absolutely lovely evening," said Zab, thanking her with one of his dazzling smiles. And to Miranda, almost bashfully, he said, "And if you ever want to have a coffee or lunch, talk about your role, I would be happy to. I know that Leni Vedette is a sort-of 'hands-off' director. Expects actors to know their blocking 'intuitively.' Maybe I could help."

"Maybe. We'll see."

He waited, but she didn't elaborate.

"Well, I guess I should be going," he said. "It's getting late." It was time to go, and he didn't seem able to come up with a reason to stay, so he left, looking a bit hound dog, it must be said.

Bea cocked her head at Miranda and asked, "Why so coy?"

"I wasn't being coy."

"He clearly likes you." And maybe it was the sushi and maybe it was that god-awful popcorn, but over the course of the evening Bea had come to accept that as handsome as Mr. Zabic was, he was no Ned Buckley. She'd come to her decision: she would step aside, leave the field for Miranda.

What Bea didn't appreciate was that Zab was no Edgar either.

"I'm married. Remember?"

She retired to the veranda, feeling wistful.

A clouded moon. A forest-scented breeze, coming down the wooded heights. The hotel above the bay. Waves along the shore. *This beautiful prison.* Miranda knew she had only to sign those papers and she could leave, would be free. So why hadn't she?

A creak from behind and Andrew appeared.

"Can we talk?" he asked quietly.

"*May* we talk. Of course. Join me." She patted the wooden chair next to hers and they sat, side by side, admiring the night view of Tillamook Bay.

"Miranda—" he began, but she stopped him.

"There is no need to apologize. What you said was right. I was being petty. A red carpet? How very plebeian of me. It wasn't the carpet, you see, or lack of, but what it represented. The rest of the cast is lounging about in the hotel, drinking champagne and laughing with gay abandon. I'm stuck here—which is perfectly acceptable.

I'm happy at Bea's. I am. It's just ... It's like a party that you don't want to attend but desperately want to be invited to." Hollywood, in other words. "I just need to be loved, I suppose."

Don't we all, thought Andrew.

She turned to him. "Do you think I am holding on to the past?"

Who among us isn't?

"It's a hard pill to swallow," she said. "To have been someone once, and now to not be. And have it again dangling in front of you. I snapped at you earlier, Andrew, and I shouldn't have."

"But you *are* someone," he said. "You're Pastor Fran, dammit! And as far as I'm concerned, you always will be. My parents fled violence and upheaval, and every Friday they watched your show—not only to learn English idioms. My dad still says, 'Miscreants beware!' It was more than that. Pastor Fran reassured them that in a world that is so often dark, so often cruel, a balance was still possible, goodness and light could still triumph. In the end. Even amid the karate chops and the miniskirts, that was the real message."

She laughed. "Bea asked me about the lab coats in that last episode."

"The one with the twins? My brother and I watched that with Mom and Pop, argued about which of us would have been the evil one. We weren't twins, and I was bigger, but it still turned into a wrestling match." His poor mom shouting at them to stop. His dad warning them that miscreants would lose their TV privileges.

"Evil twins and form-fitting lab coats," said Miranda. "I had to explain to Bea that, no, lab coats don't generally come in form-fitting, miniskirt style, that the wardrobe department would have altered them."

And there it was—the answer to the question.

She looked at Andrew, eyes wide. "The wardrobe department! That's what that chalk mark WDPT stands for. W-DPT. The jacket

Harry Tomlin died in was from the film's wardrobe trailer. Your phone, Andrew!"

"Who am I calling?"

"*Whom*, darling. Whom. I want you to dial Alan Zabic, if you please. I want to catch him before he"—gets in the shower—"goes to bed."

Andrew could hear Zab's muffled enthusiasm over his phone. He'd put it on speaker.

"Miranda, hi! I'm almost at the hotel." Car-less now, he was walking back—something unheard-of in LA, where one drove from the end of the driveway to one's mailbox. "Did you want to meet for a nightcap? I think that tiger lounge is still open."

But Miranda Abbott was all business. "Who is handling wardrobe? I didn't see it on the call sheet."

"Ah, yes, that was quite the coup. We managed to get Idelia Powell."

Andrew and Miranda exchanged mouth-gaping looks.

"*The* Idelia Powell?" said Miranda. "Idelia Powell, the fashion icon? The inventor of the fur-covered stiletto? The one who wrapped Lady Gaga in edible Silly String? Who made a 'meat umbrella' for Cher?"

"The very one! She has some amazing wardrobe concepts. She sees you in bright, bright orange. With big yellow bows."

"But—but I always wear green," said Miranda. "Preferably seafoam or tosca pear, though I can go with a slightly muted chartreuse in a pinch. Green goes best with my hair, you see." Indeed, green satin and red hair was something of Miranda's trademark.

"Not to worry. I'm sure you two will sort it out amicably," said Zab, ever the optimist. "I'm just thrilled to get her. It hasn't been announced yet. She likes to keep a low profile until the big unveiling, so keep it on the q.t."

"Understood," said Miranda. Because if anyone could have a

reasonable conversation about clothing, it would be a famous fashion designer and a former TV star.

Miranda passed Andrew's smartphone back to him, frowning.

"Why the perturbed face?" Andrew asked after he hung up. "This is great news!"

"Perhaps. But Idelia Powell only works with the finest of materials."

"So?"

"She would never deign to include the sort of cheap blend that Harry was wearing. Where did that jacket come from?"

Other fabrics.

As Miranda looked across the masts of the harbor to the hotel beyond, she recalled the sheer curtain liner that Harry had fallen through. Not from the roof or any of the floors above. He had been *behind* that curtain.

Why?

She felt as though all the pieces were in front of her, if only she could figure out how they fit together. A man in an ill-fitting jacket falls to his death. But in the moments just before that, he is hiding behind a curtain. Why?

"What was he afraid of?" she asked. "Why was he hiding? What was he hiding *from*? Inner demons? Or something more tangible?" She turned her gaze on her assistant. "Andrew, what is the single most important thing I've taught you?"

"Moisturize?"

"About investigating a murder. Ask: Who benefits? Before you go storming off to means and opportunity, look first for the motive behind it, the reasons why. Ask yourself, emotionally or financially, who benefits? Revenge. Fear. Envy. Money. Which of those drove someone to murder Harry Tomlin?"

"But he wasn't murdered."

"Wasn't he? Or was he not *not* murdered?" And before Andrew could untangle the syntax of that, she asked, with a sly smile, "Are you still deputized?"

THIS WAS A bad idea. Andrew knew it, and Miranda knew it too, even if she was trying to take advantage of a largely hypothetical loophole.

The two of them were scurrying along the harbor wall, heading for the hotel. In the night air, Miranda had a shawl thrown over her shoulders, and Andrew was in a thin windbreaker, but both of them were warm from the fast pace that Miranda was setting.

Andrew was carrying the form that Ned had filled in and signed.

"It's true I was deputized," Andrew pleaded, breathing raggedly, hurrying to keep up. "But it was only for twenty-four hours."

"Exactly!" said Miranda, not breaking stride. "But it didn't say *which* twenty-four hours, correct? It could be six hours that first day, one hour tonight, a few hours here, a few hours there."

"Common sense would dictate—"

"Not interested in common sense!" she cried, crossing the street toward the Duchess. "I am interested in *un*common sense."

He made a mental note to jot that one down later as well.

"Just glad Ned didn't give me a badge," he muttered. "You'd be kicking in doors and reading people their rights."

She stopped so suddenly Andrew almost ran into her from behind. The hotel loomed in front of them like a magnificent brick castle with the front entrance lit up and the lobby inside warm and inviting, but Miranda walked around instead, past the trampled rose-bushes, and stared up at the ivy-clad walls of the east wing. The glass atrium jutted out from the side, and directly above, three stories up, was Harry's suite. It was autumn, so the ivy had grown scraggly.

"Do you think that those vines are strong enough to support

someone's weight?" she asked, and then answered: "Probably not."

But just in case, she sent Andrew over to try. Tucking his deputy certification paper into his back pocket, he went over, tried to pull himself up. The vines pulled away from the wall instantly.

"Would've been like trying to climb gossamer," he said, reporting back.

"I thought as much, but I had to check."

The Roosevelt Suite had the only balcony on this entire wall, curving out overhead. The French windows that would have opened onto it were closed now and the heavy blinds inside had been pulled shut.

"The room was locked," she said. "There was no way in and only one way out. Those two statements seal him in, remove any chance of foul play. So, either there was no murder–"

"There wasn't."

"–or those statements are false. There *was* another way in, and–because no one was found lurking in the room when Ned entered–there is also another way out." The lights from the hotel caught highlights in her hair and a sparkle in her eyes. "The snake, Andrew!"

"Snake?"

"Flowers. Inside, remember? The snake."

"Complete sentences, Miranda. You need to speak in complete sentences."

She was getting impatient. "Rubber at first, but then real."

"I refer to my previous comment."

"I'm sure I told you about it! You must have seen every episode of *Pastor Fran* when you were young."

"Well, I'm no Bea Maracle, but sure, the first few seasons anyway." He and his brother had stopped watching as soon as they were old enough to skip out, making vague references to libraries and studying and overdue school projects, leaving their mom and dad to spend Friday night on their own, still faithfully watching every new installment–and Andrew not realizing how poignant those moments were until years later.

"So you know what I'm referring to," she said. "A bouquet of roses with a poisonous snake inside. We rehearsed with a rubber snake but filmed with a real one. The look of terror on my face earned me my second SAG nomination. Never occurred to them that I wasn't actually acting. It wasn't a poisonous viper–at least I don't think so, though one never knows with producers–but it was still terrifying. Well, I think you can see the connection."

And lord help him, he could. It made perfect sense. Maybe Marty Sharpe was right, maybe he was caught in a folie à deux with Miranda, but Andrew understood the significance of this.

"I remember that episode!" he said, with memories of his mom gasping, his dad pretending not be scared as the plucky pastor on their TV screen reached inside the– "Dumbwaiter! The killer sent the flowers up in a dumbwaiter!"

"Exactly! Now, Edgar and I honeymooned here at the Duchess, and I seem to recall that this hotel, like many older ones, had pneumatic tubes for mailing letters–but only in front of the elevators–and they also had dumbwaiters in the larger suites. They were hardly used anymore, but still charming. I remember Edgar teasing that he was going to send a rubber snake up to scare me. Those dumbwaiters were still working, or at least they were back when we stayed here."

"Ned and Holly searched that suite top to bottom, they would have noticed it."

"Unless it was hidden, and I think I know how. Deputy Andrew, follow me!"

She strode off, into the lobby and up to the front desk. A few crew members were milling about, and laughter could be heard at the bar, but the Duchess was otherwise quiet. Miranda asked for the supervisor, a nervous young woman whose blazer seemed two sizes too big.

"Yes! It is I!" said Miranda.

It was all a matter of confidence, Andrew knew, so he slapped down the paper that confirmed he had been deputized by the HRPD, and said, in his best Joe Friday voice, "We're here on police business." Hey, if you're gonna folie à deux, you might as well folie à deux all the way.

"We need to examine into the Roosevelt Suite, *tout suite*," said Miranda.

The young woman fumbled for the correct key and put the Back in Five Minutes sign up. She hadn't even examined Andrew's paperwork. He could have slapped down his JF Chen membership card for all she knew.

"It's still sealed off," she said. "But I guess that's okay, because it's not like it's, erm, a crime scene anymore. The housekeeping staff said they don't want to clean it, though, 'cause of ghosts and such."

They entered the elevator and the doors creaked shut.

"But surely any ghost would haunt the atrium below, not the room above," said Andrew.

"That's what I said, but the housekeepers are kinda mean here, and they said, 'If you're so brave, clean it yourself.'" A sigh. "I probably will have to, in the end."

The doors opened on the third floor, and the supervisor led them down the faded carpet to the door in question.

Andrew and Miranda were taken aback by the graffiti, angry words written right to the edge of the gummed tape:

"What does that mean?" asked Miranda.

"No idea. I'll probably end up having to clean that off as well." Oh, the tribulations of middle management!

The supervisor used the key to carefully split the tape along the edge and then opened the door. It felt intrusive, entering the room inside. Even when they turned on the lamp, the darkness and the gloom never fully dispersed.

Miranda crossed over, pulled the heavy blinds aside. She opened the French doors to the balcony and cold air swirled in. Using the sheer undercurrent like a veil, Miranda walked out, onto the balcony, to the very balustrade, pushing the fabric in front of her as she went.

"Easy!" said Andrew.

But she was just checking—and yes, one could plunge from behind the curtains and directly over the edge.

She then turned and faced the enormous oil painting of the lighthouse at Laurel Point in its heavy frame above the suite's dining area.

"Andrew, I draw your attention to the square of darker wallpaper above the fireplace. The same size and shape of this painting, wouldn't you say?"

He agreed.

"In fact, this painting has been moved—from there, over to here. And what lies behind this painting?"

"The dumbwaiter," said the supervisor, stealing Miranda's thunder.

"Yes, the dumbwaiter, as I shall now reveal!" Channeling her inner Pastor Fran, she reached out with both hands, took a firm grip of the frame, and yanked back dramatically.

The painting didn't budge.

So she yanked again—and again. She called Andrew over and he pulled as well, but it wouldn't move. The painting had been bolted to the wall.

CHAPTER EIGHTEEN

A Rogues' Gallery

"Why would someone bolt a painting to the wall?" Miranda asked.

"To prevent theft?" said the night supervisor in her too-big blazer.

Miranda ran her finger along the edge of the canvas. It was taut to the touch. No sneaky flap to slip through. She then peered at the sides of the frame, but it had been secured tightly with not a hair's breadth between it and the wall. She remembered when Tanvir had been renovating the Miranda Abbott Suite at Bea's, how noisy the hammering and power screwdriver had been. Bolting a painting to the wall? This wasn't something one could do quickly or quietly, certainly not in the time between a fall and a crash. And anyway, the painting's frame had been screwed into place from this side. How one could do that *after* fleeing through the dumbwaiter was unclear.

Andrew hazarded the obvious. "Harry was alone. And he fell."

"Maybe," she said, "and maybe not."

She was now fixated on the painting itself—the gaudy sunset, the pink clouds and candy-striped lighthouse—and she came right in, till her face was only inches from the surface as she studied the brushstrokes.

"I collected art," she said. "Briefly." Back when she could afford it. The art had long since been seized by the IRS and scattered to the winds, just one of the countless small humiliations she'd had to endure during "the lull." Miranda pointed to the surface of the canvas. "I can recognize a faked print masquerading as an oil painting when I see it. Do you notice how the brushstrokes don't line up with the image under them?"

Andrew stepped closer. She was right. "It's a cheap, faux painting," he said.

"Exactly. A mass-produced print with a clear latex coat of 'brushstrokes' added after."

He was having trouble following her train of thought, which was often on runaway tracks, to be fair. But her point was razor clear.

"Why would someone want to steal a cheap print? The frame alone is probably worth more than the painting–though I use the word 'painting' in the loosest sense. Do you think someone who can afford the Roosevelt Suite is going to smuggle a giant framed print out of their room?" She turned now to the supervisor. "Same painting in every room?"

"Pretty much."

"May we check?"

When she hesitated, Miranda reminded her that Deputy Andrew was here on official police business.

"It's just, the room above us is occupied."

"Below?"

"That's the family suite. Same layout as the Roosevelt, but more beds, a fold-out couch, no balcony, and windows that don't open, in case a toddler takes a tumble. It's empty right now. None of the crew showed up with their families, even though the film company paid to hold the room anyway, just in case. We could check that suite."

And so they did, trooping past the graffitied door that opened so wide it almost touched the one across from it.

"*Extra Hard*," said Miranda as she stepped into the hallway. The heavy door to the suite swung back in place behind them, locking automatically. "Could this refer to extras on a movie set, I wonder. Or stunts?"

She recalled the stunt coordinator on *Pastor Fran* classifying stunts as "tricky," "real tricky," "extra tricky," and "sure death." Might *extra hard* also refer to that sort of shorthand?

Such thoughts pursued her down the hall to the elevator, all the way to the second-floor suite directly beneath the Roosevelt. The supervisor knocked, just to be safe, then used the skeleton key to let them in.

The wallpaper was different. Yellow-and-pink stripes, with a theme of clowns along the "play area," in what had been the dry bar in the suite above. The room had a musty, dusty scent—the surfaces were coated in a fine layer, undisturbed. No one had been in here for a long while.

"Most families stay in the other wing. It's renovated. Brighter. Less spooky."

The lighthouse at Laurel Point hung over the fireplace, and Miranda went directly to it, gripped the frame, and...lifted it up. It was heavy and cumbersome, but not bolted down.

She then crossed over to the dining area and stood in front of the telltale door embedded in the wall of the kitchenette counter. The dumbwaiter. Small, even by dumbwaiter standards. The door was closed, but the lift inside would have been scarcely bigger than a very large bread box. Just enough space for a full dining tray. A tight fit, certainly, but someone could potentially squeeze in if they were tiny enough and determined enough. A child, perhaps.

"If the hotel was worried about balconies and open windows in the family suite, why weren't they worried about some irascible tot crawling into the dumbwaiter, falling down the shaft?"

"They were. We are." The supervisor explained the safety features. "Dumbwaiter doors can only open when the lift is in place. The outside door has to be lined up with the inside door for it to open. We also added a parental lock. See?" She pointed out this added feature. "Parents can lock the dumbwaiter shut if they want, the same way they might a minibar to stop older kids from raiding it."

Miranda tried the dumbwaiter door, and sure enough, because there was no lift in place behind, it wouldn't open.

"Truth be told, no one much uses the dumbwaiters anymore," said the supervisor. "They've been removed out of the other wing entirely, were boarded up and papered over during renos. Even here, in the older wing, most meals are delivered by room service staff. You can't fit much into these old dumbwaiters. Maybe people didn't have as big an appetite back then. Nowadays, guests mainly use the dumbwaiter to send their piled-up dishes back down when they're done, and sometimes housekeeping will load wet towels in them if their hampers are full, even though we've told them not to. It's not hygienic to put dirty linen in the same lifts that are used for food. But do they listen? No."

"Is this the only operating dumbwaiter left, then?" Miranda asked.

"It is. It runs up the center, through the larger suites. The smaller rooms on either side aren't connected. It's just this one shaft. Guests will buzz, or call, and staff will send up the pulley."

"Can you call one now?"

"Sure." She phoned down and, after grumbled complaints from the late night staff, they sent an empty lift up. There came a low moan, almost a groan, behind the wall as the dumbwaiter slowly climbed the two floors to their room. It clicked into place, and Miranda was now able to open the small door. She peered inside. Just a polished wooden box, really. An enclosure with nowhere to go. She pressed her hand against each of the walls in turn, but there were no movable panels, no latches in the top. Anyone who did climb in would be stuck inside until they got to another floor. If they could even fit. One would have to fold in fairly tightly for that to work. And what then? The dumbwaiter door in the Roosevelt Suite above was blocked by a very large, very unwieldy painting that had been bolted into the wall.

It was so convoluted, it reminded her of a Lachlan Todd script. His solutions were always complex to the point of incomprehensible. Maybe she could call him? But no. He and Edgar had ended on bad terms, and what would Luckless Lachlan be able to tell her anyway, other than, "Watch out for snakes hiding in the roses and trapdoors in the bullfighting arena!"

"I should probably get back to the front desk," said the supervisor, whose "five minutes" had now extended to half an hour. Prompt, by Happy Rock standards.

"Yes, of course," said Miranda with a gracious wave of the hand, like an empress dismissing a courtier. "I have only one question. These dumbwaiters, are they manual? Does someone below run the pulley up by hand?"

"No, it's a motor. You could hear it when it came up."

"The motor. Does it run on a separate generator?"

"Gosh, no. We wouldn't maintain a separate one just for a dumbwaiter that almost no one uses anymore. Even the main elevators don't have those. When the power went out, a couple of days ago, they all stopped. Fortunately, no one was inside any of them at the time. The emergency exit lights came on, but everything else was completely dark."

"That's right," said Miranda, as though confirming a theory of hers. "The power went off briefly. Ned mentioned that. Trampled roses, a scuffed side door, and darkness. Tell me, the hotel's side doors, the ones that lead outside, are they alarmed?"

"They are. Every now and then someone goes out from one of them by accident, sets it off."

"But not when the power is out."

"No, I guess not. Like I said, it was kind of scary. The eerie glow of the exit lights, people moving round in the dark, giggling nervously. I don't know if anyone came in or went out those exits. It makes you jumpy. You can't help thinking about the Hazy Girl."

"Whom?" said Andrew.

"*Who*," Miranda corrected him. "In a direct interrogative, it is *who*. Not *whom*. Now then. Whom did you say the Hazy Girl was?"

"The ghost of a Victorian child who stands at the end of hallways in a bonnet and a hoop skirt. She doesn't do anything, she just stands there. Not sure why that's so scary, but it is. I haven't seen her, but loads of other people have. Or the Glass Woman. Or the Ceiling Crawler who, well … I guess that one's self-explanatory. Point being, when the lights went out, everyone was thrilled and terrified at the same time. Lots of running here and there. Lots of squeals and *boo*s!"

"Then the power came back on," said Miranda. "And during that interim, someone could easily have slipped in without being spotted and without tripping any alarms, correct?"

"I guess. But why not just walk past the front desk when the power was on? I mean, nothing was stolen or taken during the outage. We checked."

"Perhaps it wasn't something being taken *out*," said Miranda, "but something being taken in—by someone who did not want to be recognized."

The five minutes had turned to forty, and Miranda and Andrew returned to the lobby with the supervisor in tow.

"Do I need to fill anything out?" she asked as she flipped the sign back around and returned to her post at the front desk. "For the police report."

"No, ma'am," said Sergeant Friday (aka Andrew Nguyen, personal assistant to the stars).

As they left, they bumped into Gillian Hardner, Harry Tomlin's executive assistant. Or rather, she bumped into them. She was yelling into her phone—something about getting blood from a stone—and almost mowed Miranda down. "He's dead!" she was yelling. "Don't you read the papers, for chrissake? What do you want me to do, dig him up?" She disconnected the call with a single imperious swipe of her finger, looked up, and said, curtly but not impolitely, with a nod of the head to each of them in turn. "Miranda. Abner."

"Andrew."

With a tight grimace, Gillian said, "So the shoot is going forward even without the purportedly irreplaceable Harry Tomlin. Congratulations. That must be a relief for you, Miranda." Before Miranda could answer, Gillian's phone vibrated again. "Another incoming text to Harry's number. I tell you, I'm busier since he's been dead than I was when he was alive." It was almost like she resented him for dying.

"He's still getting messages?" said Andrew, who fielded Miranda's calls as well. "Don't people know he's not going to answer?"

"Auto notifications, updates, subscription renewals, for the most part. I have to go through them as they come in and either delete, send to spam, or call them back from my own number to inform them that, yes, Mr. Tomlin has left the building— *Leni!* Wait up."

The scowling scarecrow of a director, Leni Vedette, was crossing the lobby to the Bengal Lounge, dressed as always in a hideous shade of mustard yellow. (Miranda was a redhead; she was biased against that particular color. "Would make me look like a selection of condiments," she would complain whenever they tried to dress her in mustard.)

On seeing Leni, Gillian went to catch her without an "excuse me" or a "gotta go" or a "catch you later" to Miranda.

"Something's up," said Miranda.

That was the problem with staying at Bea's: one was cut off from the gossip and inside info that would seep through a film crew hanging round a hotel bar on full expense account, getting sloshed every night and sharing careless tidbits that might easily have helped Miranda unravel the mystery of Harry's death. The *alleged* mystery.

"He fell," said Andrew.

"Or was pushed!"

"By whom? A ghost?"

"Possibly. And possibly not." Miranda strode across toward the lounge herself now. "A late night drink!" she cried over her shoulder to Andrew. "Under the tiger!"

During the day, the Bengal Lounge was manned by a fleet of elderly waiters in burgundy vests who moved so slowly as to appear to be in reverse, though that was widely acknowledged to be an optical illusion. At night, the staff was much younger–meaning, under seventy years of age–and they moved, if not with alacrity, at least in a consistently forward direction.

As one such spry fellow led them past the teak elephants and the pith-helmet palms, they did an awkward side-step when a familiar young woman cut in front of them.

"Cherise!" said Miranda, for that was the ingénue's name. "How are you, darling?" Here was a source worth pumping for information. If anyone had the inside scoop on things, it would be her.

Cherise turned. A pained smile. A gentle hand, laid across her chest in sympathy. "I'm sorry, but I don't give autographs. If you contact my publicists—just DM them on TikTok, they'll know what to do—they can send you a limited edition NFT image of me. You can pay by PayPal or crypto, whichever works. And you have a choice of messages: *Best wishes, Lots of love*—xxxs are extra—and *I am so very sorry for your loss.*"

"What? I don't want an autograph. I'm your co-star!"

"Are you! How wonderful. So very lovely to meet you. My name is—"

But Miranda had already stomped off with Andrew in tow.

"What does that even mean?" she muttered as they were shown to their table. *"Dim you with my tick-tock?"*

Andrew considered explaining it to her but decided against it, not so much because Miranda wouldn't understand but because she might. He lived in fear of Miranda Abbott discovering how to post her thoughts on social media.

"God help me, I wish *she* was a suspect," Miranda muttered as she ordered a Gunga Gin cocktail. "Alas, our ingénue was next to me at the press conference when Harry crashed the party. She was on her phone, of course, barely looked up when he smashed through. I would love to arrest her—for rudeness if nothing else!"

Andrew, meanwhile, had developed a taste for Bombay Zingers, and he swirled the pineapple slice in the frosted glass, watched the drink inside cloud over. If he thought they were going to have a relaxing night over drinks, he was mistaken.

"Look around you, what do you see?" Miranda asked, leaning in on her elbows and speaking in a conspiratorial tone Andrew knew well, as though he and she were privy to a secret no one else in the world knew.

"Um, sofas, tables, a tiger skin, ferns…"

"The people, Andrew. Whom do you see?"

A scattering of crew. The mousy interpreter, alone at her table, with a stack of papers and a weary expression on her face, looking to the door as though waiting for someone. The broken-down stunt-man Wayne Grey, slouched at the bar. The soundman at the other end, headphones on, listening intensely to an audio file of some sort. Gillian the executive assistant with Leni Vedette, the director, in a far ferny corner, caught up in a heated discussion. The chic French cinematographer, sweeping in, ignoring her interpreter and heading straight to the bar. The ingénue posing for a pouty, duck-faced selfie in front of the tiger skin.

"It's a veritable rogues' gallery," Miranda said with a low voice and a knowing look. "I daresay, a killer may be among us."

CHAPTER NINETEEN

Cleanup in Aisle Two!

An actor's craft is one of *observation*. You look for the revealing detail, the telling gesture. When first we entered this lounge, I asked you what you saw, and you listed furniture and plants primarily. You should have been observing the people. We are all of us compilations of traits and tics. One must learn to read those. Therein lies the true heart of the thespian's craft."

Andrew often forgot that, before she took the deep dive into TV, Miranda Abbott had been classically trained, had started her career on stage at the prestigious Orpheum Theatre in Minneapolis.

In the Bengal Lounge, amid the palm fronds and Kiplingesque decor, Andrew swished his Bombay Zinger, feeling pleasantly sloshed. (Had he known that the cocktail included rum, brandy, absinthe, *and* blackberry liqueur, he might not have been imbibing quite as deeply.)

"Now then," she asked. "On our way in, we passed the interpreter, alone at her table. What did you notice?"

"Um, she had papers in front of her?"

"A lot of papers. Plus pens, highlighters, a calculator, dictionaries. You would think whatever it was she was working on would be engrossing, and yet she seemed distracted, no?"

He snuck a peek over Miranda's shoulder. "She keeps looking up at the door every time someone comes in."

"Exactly. She looks at the door, but not at her watch—or even at the brass clock over the bar. What does that tell you?"

"She's waiting for someone?"

"Not waiting, *hoping*. She isn't checking the time because there was no time agreed upon. She could as easily have done her paperwork in her room, yes? Rather than in this noisy lounge, late at night, poor little thing. She's hoping someone might come in. And from the empty carafe of wine on her table, she's been waiting for some time."

Suddenly it clicked. "Chester!" said Andrew, beaming. "The hotel manager. When we took statements, she told Ned that she was outside holding the ladder for Chester when the accident occurred."

"*Murder*," she said. "When the murder occurred."

"She seemed very taken with Chester, by her own account. That's why she's working late at night in the Bengal Lounge! She's hoping he'll come in." This was fun. "She's hoping to"—air quotes—"'accidentally' run into him. I've done the same thing myself."

Andrew was very pleased with himself, but for Miranda this was only the start.

"A lovelorn heart, in and of itself, is not unusual," she said. "But the nature of her work most certainly is. The most crucial details are often sitting right in front of us, in plain sight. What is she doing?"

"Paperwork."

"Why?"

"Um, her job?"

"But she is Ms. de Valeur's *interpreter*, not translator. And you will note she has *two* dictionaries in front of her."

Andrew squinted, but couldn't quite make out the titles.

Miranda had taken note, though. "One is a lexicon of legal terms, from the title. The other is a standard and well-thumbed French-English dictionary. Now why on earth would an interpreter also be translating legal terms?"

"Moonlighting? Or maybe Jacquelyn told her to. She does seem a bit of a tyrant."

"I agree. I imagine it is at Ms. de Valeur's behest."

Miranda now turned her attention to the cinematographer in question, who was chatting away merrily with the bartender.

"I don't imagine the number of francophones on staff at the Duchess Hotel is very high. Which is to say, Ms. de Valeur can certainly make herself understood in English. So why an interpreter?"

"Oh, I can answer that," said Andrew. "When Ned and I interviewed them, they explained. The production company is paying for an interpreter for Ms. de Valeur to entice her to agree to the MOW in the first place. I mean, with a celebrated Parisian artist like her, you wouldn't imagine she'd ever be interested in a—" But Andrew stopped himself just in time. Better not to denigrate the made-for-TV fare they were caught up in, as that would have also diminished Miranda's role in it. He didn't want to open that up again.

Jacquelyn de Valeur collected her order, a fat bottle of champagne and three glasses, and waltzed over to where the director and Gillian were sitting. She joined the table but didn't seem interested in whatever issue they were hashing out.

"If I didn't know better," said Miranda, "I would almost say she is celebrating."

"Pay-or-play," said Andrew. "Even if the film doesn't move forward, they still get paid. All of them, yourself included."

The ingénue, having Snapchatted her way through OMG! photos of the Bengal Lounge, had since departed, but not Gillian Hardner. She remained in her leafy corner.

Miranda turned to Andrew. "You were with Harry's executive assistant, correct? When the murder occurred?"

"The *accident*. And yes, I was with Gillian. She had arrived late for the press conference."

"And when you heard the crash and the two of you ran outside, Ms. de Valeur and the interpreter were already there, looking up at the atrium."

"More or less. I mean, the interpreter was around the corner, holding the ladder, as I said. She came out soon after, though."

"And Mr. Cornelius–Chester, that is–he can corroborate this?"

Andrew nodded. "He felt the ladder stabilize. He was swaying pretty badly. She saved him."

Miranda sipped her Gunga Gin, frowned. "So . . . our current rogues' gallery of possible suspects has now been reduced. Unless there's something we're missing, we can remove four names from our list: the director Leni Vedette, executive assistant Gillian Hardner, cinematographer Jacquelyn de Valeur, and her overworked interpreter can all be accounted for at the time of the–"

"Accident," said Andrew.

"We shall see what we shall see," Miranda said. "And what we see, shall be seen!"

"What now?" asked Andrew.

"Now we zero in on the two people who can't account for their whereabouts at the moment of the... incident. Starting with the only member of the Happy Crew to be on set. Everyone else was paid out, and others were brought in. But not our cowboy friend Mr. Grey."

...

191

EVEN FROM BEHIND, he was the spitting image of Harry Tomlin.

Same body shape and size: wide shoulders and a tapered torso—what might be called "lanky." He was wearing a faded denim shirt where Harry would have been dressed in a Brunello Cucinelli tailor fit, but other than that, it was no wonder Wayne had been Harry Tomlin's double all those years. Even in profile he looked like Harry, but when he turned—well, the mileage showed. Where Harry had been strong-jawed and rugged, Wayne Grey was craggy-faced and creased. A lifetime of dubious choices was written on his features. A nose well-broken, a jawline the same. Haggard eyes.

Even his smile was craggy and crooked.

"Mr. Grey, hello. I don't believe we've met," said Miranda. "Even though you have saved my life on at least one occasion." She was referring to the runaway horses on *Pastor Fran*.

"Miranda Abbott, as I live and breathe. Join me."

She began to introduce Andrew as well, but Wayne waved that aside. "I know you. We've met. The deputy, right? Took my statement with that other officer after Harry did his acrobatic act. What's your poison, son?"

Andrew, weaving on his feet, said, "Zinger. Bombay." He was getting his words out of order.

The cowboy pulled out a stool from the bar. "Sit down, before you fall down."

Wayne did likewise for Miranda, though with more chivalry, standing up and pushing her seat in for her. He creaked when he moved, had to roll his bad hip onto the stool next to Miranda's when he sat.

The surface of the bar was sticky. Mr. Grey clearly did not care for coasters or other such niceties. But he asked the lady what her pleasure was in a considerate manner. "Something sweet, I imagine?"

She demurred. "Just mineral water." She wanted to stay sharp.

Unlike Andrew, who now had a bad case of the hiccups.

"If I had my bowie knife on me, I could scare those right outta you," Wayne said. "Nothing like a blade held to a throat to cure a man of hiccups."

Andrew, eyes wide. "You have a bowie knife?"

Wayne laughed. "Nah. But it scared you, right?"

Indeed, Andrew's hiccups had vanished on a sudden intake of fear.

Wayne called for JD on the rocks, a double, "and don't be stingy. I want at least three fingers' worth, my friend."

The bartender nodded, took down a bottle of Tennessee's finest.

"Mr. Grey, I would like to extend my deepest condolences," Miranda said when the drinks arrived. "I know Harry was a dear friend to you."

"Friend? Hardly. What kind of friend does that? Leaves you alone in the world?" Wayne Grey was soaked in whisky, regret—and now anger. "I won't easily forgive him, I can tell you. You heard about the note? They're calling it suicide. Leni's been blabbing it everywhere. That's bull. All of it. We talked about it often, when I was in the hospital. How best to die. I figured a fireball. He figured never." He laughed. "He was a scaredy-cat, when all is said and done. The idea of him flinging himself to his death—bull crap. If you'll pardon my language, ma'am."

"I am not of the frail variety, Mr. Grey. Manly language does not faze me. Murder does, though."

At this, Wayne Grey turned, stared at her. "What are you getting at, sister?"

"Leni Vedette may be telling everyone that Harry killed himself, but I have it on authority that the coroner's office is going to rule otherwise. They are saying it is inconclusive. The verdict? Accidental. But I have my doubts."

When he spoke, his voice was cold and flat. "No one killed Harry."

"Yes, but—"

"Let the man rest in peace, will you?" He tossed back his glass, anger growing. "Now, if you'll excuse me, *ma'am*, I gotta go take a piss."

And with that, he walked away, creaky and angry and sad.

Miranda and Andrew watched him go. They then looked down the wide mahogany swath of the bar to where the soundman Silas Ivar sat, headphones on, eyes down, at the other end.

For a man who lived in an aural world, he was surprisingly taciturn. Silent, in fact.

They decided to head over. "Hello, Mr. Ivar!" Miranda called out, scarf flipped back, hand extended from ten paces. He said nothing, just scrawled *Go away* on a napkin and slid it across.

The sheer effrontery of it!

"Mr. Ivar, really, I must protest."

Without removing his headphones or even taking his eyes off the digital sound recorder in front of him, he pulled the napkin back and added: *In the middle of something.* He then underlined the words *Go away*.

Andrew braced for an explosion, but Miranda, voice chilly, said, "I know when I am not welcome!" She always was good at picking up on cues.

They left, and Silas Ivar grinned.

They hadn't noticed the small directional mic that had been placed on an equally innocuous tabletop stand next to the recorder. A mic that was connected to his headphones. A mic that was pointed down the length of the bar to where they had been sitting only moments ago with Wayne Grey.

...

SILAS IVAR WAS chuckling to himself, a raspy, faint noise from the back of his throat. So Miranda Abbott thought the Great Harry Tomlin had been murdered? She'd said as much to that washed-up boozehound of a stuntman. She'd even sent a bumbling cop around earlier with his bumbling deputy, fishing for clues like someone casting a line in an empty pond. They had asked to review his audio files from that fateful day, and Ivar had dutifully run it past them. They'd been looking for footsteps or telltale voices or muffled screams—the fools. No. The sound of murder was much subtler than that. It could be contained even in silence, in the background hum of a room's distinct tone. They were looking. They should have been listening.

MEANWHILE, THE CRIME wave in Happy Rock continued, much to Ned Buckley's consternation. A plummeting movie star, trampled roses, a hotel door that had been pried, a suspicious character peering into cars at Owen's Garage—and now this: when Ned showed up at the police station the next morning, a call came in about a hubbub at TB Foods.

A hubbub! Before he'd even had his morning coffee! Or chamomile tea, more specifically.

Someone had smashed a bunch of bottles, sweeping them off the shelf and onto the floor of the aisle in one move from the looks of it.

"Happened soon after we opened," said the store manager, a bespectacled man with a handlebar mustache who had clearly watched too many crime shows. He had cordoned off the "crime scene" with orange cones and had told the staff not to clean up, "in case you wanted to, I dunno, dust for fingerprints maybe."

"And how many people have handled those bottles, do you

figure? Including stock boys, cashiers, random customers, the packing staff at the warehouse?"

"Gotta be a lot," said the manager.

What caught Ned's eye was not the mess on the floor, a swirling, oily puddle among shards of broken glass, but the very specific nature of what was targeted. Only salad dressing had been destroyed. And then, only one line of salad dressing: Harry Tomlin's.

"Cashier heard the crash, came running. Saw a heavyset man push past."

"Let me guess. He was wearing a homburg."

"If that's the kind of hat mobsters wear, then yes. Even stranger, when the cashier ran back to the till to page me, she found this." He extracted two crisp $100 bills from his jacket pocket. "What kind of man smashes up a buncha salad oil then leaves two hundred bucks behind?"

A man with anger management issues and poor impulse control, thought Ned.

INTERESTINGLY ENOUGH, AT the very moment that Ned Buckley was taking down the cashier's statement at TB Foods, Chester Cornelius of the Duchess Hotel was preparing to clean up a very different—but related—mess of his own.

The Portland coroner's office had now officially and publicly closed the case on Harry Tomlin's death, which meant no more disruptive press conferences. It also meant the hotel no longer had to keep the room sealed off, could finally call in a glazier to replace the missing panel of glass in the atrium ceiling. (It had been covered with a very ungainly square of cardboard ever since Harry plunged through it.)

Chief Buckley had already examined the graffiti, and Chester had instructed housekeeping to scrub the door to the Roosevelt Suite clean and remove the gummed tape Ned had put up, but they'd just stared at him, had snapped their gum and said, "That's maintenance."

The hotel's handyman was eighty-something and not perhaps as robust as he might have been—one of the reasons Chester hadn't sent him up on a ladder to scrape off the seagull droppings earlier—so it fell to Cornelius to clean the door himself. He'd filled up a bucket of warm water and taken a squeegee, and was about to make his way through the lobby and up to the third floor when he saw—her.

Paulette.

The interpreter with the tiny voice and large, fawn-like eyes. (Everyone else saw a mouse when they looked at her; Chester saw a graceful deer.) She was nested in the far side of the lobby, deep in a stack of paperwork, and he considered going over to ask if she needed anything. But he looked ridiculous, he thought, with his managerial blazer and soapy water. So he didn't. He was wrong, though. In Paulette's eyes he wouldn't have looked ridiculous. Not at all.

Tangled up in French–English legalese, she didn't look up until it was too late. She was hoping to catch a glimpse of Chester, but she missed him. Instead, with a weary sigh, she returned to her task. Why am I even doing this? she thought. I'm an interpreter, not a translator, and certainly not a *legal* translator.

Inside her, a dark resentment simmered.

CHAPTER TWENTY

Rhymes with *Catoptrophilia*

When Chester Cornelius reached the door to the still-sealed Roosevelt Suite, bucket in hand, he was surprised to find Miranda and Andrew already there. The hallway was dimly lit and they were examining the graffiti with a forensic interest. Andrew was taking photos of the writing with his phone.

"Police business?" Chester asked, startling them both.

Remembering that, as far as the hotel manager knew, he was still deputized, Andrew mumbled something that could have been interpreted as an affirmative. (What was the penalty for impersonating a police officer? Better not to think about it. And anyway, Andrew was confident that Miranda could charm her way out of anything when it came to Ned.)

Chester was even easier to disarm.

"Ah, Mr. Cornelius! Such a pleasurable pleasure." She extended her hand as though expecting him to bestow a kiss upon it. "I am assisting this fine young deputy in his ongoing investigation."

"Oh," said Chester, stepping back to let them work. "Let me know when you're done and I'll clean up the door, remove the tape."

"You're opening the room?"

"Coroner's office said it was accidental. No need to keep it sealed. I guess you must be wrapping up the rest of the evidence for your final report, eh, deputy?"

Andrew exchanged glances with Miranda. They had already been inside the sealed room the night before without finding anything conclusive. And now the suite was going to be cleaned of any possible clues? Dammit.

"Do you have any inkling who might scrawl such a cryptic message?" Miranda asked, referring to the graffiti. She was planning to collect writing samples from the various suspects, surreptitiously, of course, and see if any of them matched, though even she wasn't entirely clear what that would prove. "*Extra hard*. What could that mean?"

"I honestly don't know," said Chester. He put down his bucket like the burden it was. "It's been strange around here ever since Mr. Tomlin . . ." He wasn't sure of the right phrase. Passed away? Departed? "Checked out," he said, using a hotelier's euphemism. "It makes you wonder if the Duchess isn't haunted after all."

Just that morning Chester had gone through the suggestion box, a thankless task as most of it was from housekeeping, along the lines of "Stop making us carry wet towels down the stairs when guests are using the elevators!!!" and "We need a proper service elevator in the east wing! If you don't want guests riding with the dirty linen, let us chuck 'em down the dumbwaiter instead." (He assumed they meant the towels, not the guests.) Or: "Chester is SOO lame, I mean my god, what is up with that guy??" which was more of a comment than a suggestion, he thought.

But then, amid such enlightening commentary in the suggestion box, he had extracted an envelope with the words *MEA CULPA* written across it in bold letters.

When Chester mentioned this, Miranda asked—nay, demanded—to see it.

"The handwriting!" she cried, holding up the envelope to compare. Both were in angry block capitals. "The very same!"

And what was inside the envelope? A single, crisp $100 bill.

"What kind of person mars a door and then donates one hundred dollars, presumably toward the cleaning of that selfsame door?" asked Miranda.

Someone with a conscience, thought Andrew.

"Weird, right?" said Chester. "Haunted maybe." Though he had to admit that ghosts and ghoulies weren't known for their thoughtfulness in such matters.

"If only we had a security recording," Miranda said, rubbing her chin the same way Pastor Fran always did when mulling over a conundrum.

"Oh, but we do," he said. "Ned asked me to install one above the door once he taped it off, to see if anyone tried to break in."

Chester pointed to a small dome attached to the ceiling above them that had a bird's-eye view of the hallway. "I picked it up at Tanvir's Hardwares & Bait Shop. They've got everything! Even security cameras. They're next to the mealworms and red wigglers."

Yikes. There would be footage of Miranda and Andrew entering a taped-off possible crime scene.

"Has, ah, Chief Buckley reviewed the tape?" she asked.

"He wasn't really interested. I tried to explain, but he cut me off, saying that he had bigger fish to fry than some graffiti. Apparently, there was quite the rumpus at TB Foods."

"You haven't checked the footage to see who wrote this on the door?"

"I did, sure. But the guy never faced the camera. I can show it to you, if you like." He pulled out his phone and scrolled through.

"Uploaded it to the cloud," he explained.

Miranda was vaguely disappointed. She missed the dark, claustrophobic surveillance rooms that she—or rather, Pastor Fran—used to haunt in the day, rewinding video tapes until ... aha!

On Chester's phone, a large man in a heavy coat draped over his shoulders like a cape stomped down the hall, then stopped at the door to quickly write across it with big, angry gestures. It was only a few seconds, the image was cloudy, and the face never looked up.

"A big fella," said Chester.

"Who still wears a homburg?" Miranda wondered.

A man on a mission, thought Andrew. And then— "Wait! Can you roll it back. Look! There." Andrew pointed to the image of the man defacing the door. *"He keeps writing!* He didn't stop at the edge of the tape. He wrote across it, but the letters didn't show up. Too smooth, probably."

And as one, they pivoted to the door again. The wood was a medium walnut color, and the letters ran across to the very edge of the gummed tape. Beyond that? It was dim and hard to see.

"That's okay," said Andrew, reaching for his own phone. "I downloaded a flashlight."

He put his phone on bright and angled it across the surface of the gummed tape.

"Remarkable," said Miranda. "They truly do have an app for everything."

As Andrew shifted the light, faint marks could be seen. "It's a ... a question mark ... No! Two of them ... And an *L* and a *Y*."

What the man in the homburg had actually written was:

EXTRA??
HARDLY

They stepped back to consider this, crossed their arms, tilted their heads, chewed their lips.

"Well," said Andrew after a moment. "That was no help at all."

"No, not a bit," murmured Miranda. "If anything, it makes things more confusing. Perhaps we'll do better with this!" she said, pulling out a piece of fabric from her skirt pocket. It was a square of the same wool-polyester fabric in lime green that Harpreet and Miranda had tested their knives on. Harpreet had cut out a swatch for Miranda to take with her.

"Mr. Cornelius, would you be so kind as to show me to the room of celebrated fashion maven Idelia Powell."

"You mean the short one with the beehive hairdo? Didn't realize she was a—what did you say?—a maven. I never see her. She's holed up in our Gerald Ford Suite. He stayed here, you know. The suite is directly above us. She moved racks and racks of clothes and equipment in the first day, most of it shipped in from Milan and Paris— and not Paris, Texas. The real Paris."

A suite on the top floor! Even Harry Tomlin didn't get that. Clearly, fashion maven-dom had its privileges. (Miranda reminded herself that not only was she in the top floor of Bea's, but it was a suite named in her honor, something even Idelia Powell couldn't match!)

Chester would have accompanied them, but his radio crackled and he said, "Sorry, I have to go. Some sort of hubbub in the lobby."

If Miranda thought that she and Andrew would be welcomed by Idelia Powell on a swirl of hospitality, she was wrong. The meeting was very short and to the point. Much like Idelia herself. When Miranda and Andrew rapped on the door, they expected a waft of perfume, or a chilly femme fatale arched eyebrow, maybe a cigarette holder and scarlet lips. They got neither.

Andrew was more nervous than Miranda. He'd straightened the cuffs on his quilted jacket and classic oxford button-down, checked his flannel-lined chinos (it was autumn), had run a hand through his hair. If only he could have gotten to Unison on La Brea for a haircut, instead of being stuck out here having to visit Sharon's Klips 'N Kurls Salon and Pet Grooming Services. (As Sharon put it, "We already had the clippers and scissors and such, so why not add people?") They couldn't do a proper diagonal-part retro wave to save their lives. It always ended up looking somewhere between Ken doll and a Yorkie terrier no matter how many photos he showed them.

He needn't have worried.

The woman who stared up at them wore a simple frock in polka dots with a beehive do, more blue than black, and classic cat-eye glasses.

Miranda was not tall by any means, yet she towered over her. "Idelia?" she said, trying not to gush.

"That's right. Idelia. Rhymes with *catoptrophilia,* 'a fondness for mirrors.' Apt in my line of work."

"May we come in?"

"I don't need a turn-down service or a mint on my pillow or a complimentary foot massage, and I still have lots of club soda and Toblerone in the mini-fridge. I'm going to go ahead and close the door now."

"We're not here to clean your room or restock the wet bar. I am Miranda Abbott. It is," she assured her, "I."

"Abbott? Oh, right. The redhead, always wears green for some reason, size twelve with a bust measurement of—"

"Ten surely, and no! I am not here for a fitting. It's about something else."

"Come in, then," she said, muttering under her breath. "Green. Always with the green."

The Gerald Ford Suite had been transformed into a thick labyrinth of clothing racks, lined up in an array of colors, earth tones and pastels, bold splashes and muted dabs, and Andrew and Miranda wandered in as though entering Narnia. Indeed, the suite resembled nothing so much as an actual wardrobe that had burst open.

"I wanted to ask you about this particular fabric," Miranda said, holding it out.

Idelia winced at the sight of it. "Please tell me that you do not plan to drape that compact but curvy body of yours in something as hideous as Lime Green CD32"—she knew her colors—"because I will not do it. You would look like a misbegotten shamrock. It would be a travesty." Idelia fondled the swatch, then handed it back with a tactile disgust. "A 65-35 cross-weave poly-wool blend, as well. Ugh. Ech."

For a moment Miranda was worried the diminutive beehive of a woman was going to be physically sick.

"I was just wondering if the wardrobe department had anything in this sort of fabric," Miranda explained. "A men's jacket. One that might have gone missing, say."

Idelia vanished. Which is to say, she walked between clothes racks and in doing so disappeared behind them. Andrew and Miranda had to wend their way through to reach the rack of men's jackets.

"See?" said Idelia, running her hand along them. "All top quality. I would never stock anything so horrid, even if the character were a hayseed rube from Hicksville. I have my standards. Are any of the jackets missing? Absolutely not."

"How do you keep track?" asked Miranda. "Of your inventory?"

"I wanted to hand-tailor each role, but was told to bring my entire rack stock as well, just in case. Cost a fortune to ship them out. How do I track these jackets? Simple paper tags, pinned to the collar. See?"

They were numbered, with the initials MOTH.

"Moth?" said Andrew.

"Mystery of ye Olde Tyme Hotel. It's the abbreviated form of the film title."

"So you don't chalk the inside of the cuffs?" said Miranda. "WDPT, say, for Wardrobe Department?"

"Some might, I don't. WDPT is often used. But everyone has their own shorthand and"—in a reference to the green fabric in Miranda's hand—"their own sense of taste. You can show yourselves out."

They had been dismissed.

It would take them several more minutes and a few dead ends and some backtracking to finally solve the sartorial enclosure of Idelia Powell's Maze of Clothes and reach the door. When they turned to thank her for her time, she was gone, into the rabbit warren of her own peculiar world.

"Well," said Andrew as they stepped back out into the hallway. "That was no help at all."

"Au contraire! We now know where the jacket is not from. And if you know where it is not, you can then *not* know where it isn't!"

WHEN MIRANDA AND Andrew exited the elevator into the hotel lobby, they were amazed at what they saw. Not a mere hubbub. Not a hullabaloo. Certainly more than hoopla. This was a full-blown, flashbulb-popping media scrum!

Arms wide, Miranda sailed from the elevator like a masthead prow breaking the waves in front of her. "Yes! It is I!"

She recognized many of the microphones: Access Hollywood, CBS, NBC, Inside Edition, KGW in Portland, even—to her chagrin—TMZ. Miranda had nothing to say to those last louts! Nothing at all, and she was determined to tell them that. TMZ was the bane of Miranda's existence, mainly because they seemed determined to ignore hers. How could she tell them to stop hounding her if they wouldn't hound her in the first place? It was downright inconsiderate of them. (They only story TMZ had run on Miranda was to suggest that she and Andrew were lovers, and that she was a sex-starved cougar on the prowl. Never mind that Andrew had been engaged at the time. To a man. Those vultures didn't care!)

She grabbed the microphone of the closest TMZ toad—a schleppy guy in sweatpants and an ill-advised turtleneck. There were two of them, which was a huge crew for TMZ.

"I have nothing to say to you!" she said, refusing to let go of the mic. "Harry Tomlin's tragedy was tragically tragic. But we mustn't give up. The show must go on!"

The so-called reporter of this so-called news show wrested his mic away from her and said, "Harry's replacement on this movie—rumor is he's on his way here. Can you tell us who it is?"

"I, Miranda Abbott, cannot disclose that information at this time, because I, Miranda Abbott—that's two *b*'s and two *t*'s—am nothing if not discreet." But mainly because I don't know who it is. Maybe Marty really was "working on Clooney." That would explain the commotion.

"And you are?" the reporter asked.

"Abbott." She tilted her good side to the camera. "Miranda Abbott."

"And what is your connection to the production?"

"What? My connection?"

Andrew began his countdown . . .

"Lemme guess," said sweatpants. "Craft services?"

"I am the star! You fetid little rodent."

"*Co-star*," said Andrew, cutting in. "Ms. Abbott is the co-star. And she looks forward to working with whomever is chosen to share the marquee with her."

He scribbled this down. "Abbott, huh? And how do you spell that again?"

Fuming, Miranda pushed past him. No one was here for her, she realized. No one, except–

"Hi! Jane Bannister. *The Weekly Picayune.* Do you have a moment?"

A familiar face, and appropriately deferential. "Ms. Bannister. Always a pleasure to speak with an esteemed member of the Fourth Estate."

"Just thought I'd ask if you know which star they cast to replace Harry Tomlin."

"I cannot say." Again, because I do not know. "But it is someone worthy of the project, of that I can assure you."

A surge of excitement rolled through the lobby like a wave, and the mob crushed toward the entrance. Through the glass, Miranda could see a fleet of stretch limousines pull up, one after another. It was almost presidential in scope. To a flurry of shouted questions and flashing lights, an entourage spilled out of the first car and then moved up the stairs, through the throng and into the lobby. The paparazzi pursued. And in the middle of this gong show, seemingly serene in his sunglasses, a head taller than anyone else and moving in a slow, lumbering fashion, was that same vividly drawn widow's peak, those same sensual lips she remembered so well. It was (of course) Poe Regal.

CHAPTER TWENTY-ONE

Sealed with a Kiss

Her face flushed at the sight of him. She couldn't help it, and she certainly didn't want it. But the heart has reasons of its own, and though she didn't know it at the time, the looming love triangle Miranda was facing with Edgar and Zab was about to get a whole lot more complicated. That's how it always is. You go from having no love life to having too much.

Even from a distance, she could see that he was heavier now, and slower, with a thinning blond mane, looking like an aging Viking, or perhaps a lion stricken with mange. He was wearing a brightly colored Cossack tunic with inappropriate dragons stitched on the sleeves, more muumuu than Fu Manchu, more whale shark than Nordic warrior. His pace was lugubrious as he waded through the paparazzi in the Duchess lobby. But it was still him. Poe Regal, the one and only.

When Miranda turned, Jane Bannister was looking at her with a curious expression.

"You worked together, right?" the reporter asked.

"That was a long time ago."

The hotel manager, Chester Cornelius, followed the mob on his long Ichabod legs, and he smiled when he saw Miranda, but then—on spotting Jane—pushed past with a sour look, actively ignoring the reporter, if such a thing were possible.

"He's still upset with the feature I wrote," Jane explained. The perils of small-town journalism.

"The front-page story?" said Andrew. "On outsiders' impressions of Happy Rock? How could anyone possibly get upset over such"—he almost said *pap*—"punditry?"

"I quoted him as saying he hoped locals would also visit the Duchess. *'We have a lot to offer, both to residents and visitors.'* Well, as you can imagine, the populace took umbrage. We got a lot of angry letters—by which I mean three—saying *'How dare he insinuate that we are not supporting one of our preeminent attractions!'* And so on. My editor said it was both a storm AND a tempest."

It had bruised their pride, and small-town pride is so easily bruised.

The only thing more easily bruised is the ego of an actor. "I did notice you didn't deign to speak with *me* about *my* impressions," said Miranda with a tight smile.

"Oh. But you're not an outsider. You're one of the locals now."

Miranda was both touched and appalled. She belonged in Happy Rock.

"I had to leave a lot of good stuff out of the article," Jane said with a frown. "My editor cut everything that he thought was irrelevant. Which is too bad. Some of it was good, I thought. Added a larger context to the piece."

"Ah, yes," said Andrew. "I am sure there were a plethora of scintillating tidbits that didn't make the cut." He was being sardonic, but Jane missed the tone.

"There were, for sure. Like Harry Tomlin's salad dressing scandal. My editor said, *'Impressions, Jane! People saying nicer things about*

Happy Rock. That's the hook and the angle. No one cares about some foofaraw in Los Angeles. We are a local paper. AKILA, Jane! AKILA: Always Keep It Local Always.' I guess I still have a lot to learn about journalism."

"Scandal?" said Miranda, her interest piqued.

"Yeah. I did some digging and made a few calls and found a couple of people who would talk to me"—her voice lowered to a whisper—"*off the record.* They didn't want to be quoted or have their names used . . ." She brightened. "Hey! Those were my first anonymous sources! Keen! Anyway, it turns out Mr. Tomlin was using mislabeled products, shortchanging suppliers. He was supposed to be donating 100 percent of the profits to charity, as well, and it turns out he wasn't."

"What percent was he donating?" Andrew asked.

"Apparently, approximately zero. He was donating zero percent to charity. The rest went to his own debts, failed ventures, ex-wives. It's a shame Mr. Tomlin died," Jane mused.

"It is," said Miranda.

"Yeah, I could have asked him what he thought about Happy Rock." Her eyes brightened. "I bet he thought it was nice! I mean, before he died."

WHILE MIRANDA WAS considering Harry's shady shenanigans, something odd was happening at TB Foods. Staff at the loading dock had come in to work to discover a stack of cartons left in the bay by persons unknown. Inside were snugly packed bottles of non–Harry Tomlin salad dressing. And olive oil. An entire carton of olive oil. Olio Family olive oil. Extra-virgin, all of it.

The manager, not sure if a crime had been committed, called Ned anyway.

And Ned, in turn, brought it up that night at Bea's. Who had left those cartons at TB Foods? It had to be the man in the homburg, a Mr. Tony Olio. But why would someone smash a bunch of olive oil, replace the bottles with different olive oil, then leave a $200 "I'm sorry" payment at the cash? As far as the manager at TB Foods was concerned, it was all good. The ledger had been cleared.

Ned wasn't so sure.

Miranda, meanwhile, had returned to Bea's that night to find a sizable group had gathered for that day's Pastor Fran Friday (though technically a Saturday; it was all a muddle). New fans, it would seem! All of them guys, oddly enough. Owen McCune was there, as was Doc Meadows and Tanvir Singh, plus their buddies. The men crowded themselves into the TV room, with chairs brought in when no more of them could wedge onto the sofa cushions, amid beer and salmon jerky and loud, unprompted guffaws. Why the sudden interest in Pastor Fran? The answer was a different *P*.

"Poe is in town!" they said, giddy as schoolboys.

"Can you imagine!" said Tanvir. "The star of *Under the Law* and *Above the Siege*, here in Happy Rock!"

And you better believe they pronounced it in the proper fashion, as Re-*gal* and not Re-gull.

Miranda recalled the press tour she'd done with Poe for *The Shimmer Spy*, the one feature film they did together, and how Poe had thrown over a table when the interviewer kept—intentionally, he was convinced—mispronouncing his name. *"It's Ree-GAL, dammit!"* He'd had an explosive temper back then, though how much of that could be attributed to diet pills and protein shakes was hard to say. Male action stars had it rough in those days. The women just had to keep thin; the men had to be cartoon buff. (Unlike today, where the superhero action stars *wear* their muscles.) It was the Stallone/Schwarzenegger era of requisite six-packs and vein-bulging biceps, and she remembered Poe obsessively doing crunches in his trailer while reciting the sacred *Ohm* as they were trying to run lines.

The guys at Bea's finished an episode of *Kung Fu Sheriff* then put in one of their own. It was an early Poe Regal action flick wherein Poe battled a team of terrorists on a hot-air balloon. *Nowhere to Run*, it was called, which was true, given the lack of space to maneuver in on a typical balloon basket. (It was a sequel to the first film, *Nowhere to Hide*, which was also true.) The movie featured a procession of flailing villains being tossed over the side with nary a worry about anyone passing by below, and all via the ancient art of the wristlock. The film also featured the first appearance of Poe Regal's soon-to-be-famous catchphrase: *"Do it. Take the shot."* Which the guys at Bea's recited in unison with Poe when he said it. "Do it! Take the shot!" they shouted.

Andrew was crammed into a corner, agog at what he was seeing. "Wait. He ducked a bullet—that was fired directly at him at point-blank range?"

"Sure," said Owen. "Reflexes."

"Studied aikido in Japan for ten years, is what I heard," said Doc Meadows.

Even Ned got caught up in the excitement of it, which helped him put aside the vexing Case of the Salad Dressing for the moment.

"It was twenty years," Ned said, correcting Doc. "He studied aikido in Okinawa for twenty years. It was the Navy SEALs he was in for ten years. And he trained CIA insurgents in Central America for nine."

"Oh, right," said Doc. "Was that before Tibet?"

"The monastery? That was after, I'm pretty sure."

"Taught the Dalai Lama how to defuse a bomb," said Owen.

"And wristlocks!" someone else said.

"Why would the Dalai Lama need to know how to defuse a bomb?" Andrew wondered aloud.

"Why? 'Cause you never know," said Doc darkly, and the others nodded in somber agreement.

The explosions and wristlocks continued, but Miranda's thoughts were now distant. The past was breathing against her neck. Memories of a Burbank film lot with a rain machine and a leading man who towered so tall above her that she got cricks in her neck from looking up at him during what was meant to be a passionate embrace. So far was her head tilted back that she often got water up her nose and ended up snorking mid-take. This was not conducive to a romantic mood. Four days shooting that climactic love scene (climactic in the narrative sense only). Four days! The scene itself was a risqué move for a woman best known for playing Pastor Fran—and it wasn't working. She'd never had to film passionate love scenes during her TV stint as a lady of the cloth. Here in the rain with Poe, it was just clinking teeth and dueling noses, and a co-star who was getting sullen and resentful.

She'd shown up at his trailer that night, angrily demanding to know what exactly he thought she was doing wrong.

He'd mumbled, "You're doing a TV kiss. We need a movie kiss. We need a real kiss."

"Oh, right," she'd scoffed. "And you know all about that as well, I suppose."

He'd already told her about his time rescuing baby mountain gorillas in Uganda, and of fighting both with and against the rebels in Sierra Leone. (He seemed to have forgotten which side he had been supporting halfway through the story.)

Poe looked at her with that heavy-lidded gaze of his, somewhere between Elvis and Don Ameche, and said, "Listen, I studied the

Tantric art of the kiss at an ashram in India for four years, and I'm telling you: a kiss doesn't start—or end—at the lips. It's deeper, more filled with a sense of yearning. It needs to be ... *thirsty*. You need to quench yourself on your lover's mouth when you kiss. It should be like drinking water from a wineskin."

She was getting really tired of his esoteric gobbledygook. "Fine. You're such an expert. Show me, then."

And he did. Boy, did he.

She remembered waking up the next morning, drowsy, to the sound of Poe at his trailer's kitchen range, a towel cinched around his hips, shoulders still beaded with water. He was cooking an omelet for her, and she'd gathered up her things and joined him.

"You cook as well," she said.

"I studied at the Cordon Bleu—that's in France—for three years."

"Well, thank you," she said. "For understanding."

She had almost given in. Almost. The kiss had all but overwhelmed her, and it had been late and his bedroom had been mere feet away. But Miranda was still a married woman, even if her husband was hiding out like a book-crazed squirrel up in Oregon, so she'd placed a hand against Poe's chest. Had mouthed the word *"no,"* when the kiss had gone on just a little too long to still be considered acting. He had accepted this graciously, and she ended up sleeping on his couch—because it was late and she didn't want the crew spotting her sneaking out in the wee hours, or, even worse, the dreaded paparazzi.

She'd woken to an egg-white omelet, as fluffy as a pillow.

"Trick to making an egg-white omelet is to only use the white part of the egg," he explained.

"Let me guess," she said. "Le Cordon Bleu?"

"New York Culinary Institute."

He lied. Oh, how he lied. But he was a very good kisser, she would give him that. And his omelets were so warm, so delectable, they practically melted in your mouth...

Miranda Abbott was yanked out of her reverie by the sound of Bea announcing, "Hey everybody! Look who's here!"

Miranda hadn't even heard the doorbell. She was scrunched in between Owen McCune's side whiskers and Doc Meadow's unreasonably long legs, and she leaned forward to see Alan Zabic standing at the threshold of the TV room, looking *very* self-conscious. He was holding a bouquet of flowers—from the shoppe, no less. No TB Foods plastic-wrapped carnations for him; this was a proper bouquet. He clearly hadn't been expecting a crowd, though.

"Hi..." he said weakly.

"Hey Zab!" "Pull up a chair." "Have some jerky." "How goes the movie business?"

There was nowhere for him to sit.

"I'll go and fetch one of the chairs from the kitchen," said Bea, but he stopped her.

"I can't stay," he said, though clearly his intent had been to. Suddenly aware of the flowers he was holding, he stammered, "These are for . . ." The wheels were turning. "You, Bea!" and he shoved them at her, to her surprise (and Ned's disapproval).

"Gotta run," said Zab. "Bye. Enjoy the movie, everyone!"

Poe Regal had just flung another henchman from another hot-air balloon. The henchman shrieked as he fell. Henchmen always shrieked. It was a sign of cowardice. But Poe Regal never did, even when shot in the shoulder. How many bullets can one man carry in his shoulder? thought Miranda as she squirmed her way free.

Peeling herself from the couch, she walked Zab to the back door, thankful for an excuse to get away.

"You cast Mr. Regal in our MOW," she said. "You replaced a two-time Oscar nominee with a washed-up action star."

"Five-time," Zab said, looking down. "Harry Tomlin was nominated five times." He then looked at her, imploringly. "I thought you'd be happy. I thought you'd say, 'How wonderful, giving an old friend of mine a second chance.'"

"He sinks every project he's on."

"No! That's not true. He promised me he would be on his very best behavior. He's changed, Miranda. You'll see. He spent seven months at a Zen retreat recalibrating his inner child. He told me so."

And Zab believed him.

With his inexplicable suntan and tousled hair, his white teeth and impossible good looks, with his neuroses and his aching need to be liked, Alan Zabic was Hollywood personified, she realized. Just as Edgar in his flannel shirts and unsustainable business plan was Oregon personified.

Both were attractive. Both were repellent. Which way did Miranda fall? Team Zab or Team Edgar? Even she didn't know.

"And the rest of the crew?" Miranda asked. "Are they copacetic with your casting choice?"

"Not everyone," he had to admit. "Leni Vedette threatened to walk, said that Poe Regal's reputation preceded him. Said he was known to be notoriously unprofessional."

"Oh, come now. That's ridiculous! What could possibly have given Leni such an idea?"

"An interview he did where he said, 'I am notoriously unprofessional.'"

Miranda pshawed this suggestion. "You can take anything out of context, if you want to."

"I had to pay Leni a bonus to stay," Zab confessed. "A very healthy bonus."

This isn't a film shoot, thought Miranda, this is a shakedown. And where is all this money coming from, anyhow?

"She was the one who found the note, yes?" said Miranda. "Leni Vedette was the one who first showed it to you?"

"It wasn't suicide!" Zab said quickly. "The coroner has already ruled on that. The meaning of the note was inconclusive. Could've meant anything. And it happened during a shoot, so his ex-wives will be fine. No one will suffer for it. It will cost the production companies money, but they have deep pockets."

They were standing at Bea's back door, Zab shifting his feet and shifting his eyes.

So much for flowers and a kiss on the cheek.

"This whole situation is very curious," said Miranda.

"This film *has* to get made, Miranda. It's paramount."

"Paramount? I thought it was Pindaric," she said, but he missed the joke. "The studio behind it," she added. "Pindaric Productions, yes?"

His eyes clouded over. "They aren't all that involved in the day-to-day operations. Not directly."

"Indirectly then?"

He didn't say anything.

She had never known a production company that didn't meddle at some point. It was in their DNA. "Hands-off" never was.

Before she could pursue this line of questioning, Ned Buckley appeared, having left the TV room as well.

"Hey, Zab. Wanted to catch you before you headed out. You know anything about the Olio family? Specifically, someone who goes by the name of Tony 'The Nose' Olio?"

Even with his California tan, Alan Zabic blanched.

CHAPTER TWENTY-TWO

Therapeutic Origami

An eerie sense of déjà vu hung over the press conference the following day.

Once again, they were seated within the hotel's glass-encased atrium behind a row of microphones. Once again, the media had assembled before them. And once again, Alan Zabic was seated center table in this Last Supper arrangement. He was flanked on one side by the flamboyant French cinematographer Jacquelyn de Valeur and her diminutive, somehow overworked translator, and on the other side by Leni Vedette, scarecrow thin and smiling with the satisfaction that comes from monetizing one's moral outrage. Could she ever bring herself to work with someone like Poe Regal? Never! Never, that is, unless the price was right.

Poe Regal had shown up right on time, was the first one in. All those years working with SEAL Team Six had honed his timing, no doubt. He looked tired, though. Was heavier, had jowls now, and his billowing Cossack tunic was incapable of hiding the girth beneath. He was... meaty. And a little slack in the face, like someone who has gained a massive amount of weight, Miranda realized, only to try to lose it with an emergency crash diet. He looked, she noted, like nothing so much as a half-deflated bouncy castle. Where was that handsome man of yesteryear?

And yet, even now, even from here, there was a certain *animal* magnetism about him. More sea lion than actual lion, true. But still.

Poe was on the other side of Zab from Miranda, and he hadn't looked at her or made eye contact when she'd swanned in with feigned apologies, fashionably late. The power move of "last one in" went to the ingénue, however, who sat down and introduced herself to Miranda *again*. "And you are?" the ingénue had asked, looking up from her phone with the briefest of pauses. "The Queen of England." "Cool." And back to her phone she went.

The media were out in force today, yet understandably distracted. Everyone was keeping a wary eye on the glass above them. How could they not? A cloudy day, drizzly with wind, far different from the day Harry Tomlin dropped in. But that one clear pane of glass among the older fog-scratched ones, which had replaced the one Harry went through when he crashed the glass ceiling in reverse, was a reminder of what had happened. The reporters jockeyed for position away from the spot directly below that pane, and every creak of wind outside sent a flurry of nervous glances upward.

Zab leaned into his mic, thanked everyone for coming. The trouble began immediately. With the first question, in fact.

"Hi. Jane Bannister, *Weekly Picayune.*"

Zab had called on the local press first, before Access Hollywood, before TMZ, before even KGW in Portland. And he was right to, thought Miranda, with a certain small-town pride she didn't know she possessed. Why should the big boys get to elbow their way to the head of the line?

"My question is for Mr. Regal," Jane said—and Miranda instantly felt her chest tighten. Jane Bannister had pronounced *Regal* like *seagull*, not like Ree-*GAL*. The tension was instant.

Miranda looked down the table. Zab was staring out at the reporters, and she saw his lip twitch. Zab then said to Jane, "Can you start again, please? Correctly this time. Thank you."

Confused, Jane said, "Sure. Mr. Regal, our readers would like to know what your impressions of Happy Rock are so far."

And again she said *gull* not *GAL*.

The twitch in Zab's lips had become a visible spasm. He turned to Poe. "She has mispronounced your name. I just want to make sure that you are okay with that."

One upturned table coming right up, thought Miranda, bracing herself.

But dammit if a serene smile didn't spread across Poe's face. He spoke, and his voice was lathered and warm. "My name is not who I am. Young miss, you may refer to me in any manner you see fit, as long as you do not refer to me late for supper." It was an attempt at humor, and an uncomfortable titter rippled through the room. "My impressions of your town?" He thought about this a long while. Thought deeply. "I think ... it is very ... nice."

Jane scribbled this down excitedly. Not just nice, but *very*! This was gold!

"I have spent the last ten months studying the ancient art of life-sized origami," he said. "Paper folding. Very therapeutic. It has calmed my soul and brought me to a state of equilibrium."

The reporters seemed disappointed and began taking turns goading him, pronouncing his name Re-gull again and again, hoping to provoke a reaction. But he refused to take the bait. Like a salmon floating past a lure, he remained the very picture of calm, cool, and collected.

"I would like to address the elephant in the room," the TMZ reporter asked with a sly smile, a clear jab at Poe's weight. But again,

Poe refused to take the bait. Again the line was cast and again it was reeled in, empty. "By which I mean, the death of the beloved actor Harry Tomlin." The TMZ smile had become a smirk.

As Miranda leaned forward to watch Poe talk about the great loss that Harry's death represented, she thought, He's saying all the right words. But Miranda wasn't interested in what was being said. She was no journalist, she was an actress, and she could read subtext across a crowded room. He was happy Harry Tomlin hit the bricks. Or, in this case, the table.

She thought about Zab's reaction last night as well, when Ned had asked about the olive oil. Zab was no actor, and his panic had been evident. Yet he'd denied any connection. Had denied it vehemently. *I think the production manager doth protest too much.* What was really going on here in Happy Rock? she thought, as the press conference dribbled out to its uneventful end.

IT WAS INTERESTING that Miranda's thoughts had turned to Ned and his ongoing investigation—none of the reporters were putting any of their questions to her, though Zab had tried to include her several times—because at that very moment Ned was hot on Tony Olio's trail.

Ned had been frustrated both by the vandalism at TB Foods and by the subsequent anonymous gift left at the loading dock. No one had seen the man's face. A shoulder-draped jacket and a hat. That wasn't enough to go on. But it had to be the same guy, the one who'd been peering into Zab's car looking for something. So Ned had gone to the station and Officer Holly had printed off a picture of Mr. Olio from the Olio company website.

Ned was now at the Cozy Café, photo in hand. Even on his website, Tony looked like a mobster out of central casting, homburg firmly in place, scowling at the camera. His title was simply: *Olive Oil Expert.*

Mabel of the Funk Festival Skydive peered at the photo through her cataracts. "Not sure," she said. "Myrtle, honey! Come here a sec, will ya? Ned here is on the hunt for a gangster."

"Not a gangster," Ned said hurriedly. "Just a person of interest."

Myrtle came over, wiping her floury hands on her apron, studied the photo as well. "Seems familiar, yup. I remember a fella. Was very much like this fella, but no—not the same fella. Not at all."

Damn.

"Are you sure?"

"Absolutely. The fella what came in here was wearing fisherman's cap, not this sort of hat."

Ned resisted the urge to slap an open palm against his face, said instead, "You do realize that he could have changed his hat?"

"Oh, well then. When you put it that way, could've been the fella. Dead ringer, in fact."

WHEN THE PRESS conference at the Duchess ended, cast and crew retired to the Bengal Lounge for cocktails and chatter. Miranda wasn't talking, however. She was holed up in a fern-festooned corner reading the script, Miranda-style. Which is to say, she skipped over the title page ("Something, Something, Mystery") based on the novel by P.K. Pennington (one of the writers Edgar stocked, apparently) as written for the screen by Luckless Lachlan (actual name: Todd) and more recently revised by Stone Rockwell (aka her husband), and she turned quickly to the character breakdown. There it was, right at the top: CLOVER MCBRIDE. Miranda Abbott would be Number One on the call sheet.

She had to stop herself from hugging the script to her bosom, lest someone see.

Instead, she went back and flipped through, searching for any romantic scenes with Poe, and was both relieved and disappointed there weren't any. The script hadn't really changed at all, in fact. In revising it from a Harry Tomlin vehicle to a Poe Regal movie, Edgar had simply gone through and replaced "beloved retired school-teacher" with "former CIA assassin." An entire heartfelt monologue wherein Harry Tomlin's character appealed to the killer's better instincts had been crossed out and replaced with the words *Poe beats him up*.

She smiled. This was vintage Edgar. He'd always bristled at stupid assignments, knew that what they were asking—a full rewrite on a screenplay, after it had begun filming(!), then recasting the main actor, requiring more rewrites(!), with only a day or two to pull it off—was ridiculous even by Hollywood standards. This begrudging "revision" was a protest on Edgar's part. Knowing Edgar, he didn't expect to get paid for any of this, but wanted his objections noted nonetheless.

Zab had clearly taken the script without reading it, and had distributed copies to the cast. Under the gun as far as the schedule was concerned, he'd announced that this was it: the final shooting script.

"Whatever Edgar has come up with will be brilliant," he'd said with undue confidence. They were already breaking down the scenes. "I flew in a top graphic designer from New York to create a full-scale color storyboard as well, to really bring the script to life. Leni doesn't actually use storyboards when she directs, but I still think it's an important part of the process."

Edgar had indeed given Miranda all the best lines, as requested by Zab. However, he'd done this by simply crossing out virtually every female character's name above every line of dialogue and writing in *Clover* instead. (In a few cases Miranda would apparently be talking to herself.) The ingénue's presence had all but disappeared, and that seemed harsh. Miranda would reinstate those lines for her, would insist upon it. She remembered what it was like to be young and how you were constantly expected to step aside for older cast members. Even though the ingénue had never bothered to remember Miranda's name, Miranda would not do to her what had been done to Miranda. We have to stick together, she thought.

Edgar had also added the words *plus Clover* in the character list of every scene. So suddenly Clover McBride was in the police forensics room and also at the funeral home (even though the two scenes were intercut), and in the locked basement of the hotel and also on the roof, whilst looking out at a sailboat (which she was also on). Edgar had done exactly what he'd been asked to do; he'd made the MOW all about Miranda. Even when she had no lines, even when it made no sense, she would be in every scene. Every. Single. Scene. That's what Zab had asked for, and Edgar, pedantically, if not petulantly, had complied.

This was unworkable, she realized. I mean, they could do a double exposure to have me talking to myself, she thought—she'd done that when she played her own twin in the short-lived *Pastor Fran's Sister Also Investigates* spin-off—but this was far more complex.

Andrew threw himself down across from her. "I know why he's sad," he said, wide-eyed and breathless.

"Oh my god, Andrew. Don't do that. You startled me. Sad? Who?"

"Alan Zabic. I know why he's so stressed, why he always seems to be on the brink of despair." He was thinking of affairs of the heart as well as business affairs.

Not a mystery. *"Responsibility weighs heavy on the shoulders of*

MYSTERY IN THE TITLE

those who carry it," she reminded him. "That's Shakespeare." She thought a moment. "Or maybe Oprah. It doesn't matter. Of course Zab is stressed! This entire project is like a creaking siege tower, ready to collapse at any moment."

"Oh, it's more than that," said Andrew. "I did some due diligence, what we should have done at the start, what we *would* have done at the start—if Marty were still your agent or if Atticus knew anything about entertainment law."

"Let me guess—you used your app."

"Sort of. I did a corporate search. A to Z Film Services is under contract with Pindaric Productions, true. But Pindaric, in turn, is a subsidiary of Euro Media, which is part of a larger conglomerate whose film and television productions—including MOWs, but excluding continuing series—fall under the auspices of Valor Films."

"And?" Miranda's head was swimming. "How does that explain Zab's sadness?"

"Valor," Andrew said. "Don't you see?"

She didn't.

"Jacquelyn de Valeur. *Valeureux* is French for 'valorous.' Valor Films. It's her family's media empire. She's on the board of directors!"

"So," said Miranda, slowly unpacking this, "that would mean Zab—"

"Works for Jacquelyn. Imagine the pressure! He has to get this MOW done, and his major star offed himself! The contracts and amendments and threatened lawsuits are probably already flying back and forth, from English to French and back again. What a nightmare! And if this project goes under, everyone *still gets paid.* It's a terrible deal. Good for the cast and crew, but bad for the production companies, including A to Z."

"He's cornered," said Miranda.

"Precisely," said Andrew.

Zab's words came back to her. *You don't understand, Miranda. This film has to get made.* "That's why he hocked his watch, sold his car. He's trying to keep it afloat!"

But why? If Valor was footing the bills, and Pindaric was producing the film, and Alan's company, A to Z, was managing the shoot—including casting and crew—why would he personally be on the hook for any of it? Unless...

"If Valor wanted to shut it down, or if they were no longer going to finance it, and Zab desperately wanted to keep it going... Perhaps Mr. Zabic's dream of escaping LA wasn't simply a yearning for the simpler life in Happy Rock," said Miranda. "Perhaps he was escaping other things as well. Or trying to." He did come across as a hunted man.

Andrew thought of the, ahem, "olive oil importers" Harry had gotten mixed up with.

"Zab may have cut a deal with certain less than savory elements," Andrew said. "To keep the film going."

Was this entire production tangled up with the mob? Was Valor Films some sort of front?

"Did Zab cut a deal?" Miranda wondered. "Or was he forced into it? Threatened even?"

"By Valor?"

"Or someone else, skulking in the shadows."

A minor hubbub had broken out at the bar.

"No, not the drink! I want an *actual* screwdriver!"

Chester Cornelius was at the counter, clearly exasperated and speaking to the elderly bartender in a loud voice, asking him to turn up the volume on his hearing aid. Chester had just been handed a tall glass of orange juice and vodka, when what he'd wanted was—

"A screwdriver. A cordless screwdriver. I was told you had one for putting up liquor shelves and whatnot."

The bartender rummaged through a box under the counter.

"Yes! That's it. Thank you." Chester's radio crackled and he said, "Roger that. On my way to the Roosevelt Suite."

Now, that got Miranda's and Andrew's attention!

They intercepted him halfway to the elevators.

"Hey, Chester," said Andrew, falling in beside. "What's up?"

The manager shook his head in frustration. "Well, first I tried a regular hand tool, but the screws were in way too deep. They're like six-inch wood screws. Needs a cordless."

"What are you unscrewing exactly?" Miranda asked, though she had an inkling she knew, even if she wasn't clear why.

"The painting," he said. "The one of the lighthouse. The one that was locked in over the dumbwaiter. I'm taking the painting off again, moving it over, back above the fireplace where it belongs. Poe Regal is in that suite, wants access to midnight cravings, I guess."

"He's not scared to stay in the same room as . . . ?" Andrew didn't know how to put a deadly accident or a drunken suicide in polite terms.

"Mr. Regal? Not afraid at all. Asked for that room, in fact. He would stay there as a 'homage to Harry,' he said." The elevator pinged. "Gotta go."

Miranda stopped the door with her hand. "One last question. Who requested that the painting in the Roosevelt Suite be moved to seal off the dumbwaiter in the first place?"

"Who asked us to do that? The movie people did."

"A to Z?"

"Not sure. But the call came from France."

CHAPTER TWENTY-THREE

Torts vs. Tortes

He was treating Miranda's meeting like a date, suggesting first that they dine on the hotel patio and then, when it was too windy and cold, in a secluded corner of the lobby.

"I can send for the caterers," he offered. "Have them prepare a charcuterie board or a selection of seasonal fruit? Maybe some wine?"

Zab was referring to the film's crafts services, who had set up a capacious tent behind the hotel for the crew while they waited for production to begin.

"One of the few film catering companies ever to receive a Michelin star," he said. "I can send for them. I don't mind."

Miranda was treating Zab's date as an investigation, however, and she passed on his painfully sincere offer.

"Thank you, but no."

She waved for drinks instead, catching the eye of a slowly passing waiter en route to the Bengal Lounge, who slowly shuffled over and slowly took their order. Once again Miranda spotted Silas Ivar, seated across the lobby from them, headphones on, listening for sound levels. Everywhere Miranda went, Silas seemed to show up somewhere in the background. How much room tone could one man need?

Miranda asked for papaya cocktail. "Virgin!" she said, and she saw Zab flinch. She tried not to smile. Who knew he was such a prude? "I was referring," she said, "to the drink."

"Yes, of course," he stammered.

He ordered the same, and when the frothy drinks arrived, he raised a toast.

"You did it, Miranda. You figured it out."

"Figured what out?" She stiffened at this. She hadn't figured anything out. Not yet. Even though all the pieces were in front of her. But Zab wasn't referring to the death of Harry Tomlin, but of something more personal.

"You saw Hollywood for what it was," he said. "A cesspool of champagne. You did what we all want to do—well, what I want to do ... You left. You found a real place with real people and now you're part of an actual community, not a fake one. I wish I had that kind of courage."

It reminded her of Edgar when they first visited Tillamook Bay, how he'd fallen for the town and had decided to stay. Was Zab preparing to do the same? *You walked away from it all, Miranda! You're free!* That's what Zab had said. But did I? Am I? Or was it a strategic retreat? A regrouping of resources in preparation for another sally. A Doña Quixote of the acting set.

Zab had a confession to make. "I came here because of you, Miranda."

And damned if he didn't mean it! Miranda could see it in his face. Zab was a terrible actor. As much as he tried to be blithe about things, his real feelings always showed through. And his feelings for her were painfully evident.

"I'd seen your performance of Blanche DuBois in the 5th Avenue Theatre production of *Streetcar Named Desire*. I was there opening night. You were . . . sublime. They never took proper advantage of your talent on that TV show, Miranda. Your ex-husband"—and he said that with an emphasis on *ex*—"never did you justice. When I asked him to do the rewrite on this one, I made it very clear that the script was to highlight your abilities in every scene."

Now it was her turn to feel uncomfortable. "About that. Have you actually read the revised script?"

"There is no need," he pronounced, smiling sunnily. "I have faith in Edgar. I believe he can rise above Pastor Fran."

"And Lachlan?" She remembered Luckless Lachlan as being especially vindictive and litigious, even for a screenwriter.

"Well, Lachlan did call me up screaming, threatening to take his name off the project, refusing to share credit with Edgar. But that's okay. We're sending it to arbitration. In the meantime, I told Edgar to let his imagination run free. My job is to help make his vision come true. If we have to settle out of court with Lachlan, so be it. The film comes first."

And in that moment, Miranda knew: Alan Zabic, although he appeared to be a cog in the Hollywood machine, was in fact that rarest of birds, someone in the arts who is actually in it *for* the art, not money or fame. She could feel something shift inside her. Miranda was in the middle of an investigation, but she was also caught between the Rock of Alan Zabic and the Hard Place of Edgar Abbott. Right in the middle of a potential love triangle. But could it really be considered a triangle when one of the players actively wants you to sign divorce papers? Did she still love Edgar? Or was it only the memory of Edgar, the *idea* of Edgar? Had she been fooling herself all these years?

Perhaps it was fate. Maybe it was time—time to finally end it with

Edgar when there were still men like Alan Zabic roaming free. Zab was a genuinely sweet man, an honest man, a good man. Edgar, meanwhile, was a cantankerous old goat. So why did she still feel torn? The choice was so clear, and yet... and yet...

Zab was looking at her now with those impossible eyes, wondering what she was thinking, she could tell.

"You may have faith in Edgar," she said. "But what of Poe Regal? Surely you don't consider him of the same stature as Harry Tomlin?"

Here was a true test of Mr. Zabic's empathy. Surely he couldn't also find the good in a train wreck like Poe Regal? He could.

"People can surprise you," Zab said. "Everyone thinks of Mr. Regal as this self-destructive spent force. But when news of Harry Tomlin's death hit, he was the first to call up, the first to offer his sympathy, the first to ask how he could help. To be honest, I hadn't thought of him for the role. But after that call, I wanted to give him a chance. He's a changed man."

"A man doesn't make changes," Miranda said. "Changes make the man."

Zab didn't seem sure what she meant by this, and truth be told, Miranda wasn't entirely certain herself. No matter. The specter of Harry Tomlin's death had brought them to the crux of it.

"Why did Valor Films ask the hotel staff to seal off the dumbwaiter in Harry's suite?"

This caught Zab off guard.

"It was—it was just a precaution," Zab stammered. "They just wanted to make sure he stayed safe. He was a costly addition to the film. Very costly. They were, as they crudely put it, protecting their investment."

"Safe? From what? It seems odd to worry about the dangers of a dumbwaiter when there was an inviting balcony right there."

Zab didn't say anything. His eyes flicked nervously to the lobby.

The crew were drifting out of the Bengal Lounge now, sated on expense-account cocktails, laughing and stretching. The fear in Zab's eyes was telling. Miranda understood his silence now. It wasn't Valor. It was Zab. *He* had blocked off the dumbwaiter to Harry's suite. Not because he was worried about Harry going out. He was worried about someone else getting *in*.

"Was Harry Tomlin afraid of something?" Miranda asked.

"You have to understand, as beloved as he was, Harry had a lot of enemies. There were people who were very angry with him. Not just his exes. Leni Vedette, for example. She invested in Harry's salad dressing company under the impression it was completely vegan and gluten-free."

"And?"

"Turns out, it was drenched in animal byproducts and absolutely stuffed with gluten. Was chock-a-block full of the stuff. Gluten plus. His entire salad dressing empire was poised to collapse. There were ... threats." Then, quickly, "Frivolous, of course, nothing to worry about, and nothing he took seriously. 'Crackpots and cranks,' as Harry said."

"That's why he agreed to shoot an MOW in Happy Rock."

"The agreement he signed with Valor was a mess. Everything was translated from French into English, then from English into French, and then back again into English. It all went through Jacquelyn's interpreter. She's like the gatekeeper. Jacquelyn barely reads what's put in front of her. But her company still has to sign off on everything."

"So I heard."

"It gets worse," he said—though Miranda couldn't imagine how. "The production didn't get a proper completion clause signed before they started. Basically, we're responsible for all of Harry's fees, regardless of whether the project goes forward, even in the event of death, and for any injuries incurred by him *during the course of production*. As you know, film contracts are designed to confuse. They are intentionally rife with bafflegab and hidden land mines. It's the nature of the biz. But I still hate it. It's why teams of lawyers usually vet every single clause. I assumed Valor had done this. Valor assumed I was going to. I should have caught it when the contracts came back to me, but I didn't. The wording was so convoluted I signed off, trusting people's good intentions, and assuming Valor had done due diligence. I know, I know—trust is not something that exists in Hollywood. And now we are on the hook for everything."

"But Harry died before production began," Miranda pointed out. "He wasn't shooting a scene or on set or attempting a stunt."

"Normally, you'd be right. But in this particular contract, the definition of what 'the shoot' entailed was defined by the *dates*. It should have been by the start of principal photography, but it wasn't. So basically, anything that happens anytime during the shooting schedule or in preproduction, whether on set or not, we're responsible. That includes the opening press conference. When Harry fell to his death, he was already on the clock."

Harry Tomlin's death had been a disaster for Alan Zabic.

"Even if his death was self-inflicted?" she asked.

"If it was suicide, all of that is waived, of course. If we could have proven that Harry killed himself, it would have been very good for *me*—we would have saved a bunch of money!—but very bad for Harry's next of kin. They would've lost everything. I just couldn't do that to anyone's family."

"That's why you were distraught when Leni found that note!"

Zab leaned in close enough for a kiss, gave her a secret instead, confiding in her, "If I had spotted that note under my door first, I would have been tempted to destroy it and not tell anyone. But once Leni called attention to it, I had to bring it forward." Then, softly, he said, "I lied, Miranda." He was having trouble meeting her eyes. "Ned asked me if Harry Tomlin had been depressed or suicidal, and I said, 'Heck no.' But he *was* depressed, he was feeling down. Had started drinking again. We were worried. All of us— Leni, Jacquelyn, Wayne Grey. Even the soundman was concerned. He said, 'If Harry hits the bottle and starts slurring his words, I can't fix that.'"

Ah yes, Silas Ivar the sound "artiste." She could see him across the lobby, still immersed in his work.

Zab lowered his voice, almost as though he feared they were being overheard. "I couldn't do it, Miranda. I couldn't do that to Harry's legacy. So I lied to Ned, insisted it couldn't have been a suicide, and now we have to carry all of Harry's debts: his pending lawsuits and payouts, his fees…"

"That's what completion insurance is for."

"I wish that were true! But under the terms of the contract, the outstanding fees owed get rolled into the *actual film budget*. We have to pay. Insurance doesn't cover any of it."

"That's nuts, even by Hollywood standards. Clearly, something got lost in translation!"

Zab agreed. "It's like a game of telephone, where you whisper a message down a table and it becomes garbled along the way, English to French and back again, all muddled up. And now? Now I'm left holding the bag." He tried to smile away the pain, but his eyes were welling. "I'm in over my head, Miranda. This movie *has* to go forward. We have to complete principal photography. It's our only chance. We have to finish it, sell subsidiary rights, hope it wins some awards or becomes a cult classic. Otherwise—"

But he never got to finish his thought because, in the lobby, a hubbub had flared up.

Angry shouts—not in English—and Miranda and Zab turned just in time to see the mousy little interpreter slap Jacquelyn de Valeur across the face.

"I DON'T KNOW *the difference between torts and tortes. Don't put this on me! I studied French literature. How am I a legal expert? Ask me about Flaubert, not fiduciary default!"*

The long-simmering resentment inside her had at last boiled over in a single slap. Unfortunately, all of this was said in French, not English, so Miranda missed its significance, assuming instead it was just the interpreter's Gallic blood stirring. Never mind that the interpreter was from Soda Springs, Idaho, and had first gone to Paris on a Rotary exchange. The woman stormed off, leaving the cinematographer holding her pink cheek, smiling wryly as the French always do in lieu of actual embarrassment (or so thought Miranda).

NONE OF THIS tension and worry and debt boded well for the upcoming shoot, and yet the town was abuzz. Filming was finally going to start! The hotel was busy with crew members laying out snakelike electrical cords, setting up lights, taping out marks on floors. Zab had hired an entire contingent of locals as extras and they arrived at the Duchess in a celebratory mood, joking about their "big break" and shouting, "I'm ready for my close-up, Mr. DeMille!" approximately every fifteen seconds.

Among them was Owen McCune, he of the magnificent side whiskers, who told Miranda excitedly that he had been cast as "grubby man." No extra wardrobe required.

"But," Owen said, eyes shining, "my role got upgraded 'cause they gave me a line."

"They gave you line?"

"They gave everyone lines! And because we got lines, we were given character names in the credits too. So instead of Bystander #1 or Customer at Store, we get a name. They even let us pick ours. The name I chose was Wrench Haldex. Y'know, Wrench 'cause of wrench, and Haldex for the clutch used in an automatic all-wheel drive to disengage the secondary axle."

"Of course," said Miranda. "How silly of me not to catch that."

Owen McCune had grown out his muttonchops to win the role of the Earl of Wessex in the annual production of *Death Is the Dickens* at the Happy Rock Little Theater. Now he'd be onscreen, in all his hirsute glory, playing . . . *Wrench Haldex!* Did have a certain ring to it.

Wafting past her with a pungent yet strangely compelling presence was none other than Melvin of the manure store. (He'd played Miranda's love interest in the same aforementioned play and always gave her a "Hey, babe" wink when he passed even now.) He had been hired to assist with the boom mic. He certainly managed to clear a space for the sound crew. Silas Ivar, who lived in a world of sound, was, apparently, less attuned to his other senses, including the olfactory.

"It's tricky," Melvin assured her. "Have to remember to point the mic to the person who's doing the talking."

That was pretty much the sum total of his duties, yet still he fretted. "This could be my big break," he assured her.

The energy was palpable. And then filming began and everything went off the rails. Almost literally. The dolly tracks were laid down in the lobby. All Miranda had to do was walk down the grand stairwell of the hotel, go across the lobby, and exit. That was it. This was the first shot of the first scene of the first day of shooting. It took sixteen takes to get it.

"You're too bouncy," said the very tall and very skinny director. "Stop bouncing so much."

Miranda tried, but it was simply not possible.

"It can't be helped," she said, as Jacquelyn worked, sans interpreter, to capture the cinematic artistry that was a person walking out of a hotel lobby.

"If you were a real actor, you would know how not to bounce when you walked."

"That wasn't something they covered at theater school," Miranda said drily.

"Apparently not," mutter mutter.

In the end, Miranda held her arms across her chest as though deep in thought.

Instead of "Cut and print!" Leni would grumble, "That'll have to do, I suppose." Just as, instead of "Action!" she said, "What are you waiting for?"

Once they got the shot, they broke down the set, moved the lighting gear, camera equipment, and dolly outside the front of the hotel. Miranda then walked down the steps, still deep in thought. She had one line. She had to stop and say, "Oh my, I forgot my umbrella."

There are sixty-four combinations of emphasis one can place on the words in this line: "Oh *my*, I forgot my umbrella," "Oh my, I forgot my *umbrella*," "*Oh* my, *I* forgot *my* umbrella," and so forth.

Leni had Miranda say this line in every possible iteration. Sixty-four takes later, she decided that the very first one was "as good as any of the others, I suppose."

And then the most incredible thing happened. Leni had the crew break down the set and move everything back into the lobby again for the shot of Miranda walking back in to get her umbrella.

"But—why didn't we shoot that at the same time? We were there."

A flash of anger. "I shoot scripts in order, as a story unfolding in its true arc, not as segmented elements to be 're-constructed' later. I reject the oppressive nature of denying a narrative by atomizing it to conform to societal ideas of what is 'efficient' and what is not."

Miranda was agog. "We're filming the entire movie *in sequence*?"

"This isn't an episode of *Pastor Fran*," Leni snarled.

No, thought Miranda. It certainly isn't.

CHAPTER TWENTY-FOUR

Shimmer, Shimmer in the Night

Twelve hours to get three shots and one line of dialogue. That was Day One.

The initial excitement of the locals had ebbed, fading like the sunset over Tillamook Bay. The crew was tired, true, but they were also well-paid and well-fed, so they were fine. They were owed overtime, as well, according to union rules. "This keeps up, we're rich," was the whisper going round.

The drizzle had ended, but the wind hadn't, and Miranda had spent an entire day walking in and out of a hotel, trying her best not to bounce, and getting touched up by an entire hair and makeup team between every take. Miranda did the math. Twelve hours. Three shots. There were 120 scenes in the shooting script, which meant that even if Leni Vedette could somehow miraculously get through one scene per day—doubtful—even working through weekends and holidays, they wouldn't wrap principal photography on a story that took place "during one glorious autumn" until mid-January. The last scene specifically called for a wide, rising panorama of golden leaves falling across the path as Miranda's character walked along the shores by Ye Olde Tyme Hotel. Leni's insistence on shooting in sequence meant that by the time they reached this final crane shot, the only leaves still on the trees would be a few shriveled tokens missed by the icy winds of winter.

We're doomed, she thought.

But Zab had assured her that it would be okay.

"Things will pick up. Once she finds her feet, she'll be fine. I have faith in Leni. This is her first full-length feature. She's always done docs and short experimental films, so this is new to her."

"And why did you bring her on board?"

"She came highly recommended by Jacquelyn."

A cinematographer choosing the director? Not unheard-of, but rare. Less rare if the cinematographer's family was financing the movie.

"Leni and Jacquelyn have worked together before," he said. "They come from the same experimental school of filmmaking."

That would explain the canted angle and unusual lighting choices, thought Miranda. It would certainly explain the extensive use of "venetian blind" gobos that Jacquelyn used to throw striped shadows across every shot, however unmotivated, even when they were shooting outdoors.

Before Miranda could ask Zab about these questionable lighting choices—she'd tried to bring them up with Jacquelyn Herself, but without an interpreter the cinematographer had just shrugged Miranda's concerns away with an insouciant, *"C'est de l'art, maudite tête carrée"*—Zab was called away by yet another kerfuffle. He spends his time putting out fires, Miranda thought. And the crew spends time lighting them.

The soundman was publicly berating Melvin for dipping the boom. "The mic stays out of frame. How hard is that to remember?!" Silas was enraged, his bald head and bat-like ears pink with anger.

Melvin, fumbling amid his miasma of fumes, was struggling with the fuzzy covering when the soundman began screaming, "Wrong sock! Wrong sock!" to which Melvin looked down at his feet.

"But I'm wearing flip-flops."

"On the mic, you twit." Hollering across to Leni, who was going through the next day's shot list, he demanded, "Why are we hiring amateurs at union rates?"

She barely looked up. "Ask the production manager."

But before Silas could look for him, Zab was already there. And he seemed angry.

"I will not have you verbally abusing the crew," he said, jaw clenched.

But Silas didn't blink. He stared back at Zab with a hostility that resembled nothing so much as raw hatred and said, "Why is this klutzy teenager even on set?"

Zab replied, with real passion, "Why? Because he is part of this community, dammit. We didn't come here to impose our ways."

Ah, thought Miranda. So it begins. The hypnosis of Happy Rock was underway. This town was the greatest sedative known to man. She knew the feeling well. Time passed so languidly up here. Next thing, Zab would have woken up having spent twenty years on Tillamook Bay, wondering how that happened. She could see it in his eyes—his beautiful eyes—that the tensions crackling around the film on this first day had only served to bring out the worst aspects of the entertainment industry to Zab.

Silas left with a dismissive flick of his hand, walking off to wind up his cords. "You don't call the shots around here, Zab. Remember that."

Miranda had never heard a crew member speak so disrespectfully to senior production staff. Artiste or not, Silas Ivar was a nasty little man. And an oddball too. He kept placing boundary microphones in unusual places, as though trying to record things happening off set. Could he fit into a dumbwaiter? she wondered. Maybe. If he bent himself in tightly enough.

Miranda had given the ingénue back her lines, though no one seemed to have noticed, least of all Leni. Or the ingénue, for that matter.

"Thanks," she'd said, buried in her phone.

Miranda returned to Bea's that night feeling utterly wiped. They had a fleet of drivers for the cast, so at least she didn't have to call upon Ned to run her home.

Exhausted, she retired to the Miranda Abbott Suite. Didn't bother turning on the lights, used the small television Bea had provided as illumination instead—in more ways than one. Oh, how she longed to be back on TV again. She missed the weekly dose of affirmation that a weekly series brought. Actors often professed to prefer film over TV, but not Miranda.

"Trouble in Happy Rock???" bleated the TMZ reporter. *"M.O.W. turns O.M.G.! A terrible script, spiraling costs, bickering on set, the death of the star, the fiasco that is Poe Regal, etc., etc."* They showed shaky footage of Silas berating Melvin, of Leni berating Silas, of Jacquelyn swearing in French (subtitles were helpfully provided, with asterisks replacing key letters for purposes of decorum: *"This sh*t town, full of g*d*mned *ssh*les, is nothing but a **** with a *** and a **!"*). They then threw an image of Miranda on the screen. She was outside the Duchess, waiting for the next shot, backlit by the sun, looking wistful. *"They even dredged up TV's Miranda Abbott from the dredges of the Whatever Happened to THEM?? file."*

Her phone immediately rang.

"It's me, Andrew. In the pantry. Did you see the TMZ segment?"

"I did!" she said. "It's wonderful!"

"Wonderful?"

"Yes, I look fantastic. The sunlight really caught the auburn highlights in my hair."

"Oh. Well. Okay, so long as you're okay, I'm okay, so I guess— everything is okay."

"It is. Thank you, darling."

It was only after she hung up that Miranda realized she wasn't alone in her room. There was . . . a *presence* in the corner. A large silhouette was sitting in the armchair, was breathing in the dark.

"Miranda," said the presence in the corner. It was a raspy voice she recognized. "We need to talk."

"Poe? Dammit, you almost gave me a heart attack. How did you get in here?"

"A master never reveals his—"

"It was Bea, right? She let you in."

A beat. "Yes."

"Dammit, I've told her to stop surprising me like that. Star-struck, no doubt. Stepped aside, let you waltz right in, said 'Be my guest.'"

"She did want me to sign a copy of *Kung Fu Sheriff* for someone named Ned. A police officer, from the sounds of it. As you know, I've worked in law enforcement for—"

"You were never a sheriff, Poe. Any more than I was a pastor."

Tenting his fingers, face still enshrouded, he said, "Then how come I still have a badge?"

"Because you never returned it to props, I'm assuming. Now, please turn on the light. There's a lamp next to the chair."

A golden glow washed across his beefy face. Those same eyes, heavy-lidded, those same lips . . .

"Miranda," he mumbled. "You may have heard of some of the difficulties I have had over the years, since we last worked together."

Which difficulties? she thought. The DUIs (plural)? The protein vape Ponzi scheme? The bare-assed sea-doo fiasco? The forged

Pollock (he'd presented a painter's drop cloth on *Celebrity Antiques Roadshow* insisting it was a lost work by the famous splatter artist)? The stolen handi-bus? Getting fired from every project over the last three years or so? His misguided attempt at children's comedies? He would have to narrow the list.

The epitome of tactfulness, Miranda said, "I may have heard in passing of certain misunderstandings which you may or may not have had with the law."

"Prob'ly worried about working with me again."

She admitted she was, but he insisted that he was indeed a changed man.

"I'm trying to be a better person, and I'm here to apologize for how I might have treated you. I honestly don't recall. But I have studied meditation at a Zen monastery in Nanpuku-ji for—"

"Same place you studied the art of Tantric kissing, I suppose," she said.

This was meant to be teasing, but he tilted his head, pursed his lips, and then asked, "You're blushing. Is something wrong?"

"No, it's just warm in here." It wasn't warm in there.

"The kiss," he said—and for a moment she thought he did remember. "I studied that at an ashram in India, not a Zen temple in Japan."

He rose from the chair and she saw how creaky and ungainly he'd become, partly due to the low, attic-esque ceiling that was featured in the Miranda Abbott Suite. But more than that, it was the passage of time and the weight of a lifetime of bad decisions.

Poe lumbered over in his Cossack muumuu. "I apologize for how I may have treated you." He then leaned in and whispered, with his breath upon her neck, "Close your eyes, Miranda. It's shimmer time."

Miranda sighed. Not this again.

"Poe, come on."

"Close your eyes."

She did, and he whispered into her ear, "Shimmer, shimmer, even slimmer."

And when she opened her eyes, he had vanished. His patented ninja exit. Except she could hear him banging about at the bottom of the stairs.

Without bothering to look down, she called out, "That's the linen closet! Next door is the exit."

More clanging and banging—for a trained ninja, he was remarkably clumsy—and he was gone. *Like a whisper on the wind…* as he always said.

From her window, she watched him hurrying across Bea's backyard in a stumbling gait, shoulders hunched and head down, muu-muu billowing in the moonlight. Yeah, that'll make you invisible. Hunch your shoulders.

And yet there was something more sad than funny in all this. He had been so lean once, so young. Heck, he'd been able to fly!

And that's when everything clicked into place for Miranda, like a tumbler in a lock.

BY THIS POINT, Idelia Powell was used to Miranda banging on her door late at night. It was nearly eleven, but Idelia swung open the entrance to the Gerald Ford Suite anyway with a blunt, "What is it now?"

Once again, Miranda had the novel experience of looking *down* at another adult. She was usually looking up, but this blue beehive with the cat-eye glasses and the polka-dot skirts was a different order of diminutive.

"Hello, Idelia."

"Rhymes with Ophelia. The doomed woman driven mad by

madness itself! Come in, come in." And then, to herself: "The lady in green returns. The human shamrock."

Miranda waded in, but there was nowhere to sit, barely space to stand. Where on earth Idelia slept amid this crowded labyrinth of clothes racks wasn't clear.

"Welcome to my sartorial Knossos. Speak now or forever hold your peace."

"The men's jackets. I showed you that swatch of fabric. None of the jackets matched, and none of them were missing, either. May I look again?"

But Miranda knew there had been no empty hangers, no interruption in Idelia's inventory. Miranda wanted to check something else. When they wound their way through to the pertinent rack, she began going through the jackets, one by one, checking the backs.

"You never snip a cut into any of them?"

Idelia balked. "Why would I? Those are perfectly good jackets."

"Are you sure?"

"Of course. Unless..."

And in that moment Miranda knew what Idelia was going to say next.

"Unless it was one of the stunt jackets. Heavier fabric, those. They're over here. A looser cut, as well. Come along, Kermit." Idelia headed off into the maze, humming "It's Not Easy Being Green."

The stunt jackets had cuts between the shoulders, hidden next to the seam—almost invisible.

"That's where they run the wire," Idelia explained.

Not a crazed dagger to the back, but a careful incision made by a trained seamstress. Harpreet had been right. It had been a fabric rotary cutter, making a single decisive slice.

Could it have been a stunt gone wrong?

No. Miranda remembered those times on *Pastor Fran* when she'd been called upon to leap from a burning building or an iron beam. (Pastor Fran had once gone undercover as a stevedore.) Even with foam blocks hidden off-camera below, they'd strapped her into a safety harness and attached a wire. It was a very snug arrangement, and was one of the few times on the show she'd been allowed to wear something loose to hide the harness underneath. Poe Regal had also done his own stunts when he appeared on Pastor Fran; she remembered him flying up and over a wall at one point. He had been in a safety harness too. But when Harry Tomlin hit that table? He'd been wearing a stunt jacket—and no harness.

Could it have been a *drunken* stunt gone wrong?

She remembered the empty bottles in Harry's suite, and how Harry must have gotten tangled up in that sheer under-curtain. There was one person she needed to ask. And she knew exactly where to find him.

WAYNE GREY WAS slouched over the bar at the Bengal Lounge and had been all day. Miranda didn't imagine he'd moved once.

"*I'm going to do it,*" Miranda said, quoting the note that had been slipped under Zab's door. She pulled up a seat next to the broken-down former stuntman. "Perhaps you can shed light on what Harry meant by that exactly, Mr. Grey."

Bleary-eyed, Wayne lolled his head to one side, considered Miranda through a fog of gin. "Miss Abbott, it's an honor and a privilege, as always." He had a way of speaking that was both overtly polite yet slightly derisive.

"What sort of high jinks were you and Harry up to, exactly? The day he died. He was wearing a stunt jacket when he fell off that balcony. What was he 'going to do'?"

"Once Harry gets an idea in his head, regardless of who puts it there, he sees it through to the bitter end." He still spoke in the present tense about his friend, as though Harry Tomlin might walk in at any moment, say, *"Gotcha good, didn't I, buddy?"* But there was no Harry and there was no gotcha.

Here it was, then, the *how* of it.

"You know, don't you?" she said. "You know how he died."

A shrug. "Didn't think he'd go through with it."

"Go through with what?"

"Harry had this crazy idea I would rig him up and he would rappel down the side of the building, in full sight of the media, the way his character does in the MOW, tracking down the ghost in the hotel. He figured he could do that stunt himself. It wasn't in the original script. That Lachlan guy—"

"Todd. Lachlan Todd."

"Yeah, he added a stunt that wasn't in the original story. He was figuring I would do it, but hell, do I look like I'm in any shape to go rappelling down walls? Zab said he would fly in a team of stuntmen instead, but Harry, he says to me, 'That's a waste of good money. A simple stunt like that? I'll do it myself.' Dumbest idea he ever had, and that's saying a lot. He's had some doozies."

"You didn't try to talk him out of it?"

"Did the next best thing: I got him drunk. There was no talking Harry out of anything. I locked up the safety harnesses, got him inebriated, and sent him to bed. I guess he was still drinking come morning. I was sleeping it off in my room. But I heard that awful crash, it woke me up, and I knew in an instant what had happened. Knew it in my gut. He went down without a harness. Just a wire. That goddamn blockhead."

He swished his drink, considered another round.

"You knew it wasn't suicide," she said. "But you didn't say anything."

"Reckless endangerment," Wayne replied ruefully. "Something I am very familiar with. Funny how everyone thinks suicide is the only invalidation of a life insurance policy. If they'd known what Harry had been up to, it would've canceled the entire payment. Mary, Claire, and Charlene would've been left with nothin'."

He was referring to Harry's exes. "Harry cared about his wives. He loved them all, I'm convinced of it. Spoke about them with real affection. No children, so that wasn't going to complicate matters any more than they already were."

But here Wayne Grey was wrong. When they read out Harry Tomlin's last will and testament the next day, there would be only one name listed under beneficiaries. And it wasn't any of the wives.

CHAPTER TWENTY-FIVE

Ned vs. The Nose

She didn't go back to Bea's. It was late, but Miranda was feeling empty and forlorn. Wayne's story had affected her. Time and tide take their toll on all of us, she thought as she sat in the lounge by herself, swizzle-sticking another virgin drink.

Time and tide. She'd seen this play out on Bea's TV screen as Pastor Fran Fridays became a Poe Regal marathon. Bea enjoyed the company. (Miranda had long suspected the main reason Bea opened a B&B after Bob passed away was so she wouldn't be alone.) The "boys," as Bea called them, were always courteous, if a little raucous, crowding in and bringing beer and salmon jerky, as they worked their way through the entire Poe Regal oeuvre. They'd watched most of Bea's *Kung Fu Sheriffs* and then moved on to Poe Regal's earlier films, *Marked for Justice* and *Hard to Wound*. And they were patient with Andrew's repeated confusions over narrative consistency. *"So his mentor was really the mole. But he broke his neck before he knew that."* *"He suspected as much,"* Doc Meadows pointed out. *"Couldn't take the chance."*

Sometimes Owen McCune brought little hot dogs. *"Got 'em cheap because they were past the expiry date,"* he would say. Conspicuous by his absence was Ned Buckley, who was, in Tanvir's words, "busy tracking down a mobster."

As the boys had powered through Poe's movies, from big-budget features to the endless string of straight-to-video fare he appeared in later, Miranda had noted how much Poe had aged, how the face had grown fleshier, the fight scenes less ambitious. He was often sitting in scenes now, even when he was supposedly "the world's deadliest sniper," watching from a window, comfortably seated, without bothering to crouch for the extended sequences that would require. (He was always "the world's deadliest" something in these movies. Even in the Alaska crab-fisherman hijack story he was described as owning "the world's deadliest trawler.") He worked with Pindaric as well, she noted, on an MOW family comedy, but that wasn't entirely unexpected. In Hollywood, everyone had worked with everyone at some point. Even she and Poe Regal. And anyway, the boys skipped over that one. It would prove unfortunate. Had they put that particular VHS in, things might have unfolded very differently.

But instead of Poe's failed attempt at family fare, they'd watched *Deadly Lethal Strike Force 4: The Revengering*, and Miranda recognized the sad evolution of Poe Regal from lethal to bloated. How out of shape he was. How very tired he looked. And yet, the Poe who had slipped into her room like the clumsy ninja he was had lost a lot of weight, was less puffy-faced. He really is trying, she thought. He certainly looked healthier now than he had in any of the *Revengering* movies.

Miranda remembered how mean the press had been, calling his last flick *The Fat and the Furious*, referring to him mercilessly as "Pooh Regal." Angry yet still mumbling, oddly enough, Poe had been caught on camera by TMZ threatening the very reporter who had dubbed him Pooh.

In the shirt-pulling scuffle that followed, Poe had shouted (mumbled), *"You go around referring to me as excrement? I'll wristlock you well and good."* To which the weak-kneed reporter had quickly and cravenly backtracked, insisting, *"Not poo as in poo, but* Pooh *as in 'beloved children's character Winnie-the-.'"*

"Oh. I see." Poe had mumbled an apology and left, not realizing that it wasn't the "beloved" part of Winnie-the-Pooh they were referencing, but the body shape.

TMZ had descended on Happy Rock licking their chops, but once it had become clear that Poe Regal wasn't going to have any public meltdowns or drunken confrontations—was exceedingly attentive and well-mannered, in fact—the paparazzi had begun to drift away.

Miranda felt a sudden affinity for Poe, for his aching attempt at a comeback. She could see herself in him. He was a good kisser, she thought. I'm at the Duchess. It's late. I know where he's staying, I could pop by—not for anything salacious, she told herself (unconvincingly). Maybe just a nightcap between old friends. That's all.

Miranda realized that she was in imminent danger of entering, not a love triangle, but a love *diamond*. Diamond, in the baseball sense. Edgar on first, Zab holding second, Poe hogging third. Tic-Tac-*Poe*. And Miranda at home plate trying to decide whether to make a sacrifice punt and bring the runner home—or swing for the bleachers.

Zab was too nice. Edgar too grumpy. And Poe was too, well, too *Poe*. Zab was much handsomer than Poe, but not nearly as handsome as Edgar, she told herself (incorrectly). But Edgar did want a divorce, and ongoing legal procedures do tend to put a damper on the potential for romance.

"Oh my god," she said aloud. *Edgar Abbott. Alan Zabic. Poe Regal.* It was Edgar Alan Poe, in that order!

Poe shouldn't have even been in the running. He was creaky and beefy and full of baloney, and yet . . . there was still something there. *Hard to Wound*? No. He was, she suspected, easily wounded. Easily hurt.

Miranda Abbott had an affinity for Poe Regal, and the heart has reasons of its own. She grabbed a bottle of pinot grigio and a pair of wineglasses from the bar—the film company had an open tab with the hotel for their cast—and she headed for the elevator.

She straightened when she reached the door to the Roosevelt Suite. The graffiti had been cleaned, and the ghost of Harry Tomlin presumably banished. She would say, "A toast to our working together again after all these years!" She looked down at the carpet, roses and paisley, ugly as always, and then, with a flip of her hair, she knocked.

No answer, so she knocked again, and this time the door opened a crack.

"It is I!" she said to the face in the doorway, holding up the bottle and glasses.

He was in a dragon-embroidered silk robe and he looked very uncomfortable. "Miranda?"

"Don't tell me you're going to bed so soon!" It was only midnight. Early for actors.

She sailed past him and into the suite—and on the floor was a scarf. Not one of Jacquelyn's pastel accessories, but the hideous mustard of . . .

"Poe! Tell whoever it is to go away! I'm waiting."

Miranda recognized the brittle, demanding tone, the same one that had said *"What are you waiting for?"* at the start of every take.

Leni Vedette was in his bedroom, scarf-less.

Miranda fled, feeling ridiculous with her wine bottle and glasses, her thoughts of love diamonds. Poe ran after her in his robe and bare feet, calling, "Miranda, wait!"

He caught up to her at the elevator and for once he didn't lie. "It's . . ." He was out of breath. "It's exactly . . . what you think it is."

Face burning, Miranda jabbed at the elevator button while trying to hold the two glasses by their stems.

"Do what you like, Poe. Sleep your way to the top. I don't care."

"The top? I wish. I'm not even sleeping my way to the middle. I'm trying to sleep my way out of the bottom," he said. "A director can get you fired. A director can make or break you. I had to make sure that didn't happen."

"Is that why you were hired in the first place? Did Leni *insist*? Was that one of her *conditions*? 'The actor, here named, agrees to pleasure the director upon request.'"

"What do you think I am?"

"I know exactly what you are! This?" She was referring to the bottle of wine. "This was a peace offering, nothing more."

"I don't believe you. There are still feelings between us. I can tell. I'm very good at reading people."

"Ha! You are good at exactly three things: omelets, wristlocks, and kissing."

She hadn't meant to say that last one. It had just sort of slipped out.

A smile surfaced on Poe's face. "Really? So you liked my . . . omelets. You know, I studied at the–"

"Cordon Bleu, I know. And the New York Culinary Institute, and with Paul Bocuse in Lyon. You are a fabulist, Poe Regal, though there are less polite terms I might employ. Along with the four years you supposedly spent as a Navy SEAL–"

"Seven."

"–and your six years as an undercover narcotics agent, plus the ten years you spent touring the Deep South as a self-described 'legendary jazz guitarist,' plus the eight years you spent building orphanages in Bulgaria, plus all the other endless claims, you would've had to have been–I worked it out once–218 years old."

"Yeah, but people say I don't look a day over 214."

In spite of herself, she laughed.

The elevator finally arrived. Miranda was about to enter, when she stopped. Looked back at him standing there in his silk robe and bare feet. Thought about the faded paisley and rose patterns in front of the door to his hotel room.

"Didn't they put out a red carpet–or at least a red rug–for you when you arrived, like they did for Harry Tomlin?"

"No."

"Are you sure?"

"I would have noticed. I have heightened sensory perception from my years studying at a dojo in–"

"Yes, yes." Sigh. She got in, wished him an adventurous night. Leni, she imagined, would be very demanding.

When she got to the lobby, Miranda eschewed the fleet of sedans that were standing by outside should any cast and crew members need a ride. Walked along the harbor instead, bottle swinging loosely in her hand, trying to decide whether it was a good thing that Leni had been there. The director might go easier on the actors now that she was involved with one of them. More importantly, it had blocked Miranda from doing anything foolish. But still–the night was warm, with only a tinge of autumn in it, and the moon was very full. Ripe, almost. Miranda felt rejected, which was silly, she knew. But still.

A waft of an odor, and she came upon manure boy and the ingénue arduously entwined on a park bench, lips and hands and small murmurs in the night. Everyone else finds love? she thought. Why can't I?

THE HIDEAWAY MOTEL on the road to Nestucca Bay catered mainly to out-of-town loggers, recreational fly-fishers, and overflow in-laws one wanted to avoid putting up. It was a log-cabin arrangement, set against a wall of evergreens, with a sun-faded sign out front that still advertised *Color TV!*

Tony "The Nose" Olio rose before the dawn and was packed and dressed and ready to go with the first wash of light. When he came out of his cabin, a patrol car was parked next to his sedan. And leaning against the patrol car was a police officer, a rounded man, plump even, but not soft. No. He was anything but soft.

"Hello, friend," said Ned as Tony Olio walked toward him, suitcase in hand.

Tony recognized the man. What was his name again? Some sort of cough syrup.

"Ned Buckley," said the officer. "HRPD. We met at McCune's Garage earlier."

"Of course. How may I assist you, officer?"

"You can start by not breaking the wares of hard-working Happy Rockonians."

Tony stiffened at this. So the cop knew about the salad dressings. He placed his suitcase down. Tony Olio had his camel-hair coat draped over his shoulders like an opera cape, homburg firmly in place.

"I gave restitution," he said.

Ned nodded. "True enough. And they aren't interested in pursuing charges. They figure they came out ahead in the deal. Everyone who has crossed paths with you seems to be under the impression that you're a mobster."

At this, Tony looked genuinely hurt. "Why?"

"Well, the hat and the coat for a start, and the fact that your nickname is The Nose, and that you import olive oil."

"But I *do* import olive oil. Didn't I give you my card? I keep my coat across my shoulders because my osteoarthritis has been acting up. It's too painful to get my arms through the sleeves without help. The hat is to cover my bald spot and to avoid getting sunburned. And I'm called The Nose because I am, if you'll pardon my immodesty, one of the finest olive oil enologists in the world. I can sniff a single drop of oil and tell you the exact region, clarity, age. I have a nose for the business, you might say."

"Was that why you held a grudge against Harry Tomlin?"

"He wasn't using extra-virgin olive oil! It was a disgrace." Tony's temper flared, and he visibly fought it back down. "His oils and dressings used regular virgin oil, not *extra*. Made a mockery of what we do. But that wasn't what brought me here to your town. I'm not just another disgruntled, unpaid salad dressing maker. It was my charity work. Mr. Tomlin was keeping the profits for himself. The jig was up, as we say. And I wanted to make sure that the charities would be taken care of. He robbed from the Boys & Girls Club, for god's sake! What happened to him, he had it coming. I'm done. I'm going home."

"Funny you should say that. *He had it coming.*" It was only then that Tony realized that the officer's hand was resting, lightly, on his holster. "Because someone else clearly agreed with you."

"And you think it was me? I am aghast, officer. Aghast that you would make such an accusation. I did not kill Harry Tomlin. How could I—with these hands!" He held up his crooked fingers.

"Osteoarthritis. I can't even twist the lid off a jar of pickles, let alone wrestle a full-grown man off a balcony."

"I know you didn't. You were nowhere near the hotel when Harry fell. I have witnesses to that effect." He hesitated. "If you agree to put on a fisherman's cap, that is. You were poking around Mr. Zabic's vehicle, going through his papers, however, no doubt looking for Harry Tomlin's contract, wanting to know how much he was really getting paid."

"Fine, yes, something like that. I wanted to know how much we could go after him for. Those charities needed their fair restitution too. Harry stole millions from them."

"And now you're leaving town," said Ned. "Which makes me think that maybe you got what you were looking for, that someone agreed to pay back that money. The only question is, who? Who would have access to that much money? Who would want to cover up what Harry had done?"

He said a name, and Ned's face clouded over.

CHAPTER TWENTY-SIX

Bedlam in the Bedding

Other than the dead body that showed up unexpectedly, the second day of shooting started off fairly uneventful.

Miranda had been whisked to the hotel that morning and had run into Gillian Hardner, Harry's executive assistant, in the lobby.

"Good morning, Gillian! Such a pleasure to see you." What she wanted to say was, "You're still here?" One would have thought that, with the demise of her employer, Gillian would have departed by now.

"Leaving today," Gillian said. "I managed to sort everything out. It took several heated discussions with Leni and Jacquelyn, but I managed to convince them to go on with the project even with Harry gone."

"That was very selfless of you."

"Selfless? I don't know about that. They still have to pay Harry's estate. The full fee. The producers were thinking injury, not death, but the wording was ambiguous enough to include both. Works for me, 'cause it means I get paid as well. My salary was covered by Harry's agreement. I was part of the crew, so to speak. So you could say I had a vested interest in seeing this terrible MOW get finished."

Gillian's phone vibrated. She ignored it. "I thought that wrapped things up on my end, but no, Harry had one more trick to play. His last will and testament."

"Ah, the ex-wives."

"The three furies get nothing. Not a cent. Turns out, our beloved Harry left his entire estate, the house in Malibu, the mutual funds and stock options, even his private jets, to one person. Wayne Grey."

The news set Miranda back on her heels. "The stuntman? Harry's colleague?"

"Harry's friend." Miranda thought about the horrific accident that had left Wayne broken. "Do you think Harry felt guilty? About what happened to Wayne Grey? Maybe that's why he left him everything?"

"No idea. All I know is, I have to get down to LA right away. It's a shitstorm. Exes are hexes, as they say. And the three-headed cerberus that is Mary, Claire, and Charlene is breathing hellfire. Here he is, dead, and I'm *still* managing Harry's daily affairs for him." Again her phone vibrated, and again she ignored it. "Autodialers," she explained. "AI doesn't understand human mortality. How many subscriptions did Harry sign up for?"

With that, Gillian left.

Miranda was stunned. The film shoot could wait! It always took Jacquelyn ages to set up her key lights and gobos anyway. (She didn't believe in fill or back lighting. Everything was lit in stark key light, usually through a venetian blind effect.) Right now, Miranda needed to talk to Wayne. He wasn't at the bar, which was good, but bad because it meant she had to find him, quickly, before Leni noticed Miranda was late on set.

Fortunately, the call sheet listed his room: ground floor, service entrance, behind the loading dock. A glorified broom closet.

Why on earth would they stuff him in down here?

"Afraid of heights," he explained when she knocked. "Prefer ground floors." She couldn't be sure if he was joking or not. "Never was one for fancy suites."

"But didn't you routinely fling yourself off horses and cliffs?"

"I did," he said, motioning for her to sit on the only chair in the room. He took the cover-strewn unmade bed, amid the empty cigarette packs and bottles and Louis L'Amour paperbacks. "And I had my eyes closed the entire time. Never cared for heights, but I sure did like the horses. Did you know I bought Harry his first saddle? Taught him how to ride. The saddle was a Roy Rogers special, cheap leather, tin adornments, a cork horn. Just to learn on, y'understand. I assumed he would upgrade it. Expected him to. But he never did. Did you know that?"

She didn't.

Wayne had heard about the will; he'd gotten the call early that morning. "Ruined a perfectly good sleep."

"Harry left you everything," she said. "You're a very lucky man. He died owing money, but his estate was at arm's length, I'm sure. Standard procedure in Hollywood. The mansions and the private jets—it's all yours now."

"Sure. My best friend is dead. Lucky me."

"What happened?" she asked. "On that set that day, when you fell without a wire, when you missed the foam pit, hit the alley. Did you hold that against Harry? It happened on his film set."

"First of all, sister, I didn't *miss* the foam pit, because there was no foam pit. And second of all, I was drunk out of my gourd when I made that leap."

"Harry let you perform a stunt while you were intoxicated? That's unconscionable!"

"But I wasn't," he said. "Performing a stunt, I mean. It didn't happen during the shoot. It was after. I was showing off, and I fell. Hard.

Thought I died, and damned near did. Harry covered for me so that the studio would pay for my rehabilitation. He signed an affidavit to that effect, that I had been injured during filming. I never told anyone, and neither did he. And now he's dead, and he left me everything in the world, and I don't care. I don't want everything in the world. I just want Harry back." He ran a hand across his face. "I need a drink."

"No, you don't."

"I *want* a drink," he amended. Pulling a flask from under his pillow, he asked, "Join me?"

She declined.

Wayne took a searing swallow, and then chuckled to himself, said, "I was worried, you know, that I had screamed on the way down. That I had been scared. And when Harry came to see me, all trussed up with a back brace in the hospital, I asked him, though my jaw was wired. I rasped, 'Did I make a sound when I fell?' 'Sure,' says he. 'Splat.'"

Wayne began to laugh. He laughed so hard his eyes brimmed. He laughed so long it almost looked like crying.

Miranda reached out, squeezed the back of his hand.

But then her phone trilled and it was Andrew. "Where are you? Leni is pissed. First Silas and now you. It's only the second day of shooting, Miranda. You need to get here! We're in the hotel basement, location Number 3 on the call sheet. Hurry!"

And so Miranda left Wayne Grey alone with the sorrows of his newly gotten but strangely unappreciated windfall.

She took the back stairs, past the alarmed side door that had been jimmied open earlier, during the power outage. The mystery of that remained. Halfway down the stairs, she looked back up. The door at the top led into the lobby, right next to the front desk, she believed. What if . . . ? What if the person or persons unknown who tripped the hotel power and pried their way in wasn't trying to reach Harry's suite, as she'd always assumed? What if they were heading for the front desk under a cover of darkness that had sent staff scrambling?

But there was no time to investigate. They were waiting for her in the Duchess's laundry room.

Andrew met her with a bottle of Aquafina and a worried look on his face. "We haven't even started and already things have gone awry," he whispered.

"Lines?" she asked.

"None."

Miranda had no lines in any of today's setups. And yet she was required to be in every single scene, if only to be shown loitering in the background. Owen McCune, as Wrench Haldex!, did have a line. Just the one: "Is that blood on the actual cotton comforter?" But he kept screwing it up. It kept coming out as "the axle carbon carburetor."

As Owen paced back and forth, rehearsing his one line, trying to get it right, everyone else waited for the final member of the crew to show up: Silas Ivar. The woebegotten boom operator Melvin was already there, his oddly compelling funk having spread like a mist across the cavernous linen room. But no sign of Silas.

Leni was starting to growl, Jacquelyn was tinkering with the lights and giving halting directions to her camera crew—"*More like zis, bit not like zis, d'accord?*" (apparently the enclosed basements of hotels often featured venetian blinds just off camera)—but Silas was nowhere to be seen.

Then, on a low groan like the creaking of chains, a sound rumbled through the room. One by one, everyone turned to face the small entrance in the wall above the dirty linen cart. The dumbwaiter was descending.

"Who did that?" Leni demanded. It would have ruined the shot if they had been filming, and if their soundman had been recording.

They could hear as it slowly rattled down the shaft. It came to a labored stop. Silence. A green light blinked on, signaling that the doors of the dumbwaiter had locked into place and could now be opened.

No one moved.

"Oh, for god's sake. What are you scared of? Ghosts? Never saw such a timid bunch." Leni Vedette stumped over angrily and yanked the doors to the dumbwaiter open. Perhaps she was expecting a pile of bedding to tumble out. What she hadn't expected was Silas Ivar to tumble out instead.

The soundman had been folded into the dumbwaiter at an unnatural angle, like a human knot, with his bald head pushed down, limbs pretzeled in. He'd been strangled with his own microphone cord, and when the door was opened, he tipped out, into the laundry cart, to the screams and gasps of the crew.

Well, thought Miranda. That answers one question. Silas could fit into a dumbwaiter. If he bent himself in enough.

Amid the ensuing chaos and yelling for a doctor and the calling of police, a small slip of paper had wafted out of the shaft of the dumbwaiter. Miranda watched it land on the cement floor, and just as quickly saw Andrew step on it, hiding it under his sole.

He pretended to tie his laces and, when no one was watching, slipped the paper into his palm, and his palm into his pocket. Deputy Nguyen, on the case!

"No one touch the body!" someone screamed, just as someone else screamed, "Help him, for god's sake!"

Bedlam in the bedding room.

Miranda grabbed Melvin by the arm. "We need to speak," she said. "Before Ned gets here. Bring the sound recorder."

MYSTERY IN THE TITLE

They moved to a quiet corner of the basement, out of view of the others, as Andrew kept watch. Andrew hadn't had to flash his deputy credentials—Melvin had been happy to help—but was hanging back for reasons more malodorous than prudent.

Nothing takes more time than wrangling data, but Melvin was able to bring up the files on the sound recorder quickly enough. He was a fast learner.

"Mainly just room tone," he said. "It's really boring. You have to go through and log it by time, duration, and location. And Silas, he was really picky." Melvin didn't seem perturbed by the dramatic exit of his boss. And no wonder. Silas had been mean. Miranda was nice. An easy call. "Silas would listen to the different tones, again and again, would consider if this was a warm tone or a cold tone, a cool one or warm. Is there an echo? A faint metallic hum, a hint of outdoors through a closed window? Or is it a low tone that could be used as the drone note for a suspenseful scene? I was trying to learn, asking questions, but he kept yelling at me to be quiet. He always wanted the world to be quiet for him. I guess he got his wish."

"Can you play back the room tone from the day Harry Tomlin died? Silas was in the hallway below Harry's suite, recording room tone. Ned and Andrew checked, but they didn't find anything. No voices or footsteps or shouting."

"That was before they brought me on, but sure." Miranda gave him the date and time, and Melvin scrolled through the files on the Nagra digital recorder. "Huh. That's weird. Those files have been erased. Wiped clean."

"When?"

"Yesterday." Then, with a grin, "Good thing I backed everything up." Melvin had been so nervous about accidentally deleting files or losing data and getting yelled at by Silas that he'd saved it "on the cloud," just to be safe.

"To the cloud!" Miranda said, rising dramatically.

"It's not an actual place," he said.

She had assumed it was a storage facility of some sort. "Okay, so where is this 'cloud,' then?"

He pulled out his phone. "It's in my pocket."

Sure enough, he was able to access the deleted files, pulling them from the ether like a magic trick, and he played them back for Miranda on speakerphone. She held her breath expectantly, wondered whether she should have a pen handy to jot down any scraps of conversation she might catch. But no. There was nothing. Only the hum of a silent hallway, and then—

"What was that?" said Miranda. "Was that a *snick*?"

"Snick?"

She wasn't sure if that was the correct technical term, but when Melvin rolled back and played it again, there it was: a *snick*.

"More of a *click*, I'd say," said Melvin.

"And right after that," said Miranda. "Do you hear? A short, high-pitched *whir*, like a tape recorder rewinding."

"They don't use tape anymore," said Melvin.

A memory surfaced of Bea's, of Tanvir renovating the upstairs suite.

"A screwdriver," Miranda said. "A cordless screwdriver! The type film crews use to put up sets, maybe? Or—" It hit her. "The kind that Chester borrowed from the bar. The one he would've had to use to move the painting in the suite, when Poe moved in. The painting that had been covering the dumbwaiter."

Standing in the basement, there were four floors above them and, as far as Miranda knew, no way to tell which floor had sent the dumbwaiter with Silas's body down. It was a simple call system. No floor numbers counting down, just a basic motorized pulley system, and a set of interlocking doors for safety.

And which rooms did the dumbwaiter run through or have access to? Miranda did a tally. There were five: (1) the laundry room here in the basement; (2) the kitchen directly above them on the main floor—there would be lots of staff coming and going, impossible to lug a body through and stuff it in; (3) the second-floor family suite, empty and locked; (4) the Roosevelt Suite, where Harry had been; and (5) the Gerald Ford Suite on the top floor, where Idelia Powell had set up her fitting room. But Miranda knew from the call sheet that the ingénue was having her wardrobe adjusted today, so unless the ingénue was in cahoots with Idelia, that left... the Roosevelt Suite. Where Poe was now staying.

Miranda felt something sickly stir in her stomach.

"Psst." It was Andrew. "I think I hear sirens."

Even muffled down here in the depths of the basement, they could make out the distant mosquito pitch of a patrol car approaching, along with the frantic *wee-wah* of an ambulance.

If they stayed here, they would have to hang around to give statements to the police, and what did they have to say? They'd witnessed the same thing everyone else had: a dumbwaiter descending, and a soundman tumbling out like a badly folded towel.

"To Tanvir's!" she said. Then, to Melvin, "We will need to borrow your cloud."

"No need," Melvin said. "I'll text Andrew my account name and password. He can access the audio files I backed up from his own phone. Easy-peasy, lemon squeezy."

My, my, she thought. There really is an app for everything.

Miranda and Andrew slipped away, up the side stairs and into the lobby, where word had already spread. The crew was abuzz, rumors were flying. Wayne Grey was making his way on creaking hips toward the basement. An unauthorized stunt, thought Miranda, Silas's dumbwaiter descent. The ingénue and the diminutive Idelia appeared soon after, bursting out of the elevator in mid-adjustment, it would seem. (The ingénue's flowery skirt was still pinned up, so fast had they come down.) Zab was crowded into the same elevator, and he looked distraught. The poor man. He's exhausted, thought Miranda. Another fire for him to put out.

But stranger still was the person hanging back watching all this unfold.

"Isn't that the interpreter?" Miranda asked. "What is she doing in a hotel uniform?"

Andrew looked, but when he did, the mousy woman was gone.

"She was wearing a hotel blazer," said Miranda.

But Andrew was too absorbed in the piece of paper he'd picked up to notice. "What do you think this means?" he asked.

It was a handwritten mishmash of numbers and words, interspersed. The numbers meant nothing to them, but the words almost did: *swift check bla person.*

CHAPTER TWENTY-SEVEN

The Jacket Harry Died In

They might as well have been whittling, thought Miranda.

Tanvir Singh, of Tanvir's Hardwares & Bait Shop, *"Everything from Tools to Worms"* –the saying in Happy Rock was, "If Tanvir doesn't have it, it doesn't exist"–was comfortably ensconced on a swaybacked couch at the back of his store with several of his buddies, discussing Poe Regal's past cinematic capers, no doubt.

"Miranda! Andrew!" He gave them a wave when they entered the organized clutter that was his store. Tanvir liked them, even if he didn't understand the aura of celebrity Miranda clearly sought to impart. It wasn't like she was a proper Bollywood star, a Kareena Kapoor or a Rani Mukerji. Now that would have been impressive!

"Harpreet was asking after you," he said. "Wanted to know if you would like her to 'stab any more dummies.' I was hoping she wasn't referring to me."

"No, we won't need to stab any more dummies. You're safe for now, Tanvir."

He laughed and said, "Good to know! You just missed Doc. He got called away. Some sort of kerfuffle at the old hotel. And Ned is still out hunting down that mobster, last I heard."

Owen was absent as well, on set and still practicing his line, oblivious to the death of Silas Ivar, Miranda was sure. But even without Owen or Doc in tow, Tanvir had his Greek chorus: older men in suspenders and/or belts, with John Deere caps pushed back and sage wisdom always on tap.

"I was just saying, they should bring back Pastor Fran," one of them offered, unbidden. "But make her a spy. And a fella. And set in the future. Robots and such."

So . . . *not* Pastor Fran. She ignored this voice from the chorus, asked Tanvir, "I need your help." She didn't tell them about the "mishap" on set, had too many pieces to put into place first.

Andrew brought up the sound file Melvin had sent, and played the *click* and the *whir* on speakerphone for them. The men in the hardware store listened intently, frowned sagely.

"Do you know what that is?" Miranda asked.

"Yes," said Tanvir. "I think I do."

"And?"

He ran his hand through his beard thoughtfully. "I would say, and I might be wrong, but I'm fairly sure . . . that's a . . . *click* . . . followed by a *whir*."

He looked to the others, and they agreed. "Yup. That's what it is, all right. A *click* and a *whir*."

Miranda, exasperated, "But what kind of a *click*? What kind of a *whir*? It sounds like a cordless screwdriver."

"A screwdriver?" said Tanvir incredulously, and the others chuckled at such a suggestion, shook their heads at her naivety. *A screwdriver, as if!* "That doesn't sound *anything* like a screwdriver. I'd say that's a K 1000."

But one of the chorus disagreed. "K 1000? No, no. That's a BR-92."

"Nope, a Fleishman's 3X," said another.

"Only one way to know."

Tanvir got up and they went across—not to the screwdrivers, but to the fishing rods. They tried various automatic recoils and the consensus was that it sounded *very much* like a Fleishman's, but not *exactly*.

"So we were all wrong," said Tanvir.

"But I was the least wrong," said the fella who'd had Fleishman's on the bingo card.

Miranda thought of the fishers along the harbor, casting their lines and reeling them back in...

"Gentlemen," she said. "How much do you enjoy a good puzzle?"

Andrew brought out the scrap of paper that had flitted out of the dumbwaiter with Silas's body.

"We have a riddle that needs solving," Miranda said. "And I thought"—she did a quick nose count: there was Tanvir, his three backup singers, Andrew, and herself –"five heads are better than one." She wasn't including the "spies in space" guy.

Miranda showed them the note: *swift check bla person*, with numbers in between. Words and numbers. A code. Unfortunately, numbers were not her forte; she'd never mastered the art of balancing a bank account or maintaining a day-timer, for example. Andrew was, in many ways, her perambulatory day-timer. But she knew words, and these ones almost formed a sentence: *swift check bla person*. No punctuation to dictate how the line should be read, though.

"Perhaps," she said, "it signifies, *Swiftly! Check the blah person!*" It was almost gibberish, true, but Miranda had performed Beckett; she was used to gibberish. *Light heat white floor one sure yard never seen.* And that was one of Beckett's more lucid passages. *Swift check bla person* was the apex of clarity in comparison.

She flattened out the paper on the counter.

"It was written by the soundman," she said. "It must refer to a sound *check* by a *person* who speaks–i.e., *blah blah–swiftly*. Now. Who speaks swiftly? Well, in theater, when an actor runs their lines *quickly*, they are said to do it 'Italian.' If we can get a list of the cast and crew, we will see who has the most Italian-sounding surname and–bingo! That's our killer."

"Who's bingo?" one of them asked.

"The killer!"

"The killer's name is Bingo?"

Andrew intervened. "But there are numbers as well."

Miranda brushed this aside. "Numbers schnumbers. I'm a word person. I live by language, darling."

"Yes, but there are numbers after every word. And it's not *blah* with an *h*, but *B-L-A*."

"Hmm. You're right. That is quite the conundrum. Listen up, everybody! We are going to stay up all night if we have to, to crack this. I would brew some chamomile tea, but we need caffeine, so coffee it shall be! Tanvir?"

"I don't drink coffee, of course, but I think I have a small jar of instant somewhere in the back for guests. I could boil some water."

"Done."

It was Andrew. Miranda turned around. "What?"

"The code. It's done." He showed her his phone. He had solved it in the time it took for her to settle on which hot beverage they would be enjoying. "I entered the terms into a search engine," he said. "It's a bank account. SWIFT is the swift code–like a transit number–used for offshore deposits. *Person* and *check* must mean 'personal checking.' And BLA is the code for Bank of Los Angeles."

"Oh," she said.

There was a long pause.

"Should I boil the water?" Tanvir asked.

Miranda gave a vague wave to say no. "Whose bank account?" she asked Andrew.

"Don't know. Probably Silas's, I imagine."

"Can't you find out?"

"How?"

"You're a personal assistant. Call some people."

"Sure. I'll call my 'bank guy,' ask him for the personal information on someone else's account."

"See! There you go!"

"I was being sardonic."

"Oh. Well, stop it. It doesn't suit you."

"From the type of account, though, I can tell you that it is set up for third-person deposits."

Pastor Fran rubbed her chin. Or rather, Miranda Abbott did. "Is that so?" A sound recordist found dead with banking information on hand. "Why do I have a feeling that someone paid Silas Ivar an awful lot of money to erase those fourteen seconds of room tone, the ones that Melvin was able to retrieve? Do you think he *didn't* keep a backup of his sound files? Ha. It's like blackmailers with incriminating photographs. They always keep the negatives!" One of the many life-lessons from *Pastor Fran Investigates*. "Silas was about to hand over his banking information to the killer, but was rewarded with a broken neck instead."

"Silas?" one of the chorus asked. "Bald guy with big ears? Somethin' happened to Silas?"

"You could say that, I suppose." With a fling of her scarf, Miranda turned to Andrew. "We are off! Back to the Duchess, darling."

"Will we see you at tonight's Pastor Fran Friday?" Tanvir asked.

She smiled. "You mean to say, the woefully *misnamed* Pastor Fran Friday?" It was all Poe, all the time, now. "I suppose you shall. I do live there. It would be hard to avoid, even if I wanted to."

They took this as a compliment, for some reason.

"We're watching *The Revengering: Part Six* tonight!" one of them chimed. *"This Time It's Personal."*

"But—" Andrew couldn't help himself. "Isn't all revengering personal? Isn't that sort of the idea?"

"In this one, they kill his family."

"But—they killed his family last time."

"Those were his cousins," one of the men explained. They'd already gone through his spouse, the estranged brother, the long-lost son, the grizzled ol' mentor, and both sets of grandparents. "Now it's the nephews they're after! And, Miranda, you'll keep my idea in mind, right? A spy. In space."

"Yes, yes, robots and such."

"*Revengering Six* is the weakest of the franchise," another of the chorus complained. "Plot doesn't make a lick of sense."

Miranda and Andrew were struggling to extricate themselves from the conversational goo that was a Happy Rock afternoon. The possibility that someone might have somewhere to go didn't seem to occur to these people.

"Still better than that terrible family movie Poe made," said the third member of the chorus. "My grandkids liked it, but I couldn't make hide nor hair. I mean, leprechauns are by definition small, right?"

Miranda almost missed that. She had been slowly backing away, had almost slipped free, when she stopped. Came back. "Leprechauns?"

"Yes, *The World's Largest Leprechaun.* Poe Regal played the leprechaun. Trying to cash in on that kid-friendly movie Dwayne 'The Rock' Johnson did, where he played the tooth fairy. What was it called again?"

"*The Tooth Fairy.*"

"That's the one. Poe was flying about in that St. Patrick's Day movie and, heck, leprechauns don't fly! Everyone knows that. It's common sense."

"He was flying?" said Miranda.

"Yup."

"In a green jacket?"

"That's right."

She turned to Andrew, but Andrew was one step ahead of her. He'd already brought up the IMDB page for *The World's Largest Leprechaun* on his phone. "One of Pindaric's many holiday-themed MOWs," he said. "Straight to video." He showed Miranda the cover poster of Poe in mid-flight, trailing rainbows and gold coins behind him. "Was that the jacket Harry Tomlin died in?"

It was.

AS THE DRIVER whisked them back along the harbor to the hotel, Miranda whispered to Andrew, "Not hiding, *hidden.*"

"Full sentences, remember?"

"On *Pastor Fran*, I once leapt from a helicopter into a shark-infested swimming pool."

"Wait. What? A shark-infested *swimming pool?*"

"One of Lachlan's scripts. I don't remember the details. But in those pre-CGI days, I had to make the leap myself—at least for mid-shot. Not from the actual helicopter, of course. The long shot was of a stuntwoman. She was dangling off whatever that landing bar of a helicopter is called. The skid, I think. I don't know. I wasn't there when they filmed it. But it was me in the mid-shot. It had to be, so people could see me let go of the skid. They would cut back to long shot, of course, and then back to mid- again when I hit the water."

"But what about the sharks?"

"There were no sharks."

"Right. Of course. Carry on."

"The skid I was hanging from was a prop bar, naturally, not an actual helicopter landing gear. I was suspended maybe ten feet above the pool. And of course I wasn't *physically* hanging off the bar. You can't ask someone to support their body weight that long. No. I was rigged up with a safety harness that was then attached to the bar. The harness was hidden by a low camera angle—though I think you catch a glimpse of the wire in the background as it disengages, if you pause the video. I was wearing a flight jacket over it—undercover as a helicopter pilot, you see—but that was mainly to hide the harness. Here is the crucial part. The wire itself was released *by remote control*. A radio signal. A clunky antenna on the ground, the stunt coordinator pressing a giant red button. Today, of course, it would be much more streamlined. But that was how I plunged into a shark-infested swimming pool."

Andrew could almost see where she was going with this. Their driver pulled up in front of the hotel.

Officer Holly's patrol car was still out front, but the ambulance had left, presumably with the body.

"But Harry Tomlin wasn't wearing a safety harness," said Andrew.

She looked at him. "Why would he? If safety wasn't an issue."

"You mean?"

"He was killed by remote control. You get him drunk, run a wire through the slit in the back of the stunt jacket, loop it around his chest, just under the arms, and then out again. You attach that end back onto the wire itself, like a lasso. It disengages—with a *click*—and the wire recoils—*whir*. And poor Harry, having been propped against the edge of the balcony with only that wire holding him up—plunges. That's why he was *behind* the curtain. He wasn't hiding. He was hidden. Intoxicated to the point of oblivion and held in place by a wire, waiting for that fateful radio signal."

She remembered how calm the weather had been that day. The curtain that had been pulled over the edge of the balcony hung in place without a ripple. It would have hidden Harry from view perfectly.

"You would need to use a stunt jacket," Miranda said, "with its reinforced stitching so it wouldn't tear away under the weight of the actor against it, and with that hidden slice in the back for the wire to run through. It couldn't be a jacket from the current wardrobe department because Idelia would know."

Miranda remembered how confident Idelia Powell had been. *No jackets are missing!* She knew that before she even checked—because of course she would know if a jacket had gone AWOL.

"But Ned Buckley was inside Harry's room within minutes," said Andrew. "And the housekeeping staff in the hallway saw no one leave the room. What happened to the wire?"

"That's what I aim to find out."

With that, she headed into the hotel for her final confrontation. Andrew thanked the driver, scrambled to catch up.

"Come along, Andrew!" Miranda called over her shoulder. "We have to catch her before she leaves!"

"Catch who?" he called out.

"Gillian Hardner!"

MIRANDA BANGED THE bell several times before anyone came out to the front desk.

"Sorry," said the supervisor, reappearing, looking flustered. "I was called away. Officer Holly has cordoned off the family suite. It's empty, so I had to open it for her."

She hung the room key in the cubbyhole behind the desk.

"The family suite?" said Miranda.

She looked either way, not sure if she could say. "That's where it happened," she confided in stage whisper tones. "That's where Mr. Ivar was killed and then stuffed into the dumbwaiter. You could tell. There were signs of a scuffle. One of his shoes was still up there, a deck shoe that came off in the struggle, plus his headphones. A poker from the fireplace must have broken his neck, it was lying nearby, and he was then throttled with his own microphone cord, an act of pure rage, but—you can't tell anyone I told you."

"No cause for concern," said Miranda. "Andrew has been deputized."

The woman's voice dropped to a hush. "They're saying it was a ghost that killed him. But what kind of ghost uses a poker?"

"Entirely correct," said Miranda. "I suspect it was something—or rather, some*one*—more corporeal. Tell me, has Gillian Hardner checked out already? I understood she was leaving today."

She had indeed checked out. A private plane was waiting out at the golf course to whisk her away as soon as she arrived. Had Gillian already arranged a driver to take her there? Yes. They would be picking her up in the lobby in ten minutes.

Miranda turned, scanned the room. No sign of Gillian. Not yet.

"Can you tell me what's going on?" Andrew asked.

Miranda addressed the clerk instead. "You were also on duty the night the lights went out, yes?"

"I was!" she said, eyes wide. "I was on night shift. It was real spooky when it happened. We had to run to help the guests."

"Anything missing from the front desk afterward?"

"Our petty cash was still here when the lights came back on. I would have known if we were robbed."

"Not the cash. The keys."

The east wing still used keys.

"I—I didn't think to check. And anyway, the room keys are in the cubbyholes." She pointed to the rack where she had only moments ago hung the key to the family suite, having let Officer Holly in. "None of the room keys were missing. We would have noticed by now."

"Not the room keys. The skeleton key. The one that opens any door. The one that was used to let the chief of police into the Roosevelt Suite after Harry fell."

"Mr. Cornelius keeps it in his office, but he's not here right now."

"And there are no backups?"

"Housekeeping has their own set of keys, but those are in the basement, and maintenance has one, and we have an extra skeleton key here at the front desk in case a guest gets locked out. That happens sometimes. Just before the lights went off, someone called, asked if we had a pass key, I said, 'Sure!' Then a moment later they called back, said, 'Oops. My mistake. I found it.'"

"A man or a woman?"

"The person who called about the key? A man, I think. I don't remember well, because soon after that—"

"—the lights went out. Maybe check the drawer."

The skeleton key was missing.

"I . . . I don't understand. We always have one here at the front desk."

"We will need to borrow Mr. Cornelius's key, then," said Miranda with perfect authority. "Please retrieve it from his office. *Deputy Nguyen will sign for it.*"

If you say anything with enough authority, people respond. Plus, they would sign for it! What more reassurance did a person need?

As Andrew wrote out an official-sounding "receipt" on hotel stationery—"*Henceforth and herewith, I, Deputy Andrew Nguyen, do sequester said skeleton key, on this, the date of...*"–Miranda asked the desk supervisor one last question.

"Who was booked into the room directly across the hall from Harry's?"

She swallowed. "The Suicide Suite? Number 313? We don't, ah, usually rent out that room." Her voice dropped. "On account of the ghosts. Mr. Cornelius, he's nervous about that sort of thing. He thinks, if a guest were to run into the decayed corpse of the undead in their room while on holiday, it might dampen the experience. Could even end up affecting their Yelp review."

The clerk handed the key over to Joe Friday (aka Andrew), who said, "Thank you, ma'am."

But before he could touch the brim of his imaginary hat, Miranda stabbed a finger past him, pointing wildly to the lobby. "Andrew!" she cried. "Arrest that woman!"

CHAPTER TWENTY-EIGHT

A Challenge Is Made

Gillian Hardner was dressed in a shade of navy blue so dark it was almost black. A crisp confident suit, cut in sharp angles, it had clean decisive lapels and sublimely padded shoulders. Her hair, as always, was swept to one side and shellacked into place. It didn't bounce or flounce as she strode across the thick-carpeted expanse of the hotel lobby. Gillian always looked taller than she really was. Miranda Abbott could *portray* confidence. Gillian breathed it.

A porter was following with Gillian's Louis Vuitton bags on a luggage cart, but Miranda intercepted them before she could escape.

"Halt!"

Gillian turned the way a gunslinger might—if gunslingers wore power suits and scarlet lipstick—to face off against Miranda.

"If it isn't TV's Pastor Fran, and her assistant Alfonso."

"Andrew," he said. "My name. It's Andrew."

"Are you sure?"

And she said it with such confidence that for a moment he wasn't sure.

"Leaving?" said Miranda with a mocking half smile. "So soon?"

A shrug. "My work here is done."

Oh, I bet it is, thought Miranda.

"What do you two want?" Gillian asked. "I'm in a hurry." She was always in a hurry.

Miranda, haughty: "Andrew, do your duties."

Embarrassed, he leaned in to Miranda and whispered, "You do know I'm not a real deputy, right?"

"Fine. Raise a hue and cry, then. Alert Officer Holly! Where is she? Ah yes, she is up in the family suite—examining the dumb-waiter at the scene of *a murder most foul!*"

"For god's sake," said Gillian. "Between you and King Fool Sheriff, this film set has more than enough delusional amateur sleuths roaming around." She looked at her diamond-encrusted Michael Kors wristwatch. "I will give you precisely forty-seven seconds."

Wow. Power move, thought Andrew.

"Ha!" said Miranda. "Try twenty years. In jail!"

"What are you rambling on about?" said Gillian.

"The weather!" she exclaimed.

"You're railing about the weather? Isn't that usually reserved for small talk?"

"Not when it holds the clue to the mystery!" said Miranda. "You weren't at the press conference where Harry died, even though you are his executive assistant, because—and I quote your own words, hoisting you on the very petard you wished to wield as a shield against the helmet of truth!—*'My flight was delayed due to high winds.'* Except, it was perfectly calm that day. Blue skies, no winds. You *had* landed, but you needed time to skulk about, setting up your machinations. The red carpet! That was you as well. Oh, sure, Harry Tomlin deserved a red carpet, he is mildly more famous than I, so you had a red rug laid outside his door. But what that rug really did was hide the wire that ran from Harry's suite, across the hall,

MYSTERY IN THE TITLE

and under the door into Room 313. Which is where the wire was anchored and where it recoiled to after Harry was released in the other room, leaving the Roosevelt Suite locked and without anyone inside after Harry fell. Deny it at your peril!"

Andrew recognized that line from an episode of *Pastor Fran.* *Deny it at your peril!*

"And as for the fatally greedy Silas Ivar," Miranda continued, "when he tried to blackmail you because he had a recording of what you'd done, you killed him too! The stunt jacket Harry was wearing was from another MOW. With your connections, it would be easy enough to attain. You covered your tracks, but not well enough. Because the very jacket you happened to choose had been worn by Poe Regal himself!"

"Time's up."

The forty-seven seconds had expired, as had Gillian's patience. "I am leaving now and I hope never to see you or this collection of weirdos you call a town again." She thumbed through her phone and said, "But before I leave you to your inane and possibly libelous accusations— Here." She showed them the weather forecast for LA on the morning of Harry's death. *Severe winds. Flights canceled. Expect delays.* "Not the weather in Happy Rock, you idiot. The weather out of LA. I sat on a runway for two hours. You can check the federal aviation flight logs if you like. Now, if you'll excuse me—"

But then Gillian's phone vibrated in her hand and her aggravation level soared anew.

"Great," she said, glowering at the screen. "Just what I need. It never ends." Furiously typing. *"This is NOT Harry. Harry's dead. Read the papers, moron."* Then, to herself, "Damned charities."

"Who set up the rug in the hallway outside Harry's suite?" Miranda asked, feeling winded at Gillian's sudden ironclad alibi.

"I don't know. The hotel? Who cares? It doesn't matter. Harry's gone and still they keep texting, calling." Her phone vibrated again. She answered, and before the voice on the other end could say *"Hello, this is the Red Cross,"* Gillian was shouting, "He's dead. Okay? Take him off your list."

Autodialers, subscription renewals, annual donation requests. How many services and memberships could one man sign up for?

"You field all of Harry's calls?" said Miranda.

"Of course. I'm his executive assistant, or I was. They're all redirected through me. Harry didn't answer his own phone—I did. And once I get to LA and resolve the fiasco over his will, I am blocking every number and then throwing this phone into the ocean." A uniformed driver appeared, holding up her name. "There's my ride," she said.

Miranda stopped her.

"You would know, then. On the day of the press conference. You would know who called him just before he died."

Gillian said a word. Not a name. A single word, and with that, Miranda knew everything. She was momentarily stunned, but then stepped aside graciously. "You may go now."

"I always could. You thought you could detain me? Really?" A laugh—a cackle, anyway—and she was gone. Gillian Hardner exited stage right, still shaking her head.

After a long, thoughtful pause, Miranda asked Andrew, "This 'cloud' you always talk about. You can send messages through it. Signals?"

"I guess. If you have an app."

There is an app for everything, she thought.

...

THE KEY TO Room 313 turned with a creak. The sort of creak one hears in movie scenes set in dungeons. The lock wasn't oiled, hadn't been for some time. There was hardly cause to, considering this room was rarely, if ever, occupied. It was, after all, the Suicide Suite.

Miranda and Andrew crept in and the door closed behind them. The interior was stale and dimly lit and full of shadows undefined. They were looking for clues. Evidence of a murderer's handiwork. With everyone preoccupied over the death of Silas Ivar, it was a safe bet that this room would be empty. Safe, but erroneous.

Andrew fumbled with the standing lamp near the door, but the light didn't come on. It was only then he saw the cord lying loose across the carpet in the half-light. Someone had unplugged it. Andrew followed the cord with his eyes, and there, sitting in a chair watching them, was a darkened silhouette, like a mountain, like a man.

"Hello, Poe," said Miranda.

"You should leave," he said, his voice flat.

"I think not."

"This doesn't concern you. You should go. Now."

His heavy face was in the shadows, but the threatening undertone in his mumbled diction was clear. She calculated how far away he was. Poe moved slowly now. If he tried to lumber across the room at them, they would have plenty of time to get out. This wasn't the Poe Regal of old, and she wasn't afraid. She wanted answers.

"I'm not leaving until you tell me the truth," she said. "A rare commodity in the world of Poe Regal, I realize, but the time has come. Confess. You wanted that role badly, didn't you, Poe? A chance for redemption."

"That's all any of us want, Miranda. Redemption. You should know that better than anyone."

"A souvenir?"

He wasn't sure what she meant, and neither was Andrew.

"The jacket," she said. "The one Harry died in. The one you used in the flying scenes during your foray into family entertainment. You kept it fondly, as a souvenir, after the leprechaun movie, yes?"

"I barely remember making that picture, let alone fondly. Why would I want a souvenir? I was high on tequila and testosterone the entire time. You. Should. Go."

"Or what? You're going to employ some of your patented Navy SEAL ninja skills?"

Miranda's long-suffering assistant Andrew whispered, "Maybe we should. Go, I mean. We can call you-know-who."

"Ned?" she said, full voice. "No need!" Turning to Poe, "You were the first one to call Zab on hearing about Harry's tragic accident. Almost immediately, as though you were expecting it."

Andrew, whispering more frantically now, "Really. I think we should leave. Something's not quite right. I've got a bad feeling about this, as they say in the movies."

There was an unnatural aspect to how Poe was sitting there, arms flat on the sides of the chair, back straight, immobile in his red, dragon-embroidered silk muumuu. True, Poe Regal sat for most of his films now, even the one where he was a ballroom dance instructor turned assassin. But this seemed different, this seemed off.

"Where were you the day Harry Tomlin died?" she asked.

"I was alone on a mountaintop in Nepal, meditating," he said.

"No you weren't."

"At a remote dojo in Okinawa?"

"Try again."

"A rainforest in Paraguay?"

"Puh-leese. The closest you've come to a rainforest is the nearest buffet at Trader Joe's." Cruel, perhaps. But she was done playing around. "You were somewhere near a phone, because you called to offer your condolences."

His shoulders slumped slightly. "I was at boot camp."

"Boot camp?" Andrew asked. Cool! "Marines?"

"Dieting."

"Oh."

"And emotional therapy," said Miranda. *"Life-sized origami.* You folded Silas Ivar into that dumbwaiter easily enough, didn't you?"

"My god, Miranda. You think I killed the man? You couldn't be more wrong. That's why I'm here, to find out who did."

Miranda was not easily appeased by such protestations, however.

"The only thing I don't understand," she said, "is the timing of it. How did you manage to slip into town, unnoticed, and then throw the switch on the hotel's electrical panel, hook up poor drunk Harry into that wire, and . . ." Her voice trailed off.

It couldn't have been Poe Regal, she realized. It couldn't precisely *because* he was Poe Regal. He was too recognizable. Heck, the menfolk in town would have rushed him like fangirls at a Beatles concert. Poe wouldn't have been able to sneak around here for three days without word getting out. Everyone would have known. *Poe Regal is in town!* They would have given him the key to Happy Rock and his own parade before he could reach the hotel, and, let's face it, it's not like his ninja skills were as finely honed as they once were.

"The rug," she said. "The red rug outside Harry's hotel suite, the one placed there in lieu of a red carpet. It wasn't because Harry was the star. You took over as star of the show, and you didn't get one. I had to practically beg for mine. No, it was put down solely to hide that wire."

A creak in the next room gave away the fact that someone else was in the Suicide Suite.

"You can come out now, Zab," said Miranda.

CHAPTER TWENTY-NINE

Take the Shot

He had a gun. Of course he had a gun.

Alan Zabic stepped from the shadows, 9 mm in hand, smiling handsomely.

"It's a Beretta," he said, referring to the semiautomatic pistol he was brandishing. "I thought it apt, considering we are dealing with the faded TV stars of yesteryear." When Andrew looked at him blankly, Zab sighed. "*Baretta*? The TV show? Fought crime with his pet cockatoo? No?" He and Miranda exchanged looks with a shake of the head that said "Kids these days."

Zab waved Andrew and Miranda away from the door with the barrel.

"Over here, both of you, next to Kung Fu Sheriff. And Andrew, if I see your hand try to sneak down to your phone again to call for help, you will receive a bullet in the belly. Got that?"

Poe had been trying to warn them away, but it was too late. Miranda and Andrew came across and stood on either side of the regally seated Mr. Regal as though he were the Lincoln Memorial.

Andrew was trying not to tremble. Poe seemed immobilized.

And Miranda Abbott, star of stage and screen? Miranda Abbott was fearless.

"Not even a name," she said, her voice defiant. "A word. A single word. That's all it took for everything to unravel. When I asked Gillian Hardner who'd been calling Harry Tomlin the morning he plunged through the atrium, she said '*nobody*.' There was no one phoning Harry as we sat waiting at that press conference. Yet there you were, Zab, pretending to be frantic, dialing him up. You weren't calling Harry, you were triggering the release on the wire—*with an app!* The ingénue was on her phone as well, vanity searching; I could see her screen. But you? You were sending Harry Tomlin to his death. Poor Harry, drunk and propped against the balcony, the wire retracted like a fishing line, whipping under the door, below the red rug you had laid in the hallway to hide it, and into this very room. You set it up and then went down to the press conference. Perfect alibi. Housekeeping were making their rounds after that, and they saw no one enter or leave Harry's suite, because no one did. It was done remotely, with a *click* and *whir*."

"Very clever," said Zab. "Considering that I'm the one holding the gun."

"The trampled roses, that was Jacquelyn. But the power outage and the jimmied door? That was you. Amid the confusion, you filched the skeleton key. That was how you entered Harry's suite, how you discovered it had a dumbwaiter. It was you who asked Valor Films to contact the hotel and have the dumbwaiter blocked off behind that painting. You weren't protecting Harry from an assassin who might slip in via the shaft. No. You were making sure the room was entirely sealed so that the sole explanation for Harry's death was a drunken misadventure, a tumble off the balcony. Only thing I can't figure out is, why that hideous jacket?"

Andrew whispered, "Are you sure we should be discussing fashion choices at a time like this?"

"Ah yes," said Zab with a sly smile. "The ugly green leprechaun stunt jacket. Well, as you know, I've worked on many a Pindaric holiday classic—if you can call the dreck they pump out every Easter, Arbor Day, and Presidents' Day 'classics.' And really, when did 'an Arbor Day romance' become a thing? Anyway. Among Pindaric's family-friendly pap was, of course, *The World's Fattest Leprechaun*."

"Largest," Poe mumbled from his chair. "*World's* Largest *Leprechaun*."

"I stand corrected," said Zab. "Anyway, having been on set of *The World's Most Ridiculously Bloated Puffy-Faced Dye-Jobbed Leprechaun*, I knew I needed a stunt jacket for the wire to go through, one with the proper cut, reinforced under the arms so it didn't shred the material or have the wire get caught as it retracted, pulling Harry back instead of recoiling away from him cleanly. I knew I couldn't use a stunt jacket from this production; it might be noticed as missing. I assumed the jacket itself would get shredded in the fall, but if it didn't and someone recognized it, I figured it would lead back to Poe. Even better. Harry's replacement under investigation? That would gum up the works even more."

"And that was the entire point, wasn't it?" said Miranda. "To gum up the works."

"You're catching on," he said with a grin. "The real mystery is how Jabba the Hutt here figured it out. He was 'shadowing me,' though I use that word in the loosest sense. Not particularly stealth-like, our Poe, following me through the hotel, clumsily hiding behind potted palms when I turned around. His wheezing gave him away. It was sort of like having an asthmatic water buffalo trying to tiptoe up on you. So I lured him here, and voilà! Mr. Regal was just about to fire a self-inflicted bullet of remorse into his pachydermal skull, when who should stumble in but Queen Miranda and her sidekick,

Skippy the Wonder Boy." Zab looked to Poe, genuinely curious. "How did you figure it out, by the way? Not the murder, but the scheme behind it?"

"I read it in the twitch of a lip," said Poe. At first, Miranda thought he was getting mystical and metaphorical again, but Poe elucidated for them in that low, raspy voice of his. "When that reporter kept mispronouncing my name, I could see that you were trying to goad me into reacting. I could see it as you tried not to smirk. I know that look. I know it well. People have been treating me like a punchline—and a punching bag—for years. That gleam in your eye, that twitch of the lip, told me everything. I realized then that you wanted me to get angry, to turn over the table, storm out. You wanted me to be dysfunctional and confrontational. And I asked myself, Why? Reason seemed clear: to sink the project. Why? I figure it's a gross/net scam, where your production bonus was calculated as a percent of total revenue, not the actual profit. It's very cunning, and I should know—I have an MBA from Stanford."

"You have an MBA from Stanford?" said Zab. "No. You don't have an MBA from Stanford. Okay?"

"With a minor in tai chi."

"An MBA from Stanford with a minor in tai chi? What are you talking about? Chrissake. I would have killed you without the scheming, just to shut you up."

Miranda wanted to know who had signed off on it.

"Who signed off on it?" cried Zab. "I did! Those fools at Valor, with their legal documents translated by someone who was in way over her head, from English to French, back to English, and then vetted—by me! A mix-up between gross and net? Between total income and actual profit? Oh no, it was much better than that! I saw the real error—and the opportunity it presented—when my initial contract came back and my fee was scaled *to the final budget*. The bigger the budget, the higher my pay grade. The more expensive the film became, the more money I received. It was glorious!"

"The genuine Corinthian leather binding on Lachlan Todd's script," said Miranda. "That was why I always hesitated over your romantic overtures. I thought you were simply trying too hard, but now I see." She turned to Andrew. "I apologize. Your initial instincts were correct. When something seems too good to be true, it usually is." She looked back at Zab. "A pay-or-play contract? As an initial offer? I should have known better. An agent would've had to fight tooth and nail for that. You presented it to me on a silver cushion—and without any agent insisting on it."

"Platter," said Andrew. "On a silver *platter*."

"Yes, yes, on a silk platter. Don't be so pedantic, Andrew."

"Pedantic?" said Andrew. "You're the one who is always correcting me on whether it is *whom* or *who*."

"It's *who* or *whom*, darling."

Fortunately, Zab was able to bring the conversation back on track. "Look. We need to stay focused on the real issue here. Me murdering you. As for the 'pay-or-play' deal I offered, I'm sorry to say it wasn't just you. Every actor had the same clause. And every member of the crew had a completion provision. Generous to a fault, that's me. From best boy to key grip, they will all be generously compensated. It's why no one complained as the shoot went off the rails. I even gave the background players lines and character names, so they'd have to be paid as principal performers, which would drive up costs *and* slow down production as they struggled with their parts. The bigger the budget, the bigger my pay."

Ah, thought Miranda. That would explain Wrench Haldex. It would also explain the hiring of out-of-town security and private paramedics for the press conference.

"They'd need travel and accommodation, as well as fees," she said. "And the press trip, was that a junket too? Did you cover the travel costs for media and paparazzi?"

"Of course I did! I'm a very munificent person—when it comes to other people's money. An open bar, 24-7? For *actors??* You would have to be insane to do something like that. Fortunately, I am. Plus an entire fleet of sedans, brought in and standing by, night and day, ready to whisk people—where exactly? Not sure. It's not like we're in Vegas. No matter, the drivers were paid very well to be on call."

"That's why crafts services had a Michelin star!" said Andrew. "And that's why you could afford Idelia for costumes!"

"Rhymes with *negligent iatromelia*. Do you have any idea how much that polka-dot princess costs? And let's not forget flying in a team of graphic designers to prepare *a storyboard*—for an MOW! The audacity of that boggles even my own mind. Or renting out an entire wing of the Duchess Hotel, in the off-season and at above market rates, and paying to keep the Bengal Lounge open for the entirety of the shoot. I paid the hotel to *not* renovate. Think about that!" His eyes were shining with glee. "They got paid to *not* spend money."

"You paid off Harry's entire Happy Crew as well," said Miranda.

"And replaced them with ones that were unqualified and/or prima donnas. Talk about ballooning the budget! We were basically paying for two complete production crews—and then using the more inept of the two. I even flew in sushi and gourmet popcorn on a private jet for your silly Pastor Fran Fridays. I wanted to make sure the sushi stayed cold and the popcorn stayed warm."

"But why those horrid flavors?" Andrew asked. "Yam and wasabi, honeysuckle and lemon, even—god help us—salted caramel."

"Oh, that was for my own amusement, just to watch you fools choking it down, pretending you were enjoying it, because I am—what would you call it?—a prick. At least Bea had the good sense to 'accidentally' knock hers over."

"I liked the lemon popcorn," said Miranda. "You could really taste the lemon." Then, remembering she was facing down the barrel of a known killer, she declared, "The gig is up!"

On *Pastor Fran* that always ended things. They usually threw to commercial, and when they came back, the miscreant was already in manacles.

Zab, however, refused to play his role properly and he remained, stubbornly, angrily, pointing his weapon at Miranda despite her declaration.

"Jig," whispered Andrew. "The *jig* is up."

"Oh my god, Miranda's right," said Zab. "You're so pedantic. In this case, either works. The *gig* is also definitely up—forever."

Miranda ignored the threat implicit in this. "And Harry Tomlin? How did you manage to ensnare him in this nefarious scheme of yours?"

"Ensnare? Are you kidding me? Harry dove into my open arms. I was searching for the most expensive but financially troubled star I could find. And Harry fit the part perfectly. The Eurotrash at Valor Films couldn't believe I got him for a lowly MOW! I started adding clauses to his contract, into French and back again. And the game was on! That whole tearful speech I made to you, Miranda, how 'we're in hock for Harry's legal costs, his salad dressings are chock-full of gluten, etc.,' I basically told you what I was doing, and you were too dim to figure it out!"

"You didn't have to kill him," she said.

"Oh, but I did. He brought in that broken-down cowboy crony of his—I couldn't talk Harry out of that; he wouldn't budge when it came to Crash La Rue—and liquor loosens lips. It was only a matter of time before he spilled the proverbial beans. Harry himself suggested the manner of his own demise. He had drunkenly suggested, 'Zab, buddy, why don't I rappel down the side of the hotel, make a splash?'

He always had poor impulse control. So I checked his error-riddled contract. In case of death or injury, we would have to take over *all* of Harry's debts, *if* said death or injury occurred during production. We were acting as an insurance company, in effect. How to kill him when there were so many witnesses? It was quite the conundrum. Film sets are notoriously crowded, as you know. But in the contract, our shooting schedule was defined *by date*, not actual on-set filming. And Day One began with a press conference."

"That's why you were so upset when Leni found the note," said Miranda. "In the case of suicide, none of this would have applied."

"I was very annoyed with Leni. That note threatened the entire scheme, though she didn't realize that, of course. She was trying to—get this—have 'principles.' Who the hell ever heard of principles when it comes to the film industry? I tried to talk her out of revealing it, pled with her. 'Leni, think of his exes!' said I. 'They'd be left with nothing.' But she was adamant. Insisted I show Harry's note, *'I'm going to do it!,'* to—and I quote—'law enforcement officials.' Harry meant, 'I'm going to do the stunt, I'm going to rappel down.' But I couldn't tell anyone that, because it would give away the very manner of his death. Fortunately, this being Rubesville, Oregon, local law enforcement consisted mainly of a bumpkin sheriff and his—"

"Chief of police, thank you very much! I will not have you insulting my friends."

"Mea culpa. A bumpkin *chief of police.* When the coroner's office announced that the note was too ambiguous for them to rule Harry's death a suicide, I could have wept with joy. I almost did, in fact. I'm sentimental that way."

Miranda thought about the anguish and pain she'd often seen in Zab's eyes. At the time, she'd thought, He isn't a very good actor, he can't hide his emotions. She now realized that Alan Zabic was a very good actor. Very good, indeed.

"Of course," said Zab, "no scheme ever goes entirely to plan. What I hadn't counted on was the charity angle, the funds he owed to charities from his salad dressing and olive oil debacle. A certain charitable kingpin, one Mr. Olio, arrived on the scene. Cares about humanity and such. Really hard to bribe. Impossible, in fact. When I realized he had been snooping around my car looking for papers, I was terrified that he'd figured out the plot. But no, he was there to make sure Harry—and later, Harry's estate—paid the full amount that had been pledged to various charities. Such sticklers, these do-gooder types. In the end, I had to pay him—out of my own pocket, mind you!—to stop him from shutting down production with a lien on the funds owed to Harry's estate. It was a very large sum." Tears welled in Zab's eyes. "That part really hurt."

"Is that why you had to sell your car and Rolex?" Andrew asked.

"God no. That was to pander to your sympathy, to cast myself as a hapless but good-hearted man out of his depth and trying his best. I was playing *a role*. You should understand that, Andrew, spending your time as you do with the flamboyant Miranda Abbott. I had that greasy mechanic—"

"Owen," said Miranda coldly. "*My friend*, Owen McCune."

"I had *your friend* price my Aston Martin above blue book, so if someone was rash enough to buy it, I would still make a profit. Of course, no one did, not in this town, what with there not being a gun rack or a Greenpeace sticker on the back. As for the Rolex, I just bought it back myself. I had to make you think I was in financial straits. Couldn't let you suspect the real reason everything was careening out of control."

"But it wasn't just the car," Andrew said. "I saw you! I saw you looking at real estate postings. I know you stopped by Atticus's office to see about buying a home on Tillamook Bay."

"You thought you could tail me in Happy Rock? A town this size?

I knew you were following me. That was *a performance*, Andrew, played to an audience of one. You do stand out in this town, just a bit, not wearing any plaid."

"Well, I do have a pair of boxers with the Boy George tartan. But those are mainly ironic."

"The haircut, though," said Zab. "That certainly reeks of local sensibilities."

Embarrassed, Andrew mumbled, "Klips 'N Kurls. They do pets mainly."

Speaking of mumbling, what was happening with Poe Regal? He sat, arms on the sides of his chair, immobile and silent. If it weren't for the gentle sound of him wheezing, he hardly seemed there at all.

But now he spoke, and his voice was low and freighted with meaning. "I studied the art of pet grooming in Bangladesh. You need to ask for a side-cut feather trim, Andrew, like you might with a Bernese mountain dog. It works well with human hair too."

Zab pointed his gun at Poe's head. "I swear to god..."

"You knew I was following you, so why the charade?" Andrew wanted to know. "Why pretend that you'd found your refuge in Happy Rock?"

"Because," said Zab, "you were the only one. The only one who sensed that something wasn't quite right. I'd managed to charm and disarm everyone, except you. Pretending to be sad, yearning for a home, moping about as though I were enamored with this ridiculous town—and Miranda. Oh, I was besotted! I was appealing to the love you have for her, Andrew. I could see it in your eyes, how much you care for her, how much you want her to be happy."

It might have been a touching moment, were it not for Zab's next words.

"So I thought, he's such a sap, I'm sure I can exploit this. And it worked! I knew that once you thought I was here because of an unrequited love for Miranda Abbott, your suspicions would be assuaged. And they were. That would-be love triangle? Miranda caught between Edgar and myself? That was for your benefit, Andrew, not Miranda's."

Miranda straightened her shoulders. "That's it," she said, glaring at him. "I am breaking up with you."

"What? We're not together."

"Exactly! Because I broke up with you. I am a married woman, I remind you."

"See!" said Zab, laughing, feeling both exasperated and vindicated. "That's why I cast you! You brought that special brand of craziness to the project. Or at least, that's what I was hoping for. I remembered how you'd gotten into that drunken brawl at the Golden Globes—"

"Bea Arthur had it coming."

"I wanted to turn our MOW into a gong show. The worse it went, the better for me. I would be the captain on the SS *Minnow*, lashed to the mast, waves from all sides, insisting we sail on. Did you know that Jacquelyn de Valeur's last film was an experimental forty-two-hour single shot of a melon rotting, while nude dancers writhed about, out of focus, in the background, titled *Death Comes for Us All*? And do you know who the director was on that? Leni Vedette. I chose the worst possible cinematographer for this project, and she in turn chose the worst possible director—one who shoots her films in sequence, no less! It was sublime. This was *my* masterpiece, my magnum opus, my mise-en-scène. I arranged it, I choreographed it, I set it in motion. I was the agent of chaos—and creation!"

"When your eyes get all buggy like that, it's disconcerting," Miranda said.

"What I hadn't counted on was Poe Regal trying to become a better person," said Zab, still mystified by it. "I thought, Here is real trouble. Hell, I had to pay Leni a bonus just to work with him. She didn't ask, I offered. Other people's money, you know. And then Kung Fu Sheriff shows up and—what? He's nice now? I was *very* disappointed in you, Poe. No offense."

"None taken."

"Even Leni seemed oddly relaxed this morning," said Zab.

I bet she did, thought Miranda.

"I have to say," Zab admitted, "I was surprised with you as well, Miranda. I almost cackled when I kept you in the attic at Bea's. I expected you to throw a fit, demand a bigger suite than Harry's. It's why I kept that one suite empty, waiting for you and your prima donna tendencies to bubble to the surface. I was assuming you'd demand the room be fully renovated, with fresh flowers delivered daily, etc. But no. You accepted the attic with grace. That should have warned me. I should have known you'd changed. The Miranda Abbott who punched out Bea Arthur would never have turned down a luxury suite at a hotel just to stay in a shabby, alliteratively named bed-and-breakfast. Though I did throw in a red carpet—or rug, anyway—just to misdirect you from the real purpose of the one outside Harry's room. Hint: it was to hide the wire, as you suggested. I expected you to be a train wreck on set. Instead, you were oddly endearing. Maddening, irritating, annoying, and infuriating. But also endearing."

She glowed. *Endearing!*

"You were not nearly the difficult star I had hoped for. Again, *very* disappointed, Miranda. I even hired your estranged husband to rewrite the entire script of his old nemesis Lachlan Todd. I wanted cats and dogs, oil and water, Capulets and Montagues, Hatfields and McCoys, Letterman and Leno. I wanted turmoil and standoffs, fireworks and failures. I knew you and Poe had worked together before, on that dismally un-erotic erotic thriller *Shimmer Spy*. A *real* pastor would have shown more passion than you did. It was sort of the opposite of sexy. I also knew Poe had earlier appeared on your TV show as a background bullfighter. So imagine my delight on seeing 'Trapdoor Toreador' on the playlist when I dropped by, one of the cheesiest *Pastor Fran*s ever made. And I am an aficionado of cheesy TV. When I cast Poe, I assumed that the two of you would be daggers drawn, but no, it was almost like there was some sort of strange... connection."

Memories of The Kiss surfaced, but Miranda fought them back down. "Poe and I are professionals. We rise above such matters!"

Zab shrugged. "Okay. But did you know that Luckless Lachlan has lodged a formal complaint with the Writers Guild arbitration board? Interesting dilemma. Should we hire a team of lawyers to fight it? Or agree to pay the standard 150 percent penalty? Answer: whichever one is more expensive."

"You'll never get away with it!" This was something Pastor Fran always said.

"Oh, but I already have. It's all going to collapse, taking down the varied production companies with it, thereby covering my tracks amid the welter of lawsuits and countersuits that are sure to follow. A cluster of Chapter 7 bankruptcies. Full asset liquidation. Brutal. And did I mention, under the terms of my garbled contract, I have to be paid first, prior to any other creditors? This is usually where the villain throws back his head with a hearty *bwahahaha*, but I have more restraint than that."

"And not one murder, but two," said Miranda. "Developed a taste for it, did you?"

"Two? Oh right, the sound guy. That was my only real mistake: pissing off Silas Ivar. 'Why are we hiring amateurs at union rates?' he wanted to know. He figured something was up. When I brought in Melvin of Manure Manor to be his boom operator, that was the final straw. That malodorous kid didn't know what he was doing, which was, of course, the whole idea: to ruin as many shots as possible, to run out the clock every day. It was like a Cat Stevens riff: *I'm being followed by a boom shadow… boom shadow, boom shadow.*"

"Silas had inadvertently recorded the sound of you releasing Harry to his death while Silas was gathering room tone," said Miranda. "He worked out what had happened, began eavesdropping on the crew, putting it together. Wanted you to pay him for his silence. Ironic, considering he was a soundman."

"Artiste," said Zab, correcting her. "A sound *artiste*. And yes, he was trying to shake me down. You figured that out, did you? Well done. He wanted me to transfer my entire salary—plus bonus!—into an offshore account. Said he would delete the relevant sound files in front of me. But of course, blackmail only ever ends when there is a death—either the victim's or the blackmailer's. I met with Silas in the empty family suite, directly below Poe's room. A simple chiropractic readjustment of his neck vertebrae, courtesy of the fireplace poker—there's an actual life-sized origami for you, Poe!—and a cord around his trachea just to be sure, and I sent Silas Ivar down, in every sense, silence assured. I had to kill him anyway, so I figured I might as well do it in as dramatic a manner as possible. It guaranteed another police investigation. More delays! More cost run-ups! More money for me! It was sublime."

"And now?" said Miranda.

He smiled at her. "With you, it was always in the cards, I'm afraid to say. If the leading lady dies, we would have to reshoot everything. All of your scenes. Every one of them—from the top. Have you seen your husband's revised script? You are in every single scene. That's your Edgar. Still foolishly in love. Still trying to make you a star."

"I am a star!"

And with that, Miranda Abbott—or should we say Pastor Fran?—

lunged forward to deliver a deadly perfect three-point karate kick to Zab's jaw.

"*Haiii-ya!*"

Unfortunately, it was a "TV" karate kick she delivered. She had been trained to just miss the person she was kicking, and she did that now, expertly avoiding contact with Zab.

"What the hell was that?" He stepped back, aimed the gun higher. "Back it up, sister."

"Sister? I wasn't a nun! I was a pastor. You're thinking of Sally Field—and you, sir, are very rude!"

Andrew pulled her back beside him. "Don't escalate the situation," he hissed.

"I planned to kill you on the last day of shooting," Zab explained. "Between the Martini Shot and the Abby Singer, as they say. Right before the final setup, so no 'Ladies and gentlemen, that's a wrap on Miranda Abbott,' although your corpse would probably end up wrapped in a sheet before it was removed, which would have provided some consolation. But you've forced my hand prematurely, and now I must improvise."

"You are not going to kill us," she declared. "I won't allow it."

"I don't think it's up to us," Andrew said frantically.

"Do you know the legend of the Happy Rock newlyweds' murder-suicide?" Zab asked. "Happened right here in this room. Hotel is cursed, so I'm told." Then, to Andrew: "Such a shame that you are going to be the one to kill her. A spurned lover, by all accounts."

"I'm gay."

"Oh. Okay. Good point. Then—*jealousy*. Jealousy over Poe here. You wanted him for yourself, and she was elbowing her way in."

"Are you serious!" Andrew was mortified. "You think that *that*"— he gestured to Poe, immobile in the chair—"is my type? Not even close!" Then, to Poe: "No offense."

"None taken."

"Fine," said Zab. "Just a good old-fashioned double murder-suicide, then. As Miranda's personal assistant, you were fed up at the way she treats you."

Well, that is plausible, I suppose, Andrew thought.

"And when Poe tried to stop you from killing her by heroically sitting on his ass, you shot him too." Zab patted the pocket of his Tommy Bahama shirt. "You then died clutching the missing skeleton key. Do you see how these scenes practically write themselves?"

"Was none of it real?" Miranda asked, her voice breaking.

"You really do live in your own world, don't you? Hey. News flash, Miranda. You're an actor. You're not a real detective. You just played one on TV. Pastor Fran doesn't exist. Pastor Fran can only be enjoyed ironically."

Tears were in her eyes. "You lied—about everything. You probably lied when you said you had enjoyed my performance as Blanche DuBois in *Streetcar Named Desire*."

"No, I was being sincere about that. You really nailed the role of a neurotic, delusional narcissist."

"Thank you."

"Anyway. Time to take your final curtain call," Zab said. He moved the gun back and forth between Andrew and Miranda, trying to decide whom to kill first, settled on Miranda.

She felt her throat constrict. "I thought I knew you," she said. "I thought I might even love you."

He didn't know if she was acting, and neither did she.

And then—

Something unexpected. Poe Regal . . . rose.

"It's shimmer time," he wheezed, standing up slowly, towering above Zab. He really was a mountain of a man.

"I thought you were tied to that chair," said Andrew.

"No. I was just sitting down."

Zab, laughing maniacally, reminded Poe, "I have the gun, remember?" He leveled the Beretta at him. "Looks like Mr. Regal has volunteered to go first." (And yes, he intentionally pronounced it like *seagull*, because of course he did.) "Let's see you dodge a bullet in real time, Poe!"

But Poe Regal didn't blink. Didn't flinch. Took a giant step forward, in fact, until the barrel was pressed against his chest.

"Do it," he said. "Take the shot."

Zab snorted. "What? Are you kidding me? This isn't one of your stupid–"

And in that instant, the gun was gone and Zab was on his knees with his arm twisted back, shrieking.

"Wristlock!" Miranda shouted.

Andrew kicked the gun away and Miranda cheered. Too soon, as it turned out.

Poe was quickly winded, and he had to step back to catch his breath. "Gimme a moment," he said, sitting down again.

At which point Zab was up, gunless and nursing a twisted wrist, his eyes wild with rage. And now Andrew was upon him, tackling him to the ground and then fighting his way in and around, forcing his hands under Zab's arms and then locking his fingers behind the neck.

Zab bellowed and rolled, this way and that, and Andrew fought to stay on.

"Say, that's pretty good," Poe mumbled, still sitting. "Tae kwon do?"

"Little brother," Andrew gasped, wrestling his leg around Zab the way he had with his younger sibling when they were kids. Andrew could feel his grip begin to slip as Zab continued to buck and roar.

Miranda was jumping up and down, applauding from the sidelines. "You are doing so well, Andrew! So wonderfully well!"

"Um, li'l help?" Andrew's interlocked fingers were beginning to separate, one by one. Poe was still out of breath and Miranda was still applauding, and Andrew was losing his grip...

"That's enough, son. I'll take it from here." They turned and there, facing them, backlit in the doorway, was Happy Rock's finest: Ned Buckley, hand resting on his holster. "Good work, deputy."

Andrew let go and climbed back onto his feet. Zab, red-faced and no longer as handsome as he once was, stayed on his knees.

"Heard of some hoopla happening up here," said Ned. "I'm not a fan of hoopla. Never much cared for it." He nodded to the security camera that had been installed in the hall above the door to Harry's old suite, directly across from them. "Fish-eye lens. A perfect 360. I was asking after you, Zab, and the hotel staff said they'd spotted you and Mr. Poe on the security monitor entering this very room. It was caught on camera. And the camera never lies, isn't that what they say? Anyways. I figured you were meeting about movie business. Not really my concern. But what *is* my concern is this: Mr. Olio informed me that you had paid off Harry's debts to the charities out of your own pocket, Zab. Why? Those were Harry's shenanigans, not yours. Why would you feel responsible? Makes a fella wonder what else you're trying to hide. Now I know."

"I was so close!" Zab snarled.

"Horseshoes and hand grenades, my friend. You've produced enough of these movies. You know what comes next. *You have the right to remain silent...*"

And as Ned Buckley secured the handcuffs on Alan Zabic's wrists, he thought perhaps it was apropos that these police warnings were known as "reading someone their Miranda rights."

CHAPTER THIRTY

Till Debt Do Us Part

Miranda woke up in Edgar's bed.

She could hear the gentle snoring of her sleeping companion next to her, could feel the warmth of that body snuggled up against hers. A thought, unbidden, popped into her head: *All is right in the world.* Then her sleeping companion farted, convulsed, and began licking herself. Loudly.

Miranda gave Emmy a gentle pat. The golden Lab rolled onto her back for a morning tummy rub, the absolute best way for any dog to start their day.

Miranda remembered when she and Edgar had shared a king-sized bed with another golden Lab, Oscar, long since gone to doggy heaven, who had slept curled up quietly at their feet. Now Miranda was sharing Edgar's much smaller double bed with Emmy, who easily took up half the available room and who twitched, thrashed, and snorted her way through the night. Sometimes Emmy would chase squirrels in her sleep, whimpering with either joy or disappointment, depending on how close she'd come to catching them. Her legs would piston, her tail would thump against the mattress, and Miranda would gently stroke her until she went quietly back to a dreamless slumber.

It was interesting how a new dog could make you miss the old dog more.

She remembered Oscar as a puppy, but Emmy? Emmy was Edgar's dog, and this was Edgar's bed. She was just visiting.

The muffled jingle of the bell in the bookstore below and Emmy was up and out, galumphing down the stairs, expecting Edgar—finding Andrew instead.

"Hey there, girl, whoa! Easy!"

Miranda followed Emmy down, cinching her robe as she went.

"She likes you!" said Miranda. "How did that happen?"

Emmy was usually so growly and territorial around Andrew, but not today. Tail thumping, she was jumping up and jostling him.

"Desperate times call for desperate measures," Andrew said. "I started putting bacon in my pocket."

Sure enough, Andrew retrieved a handkerchief, unwrapped a strip, and—*whoof!* the bacon was inhaled.

Edgar had warned Miranda: *It's two-thirds dry to one-third wet. That's it. And NO more breakfast burritos from Owen the Human Garbage Disposal. Got it? I don't want to come back to a gaseous dog again.*

Edgar was at an overnight trade show for booksellers in Seattle, and it would have been too hard on the dog to make her stay in Bea's yard while he was away, so he'd left the keys to the store with Miranda and she had stayed at his place instead.

"Does bacon give dogs gas?" she mused. But didn't bother waiting for an answer. "Come, come, Andrew. To the kitchenette. I shall make you some chamomile tea. Edgar has scones, I believe, which we shall plunder with impunity."

Miranda had paid all of Andrew's back wages and what she owed

Bea for the room, plus more. Only the first payment on the MOW had gone through. The rest was in legal limbo given the criminal charges against Alan Zabic and the pending fraud proceedings against A to Z by the other companies after they'd learned what he'd done. What she had received was more than generous, though, and Miranda was now sitting on something unusual for her: savings.

"Did you see the Saturday paper?" Andrew asked, passing over the latest edition of *The Weekly Picayune.* "Chester and that French-language interpreter are getting married. It's in Obituaries— by accident, I'm sure." (*The Weekly Picayune* was a little lax on categorizing its back copy. Weddings, Engagements, Birthdays, Obituaries: it was all one and the same.) "She works at the hotel now," he said. "That's why she was wearing the blazer. She'd quit work on the film. Oversees the hotel's 'French market.'"

"Do we get a lot of French-speaking visitors here in Happy Rock?" she wondered.

"Mainly Canadians, from what I gather," Andrew said. "Walkin' around, all smug. 'Oh, our mountains are much nicer, eh?' 'Our trees are much bigger.' You know how insufferable they can be."

"True, true. I once dated Bill Shatner, remember. That was in his *T.J. Hooker* glory days, not his space-gun and alien phase."

"In entertainment news, Poe Regal will be starring in a gritty reboot of *The World's Largest Leprechaun.* And, hey, check this out." Andrew flipped back to the front page and a breaking story about Harry Tomlin's Last Will & Testament. "Turns out, Wayne Grey the stuntman has waived all claims to the Tomlin estate, has left everything to Harry's wives instead."

"All of it?"

"In exchange for one item: a saddle deemed 'of no monetary value.' Strangest thing."

She thought of Wayne and the conversation they'd had about

that Roy Rogers saddle. "Strange? Maybe. And maybe not."

The byline on the story read: *A Picayune exclusive by Jane "Scoop" Bannister!*

"Hmm," said Miranda, reading through the article. Harry's will had bumped the church rummage sale to the next page, so this was huge. "She didn't get Mr. Grey's impressions of Happy Rock, though. Pity. Seems a wasted opportunity."

The bell above the door jingled again and Miranda said, "Oh! That will be Atticus! He has some paperwork for me to sign." Calling out: *"We're in the back, darling!"*

Atticus Lawson did indeed have paperwork, which Miranda signed on the kitchenette table with an appropriately theatrical flourish.

"Perfect timing!" she said. "Edgar will be here any moment."

They heard the Jeep straining up the hill soon after. It rolled in beside the bookstore. Emmy perked up! Was it him? It was! My person! It's my person! Yay!

The golden Lab was all over Edgar as he entered. Running circles, leaping and nipping. Halfway between a mugging and a hugging, as Edgar said.

And how was Seattle? It was fine, he said, it was fine. But he had a look in his eyes that said otherwise.

"So, Atticus, what brings you here?" he asked as he joined them at the table.

It was then he noticed the documents. The ones Miranda had just signed.

"Oh."

"Fresh from the bank manager's office," said Atticus brightly. He looked very pleased, as did Miranda.

She was giddy, couldn't hold it in any longer. "I did it!" she cried, referring to the legal papers Atticus had brought.

Edgar filled his cup, took a long sip. "Did what?"

"I saved the bookstore!"

Edgar was immediately wary. "And how did you do that, Miranda?"

"Well, I heard how your check never cleared. For the work you did on the movie. And I felt bad about that."

Lachlan's objections over the rewrites had tied up Edgar's payment until it was too late. By the time it was cleared, the film had collapsed.

Miranda beamed. "I paid off the second mortgage! On the bookstore!"

He turned to Atticus. "Can she do that?"

"Certainly. The bank sold it to her at favorable terms—for them. They were worried that you might, ah, default."

"What!" Edgar, angry. "That's bull."

But it wasn't, and Edgar knew it. So did Miranda.

"A mortgage is essentially a long-term loan with locked-in collateral," said Atticus. "Creditors don't care who pays it off. They can even sell their interest in it, which is what they did with Miranda. And since she is legally your spouse, they didn't see a problem. Miranda paid the penalty for early repayment as well, so no outstanding issues with that either. This is good news, Edgar! You're off the hook for one of the mortgages."

He didn't like the sound of this. "I don't like the sound of this."

Atticus was getting nervous. "Miranda effectively bought *half* the bookstore," he explained.

Dead silence from Edgar.

"I am now co-owner of I Only Read Murder!" Miranda cheered. "Isn't that exciting, Edgar? I have so many ideas."

Edgar turned, glowered at her assistant Andrew as if to say, "You couldn't stop her?" only to get a "How was I to know?" look from Andrew in return.

He turned his attention onto Atticus Lawson instead. "That can't be right," he said. "It can't. I want you to go through those papers, right now, and I want you to check again. Surely she can't pull the ground out from under me."

Miranda was hurt. "I saved your store, Edgar. I used the last of my MOW money to do it. You should be cheering. You should be saying, 'Hurrah! How wonderful of you, Miranda.'"

"Check. Again," he said to Atticus through clenched teeth.

Miranda was already looking around the kitchenette. "This would be the perfect space for a trendy espresso bar," she said. "Or a gift nook! Some floral curtains. Maybe scented candles."

"Check. *Again*." His temple was starting to throb.

Atticus slid over a calculator and began rapidly punching in numbers. He ran the total, went through the numbers a second time to be sure. "Wait. I did the math wrong. My mistake," he said.

Whew! thought Edgar.

"I didn't carry the two," Atticus explained.

Miranda stopped. "Didn't carry the two? What does that mean, you didn't carry the two?"

Another flurry on the calculator. "It's not *exactly* 50-50. My bad. Miranda, you actually hold 50.04 percent of the store. While Edgar, through the bank, you hold the remaining 49.96 percent."

"Meaning?" said Edgar.

"She has a controlling interest. She's technically the *majority* owner."

"Oh, how wonderful!" said Miranda. How wonderful indeed.

AUTHORS' ACKNOWLEDGMENTS

The authors have noticed how movies and TV shows regularly feature closing credits but books don't. There is an entire team behind any novel you read, and this is the team at HarperCollins Canada that helped make this one possible. The credits, as it were:

Mystery in the Title

Senior Vice President & Executive Publisher .... Iris Tupholme
Editor in Chief ....Jennifer Lambert
Production Editor .... Canaan Chu
Copy Editor...John Sweet
Proofreader .... Tracy Bordian
Cover Designer .... Lisa Bettencourt
Publicist ....Shayla Leung
Marketing Manager.. Neil Wadhwa
Senior Marketing Director.. Cory Beatty
Publicity Director ....Lauren Morocco
Senior Sales Director... Michael Guy-Haddock
Senior Vice President, Sales & Marketing .... Leo MacDonald
Director, Publishing Operations & Subsidiary Rights .... Lisa Rundle

ADDITIONALLY

Salish Cultural Consultant... Steve Sxwithul'txw
Southeast Asian Cultural Consultant.................................. Jagjit Gordaya

In memory of Sue Grafton, from A to unfinished Z